THE
MIAMI FILES

I0587352

Terry Moran

TotalRecallPress.com
www.totalrecallpress.com

TotalRecall Publications, Inc.
1103 Middlecreek
Friendswood, Texas 77546
281-992-3131
281-482-5390 Fax
www.totalrecallpress.com

ISBN 978-1-59095-667-0
UPC 6-43977-36672-6

Printed in the United States of America with simultaneously printings in Australia, Canada, and United Kingdom.
FIRST EDITION
1 2 3 4 5 6 7 8 9 10

This is a work of fiction. The characters, names, events, views, and subject matter of this book are either the author's imagination or are used fictitiously. Any similarity or resemblance to any real people, real situations or actual events is purely coincidental and not intended to portray any person, place, or event in a false, disparaging or negative light.

To Sara Margaret who through years of multiple rejection slips never stopped believing and never accepted "give up" as an option.

About the Author

Terry Moran made a career in law enforcement for 28 years before retiring from Federal service in 2008. Five years were spent working undercover narcotics which gives him a unique insight in some of the stories he builds his books around. He also worked various crimes like bank robberies, kidnappings and financial fraud. After retiring he works closely with people needing high level security clearances. Terry has been married to Margaret since 1981. They have three sons, Ryan, Mitchell and Taylor. Terry and Margaret make their home in Knoxville, Tennessee.

Acknowledgment

Thanks to Jack Arms, who through a conversation after church one Sunday, planted the seed for this story.

Many thanks to Wanda Kent for her editorial assistance.

About the Book

Jack Armstrong, an up and coming young businessman in Atlanta, has paid his dues at Marlowe Plumbing and Supply. He finally gets the well deserved promotion he has sought after years of fourteen hour days and thankless nights. A misdirected shipment of supplies reveals billions of dollars worth of cocaine which could devastate the company and Jack's good name. Doing what he thinks is the right thing by contacting the FBI backfires and places him squarely in the crosshairs of the FBI Agent investigating and the mob who wants their cocaine returned. Jack races against the clock trying to evade the FBI and the mob all while trying to prove his innocence. Trekking through the southeast, he finds information which could implicate the FBI Agent chasing him and who may have more at stake than just apprehending Jack. Jack lands in Miami where he finds the information he needs to clear his name, but it may be too little and too late to save him from either side.

~ 1 ~

Quibdo, Columbia

2:30 am

Under the cover of the South American darkness, an army of underpaid servants labored without rest, hour after grueling hour. Under the watchful eye of a sleazy overseer, workers loaded crate after crate onto cargo trucks bound for an airstrip twenty-five miles away, deep in a valley tucked neatly between two tropical mountains. Twenty to thirty pounds heavier than the normal cargo they carried, the crates were bound for Miami, New York City, Seattle, Los Angeles and hundreds of cities in between.

Inside a windowless, dimly lit makeshift warehouse, a solitary ceiling fan stirred the thick sweltering air while higher paid laborers sweated as they unpacked hundreds of toilets from their original crates. Behind them came the highest paid workers, whose job was to remove the top from each commode tank and securely strap eight bricks of pure, uncut cocaine inside. Like the best assembly line in America, each laborer had their specific duties down to a science. The last group of workers completed the assignment by re-securing the tops, packaging the commodes inside the new crates, and loading them onto the trucks outside.

The highest paid employee in this phase of the operation was a big, greasy haired Columbian who sat back with his feet atop a desk in front of him, sucking on a fat cigar and talking on the phone. He spoke on the phone in Spanish with someone who was obviously higher in rank. It was really no different than anywhere else...the guy making the most money did the least work.

By five in the morning, dawn was just beginning to rise above the mountainous terrain. The trucks were loaded and ready for the hour long journey to the airstrip. As a bird flies, it was no more than ten miles. But with the heavy load and the winding mountain roads, the drivers were lucky if they made it in sixty minutes. Nervously passing several law enforcement officials on the way, they silently prayed whoever was responsible had paid the authorities whatever was required for safe passage. They had never been stopped before, and they would not be stopped this night. Whoever ran the empire was smart, efficient, and covered every base.

Upon arriving safely at the airstrip, another group of hired hands removed the crates from the trucks and reloaded them onto a fleet of sleek, shiny jets. Armed gunmen, some from the local law enforcement community, stood guard at strategic points around the airstrip.

An hour later every aircraft was filled to capacity. The trucks would be driven back to the windowless warehouse where they would sit idle for a few days until the process repeated itself.

The pilots fired the jet engines and one by one took off into the black, starry sky, disappearing behind the rolling, majestic mountain range, to points determined by men these laborers would never see.

Jack Armstrong arrived for work early on the crisper than normal September morning. Jack was an early riser. He always had been. From the time he held his first job as a bag boy at his hometown Big Star Food Mart, Jack was taught the importance of punctuality. He hated tardiness and he refused to tolerate it. It was unprofessional, and could mean the difference between making and losing a sale. As National Sales Director of Marlowe Plumbing Supply, Jack demanded his sales force throughout the entire country look professional, act intelligent and never be late. Any violation of his rules could result in immediate termination. He was a tough boss and he demanded respect. Many of his subordinates hated him for it, but he ran one of the premier sales forces in the nation and his work ethic was crucial in making Marlowe one of the top rated Fortune 500 companies in the country.

At just thirty-two years old, Jack held the most sought after job at Marlowe. The company had started in Atlanta in the garage of Samuel Marlowe in 1909. What began over a century ago as a catalogue order business for a small number of businesses in Atlanta, had mushroomed over the years into a nationwide conglomerate that supplied plumbing equipment to virtually every major contractor and do-it-yourself store in the country.

Jack started working at Marlowe when he was 16 years old. He did it the old-fashioned way by starting at the bottom. When he wasn't doing manual labor on the warehouse floor he was cleaning toilets and mopping floors. Working his way up the proverbial ladder, Jack put himself through college and earned his business degree while toiling for Marlowe. The higher-ups were impressed by his loyalty and hard work, and rewarded him with a low-level sales position the very day he earned his degree. His area of responsibility covered Northern Georgia, Eastern Tennessee, Western North and South Carolina and the Southern tip of Virginia. Jack's athletic physique, quick wit and boyish charm helped him to become the leading salesman in his region four years straight, two of those earning him National Leader of the Year.

Two months into his fifth year as a salesman, his hard work paid off. Promoted to Regional Sales Director in Birmingham, Jack took over a fledgling region that consistently finished at or near the bottom in sales statistics every year since Marlowe went national. But Jack loved a challenge. Within three years of arriving in Birmingham, he was able to transform his shoddy group sales force into the most prolific in the nation.

The brass in Atlanta kept its eye on this young, dark-haired workhorse who seemed to have what they required for the move up to an executive position within the lofty confines of the Marlowe suites, high atop Peachtree Plaza in downtown Atlanta. They carefully watched Jack's progress and rewarded him handsomely with much heftier Christmas bonuses than received by his peers in other regions. The writing was on the wall. Jack saw it. His peers and associates saw it. Although national sales were at an all time high and profit margins were soaring, Marlowe brass was not happy with the current National Sales Director, Phillip Marcus.

Marcus was a decent salesman and he produced results, but rumors were rife that he no longer fit the mold. They wanted a younger fit, good-looking, double-breasted kind of executive. Three years after he became National Sales Director, he had padded 100 pounds to his 200 pound frame. It seemed the extra bucks generated by his higher salary had gone straight to his culinary budget. Coupled with the weight gain and rapidly receding hairline, Marcus no longer portrayed the top executive image Marlowe required, or so it was rumored by employees around the country.

Jack had never met Marcus. He had heard about him through others and admired his work ethic. When Jack heard rumors about Marcus' ouster, he found it difficult to believe a reputable company like Marlowe would fire an officer simply because his looks were waning. Jack exercised daily and kept himself in excellent physical condition. His diet consisted mostly of raw vegetables and fruit. He rarely ate red meat. He did it for himself, his health, and his peace of mind... not to look attractive for the company. It seemed extremely unfair that Marcus would be dismissed based on his physique rather than be judged for his exceptional financial and business accomplishments.

Nevertheless, on Jack's thirty-second birthday and after sixteen years with the company, he was offered, and he accepted the National Sales Director position. There were periods of guilt when he thought about Marcus and moving him out of his prestigious position. But the $250,000 annual salary, company car, larger than life expense account and other financial perks, were too good to refuse. All in all, it would have been a financial blunder, not to mention a career ender, to turn down the position.

As National Sales Director it wasn't all diamonds and gold. Power lunches and golf rounds with big wig clients so often depicted in the movie business world, did not happen. Instead, there were plenty of high-level meetings with fancy hors d'oeuvres that Jack politely refused. But when he got right down to it, the work was just as hard, if not harder, than all the jobs he'd had with Marlowe since he was sixteen.

Part of Jack's responsibility as National Sales Director was supervising the national warehouse in a suburb northwest of Atlanta. The warehouse was a holding area for every piece of plumbing equipment ordered from the different regions throughout the country. What Memphis was to FedEx, Atlanta was to Marlowe. A cursory inspection was required of all shipments into the warehouse to detect any flaws, cracks or other damage to packaging before final shipment was made to its regional destination.

Jack depended heavily on Jerry Randall, his Warehouse Line Supervisor, to conduct all necessary inspections. At fifty-seven, Jerry had logged forty-one years at the company. Like Jack, Jerry was loyal to the company that hired him while still in high school. Unlike Jack, without the college degree, Jerry was destined to be subjected to manual labor until he retired. Jerry rose through the ranks because of his loyalty, but those ranks started as a bathroom cleaner in the same exact warehouse to his current position he'd held for about ten years. He certainly did not have the Marlowe look to go any further. But Jerry never complained. He was happy to have the work in a country where layoffs were a pen stroke away.

Although from different sides of the track, Jack and Jerry soon forged a close working relationship. Jack would tease Jerry about his tall, bony frame and his gray goatee which did not match his red thinning hair. Jerry, in turn, affectionately referred to Jack as B, which stood for boss. Jerry considered Jack more like a son than he did a boss. He never once resented Jack for working his way up the ladder, and in fact, respected how well he had done, and how successful the region was under his helm. Jack trusted Jerry, and gave him the freedom to do his job, which Jerry appreciated. Jack was the first National Sales Director in years that did not look down on Jerry and his crews. Everyone knew Jack was in charge and that he was the boss, but they respected the way Jack ran things and his demand for perfection. They especially respected the way he never talked down to them, even if he was upset. Jack had a way to critique without criticizing. Laborers, who were twenty-five or thirty years older than him, did not mind busting their butts for him. Although not required to visit the warehouse in his lofty new position, Jack chose to do so every morning, not only to assure things were right, but to stay in touch with the people he believed to be the backbone of the company.

It was about 5:40 a.m. when Jack arrived at the warehouse to begin his daily routine of equipment checks and perusing inventory lists, before going downtown to his plush twenty-fifth floor office overlooking the bustling streets of Atlanta to scour the national sales reports. The autumn sun was deep red as it peeked over the thick stand of Georgia pines blanketing several miles of land surrounding the warehouse. The only avenue in or out from the warehouse was a three-mile gravel road leading from the main highway.

As Jack was just finishing up cross checking the inventory list against purchase orders for a shipment headed to the Midwest region in Omaha, Jerry marched into Jack's gray, makeshift, bare cinder-block walled office. Jerry, usually a bit hyper from his fourth or fifth cup of coffee, wore a solemn look on his face. Jack glanced up briefly at Jerry's rounder than normal eyes before returning to his inventory list lying on top of the scratched gray metal top desk.

"Be with ya in a minute, Jer."

Jack, serious about detail, directed his eyes back to the list. The solid thud that cracked across his metal desk and echoed inside the empty office startled Jack. Suddenly, instead of checking and cross referencing the appropriate equipment headed to Omaha, Jack found himself staring nose down at a white brick shaped mass wrapped in cellophane and brown tape. He slowly peered up at Jerry. "What is it?"

Jerry snickered nervously. "It ain't talcum powder."

"Where'd it come from?"

Jerry motioned toward the warehouse with his head. "Some a' the boys was loadin' up a shipment a' toilets to Seattle when one a' the crates fell and busted open. The crapper fell out the bottom of the crate and broke up pretty good." With his head, Jerry motioned toward the white brick lying on Jack's desk. "That and seven others just like it were inside."

Jack rose from his desk and picked the brick up.

"They was in a shipment a' toilets from Juarez Fixtures in Columbia."

Jack chuckled slightly. "Figures."

"We been doin' business with 'em for years," Jerry said matter-of-factly.

"How many?" Jack asked.

Jerry scratched his head. "I don't know. Fifteen. Twenty. Maybe longer."

Jack stared at the brick in his hand. "How many are there, Jerry?"

"Besides this one, seven more. But we didn't check the rest of the toilets already on the trucks or those we ain't loaded up yet."

Jack paused and looked right into Jerry's eyes. "How many of the toilets came from the Juarez company?"

"All of 'em, B. Every last one of 'em."

"How many we talkin' about, Jerry?"

"Fifteen-hundred, give or take."

Jack fell back into his seat, closed his eyes and laid the brick on top of his inventory list. He rubbed his eyes, leaned back in the squeaky chair and slowly placed his intertwined fingers behind his head.

"Whataya' want me to do, B?"

"I don't know. I gotta have time to think. This kind of thing could ruin the company."

"Whataya' mean? Company ain't done nuthin' wrong. They

didn't know nuthin' bout this."

"You don't understand, Jerry. If the press gets wind of this they'll have a heyday. They'll make it sound as if Marlowe is responsible. That would be disastrous for the company." Jack covered his eyes with the palms of both hands somehow searching for an answer.

"You gotta tell somebody, B. You can't just do nothin'."

"I know, Jerry. I know!" Jack snapped back. "But we gotta do damage control first. Maybe the problem isn't as bad as it looks." Jack sprung quickly from his chair and marched out of his office with Jerry in pursuit. "Who all knows about this?"

Jerry tailed one step behind Jack. "Me and the guys that was doin' the loadin'."

"Who, Jerry? Who!"

"Well. There's Zeeb, Potato, Ryree and Mo."

"Anybody else?"

"Naw. That's it."

"Where are they now?"

"Right up here. I told 'em not to do anything 'til I came back."

Jack's primary concern was the company. Protect the company at all costs. He knew that the least bit of negative publicity could set Marlowe back years. The media frenzy that would result in the defamation of the company's one-hundred year reputation would take a lifetime to rebuild. First and foremost on Jack's mind was how to remedy the situation without any more people knowing than already did, and to try and keep the company's name out of it. Jack conjured in his mind the hit he would take if this incident was not handled properly, not only by the press, but by the Atlanta brass at headquarters. Jack had never used drugs nor ever been around them. He knew a couple of friends in college who had smoked a little weed, but he had tactfully disassociated himself from them. He wanted nothing to do with drugs and he publicly supported mandatory prison terms for users and dealers alike. Jack had worked his butt off for Marlowe for sixteen years. He wasn't about to let this incident cause his, or the company's name, get dragged through the mud.

All sorts of scenarios ran through Jack's head as he approached the shattered toilet with its spilled white bricks scattered across the warehouse dock area. Jack imagined the stares he would get and the juicy stories bound to be created by people he knew and even those he never met. He envisioned sixteen years of hard work evaporating into nothing. Jack knelt over the seven solid white bricks strewn on the floor below him. Jerry and his crew of four towered over Jack, who seemed to be praying for an answer.

"You said there're fifteen hundred toilets?" Jack's voice quivered.

"Yep. Fifteen hundred," Jerry answered, unphased.

"How many have you loaded on the trucks?" Jack inquired.

"I'd say about half," Mo answered.

Jack picked up one of the seven bricks just in front of his squatted knees. He brought it to his face, looked at it hard, and turned it around to view all sides as if it would either change or go away. He tossed the brick aside and it came to rest on the dock floor straddling another one. Jack stood and rubbed his hands to remove the powdery residue used to disguise any odor.

"Jerry. You, Mo and Zeeb unload the toilets from the trucks. Unbox 'em and check every last one." Jack barked his orders, without taking his eyes off the seven bricks still on the floor. "Potato. You, me and Ryree'll check the unloaded boxes," he said, motioning to a sea of cardboard boxes lined up nine and ten deep stretching for several hundred feet on both sides of the warehouse floor.

"You realize how long that's gonna take with just the six of us, B?" Jerry asked rhetorically.

"You got any better ideas?"

Jerry shook his head no.

"Can we at least get some more people to help us, boss?" Zeeb asked.

"No!" Jack snapped back. "The less people who know about it, the better off we are. I don't care if this takes all night. We may or may not have a huge problem, and I gotta know the best way to handle it that's in the best interest of the company."

"Screw the company!" Potato blurted, almost laughing. "Let's just call the cops."

"No!" Jack shouted. "Bring the cops and you bring the newspapers, the TV stations, radio stations, and anyone else looking for the story of their career. Besides, the cops'll screw it up if this turns out the way I think it might. It's way outta their league."

The six men stood and gazed at each other for several seconds. Each one seemed to be waiting on the others to begin the laborious process of slicing into each and every box. Finally, Jack pulled a pocket knife from his back pocket and ambled over to the first box closest to the dock. He opened the three inch blade and cut into the cardboard box which had the name Juarez imprinted with large, bold, black letters on all four sides, along with some smaller print in Spanish. Jack's five subordinates watched in anticipation as Jack sliced the four corners of the box. He removed the protective packaging neatly wrapped around the toilet. Jack looked back at the five who waited patiently like a dog waits for his master to pitch him a piece of bacon. Jack turned and eyed the top of the tank, and slowly reached for the removable lid. Jerry, Mo, Zeeb, Potato, and Ryree took one step closer. The lid made that familiar grinding noise as Jack slid it away from its position. All six heads stretched and peered over as Jack slowly slid the top away and placed it gently on the floor. Jack's mouth gaped wide and his breathing quickened when he saw eight more bricks neatly affixed inside the tank, identical to the ones discovered minutes earlier. Jack threw his laced fingers on top of his head and closed his eyes. Jerry, Mo, Zeeb, Potato and Ryree simply looked at each other. No one uttered a sound.

Jack sent every employee home except the five helping him. He provided some asinine excuse about safety violations he found, which required all but a few to go home for the day. When it became obvious he was staring head first into a major problem, he figured the less that knew or heard anything about the incident, the better. Jack had already called Margo, his administrative assistant at Peachtree Plaza, and told her there were some mix-ups regarding shipments, and he probably would not be coming downtown. Jack would lock the doors behind the last unknowing employee to leave and begin the arduous task of slicing, removing and counting over and over again.

For the next fourteen hours, the six men worked non-stop, slicing and opening every box from the truck, and those yet to be loaded. For fourteen excruciating hours, each man would remove lid after lid of countless toilets and stare at the eight solid white bricks of cocaine neatly strapped to every single tank in the shipment. The men didn't talk much to each other during those fourteen hours. A non-verbal nod of the head was about all that was passed between them during the seemingly never-ending task. These were Jack's most loyal workers, and they continued their assignment without complaint until the job was done.

When it was all over, the six had counted exactly twelve-thousand bricks of cocaine. Inside each one of the fifteen-hundred tanks, strapped securely with packing tape, were eight solid white bricks of pure uncut cocaine. The six men came together at the end of their task like a football team approaches a huddle at the end of the play. They were hot. They were sweaty. They were bone tired. Remnants of white powder clung to their shirt sleeves and pant legs. One by one they gathered, each taking a seat on the cool gray warehouse floor. When all were seated they had unknowingly formed a circle. No one said a word. The only sounds heard were the air conditioning unit clicking off when the temperature inside reached its peak, and the sound of a far away train whistle.

Finally, muddling through a thousand thoughts sifting through his head, Jack spoke quietly. "Gentlemen. What we have here is a major headache. What we have here is a monumental geographic screw-up that has somehow caught us right smack dab in the middle." Jack paused and scanned his subordinate's eyes. "Until I figure out the best way to handle this, I don't want anybody else to know about it. That means your wives, your girlfriends, your kids, your neighbors, your brothers, sisters. It means nobody."

Jerry cocked his head and looked inquisitively at Jack. "B? Are you serious? You gotta tell somebody."

"I know!" Jack snapped. "I know. I just don't know who yet."

Mo snickered. "Whataya' mean you don't know, boss? With all due respect, you gotta notify somebody."

"My next door neighbor's brother is a DEA agent in Atlanta," Potato added his two cents. "A catch like this would make his career."

"No!" Jack shouted.

"Tater's right, boss," Ryree chimed in. "DEA should know about this. They for sure would be the ones to call."

"No," Jack said, this time a little calmer.

"Why not?" Zeeb asked. "You can't just sit on this and 'spect it to go away."

Jack paused before looking squarely at Zeeb. "I don't trust 'em, Zeeb. Don't trust the DEA as far as I can throw 'em."

"Whataya' mean ya' don't trust 'em, B?" Jerry fired back. "Hell, they're the Feds."

"That's what bothers me. I've seen too many news stories and read too many newspapers to know they're not all above board."

"Oh come on, boss," Potato jumped in. "Like they're gonna waltz in here and steal 12,000 bricks of coke. Are you kidding me?"

"It's not that, Potato. Not that at all," said Jack.

"Then what?" Jerry asked.

Jack shook his head. "You've seen 'em on TV. Goin' into places. Guns drawn. Big DEA emblazoned on the backs of their jackets. It's all for show, I'm telling you. They get ready for the big bust and what do they do? They call every friggin' TV station for miles around to go on the bust with 'em. That's exactly what they'll do here. I'm telling you, fellas. Mark my words. And then you know what happens next? Marlowe is falsely implicated. Guilt by association. If they don't shut the business down, it might as well shut down anyway 'cause they'll lose client after client after client because they don't want to be associated with the name Marlowe. I lose my job. You lose yours, and right or wrong, our names are forever linked with this incident."

The five paused and stared in disbelief, first at Jack, then at each other.

Jerry chuckled below his breath. "B! You been watching way too much TV." The others snickered quietly to themselves.

"You guys go ahead and laugh. Laugh all you want. But it won't be so funny when the DEA shuts us down. Maybe not forever, but for several months while the investigation is going on. Can you afford to go four or five months with no income? I can't."

One by one, the five stopped snickering.

"I gotta sleep on this. I gotta know whatever course I take is the right one for us and the company," Jack said. "Don't worry, guys. I'll do the right thing. I just gotta figure out what that is. That's all." Jack looked at his watch and realized it was almost 9:00 p.m. His workers had busted their butts all day, but he needed to secure the drugs in a safe location inside the warehouse so when the authorities he decided to call arrived, all the evidence would be in one location and cause no headaches for him or his staff. Each man could have refused Jack's request to work a couple more hours, but in the year Jack had supervised them, they had come to respect his leadership abilities and the way he treated them as equals. None hesitated to keep helping as the night grew older.

Brick after brick was loaded carefully onto six flatbed dollies, one for each man. One dolly load was able to support around one-hundred bricks of cocaine. Back and forth for a little over two hours, each man toted twenty loads of cocaine to a secure room. When it was over, cocaine bricks were stacked ten deep and twelve wide. The parade of cocaine laden dollies going to and fro reminded Jack of soldier ants all in a line and marching one behind the other until the work was done. When the task was finished they were exhausted. Their minds and eyes played tricks on them, and they were very hungry.

Jack wrapped his tired, heavy arm around each man's shoulder as they walked to their cars outside. The sun had set hours ago, and the brisk autumn chill caused their breath to release white steam, as they discussed events of the day. Jack thanked them profusely for doing a job he could not have done by himself. He apologized for any grief they might get from angry wives for only telling them they would be just a little late coming home. Jack told them all to sleep in the next day and promised them all overtime and a steak dinner when this episode blew over.

A shade past midnight, Jerry, Mo, Zeeb, Potato and Ryree got into their respective pickup trucks, jeeps and one lime green Civic and started their engines. One after the other turned on their headlights and slowly drove away from the warehouse in one solid line that looked like a midnight freight train heading to an unknown destination. Jack watched his men drive down the one and only gravel road leading into and out of the warehouse property. In the distance, all he could detect were five sets of taillights, a few of which were busted and no longer emitting their red flicker.

Jack brought his watch close to his face as the cloudy night sheltered any moonlight which might illuminate the faded florescent hands. Jack knew Emery Carson, his girlfriend of about six weeks, would not be in the best of moods when he arrived home, if she was even still there. In the confusion of the day, Jack had forgotten the special evening his lovely green-eyed, long-legged brunette lady had planned. Emery was very understanding, but in her book there was no excuse for not phoning. Jack knew it. He knew he was in the doghouse, and there was little he could do to get out of it. But he also figured he had a pretty good excuse. If Emery didn't understand, then that's just the way it would be.

Emery was the girl Jack had waited for all his life. For sixteen years he had been married to his work. The company was number one. He'd dated a few women, but his career came first and he refused to let a woman come between him and his climb up the ladder of success. That was until he met Emery. Emery was the type of girl that could make any man do a double take. And that was unusual for Jack. He concentrated so much with furthering his career that he simply had no time for dating. But when he saw Emery, everything changed. When Jack finally caught her eye, his heart raced. This girl was different. There was something about her that made him feel like a lovestruck teenager all over again.

Jack lay on his back on his office floor with his head propped against the wall where it met the floor. His phone's battery dead, Jack set the office landline phone on top of his chest and watched it rise and fall with every breath. Jack was dead tired and could probably have gone to sleep right there. Holding the phone to his right ear, he called Emery. A click on the other end made him sit up quickly.

"Hello?" Jack said, anticipating Emery's anger.

There was no response, but the phone kept ringing.

"Hello?" Jack said a little louder.

Still there was no response, except the incessant ringing. The hair on his neck stood at attention. He heard a click, but the phone continued to ring. There was no one else at the warehouse. His heart pounded so hard he could feel it inside his head. He heard a second click. "Hello!" he shouted even louder. "Who's on here?" His heart beat even faster. His palms began to sweat.

"I don't want to hear any excuses from you, Jack!" Emery's soft voice boomed as loud as she could manage.

"Emery! Oh thank God it's you!"

"Who else would it be? It couldn't be our company. They left hours ago. Remember our company? You know....the people we invited for dinner?"

Jack slid back down to his original position and cupped his hands over his closed eyes. "I don't know what to say, Emery. It's just that things got a little crazy down here today and time just slipped up on me. I never even made it downtown. I should've called and I swear I am so sorry."

"You're sorry? It's not gonna be that easy. Do you realize the topics of conversation are extremely limited with the preacher and his wife? Do you realize that, Jack?"

"I am honestly so sorry. I don't know what else I can say. I owe you one."

"Oh, you owe me more than one, and you better have a great explanation."

"Trust me, Emery. I do, and believe me, it's a good one. I'll explain when I get there. I just got a few last minute things to do here and I'll head that way. Please don't go home until I get there, okay?"

"Oh, I'll be here alright. You can count on that."

He winced and jerked the phone away from his ear. He gently placed the receiver back onto its cradle and re-positioned his head against the wall. Within the confines of the darkened warehouse, and inaudible to Jack, was a third click.

Jack opened the gray metal drawer in the middle of his desk. He pulled out a white plastic bag emblazoned with orange lettering depicting the Home Depot logo. A day or so earlier Jack had gone to the do-it-yourself store and purchased a combination padlock he planned on using on a miniature storage unit in his backyard in north Cobb County. He pulled the padlock, still tightly packaged in its wrapper, from the plastic bag and tore the cardboard protecting it. Jack strolled to the secure room with no windows where the cocaine was stored. He figured it couldn't hurt to provide a little extra security. He pulled the lock from the package, twirled the black wheel with white numbers and notches to the left and right until the hasp opened. He placed the padlock on the already present latch and locked it down. He gave the wheel several random spins, and then pulled down hard on the padlock to make sure it was locked. Jack stuffed the piece of paper with the written combination inside his pocket. He walked back to his office, cut off the lights, then stretched and yawned.

Jack would have no problem sleeping this night.

The blue digits on the DVD player and Montgomery Gentry's song, "While You're Still Young" on the country radio station, were the only signs of life illuminating the rustic den in Jack's home. The red digits, reading 12:00, flashed on and off, showing the electricity had gone off sometime during the day. Jack's watch said 1:05 a.m., as he slithered past the deer head trophy and bass mounted prizes littering his dark paneled wall, trying to find the light switch. He knew Emery was still there. Her red convertible was still parked in the driveway of his white framed home, with matching picket fence and towering oaks that looked more like a post card than a bachelor's pad. He slid his palm across the wall until his finger reached the light switch. The lamp on the side table next to the brown leather couch lit up as Jack's finger met the switch. Emery, bundled up in a little ball on the couch and wrapped in a multi-colored quilt, moved slightly and unconsciously covered her eyes with her hand. Jack threw the switch off again, not wanting to awaken his sweetheart of just over a month.

For sixteen years Jack had labored long and hard to finally attain one of the most prestigious positions at Marlowe. He had made a promise to himself when he was hired at Marlowe that his career came first, and that he would not allow a woman to saddle him or get in the way of the pursuit of his dreams.

Jack had gone out plenty of times in the ten or twelve years he'd been on his own, but most were blind dates or group dates. Jack simply refused to let himself fall in love, although there had been opportunities. Anytime he felt someone was getting too close, he backed off. He did not want to hurt anybody, especially himself. He just believed his job came first and there was no room for anything or anyone else. It would just muddle and confuse things.

One thing Jack had promised his mother when he left home for college was that he would go to church on Sundays. He had been raised a Southern Baptist, but Mrs. Armstrong told Jack she did not care where he went, as long as it taught the Word. Jack was true to his word. From his first weekend as a freshman at the University of Tennessee to this past Sunday, Jack attended some type of Christian service faithfully. There had been a few Sundays that were missed due to a cold, flu or business travel. But overall, Jack had kept his promise to his mother. He was raised in a Christian home and was taught to fear God. And even though Jack was not one to force his views on anyone not wanting to listen, he seemed to live his life based on the morals he was taught by his parents and his church while growing up.

So it was that until six weeks hence, Jack had managed to keep his guard up. He had managed to look past the batting eyes and quick glances from the opposite sex. He had managed to avoid the coincidental introductions and accidentally-bumping-into type meetings.

It was August and a crystal clear Sunday afternoon with pleasant temperatures unusually low for that time of year in Georgia. The singles class at the church Jack attended was throwing an old-fashioned church social at one of the serene lakes north of Atlanta. There was fishing, softball, football and Frisbee. There was fried chicken, potato salad and corn on the cob all arranged neatly on red and white checkered table cloths. More tables with the same decorations held chips, dip, salsa, and various regular and diet soft drinks. All had an amazing view of the lake, and were shaded by tall pines. There were lots of single ladies and not quite as many single men. At thirty-two, Jack was definitely one of the older bachelors there. At times, he sat close to the shoreline feeling more like a babysitter than a member. He chuckled as he listened to so many goofy pick up lines being used by these recently graduated college boys with red-hot hormones. He wondered silently if he had every used the same corny lines ten years earlier.

Jack propped himself back on his elbows and watched as several stray sailboats skimmed on the calm, lapping waves. He chewed incessantly on a long, brown reed he had just plucked from the water's edge when Emery approached him and sat down beside him. Jack glanced quickly when he saw her from the corner of his eye. He glanced twice when he saw her brilliant green eyes dancing with the reflection of a passing sailboat. Her loose-fitting, white cotton blouse was tied in a knot just above her navel. Her brown skin was smooth. Her silky brunette hair blew carefree over her tanned face. Jack's heart raced faster than it ever had. Just one look into her eyes melted his heart. Somewhere in the back of his mind, in the depths of his heart, Jack knew his career had just taken a back seat.

Emery Carson was different than anyone he had ever met. She was the first girl in years that made his heart pound and his palms sweat. Emery had the same old-fashioned ideals and morals as Jack. She was pretty, but tough, straight forward, but tender. If there was anything that bothered Jack about Emery, it was her reluctance to talk about her job or her past. She seemed to not want to talk about it. Every time Jack would bring the subject up she quickly changed it. The most he could get out of her was she worked for the city.

Nevertheless, for the next six weeks, Jack and Emery were inseparable. Jack couldn't remember having this much fun since the freedom of his college days. He was like a kid in a candy store. He was quickly falling in love. Emery was protective of her feelings and Jack noticed it, but he could see in her eyes that she was also falling for him.

Emery reached for a lamp and switched it back on. She pulled back and rubbed her eyes.

"I didn't mean to wake you."

Emery shook the cobwebs from her head. "What time is it?" she said in a sleepy voice, squinting to look at her phone's time.

Jack knew what time it was, but looked at his watch anyway. "Ten after one."

Emery leaned forward and tossed the quilt to her side. "I gotta go." Jack gently pressed his hand on her shoulder as she tried to stand. "Jack. I really need to go. I've got work in the morning."

"I'm really sorry about tonight. I truly am. I should've called."

Emery rubbed her eyes. "Yes, you should've. You really embarrassed me, Jack. You embarrassed us."

"I know. And I am so sorry."

Emery stood.

Jack followed along and placed his hands firmly on her shoulders. "Emery, you gotta listen to me. I'm so sorry. I really am. But I really need to talk to you about what happened."

"Can't it wait 'til tomorrow? I'm really tired."

Jack stared deeply at Emery. She knew he was struggling to say something. "What, Jack? What is it?"

Jack pushed her shoulders downward, forcing her back onto the couch. He sat down beside her. "Something happened at the warehouse today and I'm not quite sure how to handle it."

Puzzled, Emery looked at Jack. "What happened?"

Jack took a deep breath then exhaled very slowly. "Somebody. Someone. Some group made a monumental screw-up and shipped a big…no…a huge load of cocaine to the warehouse."

Emery bolted up straight. Her eyes widened. Somehow she was no longer sleepy. "Who?"

"Don't know. It came from Columbia, but that's all we know right now."

"How much? I mean how much cocaine are you talking about?"

Jack paused and drew another deep breath before exhaling. "Twelve thousand bricks. That's what took me so long. By the time we unloaded it, counted it, and put it in a secure place, it was very late."

Emery was surprised and her reaction showed it. "You touched it? You moved it? You tampered with evidence?" She sounded agitated.

Jack pulled back, surprised at Emery's response.

"I mean you shouldn't have touched it. That's evidence. That's just common sense. You should've left it right where it was and called someone." Emery softened her tone slightly.

Jack cocked his head slightly and squinted his eyes. "Since when did you become such an expert on evidence?"

Emery stared at Jack. "It's not that."

"Then what is it?"

"Like I said. Common sense. Really, Jack. If you came across a dead body with a knife lying beside it, would you move the body and knife and hide it? It's evidence. Somebody committed a crime and now you've tampered with evidence. You don't have to be an FBI Agent to know that."

Jack threw himself back against the couch and placed his hands on top of his head which was his custom when he worried.

"I wouldn't worry about it. I mean you didn't know. You can't get in trouble for doing something if you didn't know it was wrong in the first place." Emery tried to ease his mind.

Jack looked sideways at Emery. He was confused. "You act like you know what you're talking about. That scares me a little."

Emery smiled. "I took a couple of criminal law courses as electives way back when. The law says you have to intend to commit a crime. If the intent is not there, neither is the crime."

Jack stared at Emery and shook his head. She seemed so calm about it. "I didn't do anything wrong, Emery. You're actin' as if I did something wrong."

"No, no!" she quickly responded. "I didn't say that. You just seemed concerned. That's all."

"Well, I am concerned. I'm concerned about who it was that did it and what they're gonna do when they realize their mistake. I'm also concerned about what's gonna happen to the Marlowe name when the paper gets hold of it."

"Did you call anybody?"

"You mean the police? The DEA? Are you serious? The locals wouldn't know where to start and I don't trust the DEA."

"What about the FBI?"

"What about 'em? They don't work drugs. Besides, they'll bring in the media and then it's all over."

"What about that guy at church we met."

"Who?"

"You know. That guy we met a couple weeks ago. Someone said he was an FBI Agent. You could call him and he'd know what to do."

"Who, Emery? I don't remember meeting anyone. I don't remember anyone saying anything about an FBI Agent."

Emery covered and rubbed her eyes. "Oh, what was his name? We saw him after church."

"Where? When? I have no idea what you're talking about. I have no recollection of meeting anyone like that," Jack said, almost confrontational.

"At church. It was nothing. It was very casual. We were talking to several people. It's possible you never met him. I just remember somebody saying he was an FBI Agent and a deacon to boot. If you can't trust a church deacon, who can you trust?" Emery tried to force a smile from Jack, but he was in no mood.

Jack laid his forehead into the palms of his cupped hands.

Emery touched his shoulder. "Look, Jack. I don't care who you tell, but you've got to tell somebody. If you just sit there and do nothing, don't tell anyone, it'll look like you're covering up something." Emery paused and squeezed his shoulder. "Why don't you let me call. I'll call him first thing in the morning. I'll handle it."

Jack looked at Emery and furled his brow. "How can you call him when you don't even know his name?"

"Fuentes! That's his name. Eric Fuentes." Emery seemed pleased with herself.

"That Mexican guy?" Jack inquired.

"Or Spanish. I'm not sure."

"He's an Agent?" Jack seemed surprised. "He doesn't look like an FBI Agent.

"What does an Agent look like?" Emery joked.

"I don't know. The guy on *Bones*?" Jack retorted. "I have no idea."

Jack and Emery stared at each other and then both cracked up. If for but a moment, they forgot everything and were able to smile. Jack and Emery leaned back against the smooth leather couch imbedded with button indentations. As their laughter subsided, they peered into each other's eyes. Their tanned faces moved gracefully toward the other's until their lips met. Jack's stress from the past eighteen hours was immediately released. Emery could feel the tension.

"Stay tonight," Jack whispered, coming up for air.

"I can't," Emery said, when she managed to seize a spare second.

"Why not?" Jack asked, during another lapse.

Emery softly placed both hands on Jack's face, which had more than a five o'clock shadow. She pushed slightly, just enough to separate their lips. "You know I can't. I'm just not ready."

Jack stared into her beautiful eyes that reminded him of lucid pools of Caribbean water. He leaned back against the button-studded brown couch with his fingers atop his head.

"I'm sorry," she said, stroking his cheek with one finger.

Jack smiled half heartedly. "No. Don't be. You're right." Jack rehearsed in his mind what he wished would come true. But this relationship was special and he didn't want to screw anything up. Jack knew he would regret it if they allowed their passion to dictate their emotions.

Emery rose from the couch and straightened out her wrinkled dress. Jack stood alongside her and brushed back a few strands of hair that had fallen across her eye. She smiled sweetly.

"I love you."

Emery hugged him, but couldn't bring herself to say the words.

Still holding her, Jack winced just slightly, not enough for her to notice. It killed him that she wouldn't say it back. "Why can't you say it?"

Emery slowly released her grip and stepped back. She offered him a warm, but not an 'in love' look. "I've gotta go. It's late."

Jack returned her smile, but did not try to stop her with words or emotions. He simply wondered what was in her past that was holding her back. What was it that she wouldn't let go of? Why wouldn't she open up that part of her life to him? Why did she refuse to reciprocate his feelings? Why wouldn't she let herself fall in love? He watched her slip on her jacket and flip her hair outside that had fallen between her back and her jacket. She turned as she got to the door then pressed her index and middle finger to her lips and blew him a kiss. Jack pretended that it hit him across the face, and immediately felt rather stupid doing it. Emery smiled, turned and opened the door. She looked at him one more time before stepping out into the frigid night. She closed the door behind her and gently tugged it closed. Jack stared at the closed door, inhaled deeply and exhaled. All he wanted to do now was to lie down. A board. A bed of nails. It didn't matter as long as it was flat and horizontal.

Thirty minutes later he still could not sleep. He wondered if it was true that sometimes you can't go to sleep because you are too tired. A thousand things crossed his mind while he tried to doze off. One was how he had broken his own rule about keeping this incident quiet. He had been emphatic that his crew keep quiet, and the first thing he did was tell Emery. Nothing he could do about it now anyway. He was sure it was fine. After all, she had this FBI contact and was going to contact them, so surely things would be alright. Things would be fine. Just fine.

Jack yawned and stretched for the fifth time since he had arrived at the warehouse thirty minutes earlier. The sun was just beginning to rise on a new, crisp autumn morning. The crickets' chirping slowed as darkness gave way to light. The words on the inventory lists he was checking and cross referencing kept running together. Several times he jerked himself back to consciousness while staring at numbers, like a sleepy driver jolts awake unaware of the last several minutes of driving.

Jack could hear the shuffling footsteps of the morning crew arriving as he reached for the black cup of coffee sitting on the middle of his desktop calendar. Faded brown rings decorated the calendar from many mornings past. His eyes halfway closed, he took a large gulp. A single drop rolled from the corner of his mouth and lodged, unknowingly, at the bottom of his chin. The rapping on his door caused his eyes to pop open quickly, much like a child's when he hears a creak in the middle of the night. The short dark complected man smiled and waved at Jack through the glass in the door when he realized he had startled him. Jack returned the smile and motioned the man, he now recognized from church, into his office.

Jack observed the man as he opened the door and entered his office. He was shorter than Jack remembered and was dressed in a custom-tailored pin stripe suit. He could have passed for a mobster in a movie with his black, slicked back hair and bushy eyebrows. Or maybe he was just trying to be stylish. Or maybe the fancy look covered for his short stature. Whatever, it certainly was not Jack's style.

"Jack Armstrong?"

Jack rose from his chair. "That would be me."

Pulling a black leather case with a gold badge affixed to the front, the man identified himself by displaying his open credentials. Jack could see the huge, bold FBI letters imprinted on the identification. "I'm Eric Fuentes, FBI." There was a barely detectable Spanish accent.

Jack, who was a good eight or nine inches taller, peered down on him and must have had a funny expression because, in his mind, he was thinking *Bones*. There was no way this stumpy guy could be an FBI Agent.

Fuentes smiled and closed his creds. "Yeah. I get that look all the time."

Jack shook his head. He was still very tired. "I'm sorry. It was a long night."

"Don't worry about it. Everybody expects Bruce Willis or Clint Eastwood. But we come in all shapes and sizes."

"Or, the guy from *Bones*."

Fuentes look puzzled.

"The TV show."

Fuentes looked more puzzled. "Oh, yeah." He acted like he knew, but didn't.

Jack could tell. "Never mind."

Fuentes pointed at Jack's chin.

"What?"

"On your chin. You've got a drop of coffee or something on your chin."

Jack pulled a handkerchief from his back pocket and wiped away the drip. He looked downward and smiled at Fuentes. "That's embarrassing."

Fuentes smiled and sat down in the metal folding chair situated directly in front of Jack's desk. "Emery called me this morning. She said we had met at church a couple weeks ago. I don't think I actually met you, but I do remember seeing you there on a few occasions. What do you think of our preacher?"

Jack's chair squeaked as he leaned back. "Oh, he's great. I'm never bored in his sermons. Really makes you think."

"I couldn't agree more, Jack. He hits a point and doesn't let up until he knows he has driven it home." Fuentes crossed his legs. "I heard a church over in Spartanburg is trying to lure him there. I sure hope that doesn't happen. I'd really hate to lose him."

Jack nodded his head in agreement. "Agreed. He would be very hard to replace."

"Jack, Emery called me this morning and told me a little bit about what happened yesterday and what you and your men found."

Jack looked at his watch. It was not even 7 am yet. Jack cocked his head just slightly. "What time did she call you?"

"This morning. I don't recall. Why?"

Jack looked confused. "You guys get started early, don't 'cha?"

"Well, we're pretty busy, Jack. Not a moment to spare, if you know what I mean." Fuentes uncrossed his legs and loosened his tie. He pulled out a pad of paper and a pen from inside his coat pocket and began questioning Jack about the previous day's events.

Jack explained how the misguided shipment of cocaine was discovered and how he and his men had spent the entire day, and most of the night, inventorying the stash. Fuentes commended Jack on his diligence and attention to detail, but also chided him severely for tampering with evidence. However, under the circumstances, Fuentes told Jack that he did not think there would be any major problems or issues. Jack was relieved. Fuentes did give Jack a scolding on proper and immediate notification of authorities, but since he had secured the stash, things would be fine.

After recalling in detail every tedious part of the day before, Jack escorted Fuentes to the secured room which was located about ten feet from his office. Fuentes stood directly over him as Jack knelt on one knee putting him at eye level with the padlock. Jack twisted the dial to the right several times to clear it out. Eyes closed, he looked upward trying to remember the combination. After five or six seconds, Jack peered back at the lock and twisted the dial to the right, left and back again until the hasp dropped open. Fuentes smiled when Jack looked up at him, like he needed Fuentes' approval. Jack stood, opened the door and motioned Fuentes inside. Fuentes took one step inside and was almost knocked over by the bitter aroma. His eyes scoured the storage room that was practically filled wall to wall and stacked almost to the ceiling with white bricks wrapped in light brown packaging tape.

Fuentes looked back at Jack. "Wow," was all he could say. Jack shrugged his shoulders and smiled innocently. The two then walked back to Jack's office.

Jack explained his major concern with Fuentes. "I just want to keep the Marlowe name out of this whole mess. This is all a terrible mistake on someone's part and something like this could cause a multitude of public relations problems that the company might never recover from."

Fuentes shook his head from side to side. "I don't see any reason why any of that has to come out. I'll do what I can. Obviously it will be reported, and obviously the press will want to know where the cocaine was found. Since it is an official investigation, I think there is a high probability we can keep the company confidential...at least until we have indicted someone on it. I'll talk to the powers that be up the management line and see if we can't keep a lot of the information confidential at this point. Okay?"

Jack smiled and threw his head back against his chair. "Great! Thank you, thank you, thank you! You have no idea how much pressure this takes off me. I really would appreciate anything you can do."

"Don't worry about it." Fuentes smiled and rose from his chair. "Listen. We're obviously going to need nothing short of an army to inventory and take custody of the evidence. So don't be alarmed if ten or so agents come swooping down here later this afternoon, or even tomorrow morning sometime. Most of the office was called away on an exercise and I don't know if I can round up enough agents to assist me on such short notice. That's why I wish you had called yesterday. We could have taken care of it then. But, that's water under the bridge. Anyway, I've secured the area and other than myself, you, your lady friend and your five employees, nobody else knows. We should keep it that way."

Jack thought it strange to wait a day given the enormous quantity of the stash. But he smiled, knowing the FBI was now in charge and everything was in good hands and most important of all, off his shoulders. "Just tell me what I need to do."

"Nothing at all. Just make sure that until we return no one gains access to that room."

"That won't be a problem. I am the only one who knows the combination to the lock. Do I need to stay all night to make sure it's not bothered?"

"No. I'll have one of my men stationed on the road leading to the warehouse after the last person leaves for the day. Just make sure you lock up all the exterior doors before you leave."

"Consider it done!" Jack slapped his desk.

Fuentes extended his right hand to Jack. Jack rose and reciprocated. The two gripped each other's hand and squeezed tightly for several seconds. Fuentes peered into Jack's eyes. There was a slight hesitation while the handshake continued. "Thanks, Jack. We'll be in touch."

Each man released his grip and stared at the other for a few seconds. Fuentes turned and left Jack's office. Jack watched as Fuentes disappeared from the warehouse. He sat back down and placed his interlaced fingers on top of his head. He exhaled deeply and blew out what felt to be a cleansing breath. This was now off his plate.

Jack stayed at the warehouse the rest of the day. He wanted to be there when the boys from the FBI came pouring in. He called Margo downtown and told her that he would be tied up again at the warehouse. Margo fussed at him with a tone of humor in her voice, but she was serious about how his work was piling up downtown. Not to mention, his absence at a couple of important meetings had caused minor panic. Jack promised he would be there tomorrow and would take her to lunch at her favorite restaurant if she covered for him one more day. Margo reluctantly agreed but told him he better have his American Express on hand because it wouldn't be cheap. Jack laughed. Margo didn't. He knew he was on the hook for an elegant lunch.

Jack waited around until the last employee left the warehouse for the evening. He'd hoped Fuentes and his army would have come and gone by the end of the day. He guessed it was just as Fuentes had said, not a sufficient amount of agents could be rounded up to properly handle the massive amount of cocaine. Jack stayed about an hour after the last employee left to finish some last minute paperwork. He also called Emery to see if she could meet him at the Hard Rock Café. He had a couple errands he needed to run in the area, but as usual, he got her voice mail. Jack left a romantic message and told her to meet him if she could.

Jack gathered his briefcase and picked up the keys to his three-year-old hunter green Dodge Ram pick-up. Jack could have afforded a nicer vehicle, but appearances were secondary. His primary objective was to save money now and have it to enjoy it later. He lived a practical life and believed in the importance of saving. He had always been paranoid that if suddenly everything was lost, he would have nothing for the future. Jack was very conscientious about his savings and growing older. His salary was higher than most, but he always feared it could be gone tomorrow.

Jack glanced back toward the door of the room where the cocaine was as he left his office. He stopped and turned and walked over to the door. He set his briefcase gently on the cement floor. He jiggled the padlock to assure it was secure.

There was an eeriness in the sky as Jack's truck kicked up a trail of dust speeding down the single gravel road into the setting orange sun.

~ 4 ~

Jack grinned as he sang along with Bon Jovi's "Lost Highway" playing on the satellite radio in his truck. Other than a couple of days of untouched work and a handful of phone calls he would have to return, he felt no pressure or undue stress during his twenty minute commute from his home to the warehouse. Jack had treated himself by sleeping an extra hour. He believed he deserved it.

The dull orange sun resembling an oversized basketball had just crested above the pines surrounding the warehouse as Jack made the turn off the main highway onto the gravel road. He flipped the sun visor down and grabbed his sunglasses from the dashboard. He shielded his eyes since part of the sun still peeked brightly below his protective visor.

The gravel crunched beneath the tires of the truck as he crept at a comfortable speed toward the warehouse. There seemed to be a commotion brewing on the loading dock. It was hard to tell from the sun's glare on his windshield, but it seemed that Jack's entire staff was gathered on the platform which was connected to the warehouse. Jack flipped his visor up and leaned forward to get a better look. As he pulled into the space reserved for his truck, Jack could see Jerry, Mo, Zeeb, Potato and Ryree and the remaining fifty or so warehouse employees standing around, smoking cigarettes or simply sitting on the edge of the dock with their legs dangling over the side and doing absolutely no work.

A little upset at what appeared to be the gang getting some goof off time because the boss was a little late, Jack twisted his keys back hard and cut the engine. He found his release button on his safety belt and pushed down hard but it refused to release. He pushed down four times before the latch released, causing the metal buckle to slam hard against the window. Angrily, Jack snatched the keys from the ignition, jerked his door handle upward and kicked the door open with the heel of his shoe. He was surprised that none of his employees rushed back into the warehouse when they saw him approach. It was obvious he was not a happy camper.

Jack walked up the seven or eight concrete steps leading to the ramp of the loading dock. He saw Jerry in the distance and headed in his direction since Jerry was the foreman of the warehouse staff. Jack went over in his mind what excuses Jerry would have for this work stoppage that had only happened on a handful of occasions in five or ten years. Usually it was some type of safety concern but never one which justified a total work halt by every employee.

Worried faces followed Jack as he made his way toward Jerry. A couple laborers motioned to Jerry that the boss was on his way and he didn't look too happy. Jerry turned and spotted Jack and began walking toward him. He could see Jack's displeasure.

"What the hell is going on, Jerry?" Jack half shouted to Jerry who held out his hands and cocked his head in a non-verbal gesture, telling Jack to hold on before he jumped on everybody.

"It's the Feds, B. It ain't us." With his head, Jerry motioned toward the doorway leading into the warehouse where two FBI Agents were posted to deny entrance to any employees. Jack gave Jerry a questioned look and then twisted his neck to see what he was talking about.

"They've been here since about five this morning. They were here when I got here. Won't let anybody in to work either."

Jack looked at his watch. "They've been here for two hours?"

"At least."

"Why didn't you call me?"

"They wouldn't let us call nobody. They took over the phones and confiscated all our cell phones."

Jack's concern turned to anger. "What's going on? What the hell are they doing? The agent I talked to didn't say anything about shutting us down."

"Don't know, B. Like I said. I got here 'bout five and they were already inside. They wouldn't let me in and wouldn't tell me what was goin' on either. That's why all of us are just sittin' around. They told everybody to just relax until they were through."

Jack glared at Jerry. "What was the main agent's name?"

"I don't know. I'm sure he said, but he made me nervous."

"I'll get this straightened out in a real hurry. The guy I talked to promised that nothing like this would happen. I need to find him to get this straightened out. You don't remember the name of the agent you talked to?"

"Naah. Don't recall. He was real short though. And Hispanic."

Jack didn't really need to know his name. He knew it was Fuentes. He turned and observed two agents posted at the entrance to the warehouse. He waded through several of his employees toward the two agents now standing about twenty feet away. The agents, dressed in their typical black swat gear with huge gold letters on their backs spelling FBI, stood a bit more erect when they saw Jack moving in their direction. Jack stopped two feet short of them.

"I need to speak with Agent Fuentes right now!"

The first Agent, standing a couple inches taller than Jack and obviously fresh out of the FBI Academy, tried explaining in a calm voice. "Agent Fuentes is unavailable right now."

Jack stepped back and chuckled to himself. "Is Fuentes your boss?"

"Sir, as soon as Agent Fuentes is available we will let him know you need to see him. Until then, you need to join your co-workers over on the dock."

Jack shook his head in frustration then attempted to slide between the two agents to go inside his warehouse. He was stopped immediately and placed in an arm lock.

"Sir. I'm going to do this as nicely as I can. No one goes inside until further notice," said the agent who subdued Jack.

"Alright, alright. That hurts. You can let go now."

"Are you going to behave, sir?" The other agent inquired.

"Yes. Yes. Please let go."

The agent released his grip and Jack yanked his arm free. Jack rotated his arm a few times to loosen it up. Glancing back with an evil eye toward the agents while walking away he heard a voice he clearly recognized as Fuentes.

"Jack!"

Jack turned and saw Fuentes standing in the door opening, both arms outstretched and pushing against either side of the door frame.

He was also dressed in his black fatigues. Jack couldn't help but snicker at the site of the short man dressed up in swat gear. He thought he looked like a little boy coming out to play army on a Saturday morning.

"Something funny, Jack?"

"No," Jack cleared his voice. He was still snickering. "No. Nothing funny."

"Cause if there is I'd love to hear it. I got a feeling you're not gonna be so jolly when you hear what I've got to say."

Jack's smile faded quickly. He followed Fuentes and two other agents through the door and inside the warehouse. Jerry and the majority of the laborers watched in confusion as their boss was escorted inside and the door closed behind, while the two burly agents remained posted outside.

Inside, Jack, Fuentes and the two unidentified agents moved toward Jack's office. Jack looked around the warehouse, but did not see anything unusual. He noticed that fifteen or twenty agents were gathered around the room where the cocaine was secured. A few shuttled in and out with clipboards, permanent markers and cameras. As they reached Jack's office, Fuentes opened the door and motioned Jack inside.

"I'd like to know what's going on here, if you don't mind," Jack stated angrily. "You assured me nothing like this would happen."

"You are exactly right, Jack. I did assure you. But things have changed since last night. Sit down."

Jack started to move toward his chair behind his desk, but was re-routed by Fuentes who ordered him to sit in the chair in front of the desk. Fuentes moved and assumed the cushy chair behind the desk and Jack took his seat on the metal chair. Fuentes lifted his legs and propped them on top of Jack's desk, causing papers to shuffle. Jack swallowed hard and his forehead began to sweat. He wiped the sweat off with the back of his hand.

"Nervous about something?"

"No. Should I be?"

"I don't know. You tell me. Nervous people usually sweat. It's not like its hot outside or like you've been working in a hot warehouse all day." Fuentes ordered one of the agents to post himself outside their office and the other one to sit beside Jack.

Jack watched as both agents took their positions. He looked at Fuentes' feet on his desk. "You mind telling me what the hell is going on here? Are we in some sort of trouble?"

"We?" Fuentes said. "We? Do you see any of your co-workers detained right now?"

Jack felt the blood leave his face and go directly to his belly. "What the hell are you doing? I haven't done anything wrong. Am I in some sort of trouble? I thought you said there wasn't a problem because I waited to report this."

"Oh, that's not a problem. That's not a problem at all. I already spoke to my superiors and to the Assistant U.S. Attorney and they assured me that wasn't a problem."

Jack looked around and waited for Fuentes to keep talking but he didn't. "Look. All I know is you told me yesterday that you were gonna keep this quiet and keep my name and the company name out of it. Next thing I know is you and your SS storm troopers have invaded us like it's D-Day. Will somebody tell me what the hell is going on?"

Fuentes removed his feet from the top of the desk and leaned forward. "Jack. I had every intention of keeping this on the QT but recent events have changed that."

"Recent events? What recent events?"

Fuentes leaned back and placed his short, stubby intertwined fingers across his chest. "I think you know what I'm talking about, Jack. It'd be a whole lot easier if you just went ahead and told us everything. You know, get it off your chest?"

"Get what off my chest?" Jack snapped back. "I have no idea what you're talking about."

Fuentes looked at his fellow agent who shook his head slightly and smiled.

Jack saw his expression and was enraged. "Look. Maybe if you stopped pussy footin' around and playing the Gestapo mind games and tell me what the hell is going on, just maybe I could help!"

Fuentes eyed Jack then shifted his eyes to his partner. He looked at Jack. "Fine, Jack. If you insist." Fuentes paused. "Yesterday you and your men did a diligent job. Certainly saved us a lot of time.

How many bricks did you say you counted? What was it?"

"Twelve-thousand," Jack jumped in quickly.

"Right. Twelve-thousand. And you were certain of that number?"

"Yes. We counted them when we took them out of the toilets and again when we secured them in the storage room."

"At two o'clock this morning my phone rang. My caller ID just said out of area and I don't typically get calls at two in the morning and I typically don't pick up the phone if it says out of area. But, I figured at that time of the morning it must be something important. Anyway, this voice at the other end tells me, indeed there were twelve-thousand bricks in that storage room, but that there is a huge possibility that number decreased sometime during the night. And sure enough, Jack. We have counted three times now and keep coming up with the same number over and over. For some strange reason there are only eleven-thousand, seven-hundred fifty bricks in our inventory. That's two hundred fifty missing, Jack. Somewhere around two hundred fifty million dollars worth of cocaine."

Jack sat in silence. He could think of nothing to say.

"Not to make you nervous or anything but this is an extremely serious situation we have here and we need to get a handle on it pretty quickly. You need to be honest with us and let us help you out."

"Wait a minute. You think I have something to do with it? Are you serious? I didn't do anything. Are you kidding me?" Jack suddenly felt nauseous.

"Were you the last one to leave the warehouse?" Fuentes asked.

"Yes. But, I didn't do anything."

"What did you do before you left? Did you go inside the storage room?"

"No! I mean I stopped by it to make sure it was locked, but I didn't go inside."

"Are you sure?"

"Yes I'm sure! I didn't do anything. Look. I know what you're trying to do. You're trying to get me to admit to something I didn't do. Why in the hell would I do something that stupid? Why would I tell you there were twelve-thousand bricks if I planned to steal two-hundred and fifty of them. Do I look that stupid? Hell, I'm the guy that called to report it. Why would I do that if I had some evil plan to steal it?"

"No, Jack. You didn't report anything. Your lady friend did. As a matter of fact, you sat on this for twenty-four hours and said nothing."

Jack squirmed in his seat. "Alright, fine. I didn't call you myself but I told Emery to call you. If I was going to steal two hundred fifty bricks of cocaine, why would I tell her to call you? You don't honestly believe I did this do you?"

"Somebody did," Fuentes said, not blinking once.

Jack leaned forward and banged on the desk once for each word. "But it wasn't me! I did not do it!"

"Who did, Jack?" Fuentes continued. "If it wasn't you, you must know who did."

"How would I know?"

"You're the boss. You would have to know who all has access inside here."

"What about the agents you had posted on the road all night?" Jack asked. "Did they not see anything?"

"Nothing," Fuentes answered. "Did anyone else have the combination to the padlock?"

Jack rolled his eyes and took a deep breath then slowly exhaled. "No. I'm the only one."

"See what I mean, Jack? Who else could have gotten in there? There were no signs of forced entry. As a matter of fact, the padlock was locked when we got here this morning."

"Are you sure you counted correctly?" Jack was searching for anything.

"Three times. We counted three times. Each time is the same number. Eleven-thousand, seven-hundred fifty. We could count again if it made you feel better."

Jack buried his face in his palms. "Look. I can't help you. All I'm saying is I didn't take anything. You're talking to the wrong guy."

Fuentes leaned forward. "How do you think it's going to look when I report the facts of this case and all the evidence points to you as the only possible suspect? Now's the time, Jack. Now is the time to cooperate and tell me what you know. I can help you now. As the investigation continues and I talk to more people, your window of opportunity shrinks a little each day."

"How can I tell you something I don't know? I don't care how it looks. I didn't do it and I don't know who did. You can say whatever you want. It doesn't change the fact that I'm innocent."

Jack and Fuentes locked eyes. Fuentes wanted a confession and did not want to leave without it. Jack would not give him what he wanted.

"Am I under arrest?"

"No, you're not. Not yet."

"Am I free to leave?"

"You're free to leave, but don't leave Atlanta."

Fuentes and his partner stood in unison with Jack. Fuentes' partner opened the door. Before Fuentes could step outside, Jack stopped. "I was just thinking. There is one lead you can possibly follow up on."

"Yes?" Fuentes said.

"I may not be the only person with the combination to the padlock."

"Someone else have it too?" Fuentes asked.

"If you will recall, Agent Fuentes, you were with me yesterday when I opened the door to the room to show you the cocaine. If I remember right, you were standing directly above me when I worked the combination."

Fuentes scoffed at the accusation.

Jack shrugged his shoulders. "Just a thought. Cause I gotta say, I wondered why a big time FBI agent like yourself would let over a billion dollars worth of cocaine sit overnight, unguarded." Jack looked at the second agent. "When did Agent Fuentes report this incident? Did he report it yesterday morning when he got back to the office, or did he sit on it just like I did?" Jack paused. "Like I said. Just a thought."

Jack nodded his head at both Fuentes and the other agent as he was escorted outside with the rest of the warehouse employees.

Fuentes' partner sat down in the metal chair and Fuentes sat in Jack's chair. "Well?" Fuentes' partner said.

"Well what?" Fuentes retorted.

"When did this happen?"

"When did what happen?"

"When did Armstrong find the cocaine?"

"What are you suggesting?" Fuentes asked.

"I'm not suggesting anything. I'm just saying I did not know anything about this until three o'clock this morning. Everyone I talked to didn't know anything about it until a few hours ago. If what Armstrong is saying is true, you've got some explaining of your own to do, Eric."

"You can't honestly believe what Armstrong is suggesting!"

"Course not, Eric. But I'm not the one that matters. If you didn't report this immediately, do you realize how it looks? And I hate to ask you, but was Armstrong right? Were you standing behind him when he opened the combination lock?"

"Yeah, but I didn't see anything."

Fuentes' partner shook his head in disbelief. "Reasonable doubt, Eric. Reasonable doubt. I believe you, but if anything Armstrong said is true, you may have some issues to resolve." He got up and walked out the door. "You coming?"

"Yeah. I'll be there in a minute. I just gotta finish these notes. Shut the door behind you if you don't mind." Fuentes watched his partner as he walked from sight. He said something to himself in Spanish and smacked his forehead with the butt of his hand. He shook his head, disgusted with his lack of attention. Fuentes picked up the phone on Jack's desk and quickly dialed a number. He waited a few seconds until his intended party picked up. "Hey listen. It's me. We may have a problem." Fuentes pulled a handkerchief from one of his fatigue pockets and dabbed the beads of perspiration forming on his brow. He closed his eyes and pondered his next move.

By noon, Fuentes and his quarry of agents were still busy inventorying evidence and interviewing employees. One by one, as each laborer completed his or her interrogation, Jack let them go home. It was obvious no work was going to get done this day anyway. By three o'clock, all employees had been questioned and released with the exception of the five who helped Jack two days earlier. Jerry, Mo, Zeeb, Potato and Ryree stood on the edge of the dock in a semi-circle. Mo puffed on a filterless camel cigarette while Zeeb sucked away on a skinny cigar. Jack waved away any smoke floating in his direction. The 11,750 bricks of cocaine had long since been transported to and logged into the FBI's evidence vault in downtown Atlanta. Jack and his crew turned as Fuentes and a couple of agents emerged from the door leading from the warehouse. They all maintained eye contact but no words were passed.

Fuentes walked directly into the middle of Jack and his five crewmen. "Gentlemen, I apologize for leaving you until the end but that's just the way it works out sometime. You see, we've talked to everyone and developed as much background as possible. And as it turns out, you gentlemen and Mr. Armstrong seem to have the most knowledge about this, this, stash for lack of a better term." Fuentes moved and motioned toward Jack. "I'm sure your supervisor here has briefed you on the problem that has arisen. So I am asking each of you to cooperate fully with the investigation. We will be interviewing each of you simultaneously. Does everybody know what that means?"

Jerry, Zeeb, Potato and Ryree shook their heads yes. Mo wasn't so sure.

Jack was livid. "You don't have to talk down to 'em like that. They know what you mean."

"Not talking down to anyone, Jack. I just wanna make sure everyone's on board here so there will be no confusion." Fuentes eyed the five. "We'll be talking to all of you at the same time but in separate rooms. Therefore you will not have the benefit of talking to each other or knowing who said what about who. Basically, this is your one shot to tell the truth and cooperate fully. I would be thrilled if no one here gets charged with anything, and if you tell the truth and are cooperative, that most likely will be the case." Fuentes turned and smiled at Jack. Jack shook his head, very frustrated at Fuentes' arrogance. Fuentes motioned to the five. "Gentlemen, if you come with us we will get you to whoever has been assigned to talk to you." Fuentes turned to Jack. "And Jack, as I said earlier. You are free to go." Fuentes smiled sarcastically, then chuckled.

Jack wanted to curse the cocky, dark complected agent but knew it would do absolutely no good and might possibly hurt him in the long run. Jack bit down on his lip so it wouldn't get ahead of his brain. He watched as his subordinates were escorted back into the warehouse. Jack sat down on the edge of the dock, leaned back on his hands and stared into the cloudless sky. He could not believe what had transpired in the last forty-eight hours and he wasn't about to leave until he knew his men had been cleared and the swat team had packed its gear and left.

Jack would sit for three more hours. It was almost six o'clock when Jerry emerged from the door by himself. Jack stood up and walked toward Jerry who was obviously exhausted from the lengthy interrogation. Jerry was not smiling. The half smile on Jack's face faded quickly. "What's goin' on, Jer? What'd they say?"

Jerry paused and stared at Jack. "I'm not supposed to talk about it, B. They told me to not discuss anything. Said I could be charged with obstruction of, obstruction, obstruction of something, if I did."

"Justice?"

"Yeah. Obstruction of justice. Said if I discussed anything with anyone I could be charged and could go to jail for five years."

"They're trying to frame me aren't they?" Jack asked almost emotionless.

Jerry looked at Jack but said nothing. Jack looked back and asked silently with his eyes. "I'm sorry, B. I don't wanna go to jail."

"That's okay. You just told me everything." Jack looked away. "I can't believe they're doing this to me. I've never done anything wrong in my life. Not even a speeding ticket. I don't understand why they think I would have anything to do with something like this."

Jerry looked at the ground and shrugged his shoulders. "I don't know, B. I don't know." Jerry walked down the steps leading from the loading dock and peered back over his shoulder as he approached his truck. He sighed, half smiled and half waved at Jack.

By now Mo, Zeeb, Potato and Ryree began trickling one by one from the warehouse doorway. They all sauntered past Jack with their hands in their pockets. Mo and Potato quietly told Jack they were sorry as they passed by him. Zeeb and Ryree just looked at the ground as they strolled by their boss. The four looked like kids playing follow the leader as they walked down the steps and proceeded to get into their trucks and the lime-green Civic. They all sympathetically peered back at Jack, got into their vehicles and drove away toward the orange sun sitting directly over the gravel road.

Within minutes Fuentes and eight or ten other agents waltzed from the warehouse door. Jack turned and observed a grinning Fuentes who approached Jack. Fuentes sat down beside Jack on the dock.

"You can't get away with it ya' know," Jack said passively.

"Get away with what, Jack?"

"I see what you're trying to do here, but it's not gonna work. You can turn my men against me, but at the end of the day I'm still innocent. I didn't do anything."

"If you're innocent, then you've got nothing to worry about. Right, Jack?"

"Why are you doing this to me?"

Fuentes smiled. "I'm not doing anything to you. You did it to yourself, and the longer you run away from it, the worse it's going to get. I'm not trying to implicate an innocent man, Jack. I would do no such thing. But unfortunately for you, all the facts point directly at you. If you can prove your innocence, then now is the time."

"I've told you everything I know. I don't know who did it, but it wasn't me! There's nothing else I can tell you."

"Fair enough. If that's the way you wanna play it, then fair enough." Fuentes pulled a business card from a hidden pocket and reached toward Jack's shirt where he firmly tucked it in. He patted it a couple times for good measure. "Here's my card, Jack. Should you have a change of heart and want to talk to me, you can call me any time, day or night." Fuentes and his small army of agents began walking away from Jack and toward the dock's steps. Fuentes stopped and turned back as the others continued walking toward their bucars. "But, I highly suggest you make it sooner rather than later. The sooner you talk, the more I can help you. Do we understand each other?"

Jack said nothing.

Fuentes got in his car and drove away, leaving a trail of dust behind. Jack stood up and was motionless as he watched the ten or so cars follow each other down the gravel road toward the setting sun.

A million thoughts rushed through Jack's mind as he drove down his street lined with tall oaks on both sides and down the grassy strip separating traffic. Children rode their bicycles down the sidewalks which ran parallel to the rustic wood framed homes in the shady neighborhood. Some of the kids moaned when they heard the distinct call of their moms' voice in the distance to come home for dinner or to finish homework. Dusk was just about to give way to darkness.

In the distance, Emery's red convertible jutted out just far enough from his driveway for Jack to see it. The feeling he got when he knew Emery was there was the only pleasant thing that had happened to him all day. He drove slowly through his pristine neighborhood and wondered if the good life was slowly beginning to crumble around him. As he drove into his driveway and parked behind Emery's car, he thought of the events of the day and how he had absolutely no alibi. Nothing, nor no one, to prove him innocent.

Jack opened his car door, climbed out and gently shut it. He leaned back inside through the open window and pulled out his briefcase. He turned and headed for his house hoping to see Emery on the front porch swing waiting for him. But, she wasn't there and this was strange. Usually, once or twice a week, Emery met Jack at his house after work and would patiently wait for him on the porch swing. Her lovely smile would turn into a gigantic grin as he drove into the driveway. Walking up the steps to his wood-planked front porch, Jack assumed Emery had gone next door to see the elderly couple she had befriended in the last couple of weeks. After all, it was later than normal and he figured she had probably become bored after waiting for him. He was just glad she hadn't left.

Jack fidgeted with his keys and manually chose the right one by touch. He positioned his house key between his thumb and index finger and aimed it toward the keyhole. As the key was inserted, the door eerily creaked open. Jack quickly straightened up, at first suspecting a burglar and then remembering that Emery might be inside. He positioned his truck key, the largest one on his key ring, between his thumb and index finger and readied it for use as a possible weapon. He set his briefcase down on the porch and slowly pushed the front door open, inch by inch. When it was sufficiently wide enough, he bobbed his head in quickly to get a peek and then back out again. He saw no signs of any intruder but still sensed something was not right. He poked his head in again and left it there. His body was shielded by the door and he could make a quick exit should someone be there who was not supposed to be. As he scoured the living room with his wide open eyes he was greeted with couch cushions obviously thrown to the floor, chairs overturned and some gutted with their foamy insides spewing out onto the hardwood floor. He heard no signs of possible intruders and figured whoever had been there was long gone. His main concern was Emery's safety. He imagined finding her sprawled out on the floor. He prayed he would not.

Jack moved carefully inside the house, but did not close the door behind him. Should someone be there, he needed a quick exit. Jack was confused as he crept very slowly into his den. The ceiling fan whirred above, gently blowing pages of newspapers indiscriminately scattered across the floor. Books were thrown from a bookcase and left open on the floor. Jack kept his ears open for any sound and squeezed his key weapon firmly. He stopped in the middle of the hallway when he heard a single footstep from inside his bedroom. His heart raced so fast he could feel it in his temples. His face burned and his legs froze like they do in a dream. He leaned back against a wall and could not feel his legs. He was terrified any sound he made would be heard by whoever was in his room. Jack blinked hard when he heard a second step, then a third and fourth. He inhaled deeply but quietly. He knew he could not just stand there and do nothing. He had to make a move, whether it was to his bedroom or the opposite way to get the hell out of his house. He thought of Emery and that she might be hurt. He clinched his fists, closed his eyes and tensed every muscle in his body. His mind said yes, but his legs said no. His mind raced to a time when he bragged 'pity the poor fool who comes uninvited into my house'. Now it was time for action.

Either stay and fight, or run. Male pride made him choose the former. His trembling legs bumbled closer to his bedroom door. As he got closer he could hear the culprit rummaging through his drawers. He prayed Emery was next door and not dead. Several steps away from the door he could detect a shadow filtering from the bedroom onto the hallway floor. Jack froze as the shadow seemed to move slowly toward the door. Maybe whoever it was had also heard him. His pulse quickened and his heart felt like it was going to explode. Just as it seemed his heart would go in arrhythmia, a hand grabbed him suddenly on his shoulder.

"Jack!"

Jack about jumped out of his skin. He held his car key in the air, ready to attack. "Oh, crap, Emery! What're you trying to do, give me a heart attack?" He pushed back against the wall and exhaled. As his heart raced, and the possibility of an underwear change loomed, the sound of bolting footsteps and shattering glass reverberated from Jack's bedroom. Almost forgetting the shadow, Jack bound into his bedroom, but could only make out two dark colored tennis shoes with white lettering on the back as whoever it was sprinted quickly down the street. Jack stared out from the broken glass of his bedroom window, with shreds of bloody denim and a piece or two of torn skin hanging on a shard of glass.

Emery strolled to Jack's side and nervously peered through the shattered glass. "Who was it?"

Bewildered, Jack glanced at Emery. "How would I know?"

"Maybe it was the FBI."

"The what? They wouldn't run. And they sure wouldn't bust through a window. It wasn't the FBI. Trust me. I think every agent in Atlanta was at the warehouse today."

Emery held up a white form for Jack to see. "This was on your kitchen table."

Jack snatched it from her hand and read it. "A search warrant?"

"What's happening, Jack? Why would the FBI search your house?"

"Because for some stupid reason they think I stole two hundred fifty bricks of cocaine from the warehouse." Jack stared out the window.

Emery put her hand on Jack's shoulder. "Was there anything for them to find?"

Jack glared at Emery. "What's that supposed to mean?"

"I don't know, Jack. They searched your house. They had to have a reason. They can't just come in here and search for no reason."

Jack sighed and peered back through the broken window. "I can't believe you'd even think such a thing. They got you believing it now."

Emery gently touched his chin and turned his face toward hers. She peered sympathetically into his eyes. "You know how I feel about you, Jack. It's just that..."

"It's just what? You don't believe me. Is that it?"

"No. That's not it."

"Then what?"

Emery paused. "I barely know you. That's all. If you say everything's okay then I believe you. Okay?"

Upset, Jack looked at Emery and exhaled hard through his nostrils. "Don't you think if they'd found something or they had a shred of evidence that I'd be sitting in the Fulton County Jail right now?"

"I guess," she said, turning away from Jack and peering out the jagged glass.

Jack joined her. "Thanks for the vote of confidence."

"I'm sorry. I really am. It's just..."

Jack interrupted. "Don't say anything. Just don't say anything."

Emery peered sadly at Jack, but he just stared outside. He had been violated by the FBI or someone, and now by the one person he thought would believe him. His entire world was crashing down on him and there was nothing he could do about it. "I'd better go," she said sheepishly. She looked down and saw all the glass on the floor. She knelt and began to clean it up.

"Just go. I just want you to go," he said, while still staring outside.

Emery paused momentarily thinking of the right thing to say. But now wasn't the time for talk. She turned and walked away. As she got to the doorway, she turned to Jack. "Call me?"

"Sure," Jack said, but not really meaning it.

Emery sighed, turned and walked away. Jack watched as she maneuvered her convertible around his truck which had her partially blocked in. Her tires screeched as she floored the accelerator and disappeared into the night. Jack watched as her tail lights faded from view. He turned away from the shattered window and walked over to the only friend he believed was on his side. Jovi, an overweight, white-and-brown-spotted floppy eared basset hound, was rescued from an animal shelter just hours before it was to be euthanized. The lazy canine was so named because Jack rescued Jovi on the day Bon Jovi's latest album was released. Jovi weighed about a hundred pounds and did little more than sleep. But Jack loved him like a child. Every afternoon when he returned from work, there would be a slumbering Jovi on the area rug near the fireplace. He would take about three seconds to gaze up with those familiar sad eyes and yawn, his way of welcoming Jack home. About the only sound Jovi ever made was a low moan when he would wake up for a few seconds, yawn, and then lay his head back down.

Jovi looked up at his master, his mouth open, tongue draped over the right side of his mouth. A loyal friend, he was. A watch dog, he wasn't.

"Did you show them where all the jewelry was too, Jovi?"

Jovi yawned and laid his head back down. He rested his snout on top of his left paw.

Jack kneeled down and stroked Jovi on top of his head. "All this excitement just wore you out. Huh boy?"

Jovi was fast asleep.

~ 5 ~

The *Atlanta Journal Constitution* held nothing back. In bold black letters, the front page headline leaped out at Jack as he sipped his morning cup of coffee. **PLUMBING COMPANY EXECUTIVE IMPLICATED IN HUGE DRUG HAUL.** It wasn't an indictment, but it certainly led the reader to believe Jack was involved. The story began with Jack's exemplary career with Marlowe and of his squeaky clean past. Although he had not yet been charged, the article clearly suggested Jack's arrest was imminent.

Angrier by the minute, Jack drove to work as the sun barely peeked above the horizon. He began to realize the FBI would not back off until they got him. For whatever reason, he was their man and their sights were focused squarely on him. The phrase "presumed innocent" meant absolutely nothing. He knew it was up to him to find anything that would exonerate him.

Halfway to work, Jack flipped on his favorite radio station to help take his mind off of the situation. But even the deep-voiced announcer was enjoying commenting on the most recent developments of the largest drug haul in the history of Georgia. Enraged, Jack ripped the volume knob from its stem and threw it to the ground a fraction of a second before his name was blurted over the airways for all Atlanta to hear. "Dammit!" Jack pounded hard on his steering wheel.

Folded newspaper in hand, Jack slammed the door to his truck so hard the side view mirror popped from its socket and crashed into the gray gravel below, shattering on contact. He looked at the shards of glass, muttered a silent profanity and quickly made his way up the loading dock steps. Inside, several workers scattered back to their work stations after curiously watching Jack, now an implicated criminal. They wondered how their boss could have committed such a crime and violate their trust of so many years. They already had begun to believe what they were hearing and seeing.

As he entered the warehouse, Jack could tell he was being watched. The employees pretended to work, but it was obvious from the quick peeks that work was not foremost on their minds. Jack stood alone and watched in all directions. Eyes that watched him quickly snapped back to whatever make-believe task they were doing when he looked their way. Jack's patience reached its boiling point as he shouted verbal orders at every employee in sight. Workers witnessed a side of him they had never seen. A normally cool and calm man who never became ruffled was suddenly losing all composure. As he shouted his demands at anyone listening, they began to confirm in their minds that it was all true. Maybe he had cracked and what they were seeing was the real Jack.

Some employees found it all hard to believe. They found the news very hard to swallow. More likely he was being made a scapegoat for some larger organization. Maybe he was just caving under the pressure. They did not want to believe their boss, who'd been a friend to so many, so kind to everyone and more like a peer than a supervisor, could possibly be involved in something as serious as this. But logic seemed to suggest the FBI was right. The gossip at the warehouse centered around how Jack sent everyone home when the drugs were found without reporting it to the police. Why not? Jack was the last one to leave and the padlock he provided to lock the room belonged to him. Jack was the only one with the combination and the padlock was locked when the FBI arrived the day before. There were no signs that anyone broke into the room. As much as the employees did not want to believe it, the evidence mounting against him suggested Jack was the only one who could have stolen the cocaine.

After another barrage of senseless demands and wary stares from his subordinates, Jack realized he was taking his frustrations out on his employees. He quietly apologized and disappeared to his office. He tossed his folded newspaper on his desk where it landed face up. The glaring headline only reminded him of his predicament. Jack leaned against his closed door, inhaled deeply then exhaled. He sat down at his desk, placed his folded hands across his face and thought for a few seconds before he picked up the phone and dialed information.

"What city?"

"Atlanta," Jack said.

"Go ahead."

"I need the number for the FBI," he said, in a monotone voice.

"One minute, sir." After a slight pause, a number was provided.

Jack pushed the cancel button with his finger and waited for a dial tone. He kept the receiver to his ear and forcefully punched the seven buttons.

After three rings, a confident female voice answered. "FBI. How can I direct your call?"

"Eric Fuentes," Jack mumbled.

"May I tell him who's calling?"

"No you may not."

"Excuse me?" The receptionist was surprised at the response.

"You asked me if you could tell him who's calling and I gave you an answer. I said no." He had always wanted to say that to someone but out of courtesy never had. But he was in no mood for anyone to test him. He kept talking. "I never understood why you receptionists always ask that question. May I tell him who's calling. Why do you ask that? Are you not gonna let me talk to him if I don't tell you? I will tell you this. If you don't put me through to Agent Fuentes, he will probably be royally pissed off that I wasn't put through. Now I'm sorry, but you've got no business knowing who I am. Are you gonna put me through or not?"

"Please hold, sir."

Jack smiled for the first time in two days. He listened to ten or fifteen seconds of elevator music while on hold when an obviously agitated Fuentes answered. "Fuentes."

"What the hell are you trying to do to me?" Jack said forcefully, but not loud.

"Good morning, Jack. Well, so far in two days, you've managed to steal two hundred fifty million dollars worth of cocaine and bully our receptionist. Personally, the latter is probably the most serious."

"Very funny, Fuentes. Very funny. Why are you doing this to me?"

"Jack, whatever you've done, you've done it to yourself."

"That's a load of bull and you know it."

"Look, Jack. I'm not going to get into an argument with you. Alright? That's not going to do anybody any good."

"How can you sit there and let this happen? I had nothing to do with this and you know it."

"Then who did, Jack? If you didn't do it you have to know who did. You were the only one who knew the combination and that padlock was locked when we got there. Somebody got in there between the time you left and the time we got there. If it wasn't you, who was it?"

"I swear to you, I don't know!" Jack was almost pleading.

"Fine, Jack. Look. All I know is what the evidence tells me. If it wasn't you, then you must be protecting someone. You're gonna go down for this all by yourself while your partner flies away to the Caribbean a multi-millionaire. Is that okay with you?"

"Partner? What partner? There is no partner."

"So you acted alone?"

"No! You're twisting my words."

"Then who, Jack, who? Who are you protecting?"

"I'm telling you, there is nobody! I didn't do it! I swear to God, I don't know who did!"

Fuentes paused. "Not good enough."

"What do you want from me? I've never broken the law in my life. Why would I risk my career and my life?"

"That's what they all say. You tell me."

Jack's voice broke. "What do you want from me?"

"A signed sworn statement, Jack. I want a full confession. That's the only way I can help you. Anything short of that, I don't want to talk to you."

Jack paused. "There's nothing I can tell you. Nothing."

"Jack. Let me tell you something. A special session of the Federal Grand Jury has been called specifically for this case. I will be testifying before it in about an hour and forty-five minutes. It's about a ten minute walk from my office to the Federal Building where the Grand Jury will convene. That means I'll be leaving in about an hour and a half. If you are unfamiliar with the Grand Jury process let me try and explain it to you." Fuentes was feeling more powerful by the second. "You see. I go in and tell the members of the Grand Jury what facts and evidence I've obtained regarding the case. There are no defense attorneys and no objections. I don't even have to have a whole multitude of evidence which would convict you. All I need is a preponderance of evidence which says you are most likely responsible for the theft of the cocaine. What that means, Jack, is a majority. If the majority of the Grand Jurors believe I have sufficient evidence, they will return what's called a true bill. That means they hand down an indictment. You know what an indictment is, right?"

Jack was silent.

"I'll take that as a yes. Tell you what. You've got about an hour and twenty-eight minutes before I leave. If you feel lucky and think the facts won't result in an indictment, then you just go ahead and take your chances. But don't think for a minute that I'll stop investigating this. I'll keep going until I can get an indictment. On the other hand, you can end this today and I won't hold any of your lies up til now against you. If you will just cooperate and tell me what happened, I will tell the AUSA and he will cut you a sweet deal. Alright?" Fuentes paused. "Alright, Jack. You've got a little less than an hour and a half. I'll keep my line clear."

"Why would I confess to something I didn't do?"

"You heard my offer. Once I'm in there, it's too late. All offers are off the table."

Jack was silent.

"Are we clear, Jack? Jack?"

"You did it, didn't you?" Jack asked Fuentes.

"Did what?"

"You stole it, didn't you?"

Fuentes paused at first but then started laughing.

"Go ahead and laugh. It all makes sense now. No witnesses. You made sure of that. All the evidence points to me. Why not make me the scapegoat?"

Fuentes could hardly control his laughter. "Jack, Jack, Jack. Are you serious? Do you seriously think anybody in their right mind would ever believe such an accusation?"

"I hear your accent. You're not a natural born citizen. Where are you from anyway? Huh? Who do you associate with? Who are you related to?"

Fuentes stopped laughing.

"Struck a nerve, did I?"

Fuentes paused. "I'm done, Jack. Maybe you can plead insanity after you are indicted this afternoon." Fuentes paused. "You've now got about an hour and twenty-five minutes before I get up and make my way to the Federal Building. "Don't call me back unless you plan on fessing up. And, by the way. You may want to call an attorney. You'll need a good one before the day is out. So long, Jack."

Jack hung up the phone, leaned his head back and covered his eyes with both hands.

Most of the members of the Grand Jury were seated behind long straight oak tables fashioned into a square. There were a few seated in metal chairs situated against the wood paneled wall. The room was small, but most of the Grand Jury members would swear it was never meant for gatherings of more than ten. The room had two large windows which made the room seem larger than it really was. But Assistant United States Attorney Russ Waters always drew the curtains closed because he wanted the full attention of all the members on whatever case was being presented. Any distraction could be unfair to the Government, or the subject of a case, and AUSA Waters was a stickler for truth and justice no matter which side it fell.

AUSA Waters became an attorney by fate. In college, some twenty years earlier, he was a six-foot three, 245 pound All-American linebacker. With dark hair and deep-set eyes, he was not only projected to be a first round draft pick in the NFL, but most figured he would land in Hollywood after his playing days were over. But a devastating neck injury in the final game of his senior season ended his dream. He laid around in a desperate state for a year until one afternoon he flicked on his television and watched an episode of *Law and Order*. He was enthralled by what he saw. He pulled himself out of his doldrums and entered the University of Tennessee Law School envisioning himself making a six figure income working for some prestigious law firm. The only problem was criminal law was the only area that interested him, and he couldn't imagine ever defending a murderer or rapist. Hence, his only option was the U.S. Attorney's Office or the District Attorney's Office. Because his father was friends with the FBI Special Agent in Charge who was good friends with the U.S. Attorney, Russ filled a slot as an Assistant one year out of law school. There was quite a bit of resentment from some of the other Assistants who had paid their dues, but that would soon fade when they saw Russ putting in sixteen and seventeen hour days. And never once did he drop a name or expect special treatment. His deep and booming voice became his trademark, perfect for the courtroom and for keeping a jury interested.

Waters stood and turned his whole body as Fuentes entered the Grand Jury room. Ever since his football injury Waters had been unable to turn his head in either direction. Very annoying, but he soon got used to it. Waters half smiled at Fuentes and motioned for him to sit down in the empty seat behind the table which faced the Grand Jury members. Before he could sit, the clerk swore him in.

Fuentes swore to God to tell the whole truth and nothing but the truth. Waters expected he would do no less. Fuentes was seated and began reciting why he should be believed as a credible witness. Fourteen years as a Special Agent with an exemplary record. Most of the Grand Jury members recognized him from pictures in the papers on several occasions on headline making cases. Fuentes had name recognition, the credentials, the stats, not to mention the aura that goes along with being an FBI Special Agent. In short, he was very believable. Agent Fuentes was a very credible witness.

Fuentes cited all the facts he'd gathered in the investigation. He answered all of Waters' questions with precise detail. He was an excellent witness. Fuentes discussed a multitude of circumstantial evidence which could be considered by the Grand Jury. He even politely answered several questions from a couple of Grand Jury members who were intrigued by the case.

After Fuentes was excused, Waters reminded the Grand Jury of its obligations and that only a preponderance of evidence was needed to return an indictment or true bill. Waters thanked them for their attention and left them to deliberate the case. Waters ducked out a side entrance to the room and literally bumped into Fuentes. "Excuse me, Eric. Didn't look where I was going?"

"That's alright," Fuentes paused. "So what's your feel?"

With several folders tucked neatly under his left arm, Waters began walking away. "Walk with me, Eric. I've got ten minutes to walk four blocks."

Fuentes began walking and offered to carry the folders.

"Thanks. I'll let you."

They walked briskly to the elevator. Waters pushed the down button over and over somehow hoping that the more he pushed it the quicker the elevator would arrive. "I think it went well in there. But you can never tell. Grand Juries do funny things sometimes. Evidence is certainly overwhelming."

"I can't help but sense a little doubt in your voice." Fuentes frowned at Waters, who eyed the elevator numbers lighting up as it got closer and closer.

"C'mom, c'mon, c'mon," Waters impatiently chided the elevator. "It's not that I'm not sure, Eric. It's just that ninety-five percent of your case is based on circumstantial evidence." The elevator doors popped open and the bell dinged. "Finally." Waters eyed his watch as half of the full load emptied out past him and Fuentes. "C'mon, c'mon." After the last person exited, Waters and Fuentes stepped inside. Waters pushed the button for the first floor four or five times, once again, assuming the doors would close quicker if he did. Waters checked his watch as the doors closed.

"But the Grand Jury can return an indictment based on hearsay and circumstantial evidence. So what's the problem?"

Waters only half listened. He was more concerned about his next appointment and he knew he was going to be late. "What? Sorry, Eric. My mind is somewhere else."

"Circumstantial evidence. Don't you think we have enough to indict?"

"Oh yeah. Probably. I'm just saying your case is weak right now and there's no way I'd take it to trial with what you've got. An indictment's enough to charge and arrest your boy, but it's not enough to convict. Grand Jury will probably indict. But based on what I heard in that room, you raised more questions than you answered."

"But you're looking at it from an attorney's viewpoint and not a layman's."

"True. But if they indict Armstrong, he'll have an attorney that will also view it like me. With what you've got now, you'd get chewed up and spit out in court. Sorry to be blunt, but that's the way I see it at this point. I need more, Eric."

The numbers on top of the elevator doors signaled the first floor. The doors seemed to open in slow motion for Waters. He snatched his folders from Fuentes and fled quickly out of the elevator. Fuentes stood frozen inside. Waters wheeled around to Fuentes. "Don't worry. You'll get the indictment. You'll get the arrest. I'm sure of that. Armstrong will be in custody in less than forty-eight hours. But you gotta bring me more than you've got right now or we'll never make the case." Waters looked at his watch, spun around and began jogging out of the building and to his next appointment.

Fuentes remained frozen inside the elevator, watching Waters disappear onto the crowded Atlanta sidewalks. Even after Waters had vanished, Fuentes stared straight ahead, not realizing he was staring straight into the elevator doors which had closed several seconds earlier and beginning its upward climb with a brand new set of passengers.

Jack pretended to busy himself behind a pile of papers. His eyes were down, his pencil actively jotting down unintelligible numbers and doodles. It was the best way to avoid any embarrassing eye contact with any employee happening to walk by his office window. But the sudden hard rapping on his window brought his mind back to the situation. Startled, he lurched forward and looked up to see Jerry saying something inaudible and pointing outside. Jack rose and strained his neck to see if he could see what Jerry was pointing at. There he was. Jack knew it was inevitable. Stepping out of the front passenger door of the shiny black BMW was Samuel P. Marlowe III, President and CEO of Marlowe Plumbing and Supply.

At sixty-two, Marlowe III was the third generation to head this prestigious company which had outlasted a phonebook full of competitors since its inception. Marlowe III had worked for his father and grandfather since he graduated college. Like most, he had to work hard to earn his salary and position. It wasn't just given to him because of his name. But unlike most college graduates, he wasn't required to start at the bottom and work his way up. He started in a lofty position that very few without the Marlowe name could ever hope to obtain. When he turned seventy-five, Marlowe II retired and turned over the reins to Marlowe III, who had just turned fifty.

The first five years of Marlowe III's command were disastrous. National figures spiraled downward. His ouster seemed imminent. By the time Marlowe III reached fifty-five, he was fully gray from the stress caused by the day in and day out pressure running a perennially successful national company which was quickly heading in the wrong direction. But in the sixth year of his reign, Marlowe III began to travel extensively, supposedly to meet old and new clients face to face. Figures picked up dramatically and practically quadrupled by his seventh year as CEO. He was hailed as the company's savior and his position was solidified.

Marlowe III placed his left hand on the hood of the luxurious car, poked his head inside the front passenger window and said something to the driver. He motioned with his head to the third person sitting by himself in the middle of the back seat, at first unnoticed by Jack.

Jack squinted from inside his office as the man in the back seat with white, slick hair pulled back tightly into a small pony tail, handed Marlowe III his sport coat. Jack knew that Marlowe III never drove himself anywhere, but he could not place the man with the pony tail. He didn't even look familiar, but assumed he must fit somewhere into the hierarchy of the company.

Marlowe III put his sport coat on as he walked away from his BMW. He turned around when he was about ten feet away and held up a hand telling the man with the pony tail to get back into the car. Employees scrambled about and avoided eye contact as Marlowe III spun and made his way up the dock steps.

Jack's heart pounded as Marlowe III opened the door and entered the warehouse. Jack knew the CEO must have been upset over the incident. He knew something like this could destroy the company's image and maybe the company itself. Jack assumed that other than a serious dress down and possible demotion, Marlowe III was thinking damage control and what could be done to counter any negative publicity.

Jack opened his office door, walked out and met him halfway. "Mr. Marlowe. It's been a while," Jack said extending his right hand.

"To hell with the niceties, Armstrong," a frowning Marlowe III said, walking briskly by Jack. "In your office, now!"

Jack took a deep breath and followed behind Marlowe III, who by now was making himself comfortable in Jack's chair behind his desk. Jerry and several other employees pretended to be busy but secretly watched and wondered if the boss they revered so much would still be employed when this meeting was over.

Jack closed the door behind him and sat down in one of the two metal chairs positioned in front of his desk. They stared at each other for several seconds. Marlowe III's ten fingertips touched each other in front of his face. "Why didn't you call me, Jack?"

"Sir?"

"You heard me. Don't make me ask again."

"I don't know, Mr. Marlowe. I guess I didn't believe things would turn out the way they have."

"I don't give a shit what you think. What the hell were you thinking anyway? The company is the only thing I'm concerned about. What the hell were you thinking? Over a billion dollars of cocaine shows up here and you don't call?"

Jack paused. "I don't know what to say. I guess I did what I thought was right at the time."

"What *you* thought was right! What *you* thought was right! I don't see the initials CEO in front of your name, Jack! You're a frickin' salesman! You made that kind of decision on your own? What the hell were you thinking? Did you even stop to think the public relations nightmare this would cause?"

"That's why I made the call to keep it quiet."

"Well you were wrong, Jack. Dead wrong. It was a stupid move on *your* part. It's not bad enough this happened, but you gotta go and make a dumb ass mistake and implicate the company."

Jack shook his head slightly. "I'm sorry. I really thought…,"

"You thought!" Marlowe III interrupted. "You thought what, Jack? That you could handle something major like this on your own? Or that you were going to be some kind of hero? Huh? Is that what you thought, Jack?"

Jack's face was hot and he could feel beads of sweat right at his hairline. "No, sir."

"What took my grandfather a half century to build you may have managed to bring down in a day with one bonehead decision."

Jack said nothing. He could think of nothing to say except sorry, and he'd already done that.

"The press is hounding me. They want a statement. What the hell am I supposed to tell them?"

"Tell them the truth."

"And just what is the truth, Jack? Did you steal the cocaine or not?"

Jack paused and leaned forward. "All that really matters is what you think. Right, Mr. Marlowe?"

Marlowe also leaned forward. "I'm not going to fire you, if that's what you're asking."

Jack smiled. "You probably won't have to. If the FBI threats are real, this time tomorrow I won't be here anyway. Then you won't even be faced with the decision."

The corners of Marlowe III's lips curled slightly. "Have you talked to anyone else about this besides the FBI?"

Jack cocked his head slightly. "No. Why?"

"Are you sure? What about the company? Have you talked with anyone in the company besides me?"

Jack thought for a moment. "Except for the guys that helped me stack it all up the day it happened."

"That's alright. That's not a problem."

"I don't understand." Jack was confused.

Marlowe III leaned back in the chair. "Can I trust you, Jack?"

Jack looked around, then back at Marlowe but said nothing.

"Can I trust you?"

"Yes. I guess."

"Yes or no, Jack?"

"Yes. Of course."

Marlowe III rose and extended his hand to Jack. Jack stood and shook his hand. "I'll be in touch, Jack. In the meantime, don't discuss this with anyone."

Marlowe III turned to Jack as he opened the office door. "Of course the company will provide you an attorney. Won't cost you a dime. Okay?"

Jack nodded in appreciation.

Jack watched from inside his office as the man with the tightly pulled pony tail climbed outside from the backseat and opened the front passenger door for Marlowe III. He was taller than he looked from when he was seated in the backseat. He was also formidable looking, dressed in a black suit and black t-shirt. Jack didn't give it much thought until the man with the pony tail shut Marlowe III's door and glanced in Jack's direction and grinned. Jack pulled back quickly from his window to where he could still see, but didn't think he could be seen. The pony tailed man climbed back into the back seat, never taking his eyes off Jack's general position. Jack sat down behind his desk as nothing but a dust trail was now visible. He threw his head back, looked up and tightly closed his eyes. He let out a slow but purging breath.

Jack stared at his peas, carrots and apples in front of him on the coffee table. An old episode of *The Andy Griffith Show* blared from his TV. The fruit and vegetables in front of him were not appealing in the least. He always ate healthy, but now a greasy hamburger seemed more appropriate. It didn't matter anyway because he had no appetite to speak of. His mind wasn't on dinner. And it for sure wasn't soaking in the hilarity of Barney chastising Otis for another night of too much drinking. Jack paid no attention to the noise the window repairman made as he knocked the shards of glass away from the bedroom window broken the day before.

The headlights from a car outside illuminated the light blue walls of Jack's kitchen. He noticed but didn't pay attention. He picked at his peas and carrots and stabbed one with his fork every now and then. He paid no attention to the sound of the car door shutting. Jack's mind was anywhere but present. He smashed an imprint of his fork into his peas and halfway laughed at something Barney Fife said as a soft rapping was heard at his front door. He glanced toward the door, but couldn't see who was there. He leaned forward and craned his neck just enough to look out the window and see Emery's convertible in the driveway. Still upset at her lack of trust, he didn't acknowledge her presence at the front door.

Emery knocked a little harder then moved to the large window next to the door and peered inside. The sun was just going down so with the darkness setting in, and combined with the lights inside, she could see Jack on the couch. She tapped lightly on the window. Jack looked up and mouthed the words the door was unlocked then motioned for her to come in.

Emery walked in, almost sheepishly, and wiggled a pinky extended three fingered wave to Jack, who didn't wave back. He just piddled with his peas and carrots.

"Hey," Emery said in a half whisper. She stood ten feet away and was unsure if Jack wanted her any closer.

"Hey," was Jack's response as he glanced at her quickly then ate a mouthful of carrots.

"How're you doing?" She asked, her hands folded neatly in front of her.

Jack spun in his seat to face her and chuckled. "How am I doing? How am I doing? Well, I'm eating tasteless vegetables and facing an indictment and arrest for something I didn't do. So I guess I'm doing great. Never better. And you?" he said facetiously.

Emery stared at Jack not at all amused at his sarcasm. "I came here because I was sorry and because I wanted to tell you I was wrong to doubt you. If you want me to leave I will."

Jack felt three feet tall. Emery turned and started walking away.

"Wait," he said.

Emery stopped, but did not turn around.

"I don't want you to go."

Emery spun slowly and looked across the room at Jack. "Tell me why I shouldn't."

Jack stood motionless. "Because I need you."

They peered deeply into each other's eyes and almost on cue rushed to each other and embraced. Everything that had happened had built up inside Jack like air in a taut balloon. His emotions exploded, and as he held on to his only support system, he opened up completely and cried like a newborn baby. Tears flowed down his cheeks. Emery held him tightly and gently stroked the back of his head with her fingers.

"I don't know what I'm gonna do," he said trying to regain his composure. "I don't think there's any way out."

"Let's don't talk about it now. Let's just go somewhere tonight and forget it all for one night." She pulled away gently and caressed both his hands with hers. "I just wanna be happy tonight. That's all. I don't wanna think about anything tonight except us. Okay?"

Jack smiled. "I keep hoping this is all a bad dream. That I'll wake up in a cold sweat and that relief will finally come." Jack paused. "But I don't wake up and the nightmare just gets worse and worse."

Emery put her arms around Jack and they embraced once more. "We'll think of something. We will. We'll figure out something," she whispered softly in his ear.

Jack squeezed her tightly and shut his eyes. He knew deep inside there was nothing he or Emery could do. The evidence against him was overwhelming. He knew there was no way out. But nothing or no one could take this moment away from him. No matter what lay ahead, Jack wanted to hold on to this moment forever. When he was with Emery, nothing else mattered. He wanted to hold her all night. The sudden ringing of the phone threatened their embrace.

Jack pulled away slightly, but Emery refused to release her grip. He tried again after the phone rang for the third time.

"Don't, Jack. Don't answer it."

Jack looked over his shoulder as it rang four and five times. He pulled away again.

"No!" she ordered. "I won't let you answer it."

But the phone kept ringing and Jack kept his eye trained on it. He pried her hands away. "It might be important."

"More important than me?"

Jack gave her a sheepish grin and moved toward the phone.

"Go ahead. Don't worry about me," she said, a hint of anger in her voice.

The phone continued to ring. "Whoever it is isn't giving up."

Emery didn't like it but she understood. She sat down where Jack had been sitting and gave a 'yuk' expression at the bland looking vegetables on the plate sitting on the coffee table.

Jack picked up the phone. "Hello."

A low voice at the other end, with a distinctive, heavy foreign accent, alarmed Jack. "I know you're home, Jack. What took you so long to answer? Did the pretty little lady inside want you all to herself?"

Jack glanced at Emery. "Who is this?"

Emery stood when she sensed his concern. She inched slowly toward him.

"You don't want to know who I am, Jack. Nor do you need to know," the voice on the other end warned.

Emery had reached Jack by now and entangled her arms with his.

"Let's make this quick. You have something I want."

"And what would that be?"

"Don't be stupid, Jack. You know exactly what I'm talking about. You took something that belonged to me and I want it back. We can do it the easy way or the hard way, whichever way you prefer."

Jack was silent. His face flushed, his mouth became suddenly dry.

"Are you there, Jack?" the deeply accented voice asked.

Jack looked at Emery. She could sense his fear.

"Jack," the deep voice continued.

"I'm here. I'm here."

"I want you to relax. Okay. Just relax. What has transpired can be easily fixed. What you've done can be forgiven."

"But I haven't done anything."

At the other end was silence then laughter. "Jack, Jack, Jack. Do you think I'm stupid? I've read the papers. I've seen the news. I know people. I don't have time to play your games."

"But it's the truth."

The man on the other end laughed again. "Sure it is, Jack. Sure it is. You keep telling yourself that and maybe you'll convince yourself." He paused slightly. "Look. I'm going to give you one opportunity to make this right. One opportunity to make things right and you'll never hear from me again."

"Look. I did not take your dope. I don't know who did, but I had nothing to do with it. Someone is trying to set me up."

"I'm looking at my watch right now. It is 7:12 p.m. By midnight tonight, I want my property you stole back in my possession. I want two hundred fifty bricks and not one less. Do you understand? I've lost more than I care to think about, and you are holding over a quarter billion dollars of property that belongs to me. In a small way I am glad you took it. That's at least part that isn't with the Feds. I can salvage something from this debacle. You can make this right and you will never see or hear from me again and I will guarantee nothing will happen to you."

"I don't have it! I didn't take it! Why won't anyone believe me?"

"Do you know where the old L&N yards are just south of the city?" the man with the deep accent asked.

"No! Yes! No!" Jack didn't know what to say. "Look. I know where it is, but I don't have anything to bring. I didn't steal anything. Why can't you understand that?"

"What are you telling me, Jack? Are you telling me you've already sold it? You've unloaded it?"

"No!" Jack interrupted. "I'm trying to tell you you're talking to the wrong person. I didn't take it!" he screamed.

Suddenly silence. Jack could only hear breathing.

"It's now 7:13. That's one less minute you have to deliver what belongs to me. If you produce, and I know you will, and everything is present and accounted for, all will be forgiven. If you fail to show, or if even one brick is missing…well, I'm sure you won't disappoint me, will you Jack?"

Jack had nothing more. He knew he wasn't convincing whoever this man was.

"At the yard there is one car that sits by itself off the track. You'll drive up to that car and unload my property into it. You will then close the door of the car and get back into your car and drive away. You will never see me, nor will you ever hear from me again. Unless of course you don't show. But I'm sure you will."

Jack stared straight ahead and whispered. "I don't have it."

"It's 7:14, Jack."

The next sound he heard was the clicking of the other party hanging up. Jack slid the receiver down the side of his face, his eyes wide open.

"Jack. What is it? What's wrong?" Emery asked, touching his cheek.

"I don't know. Some man. He said the cocaine was his. He thinks I stole it," Jack answered, with a distant stare.

Emery's eyes widened. "You have to call the FBI."

Jack broke his blank stare and looked at Emery. "The FBI? For all I know that *was* the FBI. Maybe Fuentes thought he could coerce a confession or something."

"That's crazy, Jack. They can't do that." Emery paused. "Look. Whoever that was could be dangerous. You need to call the FBI."

"No offense. But the last time you told me to call the FBI, I got indicted."

"You haven't been indicted."

"Not yet. But it's only a matter of time."

"You've gotta do something. You can't just sit there and do nothing."

"There's nothing else I can do, Emery." Jack peered into her eyes. "I'm going to call their bluff."

Emery paused. "And what if they aren't bluffing?"

~ 6 ~

Jack did not sleep a wink. He went to bed but lay there all night looking out his window. He especially watched the clock as it struck midnight, wondering if a contract was being taken out on his life at that very minute for being a no-show at the railroad yard. Around 5:00 a.m. mental exhaustion gave way to a semi-conscious doze. When the alarm blared at 5:30 a.m., he felt like he'd slept for about ten seconds. He slapped the doze button with his left hand and threw off the covers with his right. Sitting up on the side of the bed he rubbed his eyes. His body was tense and it ached from the lack of sleep. He felt like crap, but he'd made it through the night with no uninvited visitors, and that was a small victory. He stretched his arms high over his head and yawned. He badly wanted to lie back down and try and sleep, but regardless of everything that had happened or was about to happen, he had a job to get to. He stood, stretched again and walked to the linen closet in the hallway just outside his bedroom and grabbed a big blue towel and green wash rag.

Stumbling back into his bedroom, his eyes still half closed, he walked gingerly toward his master bedroom shower. He flipped the light on and hung his towel on the rack above the toilet. Reaching around the closed shower curtain, he turned both the cold and hot water controls and let the water run over his hand until it was the perfect temperature. When it was just right, he stood and stripped away his tee-shirt and boxer shorts. With a quick jerk of his right hand, Jack pulled back the shower curtain and was about to step in when what he saw made him gag. He choked back a surge of nausea and swallowed hard. Hanging upside down by a thin thread from the shower head was Jimmy, his Red Macaw he'd had for ten years. He named it after Jimmy Buffet. Jack had taught Jimmy to say nine or ten words. His favorite line was "Welcome home, boss." Jack took a deep breath and reached for Jimmy's lifeless body. He placed both hands under his back and lifted him slowly so he could cut the thread holding Jimmy's limp body. His neck, obviously broken, flopped over Jack's hand. Jack fought back a tear as he jerked the thread to snap it from the shower head. A note tied to one of Jimmy's legs read 'A second chance is rare, but you get one'. Jack sat down on the side of the tub and stared at his dead pet. A burning sensation developed in his stomach when he realized someone had been right there, perhaps in one of the few minutes he was able to doze. As much as he loved his bird, he knew it could have been him. A sense of relief gripped him, but just as quickly, he was consumed with fear knowing how close they were.

Jimmy's lifeless body lay frozen inside a shoe box on top of Jack's desk at the warehouse. Jack planned on giving him a decent burial later that evening when he got home from work. Jerry and some of the other employees that happened to venture inside did double takes at Jack's deceased pet. The only explanation they received was that Jimmy had died during the night. Jerry didn't believe Jack but didn't press him for details. Jack didn't even know why he brought Jimmy's body to work. He guessed it was an emotional thing. He didn't want to leave Jimmy alone.

Jack was busy completing forms that had begun to pile up on his desk. The only thing he could think of was the trouble he was in and how everything and everyone seemed to be mounting up against him. Even the strange looks from his employees he interpreted as mistrust and their pre-conceived belief of his guilt.

Around 9:00 a.m., Jack was scheduled to hold a meeting with Jerry to receive a daily report on all shipments. He stood and as he began to put his jacket on, the phone rang. Fitting his right arm through the sleeve, he grabbed the receiver. "Armstrong."

"Jack," the low voice with the heavy accent, said quietly.

"Hey, I'm gonna put you back to my secretary," Jack said, not paying any attention to the voice. "I'm running late for a meeting."

"Wait," the voice said quickly. "I thought you might want to talk about your bird."

Jack froze, one arm in his jacket, the other out. Jerry and his crew stood outside Jack's office waiting on him. Jack motioned for them to go on without him.

"Jack. Are you there?"

Jack loosened his tie, took his coat off and sat back down. "I'm here."

"Very good, Jack. Very good."

"Why?"

"Why what, Jack?"

"My bird. Why did you have to kill it?"

"So sorry about that. Would you rather it been you?"

Jack was silent.

"I didn't think so. You see, Jack. If it'd been you, then my property would be lost forever. And I don't want that. You are worth a lot more to me alive than dead. At least right now. And if you will just cooperate, you may just stay that way." The man with the accent paused. "Unfortunately, for your bird. Well, let's just say he was expendable. Collateral damage if you will. Anyway. Enough about that. You can get another bird."

Jack swallowed hard.

"About second chances. I'm going to assume you either didn't take me seriously or you lost your way to our little meeting, or maybe that pretty little lady detained you. Whatever the reason, I really don't care. You are getting something I usually don't allow. I'd really just as soon kill you. But unfortunately, I can't do that. Seeing as how the FBI has whatever you didn't steal in their custody, the next best thing for me is to get back what you took. I can still salvage something. I think even a little pea-brained shit like you can understand that. Right, Jack?"

Jack thought for a moment and said calmly. "I don't have it. There's nothing else I can say or do."

Jack could only hear breathing. "I'm going to give you one more opportunity. One more chance to give me what is mine, or each hour that goes by, your life will become a little more unraveled. Don't fuck with me, Jack. You do not want to fuck with me."

"Look!" Jack pleaded.

"No, Jack! You look. No more games. I'm tired of playing your stupid games. I know you have it. I know you have what is mine and if I don't have it back by midnight tonight you will understand I'm not playing with you. Tonight, at midnight. Same place. No questions asked. You will never see me."

Jack let out a sigh. "I. I don't have it."

"If you fail to show tonight, this time it won't be your bird."

Jack's hands trembled as he watched his secretary escort Fuentes and three other agents toward his office. His heart pounded and his sphincter tightened. "I'm afraid the FBI has beaten you to the punch."

"Whattaya' mean?"

Jack was almost relieved to the point of humor. "I don't have your cocaine. I don't know where it is, and I really don't give a damn. But the FBI believes I have it too, and I do believe they are here for me now. Maybe you should take it up with them. You want to talk with Agent Fuentes? You may know him. Your accents are strikingly similar."

Fuentes and his three agents waltzed into Jack's office. One agent stood in front of Jack's desk. Two others stood on either side of his desk. Fuentes moved to where he was standing directly behind Jack.

Jack smiled and handed the phone to Fuentes. "Here. This is for you. I think it's your cousin."

Fuentes took the phone and placed it to his ear for a few seconds. "Fuentes. Fuentes." He pulled the receiver away from his ear and hung it up. "There's no one there."

Jack smiled. "I guess he had better things to do."

"You're a scream, Jack. A real comedian. It's a real shame I'm getting ready to wipe that shit eatin' grin off your face."

The smile Jack wore to protect his real fear faded. "I figured you weren't here for tortilla de potatas."

"Damn, Jack. You're just hilarious. I can hardly contain my laughter," Fuentes said with a straight face. "So you're a racist too, huh?"

Jack rolled his eyes. "And here we go."

"Stand your ass up, Armstrong. You are under arrest." Fuentes pulled his handcuffs from the back of his belt and slapped them on Jack's wrists. "You are under arrest for possession of an illegal substance."

"Possession? I thought you had to have it to possess it." Jack winced when Fuentes clinched the cuffs as tight as they would go.

"You have the right to remain silent. Anything you say can and will be used against you in a court of law. You have the right to an attorney. If you cannot afford an attorney, one will be appointed to you. Do you understand these rights?"

Jack stared straight ahead trying to adjust his wrists to a more comfortable position.

"Do you understand your rights?"

Jack paused and looked directly into Fuentes brown eyes. "Yeah. I understand my rights, but why here? Why did you have to do this in front of everyone? Does it make you feel like a bigger man to embarrass me? To humiliate me like this? Huh? Does it?"

"You did this to yourself, Jack. You've got no one to blame but yourself." Fuentes forced Jack out of his office. "Let's go." Fuentes guided Jack through a maze of warehouse employees who had gathered around to watch. Fuentes leaned in and whispered in Jack's ear. "So sorry to hear about Jimmy." Fuentes smiled.

Jack stopped abruptly and glared at Fuentes. "How did you know my bird's name?"

Fuentes said nothing. He forced Jack to keep moving.

Some of Jack's co-workers shouted words of encouragement, inciting Jack to hang in there. That this would pass. Others watched in confusion, silently assigning guilt, while others were convinced of his innocence.

Fuentes gently guided Jack into the middle of the back seat of his bucar and climbed in beside him. Another agent sat on Jack's other side. The remaining two took their place as driver and passenger. Most of the warehouse employees stood on the dock as their boss was whisked away by the four "suits". Some stayed awhile and discussed the happenings. Others trickled back inside. Some talked about how he was framed. Others were convinced he was guilty. One thing for sure, there were plenty of questions but no real answers.

Jack stood before the United States Magistrate. His arms were neatly folded in front of him. He felt alone, totally abandoned as he listened to the U.S. Magistrate. Fuentes and AUSA Waters stood behind Jack.

"Are you Jonathan Terrell Armstrong?" the Magistrate asked.

"Yes, sir," Jack replied, just above a whisper.

"You also go by Jack?"

"Yes, sir."

"Are you the same Jack Armstrong named in the indictment?"

Jack looked at Fuentes who nodded his head. "I would assume that is correct your honor."

"Mr. Armstrong. I want you to understand that this proceeding is not a trial, nor do we hear arguments or look at evidence. It is nothing more than an initial appearance to ensure you are the person named on the indictment. Do you understand this?"

"Yes, sir."

"Very well. I want you to know that I am not going to ask you for a plea or anything of that nature. That is something that you will discuss with your attorney. Do you understand?"

"Yes, sir."

"Very good, Mr. Armstrong. After a careful review of the affidavit and warrant written by Special Agent Fuentes, I have no choice but to remand you to the custody of the United States Marshall." The Magistrate motioned to the two Deputy U.S. Marshalls standing to the side of the bench Jack was standing behind. "These two deputies will be escorting you downstairs where you will be processed. You will have an opportunity to obtain legal representation and meet with your attorney. You will remain in the custody of the Marshall's service until your bond hearing. If no bail is set or you cannot make bail, you will be remanded to the custody of the Fulton County Sheriff's Office until a trial date is set. Do you understand all of this Mr. Armstrong?"

Jack's mind wanted to shut down. He'd seen this in the movies, but never in a million years did he ever think he would be standing in this position. "Yes, sir," he answered, his voice shaking.

"Do you have any questions?"

Jack was numb. He didn't answer.

"Mr. Armstrong!" the Magistrate half shouted.

"Sir," Jack shook his head no. "No, sir. I don't have any questions."

"Very well, gentlemen." The Magistrate motioned for the deputy Marshalls to take Jack away.

Once again, Jack was handcuffed behind his back. He was spun around toward the back of the courtroom where he came face to face with a broadly grinning Fuentes. His insides burned at the sight of the gloating agent. As the deputies escorted him toward the entrance, Jack looked back at Fuentes who had never taken his eyes off Jack. Fuentes winked at him as they disappeared through the large double doors of the courtroom.

"Relax your hand," the deputy Marshall demanded as he tried to roll Jack's thumbprint. "We'll stay here all night if we have to."

Jack was humiliated. This is what happens to thugs, murderers, rapists, thieves and other lower life forms he thought, as the deputy rolled his entire palm with ink. Finally finished, he dipped his fingers into the creamy brown goo and vigorously rubbed his hands together. The ink seemed to magically dissolve from his hands and fingers.

"Sign here," demanded the deputy.

Jack grabbed three or four paper towels to wipe his hands then tossed them into the circular trash can at his feet. He picked up the pen and signed the card. It now seemed official. He officially had a record. He was a prisoner of the state. Now he would be entered into the computer with a mother lode of other deviants. He was a marked man. Innocent or not, he was forever labeled as a criminal. Even if innocent, he was guilty by association. Fuentes had made sure of it, and now the Atlanta media followed along. He wondered if he would keep his job after this was all over. He had worked so hard to get where he was. Would friends look at him differently than before? What would Emery think of him now? Would she abandon him in his time of need? Would his family disassociate themselves?

The bright flash made Jack blink.

"Turn to your left," the second deputy barked his order.

Jack turned slowly. The next flash temporarily made him see stars.

"Now, to your right."

Jack faced the other direction as the camera snapped his profile. He inhaled deeply and blew out a long breath of depression. He kept praying he'd wake up. He tried not to imagine the deep shame he was about to bring on himself, his family and his friends. How people would say 'not Jack Armstrong, that's not the Jack Armstrong we know'. Or 'he was a quiet fellow, never caused any trouble in the neighborhood'. How people would try to imagine how he couldn't have done what the papers say but would believe it anyway.

"Okay. You're through for right now. We're gonna take you back to your holding cell."

Jack stepped in between the two deputies. "This is unfrikkinbelievable."

"You don't like our home? I'm so sorry it doesn't measure up to your standards," one deputy said sarcastically as they escorted Jack toward a square cage in the middle of the room.

"Would you want to be here if you were innocent?"

Both deputies looked at each other and smiled. "Never heard that one before. I think you're the first guy we've had in here who claimed he was innocent. Go figure."

"Big difference in me and the others. I *am* innocent."

"Sure you are." the second deputy said.

The first deputy unlocked the door to the cell and motioned Jack inside where two other prisoners sat on a wooden bench. "Here you go, Jack. You need to wait here with these other two innocent guys." Both deputies laughed as the door clanged shut.

Jack sat down and folded his arms across his chest. He jumped when the cell door shut. "What now?" he shouted to both deputies who were walking away.

"Just sit tight," the second deputy shouted. "Enjoy the scenery."

For an hour, Jack thought about everything from when he was a little boy and was taught the difference between right and wrong. From lectures of how it was better to walk away from a fight to Sunday morning sermons about taking responsibility and how irresponsibility, not money, was the root of all evil. He tried to take every lesson he ever learned and apply it as an adult. The last thing he ever wanted to do was to cause embarrassment to his family and friends. He felt his whole world crumbling down around him and he had no idea how to stop it.

Jack dozed in and out of consciousness for what seemed like days but was really no more than an hour or two. The lack of sleep, and the darkness of the dimly lit cell actually helped him relax, if only slightly. The semi-conscious doze was never sound though, and after a brief respite he was rudely awakened by the key turning the tumblers.

"Wake up, Armstrong. You got a visitor," the second deputy called out as he opened the cell door. He smiled for the first time all day anticipating the sight of Emery. Instead his hopes were crushed as Harrison Jackson, the Chief Counsel at Marlowe Plumbing, entered through the cell door but froze one step into the cage.

Jackson looked at the deputy. "You don't expect me to go in there, do you?"

The second deputy looked at Jackson, then Jack, then back to Jackson. "Is that a problem?"

"Yes, it is a problem. My client and I would like some privacy."

"That's not a problem." The second deputy pointed to a desk about thirty feet away. "See that desk over there?"

Jackson smiled at Jack believing he had made his point. "Yes."

"That's where I'll be if you need me. That should give you all the privacy you need."

Jack snickered to himself because he had never been very fond of Jackson. He didn't like his name because it sounded more important than it was. Jackson went by T. Harrison Jackson and Jack knew the only reason Jackson did was because it sounded more attorney like. He didn't like the way he talked or the way he looked. And he didn't like the way he acted. He didn't like his hair because it was way too long and it was gray, and Jack felt gray-haired men shouldn't have long hair. Besides, Jack felt the only reason Jackson had long hair was because he had probably seen some famous defense attorneys on TV with long hair, and therefore felt he had to look the same. Jackson thought he was better than the person he happened to be with at any given time. Jackson was a know it all who expected praise from anyone he came in touch with. In reality he was nothing more than a pompous ass in a thousand dollar suit. Jack thought he looked more like a slick TV money grubbing evangelist than a corporate attorney. If truth be told, Jackson didn't think much of Jack either.

Jackson waited for the deputy to reach the desk before he turned to address Jack. "Well, well, well. Just what have you gone and gotten yourself into now, Jack? What kind of trouble did you make this time?"

"I just have one question, Harry."

Jackson despised being called Harry. If you weren't another attorney or a Marlowe executive, you called him Mr. Jackson. The first initial in front of his name indicated he was a very important attorney, at least in his own eyes. Jack knew that and called him Harry every chance he got. He loved getting in a shot any time he could.

Jack continued. "I'm obviously gonna need an attorney so I was just wondering if you brought one with you." Jack smiled at his stab at humor.

"Hilarious, Jack," Jackson said, as he sat down in the metal chair the deputy placed in the cell for him. "Maybe when you get out you can start your career as a stand-up comedian." Jackson paused. "That's assuming you get out. Oh, and you go ahead and joke all you want. Just remember, when we're done here, I'll be going home, eating dinner with my wife and sleeping in my own bed. Tell me again where you'll be spending tonight."

Jack grimaced. He thought to himself, 'touché'. Jackson one-upped him. "Point taken." Jack swallowed his pride.

"Good. Whether you believe it or not, I'm here to help you."

"I know. Sorry 'bout the jab."

"Apology accepted. The first thing we gotta do is go to your bond hearing in about thirty minutes."

"Forgive me for asking, but shouldn't I be talking to a defense attorney? I mean no offense Mr. Jackson, but you're not a defense attorney."

"You're right. And the company is working on retaining you one as we speak. But if you expect to post bond, you need an attorney right now and I can help out there. Once all the proceedings start, the company will have retained you an attorney, an excellent one at that. One of the best in the country."

"What do you mean *if* I expect to post bond? Isn't the company going to post my bail?"

Harrison looked around before answering. "Jack. You need to understand. That would not look good for the company."

"The company!" Jack shouted, rising quickly from his chair.

The deputy heard Jack shout and stood up to assure everything was okay. Jackson saw him and motioned everything was alright. Jack sat back down then leaned forward in his chair toward Jackson. "What about me? What am I supposed to do? Sit in here for two years until my trial comes up? You know there is no way I'll be able to afford the bail they set."

"Jack, you've got to think sensibly. You've been with the company a number of years. You know what it's all about. Appearances. Images. It just wouldn't look right if the company posted bail."

Jack grew angrier by the second. He pointed at Jackson as he made his point. "I've been loyal to Marlowe for almost twenty years. I'm innocent of everything I've been accused of. Are you telling me they're not gonna support me here?"

"Look, Jack. What I'm telling you is you're gonna have one of the best defense attorneys in the country. The company is behind you a hundred percent. But you know as well as I know that no matter what the law says, you're guilty until proven innocent. If the company bails you out, it appears it's condoning what happened whether you did it or not."

"But I didn't do anything!"

"Appearances, Jack. Appearances are everything. You know that as well as anyone."

"So that's it. I'm all on my own here?"

"Absolutely not. The company is behind you a hundred percent."

"Except they're just gonna leave me in here to rot."

"If that's the way you want to look at it. Your words Jack, not mine."

Jack leaned back, put his folded hands on top of his head and glared at the lawyer. "Unbelievable. I see now how all you stuffed shirts up there on the top floor care about the guts of the company. All that matters is appearance. To hell with the truth."

"I'd be careful what I say. The company is being a lot more supportive than it has to be. If it felt you were the least bit ungrateful, it would fire you and then you'd be all on your own for your defense. As it sits right now, the company will continue to pay you your salary whether you are in here or out there."

"How very kind of them."

"What do you want me to do, Jack? What do you want me to say? Most companies would have fired you two days ago. I think Marlowe has gone above and beyond. Please don't mess that up and say something out of anger that you really don't mean."

Jack thought a few seconds and realized Jackson was right. Most companies would never give anyone the benefit of the doubt. Maybe Marlowe had gone above and beyond in helping him. "You're right. I'm just upset. Very stressed right now."

"That's okay. It's understandable."

Jack closed his eyes and covered them with both palms. "So how much do you think bail is gonna be?"

"I don't know. Charges are pretty damn serious."

"Any guess?"

Jackson paused. "A million. Maybe two."

Jack leaned over, planted his elbows into his knees and buried his face in his hands. "Holy shit. I'll be in here forever. I can't come up with one percent much less ten."

"Like I said. These are pretty serious charges. If you're guilty."

"I'm not guilty!" Jack interrupted.

"Easy, Jack. I'm not saying you're guilty. I'm just saying the court looks at these type charges and looks at the flee risk, which in this case is highly probable. The motive is to make bail so high you can't get out and flee."

"I'm not gonna flee. I've got nowhere to flee to."

"I know that and you know that, but the court doesn't." Jackson paused and leaned forward and said just above a whisper. "Look, Jack. I probably shouldn't say anything but, uh, don't be surprised if you get bailed out. Okay?"

Jack looked up at Jackson. "Whattaya' mean?"

"Just don't worry about it. Just be, well, just be thankful if it happens."

Jack looked totally confused. "But you just said the company wouldn't..."

Jackson interrupted. "That's right. The company won't." He paused. "Look. Forget I said anything. Okay? Just forget I said anything." He looked at his watch. "It's almost time for your bond hearing." Jackson stood and motioned to the deputy. "The deputies will be taking you to the hearing. I'll meet you there. I don't know what the Judge will set your bail at, but we'll argue to get it as low as we can." Jackson waved and shouted at the deputy. "I'm ready." He turned back to Jack and looked at him sympathetically. "Hang in there. I know this isn't easy. Rest assured the company's supporting you all the way."

Jack cocked his head slightly, then nodded.

"Two million dollars. I'll never see the light of day," a dejected Jack told Emery, who sat on the opposite side of a clear fiberglass barrier at the Fulton County Jail visiting area.

After setting Jack's bail at two million dollars, the Judge remanded Jack to the custody of the Fulton County Sheriff until trial, or until he could make bail. Jackson managed to persuade the Judge to lower his original idea of ten million to two million. But that was like lowering the value of the Hope Diamond from $200 million to $100 million. You still couldn't buy it. Lowering the bail to two million did Jack no good.

"I wish there was something I could do," Emery said. "Is there anyone you can think of that has that kind of money?"

Jack laughed. "You're joking, right? Two-hundred thousand dollars?"

"There has to be someone."

"Forget it, Emery. There is no one with that kind of money that I know other than the company."

"I just feel so helpless."

Jack forced a smile. "Try it from this side."

While Jack and Emery tried to encourage each other, a flurry of activity was unraveling just out of their sight. Just beyond the door where Emery was led through to see Jack, deputies were counting and checking the authenticity of the $200,000 in one hundred dollar bills neatly tucked inside a metal briefcase delivered by a local bail bondsman. The official document stated the money was earmarked for Jack's bail. After some discussion between high level officials, it was determined the money was legitimate and there was no way they could keep him locked up.

Emery was standing to leave when a deputy walked through the door behind Jack, approached him and whispered in his ear. Jack's head jerked quickly, placing him face to face with the deputy. "Who?" Jack said, obviously surprised.

The deputy shrugged his shoulders nonverbally telling Jack he didn't know who posted bail.

"What is it?" Emery asked.

Jack stood, turned to Emery and peered through the fiberglass window. "Somebody out there loves me!"

"Are you serious?" she asked excitedly. "Did Marlowe decide to do the right thing?"

"I don't know. Maybe. I guess." Jack put his hand against the fiberglass window. "Meet me wherever they're going to release me."

Emery nodded and grabbed her purse and jacket then rushed out of the door, the sound of her heels clicking down the hallway. Jack was led back to his cell where he retrieved his jacket.

Approaching the Chief Deputy's station where he would receive his personal belongings, Jack saw Harrison Jackson talking with the deputy assigned to the custodian desk. Jackson aimed a wide grin when he saw Jack a few steps away. "What'd I tell you? Huh? Did I nail it or what?"

Still confused about everything, Jack squinted his eyes and stared at Jackson. "Yeah. Guess you did."

"Just a few forms to sign and you'll be out of here," Jackson said, as he scanned the triplicate forms the deputy placed side by side on the desk.

Jack picked up a pen from the desk. His eyes darted back and forth at the four or so forms in front of him. "Where do I sign?"

The deputy pointed to specific places on each form. "I put a red X everywhere you need to sign."

Jack started signing the two or three places on each form. "Who posted my bail?"

"We'll talk about that later. Alright?" Jackson said, a little tension in his voice.

Jack stopped his pen in mid stroke. "What? What's the big deal, Harry? Did Marlowe post it?"

Jackson's eyes blinked quickly several times. He motioned with his head. "I said we'll talk about it later."

Jack paused for a few seconds and stared at Jackson. He then signed the second form. When he was through, he stared again at Jackson. "Why not now?"

"Because it's not a good time. Okay?" Jackson snapped back.

Jack continued to stare down Jackson for several seconds before turning to sign the third form. "What difference does it make? I mean did Marlowe bail me out or not? It's a pretty simple question."

Growing visibly upset, Jackson glared at Jack. "Just sign the forms, Jack. We'll discuss the details later. Just be glad you're getting out."

Jack signed the third form and peered up at the deputy while still signing. "Do you know who posted my bail?"

Not sure if he could provide that information, the deputy looked at Jackson, then at Jack. Jackson shook his head no. The deputy called back to another deputy. "Hey, Joey. Can I give Armstrong info on who bailed him out?"

"Sure. Ain't no rule against it."

Jackson threw his head back and rolled his eyes.

The deputy at the desk opened the manila folder and perused it with his fingers while Jack signed the fourth form. "Says here that a Mr. Matthew Armstrong posted your bail."

Jack's hand froze in mid-signature. "That's my brother." Jack turned to Jackson. "Matt's my brother. Lives in Seattle."

Jackson became suddenly nervous and avoided any eye contact with Jack. "Yes, right. You need to finish signing the forms." His jittery hands shuffled the remaining form toward Jack.

Jack never took his eyes from Jackson. "What's goin' on, Harrison?" Jack turned serious. He'd never called him Harrison before. "My brother could no more afford this bail than I could."

Speechless, Jackson stared at Jack.

"He manages a grocery store. He makes thirty-five grand a year, if that." Jack paused, pen fixed between his fingers. "Who posted my bail, Harrison? Who?"

Jackson refused to look at Jack. "Just sign the damn form, Jack. You can take this up later with people in much higher places than me."

Jack glared hard at Jackson. His nostrils flared with every breath. He jerked the remaining form toward him and bore down as hard as he could, then briskly signed his name.

Holding a paper bag with his personal possessions, Jack embraced Emery tightly in the lobby of the Fulton County Sheriff's Office. Jackson, who stayed behind with the deputy for a minute to assure all the t's were crossed and i's dotted, approached them. He stopped and looked at Emery. "Don't believe I've had the pleasure."

Jack released his grip from Emery. "Oh. Sorry. Uhh. Emery Carson. This is Harrison Jackson. Harrison, Emery Carson."

Jackson extended his right hand toward Emery. "Emery, my pleasure."

Emery reciprocated by extending her right hand toward Jackson. "Likewise."

Jackson turned his attention to Jack. "Jack. I need to talk with you privately for a minute."

Emery started to walk away just as Jack pulled her back. "No!" he said forcefully. "I'm tired of talking alone with you. If you've got something to say, you can say it right here."

"I don't mind, really," Emery said.

"No. Whatever he has to say, he can say it to both of us." Jack desperately wanted to show Emery his solidarity with her.

Jackson eyed Jack, glanced at Emery then back at Jack. "Fine. Fine. Whatever you want. Frankly, I'm getting a little tired of this myself. Mr. Marlowe will be wanting to see you."

"Fine. I'll call him tomorrow," Jack relented.

"No, Jack. I don't think you understand. I mean now. He needs to see you today. As in now. As in immediately."

Jack patted Jackson on his shoulder and straightened his lapel. "You know what? I've been through quite a bit the last day or so. Mr. Marlowe can wait."

Concerned, Emery turned to Jack. "Jack, maybe you should…"

"No!" Jack interrupted. "Look. I haven't been home in almost two days. I haven't shaved. I haven't showered. I haven't slept. All I want to do right now is go home. If Mr. Marlowe has a problem with that, then fine. He'll have to deal with it. You can tell him, Harry. That's why you make the big bucks, right?"

"I don't think that's such a good idea, Jack," Harrison answered, while shaking his head. "I don't think you should keep Mr. Marlowe waiting."

Jack nudged himself as close to Jackson as possible. "Look, Mr. Jackson. No offense. But something's not right here and you're being a little less than up front with me. My brother, who by the way can barely afford to pay his rent, comes up with two-hundred grand to bail me out, when as far as I know doesn't even know I was arrested." Jack patted Jackson in his chest. "Doesn't that sound the least bit fishy to you?"

Jackson was visibly shaky. He motioned his head toward Emery. "Maybe she told him."

Jack glanced at Emery who nodded that she hadn't. Jack turned back to Jackson. "Nice try." Jack paused slightly. "Look. I don't know what's going on, but I intend to find out. You told me the company wouldn't bail me out because it would look bad. But then you did an about face and said don't be surprised if I make bond." Jack squinted his eyes and peered directly at Jackson. "What did you mean by that? Who bailed me out?"

Jackson leaned back trying to avoid Jack's probing glare. "I think its best you speak with Mr. Marlowe."

Jack stepped away from Jackson. Jackson straightened up and smoothed out his coat jacket. He then backed a step or two more away from Jack. "Look. I'm tired. I'm hungry. I stink. I smell like, like, prison. I'm going home. If you see Mr. Marlowe, just explain it to him. I'm sure he'll understand."

"I'm not so sure he will."

"He'll have to," Jack declared boldly.

Jackson sighed and shrugged his shoulders as Jack and Emery walked outside and down the steps of the county building. The sun was just beginning to set and cast its orange tinted rays on the mirrored glass of the Atlanta skyline.

~ 7 ~

The coastal estate expanded out and overlooked thousands of lush, green acres of tropical forests. The monstrous white mansion, that looked more like a fortress than a home, was surrounded by twelve foot high, five foot thick security walls of white painted cement. Posted every one hundred feet were guards armed with AK-47's. Surveillance cameras sat atop the security walls at strategic locations and angles. Ten Doberman Pinschers lived in a large kennel just outside the main quarters and close to the main guard post. They could be released instantly by touching a button. Water fountains of Victorian architecture dotted the inner, confined landscape. A large, black iron gate that was electronically monitored and operated to allow any necessary traffic, was the only entrance through the fortified walls. The only other entrance to the property was a computer controlled thick metal door leading to the white sandy beach and deep turquoise ocean. Hector Raes owned every piece of visible real estate to the south, north and east of his massive estate. He had enough money to buy the sparkling coastline and crystal clear ocean on the Quibdo shoreline. Unfortunately for Raes, it was not for sale. However, it was like he owned it anyway because everyone knew who lived there and would never dare to infringe on his privacy.

Inside the immaculate fortress was a little over one hundred thousand square feet of pure luxury. Aside from the fifteen or so bedrooms furnished with rare European artifacts, the home consisted of two large kitchens that would put any five star New York restaurant to shame. Raes' full time culinary staff not only cooked five or six course meals daily, they kept the kitchen completely sanitized. That was a requirement of Raes. He hated dirt. He required all his possessions to be cleaned three and four times daily.

Raes wore white. Everything was white...shoes, socks, pants, shirts and the hats that he wore, only occasionally. He was so concerned about cleanliness that if he put on a shirt and decided a minute later he wanted another one, the first one went immediately to his laundry staff which consisted of three full time servants.

Raes spent most of his time inside his business office located on the second floor overlooking the tranquil Pacific Ocean. Bigger than most family dwellings, his office alone spread over 3000 square feet. Equipped with several large screen, flat paneled televisions tuned to news channels throughout the United States and Europe, Raes kept abreast of current events and other happenings that directly affected him. His association with an international drug cartel had made him a very wealthy man. It also turned a once gentle and kind man into a cold and ruthless killer.

Standing a little over six feet tall, Raes was a handsome man for his forty years. A head full of black, curly hair and a trim body kept in shape by twice daily workouts in his fully equipped gym, Raes had ironically become a prisoner of the world that had made him so rich. His link to the outside world was fifteen or twenty different telephone lines made necessary by the constant flow of calls originating worldwide to discuss "business" transactions.

Other than his personal staff of household servants and four or five of his top security officials, Raes lived in the immense mansion alone. He had no children. He had only a few friends. He had no female visitors. He was faithful to only one woman, his wife, who he rarely saw. She knew what he did and accepted it but she did not like the isolation he chose to live in. She loved the lifestyle and all the material riches it brought but hated the loneliness. She didn't visit often… maybe once every month or so for a few days. After that she got cabin fever. She had to do something besides sit around and do nothing all day. But she still loved him and there were a handful of occasions she actually worked for him. She definitely enjoyed the benefits of his business.

Most everyone else he considered a security risk and that was something he refused to deal with. His vast fortune was spent on a variety of investments throughout the world. He was also a local hero because he gave away millions of dollars to the locals, who were, for the most part, extremely poor and lived in squalor. Raes had become so paranoid, so insulated, that he could hardly enjoy the fruits of his trade. But that did not matter. What mattered was he had it.

There were many people throughout the world who wanted to see Raes dead. Raes saw no reason to increase that likelihood by socializing outside a small group of accomplices. Occasionally, Raes was known to entertain foreign dignitaries at his palatial estate. His cover was his family had earned their wealth over years of good investments. Everyone knew the real truth but played the game. Unlike many of his counterparts, Raes did not like exposure nor did he crave the attention. Basically, he was a loner that had reluctantly taken over this billion dollar empire when his brother was killed in a shootout with local authorities. So even though he loved the money and his lofty lifestyle, he despised the life it had created, one of loneliness and fear.

The oversized, hazy orange sun ducked halfway into the Pacific horizon. Raes peered out of his window into the expansive blue sea and spoke in Spanish in a low, monotone voice into one of his numerous phones. "I don't want to have to take matters into my own hands. Do you understand that? That is what I pay you for."

"I understand," announced a raspy voice in Spanish on the other end.

"I need you to take care of this matter in an expeditious way," Raes continued.

"Do you want me to eliminate the problem?" the raspy voice asked, in an obvious style to mask what the conversation was really about.

"I want you to do whatever is necessary to retrieve my property."

"I've given him two chances. He's failed on both."

"Let me make myself clear one more time. Do whatever is necessary."

"He says he does not have it."

Raes stared at the perfectly round sun as it dipped even further into the ocean. "Does he?"

"He's the only one who could have it. No one else had access to it."

"Call him again and this time let him know the seriousness of the situation. I don't think you have done that very well."

"Yes, sir."

"Assure him this will be his last opportunity. There will be no more."

"Yes, sir."

"I want him to know how important it is for him to cooperate fully with you."

"Yes, sir."

"If he does not see the error of his ways, then eliminate him and anyone else who gets in your way. Do you understand? I don't have any more time to fool with him. I'll just write it off as a bad investment and move forward. But I will not allow him to take what is mine."

"Yes, sir."

"It is my understanding you arranged bail."

"Yes, sir. We took care of that. He should be on his way home as we speak."

"Perhaps you should be there when he arrives."

"I already have two men there, sir. Sort of a homecoming party you could say." The raspy voiced man chuckled at his own joke.

Raes was not amused. This was not funny. The cocaine the FBI seized was the price of doing business and Raes understood and accepted that. And even though the coke they believed Jack had stolen was worth only a fraction of Raes' net worth, it was the principle. Raes believed Jack had something of his and whether it was worth a thousand dollars or a hundred million, he wanted back what rightfully belonged to him. Raes was a drug dealer and murderer, but to him the worst kind of criminal was a thief. And no insignificant thief was going to beat him. Raes didn't care who suffered as long as he won in the end. "I want it back! All of it!" he shouted. "Or I want his head! Do you understand!? Don't come back until you have one or the other!"

"Yes, sir," the man with the raspy voice answered, his voice slightly cracking.

Raes hung up the phone and watched the dull orange sun drop all the way into the sea as one star appeared brightly in the Columbian dusk just above the horizon.

~ 8 ~

Emery's hair blew wildly as she drove north on Interstate 75 with the convertible top down. Jack followed closely behind in his pickup truck, trying to smile at the sight of her smooth locks whipping into the air and across her face. After leaving the Fulton County Jail, Emery had taken Jack to the warehouse to get his truck. They were now on their way to Jack's house.

She took the West Paces Ferry exit and began making the six or seven turns necessary before reaching Jack's house in All-American suburbia. Emery rolled to a stop just past the driveway and parked her car on the street in front of his house. About five seconds behind her, Jack pulled his truck into the driveway, which sloped ever so slightly. He exited his truck and walked toward the street where Emery was checking his mailbox.

"Anything?" Jack inquired.

"Looks like bills," she answered, flipping through the seven or eight pieces of mail.

Jack snickered. "Tell me something I don't know."

Jack and Emery stood about five feet apart.

"Jack?"

"Yeah."

"I'm really sorry you had to go through all this."

"Me too. I never thought something like this could happen in America. Land of the free. Home of the brave. Innocent until proven guilty. Certainly didn't think it could happen to me. You only see stuff like this in the movies. Ya' know?"

Emery smiled. "For what it's worth. I believe you."

Jack smiled back. "It's worth everything. I think you may be the only one who does believe me."

Emery waltzed slowly to Jack and embraced him around his

waist. He wrapped his free arm around her back and kissed her lightly on her cheek.

Emery pulled back. "Are you hungry at all?"

Jack smiled. "Starved."

"Let me take you to dinner."

Jack laughed and gently pulled away. "Like this?" He motioned to his disheveled clothes and stubby whiskers emerging on his face.

"Why not? Besides. Who's looking and who cares?"

"Lemme' at least shower and shave real quick. Then I'll take you up on it."

"You're not too tired?"

"I'm dead tired. But I'm more hungry than tired." Jack turned and began walking up his driveway toward the sidewalk and to the front steps. "C'mon inside and wait. I won't be more than five or ten minutes."

Emery trotted to catch up with him and affectionately wrapped her arm around his waist as they sauntered up the steps to the front door.

Jack turned the key and the lock popped, causing the door to creak open just slightly. He pushed the door open with his right foot and politely waited for Emery to enter first. He followed closely behind and closed the door with a swift back motion from his left foot. Jack flipped the light switch on.

"Good evening, Jack," said the dark haired, dark skinned man standing nose to nose with Jack as the light illuminated the darkened foyer.

Jack jerked upright at the unexpected sight of this intruder whose face was covered with pock marks. His heart raced rapidly and pounded so hard and fast he could feel it in his throat. Jack glanced quickly at Emery who froze in her tracks. Jack was afraid to flinch.

"Congratulations on your release. You must feel very good about now," this well over six-foot, bulky, but muscular foreigner said facetiously in a thick Spanish accent which was very similar to the one Jack heard on the phone. "I trust we haven't spoiled any plans the two of you may have had tonight."

Jack and Emery remained silent.

"We have some things to talk about, Jack," the imposing

Columbian stranger said, still standing face to face with Jack. "Why don't we retire to your den where we can sit down." The stranger took one step away and motioned Jack and Emery into the den situated at the end of the foyer.

Jack glanced at Emery as if to question the command, but he had no choice. Running was not an option. He knew they wouldn't make it to the front door before being gunned down. Jack wasn't worried about himself as much as he was Emery. He followed the stranger's demand and began walking toward his den that was still darkened. Only the light from the fish aquarium could be seen faintly filtering through the door now only several feet away. Approaching the doorway of the den with Emery nudging up to his back and the stranger several feet behind, Jack reached around the wall and flipped the light switch on.

"Hello, Jack. Ms. Carson," a second dark haired, dark skinned man with a Spanish accent said, rising from his seat on Jack's leather couch. "Let me apologize for the intrusion. But you must understand that business is business."

Jack's heart, which had settled somewhat from the first encounter, started pounding once again. Emery's hands trembled and her heart pounded as hard as Jack's.

"Please. Make yourselves comfortable," said the second stranger. He was dressed in a coat and tie, unlike the first stranger in dark jeans, long sleeve tee shirt and army boots.

Jack and Emery moved together and sat closely by one another but in two separate chairs. The second foreign stranger, who was in his mid-forties, was very neat and handsome. He sat back down while the first stranger stood at the doorway of the den, hands neatly crossed in front of his beltline.

Jack looked back and forth at the two strangers. Somehow his mind still had a touch of humor left because he mentally named the two strangers Guido and Sarducci from a *Saturday Night Live* sketch he'd watch years ago. Sarducci was the well dressed stranger on the couch and obviously the brains of the outfit. Guido was the muscle.

"I wouldn't normally discuss business in front of a lady, but I assume that Ms. Carson is well aware of the sensitive position you've placed us in," said Sarducci.

"The sensitive position *I've* placed *you* in?" Jack said, emphasizing the two words. "Look. If what you're intending to do here is scare the living crap out of us, it worked. But I don't know what else I can say or tell you to convince you I had nothing to do with it."

"Where is it, Jack?" Sarducci continued without blinking an eye. "Where's the cocaine you stole?"

Jack stood quickly. "Dammit! Don't you get it? Don't you understand? I don't have your fucking cocaine! I don't have it!" Jack punctuated each word.

Guido moved slightly toward Jack to avoid a possible altercation. Sarducci remained quiet and calmly seated on the couch. "Please sit down, Jack. No need for dramatics."

Jack smoothed out his shirt, glared at Guido then slowly sat back down. "I don't have it," he repeated in a much softer tone.

"Then who does, Jack? If you don't, who does?" Sarducci asked.

"I don't know. Don't you think I would have told the FBI if I knew? I mean do you think for a minute that I'd subject myself to arrest, much less spending the night in a seedy, God forbidden jail if I knew who took it?"

"A lot of people would put up with a lot more than that knowing that they were going to be rich beyond their wildest dreams. What about you?"

Jack frowned and sighed. "Look. I've just been through the most humiliating experience in my life. No amount of money is worth what I've been through. If I knew who took it I'd tell you. Hell! I would've told the FBI. But the honest to God truth is I don't know! There's nothing else I can tell you. How many more times have I gotta say it?"

Sarducci sat strangely quiet on the brown, button studded couch. He looked straight into Jack's eyes, almost penetrating his thoughts. "I don't believe you. My sources say you are lying."

Jack glared back at Sarducci. "Then you've got bad sources."

"My sources don't lie."

Jack stared hard at Sarducci. Sweat beads formed on his head.

"Is there something you want to tell me? Something you need to get off your chest?"

"No!" Jack snapped. "Look. I swear to you. I didn't take your damn drugs. I don't care what your sources say. I don't give a damn what the FBI says. I'm innocent. I haven't done anything wrong. The only thing I'm guilty of is not having an alibi. I wish I did. I wish to God I did. But I don't and there's nothing I can do about it. The only thing I have is my word. It may not be good enough for you or the FBI, but it's all I've got. You can kill me now, but it won't change the fact that you've got the wrong guy and killing me won't get you your cocaine back."

Guido listened to Jack's plea but still stood at direct attention at his post guarding the doorway. Sarducci sat calmly on the couch staring at Jack. Emery simply listened and tried to calm Jack by rubbing his knee.

"Jack," Sarducci finally spoke again. "I gotta tell you that you are a very convincing guy. Very convincing, indeed. But you know what?" He paused. "I don't believe a word you are saying."

Jack slumped in his chair grasping for anything that came to mind to prove his innocence.

"You see, Jack. No matter what you say. No matter how many times you claim your innocence. The bottom line is you are the only one who could've done it. Now, we have been very, very patient with you but our patience is wearing thin. You've been given ample opportunity to cooperate and you simply haven't done it."

Frustrated, Jack looked at the ground. "I can't cooperate with you because I don't know anything."

Sarducci ignored Jack's comment. "As I was saying. Your cooperation is essential to our mission. I've been authorized to allow you a very rare opportunity. An opportunity rarely afforded to anyone in a situation such as you find yourself right now. But the people I work for are compassionate human beings and want absolutely no harm to come to you." Sarducci glanced at Emery then continued, "Or anyone close to you. We are willing to give you one last chance to tell us where you've hidden it."

It suddenly dawned on Jack that he knew his safety was secure as long as they believed he had the cocaine. If they determined he didn't have it, they would surely kill him. He raised his head and blew out a long breath. He stared at Sarducci. "Alright. Alright. But I need twenty-four hours."

Emery's head jerked quickly toward Jack. He winked at her to play along.

Sarducci burst into a wide grin. "That's more like it, Jack. That's what we want to hear. We don't want anyone to get hurt. We just want back what belongs to us. There's one glitch though. We don't have twenty-four hours to give you. I need you to take us to it now. We are on a very tight schedule with strict instructions."

Jack glanced at Emery with an expression that said "What now?"

Sarducci rose from the couch and motioned toward the door. "After you."

Jack and Emery stood at the same time and looked at each other. Jack thought quickly. "Can I at least go to the bathroom? I haven't been since this morning and I really gotta go bad."

"No!" Sarducci barked. "I've had enough of your games. You can go when we get there."

Jack had run dry of excuses and delay tactics. As Guido and Sarducci quickly escorted Jack and Emery through the den doorway and into the foyer, Jack glanced at Emery and winked, trying to convey his non-verbal message to follow his lead. He knew if they got into Guido and Sarducci's car, wherever they had parked it, it would mean certain death. There was no way he or Emery would make it out alive. Jack didn't know a lot about the underworld, but he was smart enough to know that witnesses were better dead than alive. He knew the only possible means of escape was to bolt as soon as the front door opened. He and Emery knew the neighborhood better than Guido and Sarducci, who were strangely laid back and walking rather loosely five or six feet behind.

Jack caught Emery's eye again as they approached the front door. He shifted his head slightly back and forth and did the same with his eyes, hoping she would understand he meant for them to run in different directions as soon as he opened the door.

Jack glanced again at Emery as he slowly reached for the ivory doorknob. She winked to assure him she knew what to do. Jack grasped the doorknob and slowly twisted it until it popped slightly free from the jamb. Jack peered at Emery one last time, wondering if it would be the last time, before he flung the door open with all his strength, making it career and bang loudly against the inside wall.

Jack and Emery prepared to run for their lives when their pathway to the free world became suddenly obstructed.

"Jack. I heard you were out. Just wanted to make sure you were adjusting to freedom, however short that might be," a grinning Agent Fuentes said, standing by the front door with his partner.

Jack and Emery jumped back. Once again, his heart pounded rapidly, as if it were going to explode. "Agent Fuentes! Are we ever glad to see you!" Emery said, breathing quick and heavy. "It's Agent Fuentes with the FBI," she announced boldly to Guido and Sarducci.

"Uh-huh. I'm sure you are," Fuentes replied sarcastically. "Oh, I'm sorry, Jack. I didn't realize you had company. Are these friends or business associates? We can always come back."

"No! They were just leaving. Come on in."

Guido and Sarducci stood quiet, not quite sure what to think of the ongoing conversation.

Fuentes eyed the two Columbians. "I think we need to talk, Jack."

Jack had no intention of telling Fuentes anything but he did not want him to leave. "Yes. Come in. Please." Jack turned to Guido and Sarducci. "You fellas were just leaving, right?"

Guido and Sarducci looked at each other and then at Jack. "Yes. I guess we were," Sarducci replied in his thick accent.

As they exited the front door, Jack slapped Sarducci on the back. "You boys come back when you can stay longer. Ya' hear?"

Guido walked out the front door and gave Fuentes a dirty look as he passed by. Sarducci stopped, turned and whispered as soon as he passed Jack. "You should call your brother in Seattle and thank him for your bail." He patted Jack on the shoulder and grinned. "We'll be in touch," he said, as he crossed Fuentes and his partner. Sarducci stopped suddenly, walked back and stood face to face with Jack. "Don't forget to ask your brother if he likes the Columbian necktie we gave him. Maybe we can get you one too."

Jack frowned, unsure of what Sarducci meant. Sarducci ambled past Fuentes, turned and grinned at Jack. He turned and eyed Fuentes. "Have a nice evening." The smile never left Sarducci's face.

Jack watched as Guido and Sarducci walked down the driveway and down the road out of sight. "Come on in," he said, motioning Fuentes and his partner inside.

"That's alright, Jack. We can talk out here."

"No. I insist. I'll be much more comfortable inside. I can fix you a coke or coffee. Iced tea maybe."

"Fine," Fuentes relented. "Whatever makes you happy."

Still standing in the doorway, Jack motioned them inside. As Fuentes crossed Jack and moved through the doorway and into the foyer, he peered up at Jack and shook his head. Jack shut and locked the door and immediately fell back against it as soon as Fuentes and his partner were inside. Emery leaned against another wall and slid down into a seated position on the hardwood foyer floor.

"Thank God you showed up when you did," Jack said, still trying to catch his breath from his increased heart rate.

"What was your friend telling you?"

"He's not my friend!" Jack barked as he pulled his jittery body away from the door.

"Fine," said Fuentes.

Jack shook his head. "He said something about a Columbian necktie."

Fuentes and his partner glanced quickly at each other as Jack moved past them and into his den. Emery eyed Fuentes and followed Jack into the den. Fuentes and his partner followed. Jack and Emery were seated on the couch. Fuentes and his partner remained standing in the doorway.

"Look, Jack. I know you don't like me, and that's understandable. But I gotta tell you. I believe you're in way over your head and don't realize it. You don't have to talk to me, but I feel I need to tell you we can't protect you on the outside. You probably don't realize it, but you were probably safer in jail."

Jack shook his head. "Look. I don't know how many times I gotta tell you. I didn't do anything. I don't know those men who were just here. I don't have their cocaine. I don't know where it is. If you and the Government want to put me away for something I didn't do, then so be it. I can at least go with a clear conscience." Jack paused and looked squarely into Fuentes' eyes. "Can you?"

Fuentes shook his head and snickered. "Why do you keep insisting I'm somehow involved Jack? Why can't you just own up and take some responsibility?"

"Cause I didn't do it. That's why." Jack paused. "You were there just like me. You saw me work the combination. You were there. You know as much as I do." Jack didn't blink an eye. "Have you been questioned by anybody? I seriously doubt it. Hell, maybe I should have told my, my, friends who just left, that you were there that night too. I told them they had the wrong guy. Maybe I was right. Maybe they should be talking to you instead."

Fuentes looked at his partner, shook his head and smiled. He looked back at Jack. "Look, Jack. I didn't come here to argue with you. And how you choose to defend yourself is strictly up to you. I simply came here to offer you one more shot at cooperating with me."

"I don't think my attorney would appreciate you coming over here without going through him first."

"What attorney? You haven't retained one yet."

"And just how the hell would you know that information?" Jack inquired.

"You have no idea all I know. No idea."

Jack sat back.

Fuentes walked toward the chair and sat down on the edge of the table across from Jack. "Your buddies that just left. Tell me who they are."

"I have no idea. Never seen them before."

"That's bullshit and you know it." Fuentes leaned in closer. "You're small time, Jack. Small time. I really don't give a rat's ass about the stuff you stole. Or you, for that matter. It's small potatoes compared to what these guys are doing."

"I didn't steal it!"

Fuentes laughed. "That's right. I keep forgetting. You're innocent." Fuentes paused. "Look Jack. It's not you I want. I want the people responsible for the shipments. If you help we can make this all go away."

"Shipments. What shipments?"

"Oh come on, Jack. Are you serious? You gotta stop playing these games with me. I know you know all about the shipments. Look. I can't speak for the U.S. Attorney. But we want Raes. We're gonna bring his empire down, and you are the man who can help us do it. If you give us Raes, I am certain the Government will drop all charges against you."

Jack laughed and looked at Emery who was not laughing. "How can I cooperate when I don't know anything?" Jack paused and then said sarcastically, "Listen very closely and read my lips. I'll say this one more time very slowly so even you can understand it. I don't know anything. I did not do it. I am innocent. I don't know who Raes is. I don't know anything about any shipments. Someone, for some reason, is trying to frame me." Jack slid to the edge of the couch and was almost face to face with Fuentes. "How many times have I got to say it? If I knew anything I would tell you. But I don't."

Fuentes reached into his coat pocket and pulled out his business card. He tucked it into Jack's palm. "Here's my card. The Assistant U.S. Attorney authorized me to tell you you've got one more chance to cooperate. You've got twenty-four hours to decide or you can forget any immunity deal. Are we clear?" Fuentes looked at his watch. "Tomorrow at 6:00 p.m. any deals are off and you're on your own. You'll have to deal with a judge and jury on your own terms. More importantly, you'll have to deal with your friends that just left. And I can assure you, Jack. Your friends are to be feared much more than a jury of your peers."

Jack stared at Fuentes and flipped his card over and over between his fingers.

"Twenty-four hours. That's it." Fuentes and his partner turned to leave then turned back to Jack. "Don't blow this opportunity. I know you're guilty. You know you're guilty. The evidence is mounting hour by hour against you. You're going to be convicted, that is if your friends don't kill you first." Fuentes paused. "It's a golden opportunity, Jack. Don't screw it up." Fuentes and his partner turned and left Jack's house.

Jack laid the back of his head on the couch and stared at the ceiling. "I can't believe this is happening to me."

"Maybe you should call him tomorrow."

Jack turned quickly to Emery. "And tell him what?"

"I don't know. Anything to show you're cooperative."

"I don't know anything, Emery!" Jack said passionately. "I have nothing to tell him. The only other person besides me that could possibly know that combination was Fuentes."

"Then tell someone that."

"Oh, yeah. Like they're gonna believe me."

"Do you think Fuentes took it?"

Jack reared his head back against the couch again. "I don't know. I don't know what to believe anymore."

Emery stroked Jack's temple. She could feel the tension. He shut his eyes, desperate for sleep. He somehow wished he would never wake up once sleep came, but the brief respite of relaxation only lasted less than a minute. The shrill ringing of the phone caused him to jerk from his semi-conscious state. Jack pulled his head upright and edged his bottom to the edge of the couch. He rubbed his eyes as it rang three and four times.

"You want me to get that?" Emery asked.

"No. No. I'll get it." Jack leaned way over and picked up the phone that rested on a small table at the other end of the couch.

"Hello."

"Jack?" said a desperate female voice at the other end.

"Kelly?" Jack said, concerned for his estranged sister's tone of voice. Jack and his sister had not spoken for several months after a falling out over something silly. Both had refused to take the first step to reconciliation.

"Thank God you're there. I've been trying to find you."

Jack shook his head at Emery and mouthed the words that it was his sister. "Is everything okay, Kelly?"

"It's Matt."

"What about him? Is something wrong?"

"He's." Kelly paused. "He's dead, Jack. Matt's dead." Kelly struggled to say the words as she sobbed. "He was murdered."

"Oh, God," Jack said, leaning his head back against the couch, staring at the ceiling. Jack placed his free palm across his forehead. He tried to choke back his tears. "Why? What happened?"

Kelly struggled to regain her composure. "They don't know. The police are investigating. All they're saying is that it was drug related."

Jack jerked forward to where he was sitting on the edge of the couch. "Drugs? Matt didn't use drugs. That couldn't be right."

Concerned, Emery moved to the edge of her seat and rubbed Jack's thigh.

"All I know is what they're saying. The police said the style of the murder leads them to believe drugs were involved."

"Whattaya' mean the style?"

Kelly started sobbing again. "I don't want to talk about it. It was awful. You just need to get out here as soon as you can."

"Kelly!" Jack snapped. "I need to know. What did they do to him?"

"I can't, Jack. I can't." Kelly choked back her tears.

"Yes you can! I need to know, Kelly! What happened to Matt?"

Kelly paused long enough to control her emotions. "Whoever murdered him. They slit his throat and..." she tried to finish, but broke down.

"Kelly! Please. You gotta get a hold of yourself. What did they do?"

"They...they...slit his throat, Jack. They slit his throat and pulled his..." she sobbed again. "I'm sorry. I just can't say it."

Jack stared at the ground and briskly rubbed his forehead. "Dammit, Kelly! What did they do?"

Kelly sobbed hysterically. "His tongue. They pulled his tongue out of his throat." She struggled to get the words out. "The police called it a Columbian something."

Jack straightened. "Necktie," he said, finishing his sister's sentence.

"Yes," Kelly said, again gaining control of her emotions. "What're we gonna do? Matt's wife. The kids. What're we gonna do? You've gotta get out here now. The family needs you."

Jack stared blankly across the room. "I'll get there if I can."

"Hurry, Jack. Please hurry."

Jack handed the phone to Emery who placed it back into its cradle. Jack never broke his distant stare. "I've gotta get out of here."

"Your brother?"

"They killed him. They murdered my brother for something he had nothing to do with. If I don't get out of here I'll be next."

"Maybe you should ask for protection."

"From who? Fuentes? Who may be in this up to his eyeballs? No thanks."

"Jack. There's nowhere you can go. You can't run or you'll be a fugitive. Your picture'll be plastered everywhere. I don't think leaving is such a good idea."

"If I stay I'm a dead man. If Fuentes hadn't come when he did, we'd both be dead. Don't you get it?"

Emery nudged slightly closer to Jack. "Just call Fuentes and explain everything. He'll understand." Emery paused. "Running won't solve anything, Jack."

"No. But it'll buy me some time until I can prove my innocence." Jack paused. "I'm going. It's the only choice I've got. I'll call you when I get to wherever I'm going."

"No," Emery said matter of factly. "I'm going with you."

Jack wrinkled his eyebrows and looked at her like she was crazy. "I don't think that's such a good idea."

"Why not? I'm in as much danger as you are. They saw me. They know who I am. If you go and I stay, who do you think they're gonna go after next?"

Jack smiled at Emery. "I don't even know where I'm going."

"I don't care. All I know is I want to be with you."

"Look," Jack said shaking his head slightly. "I can't be dragging you all over the state or anywhere else. I can't do that to you."

Emery backed away. "You'd rather me stay here and face those two goons alone?"

Jack paused and grasped her hand tightly. "Are you sure?"

Emery nodded.

"When can you be ready? We don't have much time."

"I'm ready now."

They both stood. Both were scared. Jack scoured all his drawers and underneath sofa cushions and pillows for any long lost dollar bills or change. He turned to Emery who was combing the kitchen drawers for any hidden coins. "You know they'll be watching us," Jack said from another room.

Emery continued her search but acknowledged his assumption.

In the bedroom closet, Jack searched through every pocket for hidden money. Emery joined him and stood close by. He wished silently he hadn't postponed that trip to the bank a few days earlier. His billfold was nearly empty. "We can't just drive away, you know," Jack said. "We've gotta throw them off somehow."

"Any ideas?" Emery asked.

In the next few minutes Jack devised a quick plan he believed would throw both the FBI and Guido and Sarducci off their track. Jack and Emery agreed to meet at a seedy biker bar on the outer edge of the county after switching or dumping their vehicles. From there they would hop into a borrowed car and drive away into obscurity. Or so Jack hoped.

After Jack threw a few things into a small army duffle bag and had scrounged together as much cash as he could, he and Emery walked leisurely out the front door. They did not want to cause undue attention should someone be watching, which they both strongly suspected. Jack walked Emery to her car on the curb and opened the door for her as the darkness crept on the horizon. He leaned over, planted a light kiss on her cheek, and whispered something into her ear as Agent Fuentes, his partner, and Guido and Sarducci watched from two strategic, yet undetected places a hundred or so feet away. They watched closely as Emery drove away by herself in the direction that her car was pointed. Jack walked casually back toward his truck in the driveway and climbed in and shut the door. He waited ten or fifteen seconds, sure that the FBI or Guido and Sarducci would drive by in loose pursuit.

Jack watched in his rearview mirror as Fuentes and his partner rolled slowly by the driveway soon after he got into his truck. The agents looked at him a moment, and then drove off in pursuit of Emery. As soon as they were out of sight, Jack started his engine, backed down the driveway into the street and headed in the opposite direction of Emery. Jack looked for Guido and Sarducci as he drove down the street, but could not spot them. Nothing seemed unusual or out of place, but he refused to have a false sense of security. He knew they were out there somewhere watching everything he was doing.

Emery pulled into her apartment complex which was about a twenty minute drive from Jack's house. She looked around as she got out and quickly shut the door. Leaning over, she stuck her head inside the window and grabbed her purse from where it rested on top of the pull-up emergency brake. She did not take the time to put up the convertible's top. She hurriedly bolted up the one flight of stairs at the end of her unit and then ran past four or five apartments until she reached hers. Fumbling with her keys until she found the right one, she opened the door, quickly glanced over her shoulder and then shuffled quickly inside, shutting the door behind her.

Down below Fuentes pulled into a parking space a good distance away from her apartment. He got out of his car and propped his elbow on top. He watched Emery's unit for a minute or so and told his partner to stay in the car before lightly closing the door and walking toward the same stairwell Emery had ascended moments before. Obviously in no hurry, Fuentes walked the thirty or so feet to her door and knocked lightly three times. About ten seconds passed when the door cracked open just slightly. His partner watched from the car as Fuentes said something to Emery. Emery poked her head out and looked both ways before opening the door and letting Fuentes inside. Fuentes closed the door behind him.

Jack steered his truck into the Greater Atlanta Greyhound Bus Station in downtown Atlanta and jumped out as quickly as he could throw the gearshift into park. He bolted inside the bus station as fast as his weary legs could take him. He assumed Guido and Sarducci were close behind if not already there.

Inside, Jack immediately headed for the women's bathroom and the small package he knew awaited him inside the first stall against the wall. He figured this would buy some time because even Guido and Sarducci would check the men's room first. Jack checked to make sure no females were using the facilities before barging in. When the coast was clear, he stepped inside feeling somewhat strange and perverted. He stepped inside the first stall against the wall and saw the brown grocery bag tucked neatly behind the toilet. Quickly latching the stall door, he pulled a tattered, putrid brown skirt and a torn and dirty tan sweater from the bag. He shook his head and sighed, trying to think more of his well being than his male pride. Reaching deeper into the bag, he pulled out a haggard looking gray woman's wig, a pair of white socks and a dingy white pair of tennis shoes. Thinking it could never happen to him, Jack was about to become a homeless bag woman. The only thing lacking was a grocery cart. The thought sickened him, but his very life could depend on it. Jack thought of the times he would inconvenience himself and cross the street just to avoid one of these 'deviants' as he often called them. Now, suddenly, he sympathized with them.

With a solid blow from the heel of their shoes, Guido and Sarducci took turns kicking open each stall in the bus station's men's room. At each stall they poked their heads inside and then moved on to the next stall. They stared at each other wondering where Jack could be. There was nowhere inside the men's room, other than the stalls, he could hide. They had already checked the lobby area of the bus terminal. There was only one other place he could have hidden and they had already checked the janitor's closet and found nothing but cleaning supplies.

Guido and Sarducci pushed the men's door open hard and stepped back into the waiting area. Angry and growing angrier by the minute, they both scoured every square inch of the bus station which was shaped in a semi-circle. Sarducci twisted his neck far to the right and noticed the women's room. A fleeting thought crossed his mind, but he dismissed it. He stared at the door for a few more seconds before approaching it very slowly. He motioned over his shoulder to Guido to follow. They both stepped to the door and heard some strange noises from within. They looked at each other before making the bold decision to go inside. Each expected the other to go first. Finally, Sarducci, who was obviously the leader of the two, motioned Guido to go in first.

Guido pushed the door open slightly, just enough to poke his head inside. He retreated and told Sarducci in Spanish, that nobody was inside. Perturbed, Sarducci rolled his eyes and lightly pushed Guido away. He then pushed the door hard, causing it to fling open and bang loudly against the wall, making an echo inside the terminal.

The ten or fifteen people inside the terminal seated on the hardwood benches and chairs glanced at Guido and Sarducci, but thought nothing much of it. They'd all seen much stranger things inside bus terminals before.

As they stepped into the bathroom they were immediately split by a genuine female who gave them a look of disgust. She walked away, but not before glancing back several times shaking her head.

"Shut the door," Sarducci ordered Guido in Spanish.

Guido complied.

"Don't let anyone in," Sarducci barked.

Guido backed up against the door and remained silent while Sarducci ambled slowly toward the five or six stalls neatly aligned down the inside wall. Bending over, Sarducci checked all the stalls in one quick glance and could only see one set of female legs donning white socks and white tennis shoes, her dress all bunched up and wrinkled around her knees. He straightened himself up and motioned to Guido that it was time to leave the bathroom and search elsewhere. Exiting the women's room amid penetrating stares from a handful of patrons and a few winos halfway dozing on the floor, Guido and Sarducci straightened up and walked to the reservations desk. There a tall, bony man with a red goatee dressed in a white, short sleeve shirt and skinny black tie, stood ready to assist them.

"Have you seen this man?" Sarducci asked in broken English, showing the clerk a photo of Jack.

The clerk took the picture and looked at it for several seconds. He set it down on the counter, grabbed his reading glasses from his pocket then squinted his eyes squarely at the face on the photograph.

"Well?" Sarducci asked, becoming a bit agitated.

"Yep. He does look familiar. Sure does," the clerk said in a thick southern accent.

"Have you seen him tonight?" Sarducci asked in a thick Spanish accent.

The clerk peered at the photo one more time. "Well. Ya' know. Maybe he was here tonight. I think maybe he bought a ticket. Yep. As a matter of fact, he did. He seemed to be in a real hurry, too. Seemed kind a' worried 'bout something."

"Where did he buy a ticket to?" Guido asked the clerk.

"I do believe he was going to Seattle. Yep. Seattle, Washington."

"Has it left yet? Has the bus left yet?" Sarducci asked hurriedly, his voice tuned up a pitch.

"No. It's right out there," the clerk said. He pointed to a bus. "But it's leaving in about," he looked at the large clock on the wall behind him. "Three minutes."

Guido and Sarducci quickly darted away from the counter and began running toward the door.

"Wait!" the clerk shouted.

Guido and Sarducci stopped in their tracks and looked back at the clerk.

"You can't get on that bus without a ticket. It ain't allowed. The guard won't let you on without a ticket."

Guido and Sarducci looked at each other and ran quickly back to the reservations counter. "How much?" Sarducci asked. He pulled out a long black envelope shaped billfold, thick with cash from inside his jacket.

"You want one or two tickets?"

"Two," Sarducci barked, constantly looking back at the bus making sure it was still there.

"You paying for one or both tickets?"

"Both," Sarducci answered as he pounded his fist on the counter. "Hurry!"

"Just trying to do my job, sir," the clerk insisted.

"Just give me the tickets," Sarducci ordered, becoming more and more irritated.

"Will that be one way or round trip?"

Guido and Sarducci glared at the clerk and both shouted, "One way!"

The clerk bobbed his head slightly and furled his eyebrows at the two foreigners. "Hey. Chill out, will ya'. No need to get your panties in a wad. I'm just doing my job. That's all."

Sarducci leaned across the counter and grabbed the clerk's collar and pulled his skinny frame halfway across the counter to where he was almost laid out flat. His legs dangled from the back of the counter.

Concerned, Jack watched from a crack in the ladies room door.

Sarducci pulled the clerk to where the tips of their noses touched. "Listen very carefully. You don't want to fuck with me. Are you fucking with me?"

The clerk was scared to death. His voice shook. "No. Absolutely not. I wouldn't do that. No, sir."

"Very good, then. I'm going to say this once. We want two one way tickets to Seattle. I am paying cash for both of us. Is that clear?"

"Crystal," the clerk said, his voice shaking.

Sarducci pushed the clerk back softly until he landed on his feet behind the counter.

The clerk straightened his tie and collar and smoothed out his shirt. "Two one way tickets to Seattle comin' up." He reached inside a drawer and pulled out two tickets, placing them on the counter. "Two one way tickets from Atlanta to Seattle. "That'll be three hundred and fifty-one dollars please."

Sarducci grabbed up his wallet from the counter and sifted through fifteen or twenty one hundred dollar bills before pulling four of the bills from inside and handing them to the clerk. The clerk slid the two tickets toward Guido and Sarducci and picked up the four crisp one hundred dollar bills. Guido and Sarducci snatched the tickets from the counter and darted toward the bus entrance.

"Wait!" the clerk shouted as he waved forty-nine dollars in change in his hand. "Your change!"

Guido and Sarducci paid no attention to the clerk. They bolted out the door and ran toward the Seattle bound bus that had just closed its doors, was backing up and preparing to depart. When the bus driver saw the two foreigners waving frantically, he stopped the bus and opened the door. Guido and Sarducci stepped up into the large silver bus and handed their tickets to the security guard in the front seat. The bus driver closed the door and began maneuvering it into a position where he could begin his journey. Guido and Sarducci ambled slowly down the aisle, looking closely at every person on the bus. Two or three passengers were quite upset when Guido slapped their newspapers away so he could see their faces.

Inside, Jack emerged from the ladies room still dressed in drag. He felt immensely stupid, but knew it probably had saved his hide. He started toward the door but stopped and glanced at the clerk who had done a superb job at stalling the two Columbians until the Seattle bus was pulling out. The clerk acknowledged Jack's slight smile.

"Thanks, Jer," Jack mouthed toward Jerry, his longtime and faithful head foreman whose brother-in-law just happened to be the night manager of the bus station. Earlier in the evening Jerry had received a frantic plea from Jack for help. A quick, but efficient plan was hatched that would shake Guido and Sarducci should they follow Jack. At least for the time being, some time was bought to ensure an escape.

Jack walked outside, somewhat awkwardly, in the women's tennis shoes Jerry had taken from his wife that were three sizes too small and beginning to cut off Jack's circulation.

The Seattle bound bus finally backed itself into position where it could safely merge into the downtown street at the same time Jack approached his pickup truck. Jack noticed the black Lincoln Continental marked "Rental" parked next to his truck. He laughed to himself thinking that at least the Columbians did it up right when they came to town on business. When Marlowe Plumbing sent Jack on travel he would have to pay for his own upgrade from economy to mid-size. Now he was only concerned about getting the hell out of Dodge. He did not pay attention that the Seattle bus was just departing. He assumed it would be several miles away when Guido and Sarducci realized he wasn't on the bus, and by the time they got back he would be long gone.

Guido and Sarducci made their way to the back of the bus and were growing more and more frustrated when there was no sign of Jack. Suddenly Guido spotted the lavatory at the very back of the bus. He motioned to Sarducci.

"What?" Sarducci said in Spanish.

"He's in here," Guido beamed. He was proud of himself.

Sarducci smiled back. "Open it."

Guido firmly grabbed the handle of lavatory door. Sarducci nodded for him to open it. Guido jerked down hard on the handle and pulled the door quickly which resulted in total embarrassment to the middle aged man reading the sports section of the Atlanta Journal Constitution while doing his business and smoking a cigarette.

"What the...!" the man yelled at Guido, which caused every

passenger to turn their heads back and watch. "It's occupied. Do you mind?"

Guido looked at Sarducci. Sarducci looked at Guido and motioned for him to close the door.

Guido closed the door about three quarters of the way and stuck half his body inside the lavatory. He pulled out his black 9mm Sig Sauer and stuck it in the cheek of the man who immediately finished his business. "Greyhound Security," Guido said, with his thick accent. "Can't you read?" Guido said, motioning with his head toward the no smoking sign posted above the door.

The man looked at the sign, nodded his head affirmatively. He immediately removed the cigarette from his lips and dropped it in between his legs and into the commode.

"Greyhound thanks you," Guido said smiling at the man. "Have a nice trip."

Jack slapped at his pants pocket underneath his dress in a frantic search for his keys, just as the bus had a clearing in traffic and finally merged itself into the heavier than normal traffic for that time of night. Jack lifted up his skirt and checked his pockets, but the keys were not there. All he had was a pocket knife. He tossed the knife on top of his truck.

Inside the bus, now almost a football field away from the bus station and moving slowly with the traffic, Guido and Sarducci were dumbfounded about where Jack could be. Sarducci peered through the large tinted window in the back of the bus toward the bus station. He squinted his eyes and leaned over the very last seat in the bus which was not occupied. He watched as a man standing beside his truck began stripping away his wig and other women's clothing and tossing them into the bed of his truck.

"It's him!" Sarducci shouted. "It's him!" Sarducci pushed himself away from the seat, almost knocking Guido over, when he turned and bolted up the aisle toward the front of the bus. They shouted at the driver to stop the bus. Guido looked out the window and could barely make out Jack who was stooping over and looking underneath his truck. Guido smiled, turned quickly, and followed Sarducci.

By now Jack realized he must have dropped his keys in the ladies restroom while he was getting dressed. He had already checked all over, even the most obvious place, the ignition, without luck. Jack trotted quickly inside the terminal feeling much better now that he had shed the filthy clothes. He jogged over to the ladies room and cracked open the door. "Cleaning," he announced. "Is anyone in here?" Unfortunately, Jack got an answer. "Damn," he whispered under his breath. He looked over his shoulder and saw there was only one lady in the station. Jack approached her. He wondered how he was going to ask her, but he didn't have time to think of some lame excuse. "Excuse me, ma'am," he said to a lady in her early fifties, who was reading a Stephen King horror book.

"Yes?" the woman said, peering above her paperback.

"I think I may have dropped my keys in the ladies room a few minutes ago. Would you mind going in there and checking for me?"

She laid the book in her lap and gave him a 'you pervert' type look.

"I know what you're thinking, and I know it sounds crazy. But it's a long story and I wish I had time to explain. But I don't. I'm not a pervert or child molester or transsexual."

The woman peered down at Jack's tennis shoes with two pink stripes running down the side. Jack followed her eyes. She peered back up.

Jack smiled sheepishly. "I just need my keys and I'm pretty sure they're in there somewhere."

The woman smiled a smile that really wasn't a smile at all. She picked up her novel and put it inside her bag. "Sure. What the hell. I've seen stranger things."

Guido and Sarducci stood beside the bus driver shouting orders for him to stop the bus. They refused to listen to him state emphatically that stopping the bus was against regulations unless it was an emergency.

Guido pulled out his 9mm pistol and placed it against the temple of a passenger seated in the first row behind the driver. "Does this qualify as an emergency?"

The bus driver looked in the rearview mirror and immediately slowed down the bus. It rolled to a stop alongside a curb and now was about two-hundred yards away from the bus station.

"I thought it might," Sarducci said in his Columbian accent. "Open the door."

Guido and Sarducci shot out of the door and onto the sidewalk like thoroughbreds lunging from their gates at the Kentucky Derby. They could see the Greyhound sign illuminated in the darkness and bolted in that direction.

Jack tapped his foot impatiently waiting for the lady to emerge from the ladies room with his keys. He would have liked to have asked Jerry for help, but he had already gone and turned the reins back to his brother-in-law. Finally, the lady came from the bathroom with the circular key ring slipped over her index finger. Jack sighed and smiled. "Thank you so much," he said as the lady handed him his keys. Jack turned to leave.

The lady called out to Jack. "You must have lost this too. It was next to your keys."

Jack turned around and looked at the lady's extended left hand that was open and holding a lipstick tube. Jack smiled and snickered. "No. Not my color."

The lady snickered back as Jack wasted no time running to his truck. Somehow she knew he was alright.

Jack inserted the key into the lock on the driver's side door. He heard the sound of hard-soled shoes running quickly across the concrete sidewalks but he didn't look up. He keyed the lock, opened the door and pulled the key from the lock. He took his time as he turned to climb inside.

The quickening thud of the footsteps grew louder and faster as Jack shut his door and put the key into the ignition. He threw the gearshift into reverse and turned to check behind him before backing up. His heart leaped into his throat and the thumping penetrated his ears when he saw Guido and Sarducci were closing in, guns drawn, descending on him at a quickening rate. He floored the accelerator and his truck shot back almost plowing into a parked bus. He stomped on the brakes hard, jolting his truck to a dead stop which catapulted the pocketknife from the top of his cab into the bed of his truck. Jack turned quickly to see what the clanging was and saw the knife. A thought quickly crossed his mind. Looking out the passenger window, Guido and Sarducci were about two hundred feet away. As fast as he could, Jack jumped from the truck leaving his door open. He grabbed the pocketknife from the truck bed and pulled the blade out, then quickly bolted towards the Lincoln Continental he hoped was theirs.

Guido and Sarducci chests heaved as they bore down within a hundred and fifty feet of their target. Jack kept his eye on them as he plunged the blade deep into the right front tire. Pulling the blade out, Jack heard a slow hissing as he rose and darted back to his truck. But before he made it halfway, he saw Guido and Sarducci equidistance on the other side of the truck as he was on his side. The only difference was they were running in full stride, guns aimed squarely at him. Jack froze for a fraction of a second but then bolted toward the open door of his truck. Six feet away now, Jack dove head first toward the seat at the same time Guido grabbed the passenger door handle and Sarducci rushed around the front of the truck to catch him before he could get inside. Jack lurched upright and pounded his foot on the accelerator, pushing so hard his toes hurt as they were forced backwards.

Guido opened the passenger door and busted out the window

with the butt of his gun, wrapped his arms around where the glass used to be, then hung on for dear life as Jack screeched out of the bus parking lot and onto the downtown street. Sarducci dove for the bed of the truck but didn't make it, causing him to fall face first into the pavement. He picked himself up off the pavement and quickly jumped into the Lincoln Continental and took off after Jack who was driving like a maniac through the streets of downtown Atlanta. Guido hung on precariously to the passenger door, swinging and swaying with Jack's quick maneuvers. He held tightly to his gun but was unable to take aim at Jack.

Jack looked at his speedometer as it flirted with sixty-five miles per hour. Guido tried his best to climb into the cab, but every time he extended his leg to get a grip, Jack would jerk the steering wheel hard to the left, then to the right, causing Guido to swing rapidly out as far as the open passenger door would go.

In his rearview mirror, Jack kept an eye on Sarducci who was unaware that the air in his right front tire was slowly escaping.

Jack rounded the corner going about seventy, which caused his truck to roll temporarily onto the two left tires. The tires on the right side lifted about two feet off the ground sending the top half of Guido's body onto the top of the cab and the other half dangling inside. Jack swung out sharply again to his right, making Guido's legs fall hard against the pavement. Guido looked back at both his knocked off shoes flipping over and over in different directions.

Sarducci rounded the same corner going faster than Jack, causing his Continental to fishtail into oncoming traffic. He straightened it back up and floored the pedal. He could see he was closing in on Jack now who was about seventy-five feet away.

Jack kept swerving to keep Guido from gaining entry into his cab. Guido spouted a few curse words in Spanish while trying to point his 9mm pistol at Jack. Each time he tried, Jack swerved, making Guido grab on for dear life to keep from being thrown from the truck and becoming part of the pavement.

Sarducci's tire was getting smaller and smaller as he closed the gap to fifty feet. Even though Guido couldn't hear him, Sarducci kept urging his partner to hang on until he could pull even.

Jack saw the sign indicating the ramp to Interstate 75 was the next street up. He tried to fool Sarducci by switching quickly to the inside lane, hoping Sarducci would think he was going to go underneath the interstate overpass. Suddenly, just at the last second, Jack swerved across two lanes and cut off traffic, then sped up to the merge lane to I-75 North. But Sarducci wasn't fooled. With traffic stopped and a couple of hotheads standing outside their vehicles cussing and offering Jack their one finger salute, Sarducci simply cut in front of them and drove his slightly leaning-to-the-right Lincoln onto the entrance ramp. He smiled, thinking Jack had just made a tremendous tactical error. All he had to do now was to keep Jack in his sights and catch up. Coldly, Sarducci didn't care if Guido hung on or not. He knew he had Jack.

Jack zigged and zagged his truck, now pushing a hundred miles an hour. He weaved in and out of traffic causing Guido to bob back and forth on the door over and over. Jack knew if he stayed straight, no matter how fast he went, Guido would manage to pop off a round or at least work his way inside the cab. And then it would be over.

Following close behind, Sarducci weaved in and out of the five or six lanes of traffic. But with each sudden movement, his right tire lost a little more air. His eyes went back and forth between the front of his car and Jack's.

Jack pushed the accelerator as far as it could be pressed against the floorboard. His speedometer topped out at 130 miles per hour and that's where the red needle pointed. He couldn't believe that Guido had the endurance to hold on, considering the beating he was taking. Jack checked his rearview mirror and confirmed that Sarducci was there. His only hope was that the tire would finally give way. With each mile it was losing more and more air.

Sarducci's speedometer read 125. He knew he had to catch up and force Jack off the road. The accelerator was already floored but he pushed harder anyway. Inch by inch, foot by foot, Sarducci weaved his way in and out of traffic until he was right on Jack's bumper.

Jack was amazed that the tire had not blown, especially at the speeds they were traveling. He weaved back and forth from lane to lane, worried that his small blade on his pocket knife had not pierced deep enough to create the damage needed for a full blowout.

Sarducci was two inches away from Jack's bumper. He was so close Jack could see him grinning in his rearview mirror.

Sarducci edged his car slightly forward, barely bumping Jack's back bumper. He did this several times, each causing Jack's head to jerk forward slightly, and making it nearly impossible for Guido to continue holding on.

Jack's heart began to pound so hard he could feel it in his temples. Guido wasn't letting go and Sarducci refused to give up. Suddenly, while trying to weave around a car in one last attempt to elude Sarducci, Jack heard a loud pop and the screeching of tires. He quickly glanced in his rearview mirror and saw Sarducci's car spinning wildly out of control. Cars all around were slamming on brakes and coming to screeching halts. Jack slowed just slightly and watched in his rearview mirror as sparks shot from the Continental's tire rim as it scraped and slid hard and fast against the interstate's dark pavement.

"One down and one to go," Jack said, as he slowed his truck to eighty.

Just ahead of Jack in the far right lane was a tractor trailer. Jack passed a few cars while bobbing right and left just enough to keep Guido bouncing back and forth. Edging his truck alongside the tractor trailer, Jack maneuvered his vehicle and Guido closer and closer to the tractor trailer's fast moving wheels. Guido saw what Jack was trying to do and tried to arch his legs toward the cab or to anything he could find to grab with his feet and pull himself away from the tractor trailer. But Jack simply jerked the steering wheel or tapped his brakes slightly, causing Guido to pop back out with the open door.

Guido straddled his legs and crossed them through the broken window. His muscles burned and he did not know how much longer he could hold on.

Jack edged his truck closer and closer to the dangerous churning wheels of the semi. The truck driver could see Jack in his side view mirror and wondered why he was getting so close. He thought maybe Jack was intoxicated. He could not see Guido, who was now inches away from the hot, spinning tires. Guido tried unsuccessfully to point his gun toward Jack.

Jack stuck out his arm toward Guido. "Give me the gun! Throw it in here!" he yelled at the top of his lungs.

Guido shook his head no, his face immersed with pain.

"Throw me the gun!" Jack shouted again.

Guido shook his head vigorously, still clinging his arms and legs tightly around the door's window frame.

Jack clinched his teeth and edged closer to the semi's spinning tires. Guido could feel the heat on his face from the friction of the speeding wheels against the pavement. He squeezed his eyes shut, waiting for impact.

Jack darted his head back and forth between the road and Guido. The driver in the truck kept an eye in his mirror, wondering if it was a drunk or a maniac. He tried to slow down, but Jack just kept pace dangling Guido dangerously close to the ominously spinning wheels. "Throw me the gun now!" Jack yelled again at Guido.

Guido thought about a second or two before screaming, "No!"

Jack inched closer to the semi's tires. The burning rubber spun violently as it barely skimmed Guido's back. He tensed his entire body. He believed the next sound he heard would be the crunching bones of his body between the truck's giant tires and interstate pavement.

"Toss me the gun, Guido!" Jack shouted as loud as he could. "Now! Or the next time you'll become part of the wheel! Now throw it in here!"

Guido looked at Jack and then at his gun. He turned his head and saw the churning tire only an inch or so from his nose. He looked at his gun again, and then at Jack.

Jack reached out his hand toward Guido and said softly, "Give me the gun."

Guido sighed and carefully transferred his weapon from his right hand to his left, never losing his grasp of the door. He slowly softened his grip he held with his left arm and extended the weapon toward Jack, before tossing it into the middle of the seat. Jack looked at it a second and then quickly grabbed the butt of the gun. He picked it up and pointed a shaky barrel toward an exhausted Guido.

When Guido saw Jack had taken dead aim, he figured he'd made a stupid mistake. On the other hand, he believed a bullet to the head would be less torturous than being mangled between the pavement and the roaring wheels of a semi-truck. Suddenly he felt the pickup truck slow its pace. It moved away from the semi and eased into the right lane directly behind it. Guido looked at Jack, who stared back at him, still nervously pointing the gun directly at his head.

Jack tapped his brakes and slowed his truck to forty-five. He stretched the index finger of his left hand, the one holding the steering wheel, toward the turn signal and pushed it up. Easing his pickup onto the shoulder of the interstate, Jack brought it to a complete stop. Guido looked at Jack, and squinted in disbelief. He planted his feet firmly on the ground and unwrapped his exhausted arms from around the door frame. His biceps seemed to hurt more now than they did when he was hanging on. Guido rubbed his arms and legs, never taking his eyes off the barrel of the gun still pointed directly at his head.

Jack lowered the gun slightly and looked over the top of the barrel at Guido. "Go on. Get out of here," Jack said, motioning with the gun.

Guido stood frozen. "Why?"

Jack stared back. "Because I'm not a murderer." He paused slightly and lowered the gun before re-aiming at Guido's head. "You better go before I change my mind."

Guido smiled. "You know we'll find you."

Jack squinted then pulled the trigger back. "Yeah. I reckon so."

The faint smile faded from Guido's face.

"Go," Jack ordered.

Guido's smile returned. "Until the next time, my friend," he said with his thick accent. Guido turned and quickly disappeared down a hill and into a dense thicket of pine trees.

Jack released the trigger and folded his arms across the top of his steering wheel, resting his head on them. His breathing was heavy. Sweat poured from his brow. He rested less than a minute before shoving himself back against his seat. He looked at his watch, remembering the plan he'd hatched to make his getaway and the proper timing it would take. This had thrown that off. He knew Emery would be waiting. He tossed the pistol into the passenger seat next to him. He checked his side view mirror for oncoming traffic and merged slowly back into the right lane when all was clear. Jack marveled at the huge orange moon just above the horizon as he passed the next sign indicating Dalton was eighty-one miles away.

Emery had long since raised the top on her convertible. Now that the night had set in, it was a bit too cool to be driving with it down. She pulled into the parking lot of the seedy looking biker bar just on the outskirts of Atlanta and parked her car next to fifteen or twenty Harley-Davidsons. Stepping out of her car, she could hear loud music and shouting coming from inside the bar. She was dressed casually, but nice. Nicer, at least it would seem, than some of the females inside the less than reputable biker establishment. She looked around in every direction, clutched her purse tightly to her breast, and reluctantly began making her way toward the front door where two burly bikers waited just inside to assure no unwanted guests could enter.

Across the street about a hundred feet away, Fuentes and his partner watched through binoculars as Emery entered the bar. They scoured the parking lot for any signs of Jack's pickup truck, but could not spot it. They wanted to be closer, but obviously did not fit into the surroundings. Fuentes had to settle for an occasional peek through the binoculars in hopes that Jack and Emery would soon emerge.

Emery closed the door behind her and was rudely greeted by both the putrid smell of cigarettes, marijuana and stale beer. She sighed and shook her head slightly as two scantily clad girls danced erotically around a pole on a makeshift stage. Most of the bikers stood around the outer wall of the bar smoking, drinking or playing pool on several billiard tables. A few men in shirt and ties sat around the stage drinking their beer and shoving five dollar bills inside the g-strings of the dancing girls.

Emery was repulsed at the sight of grown men acting like this. She figured this was the Neanderthal in all men she'd heard about all her life. She shook her head, waved her hand in front of her face to brush away the smoke, and began scanning the room for Jack.

"Lookin' for someone sweetheart?" one of the bikers by the door said.

Emery glanced back at the biker who flashed his toothless smile. She said nothing and turned away. As she walked a few steps deeper into the bar she was approached by another biker about twice the size of a tank. Dressed in tattered blue jeans and a black leather jacket studded with silver buttons, the gray bearded hood blocked Emery's path when she tried to go around him. She tried the other direction, but he stepped to that side blocking her movement. Emery looked up at the giant who seemed to tower ten feet above her. "Excuse me," she said softly.

"Come with me."

Emery balked. "Uhhhhh. I don't think so. I'm with someone," she said curtly, squinting to catch a glimpse of Jack through the smoke filled room.

"You're here for Jack, ain't ya'?"

Emery's head jolted upward toward the massive man. "You know Jack? I mean, Jack knows you?" She couldn't believe Jack would know anyone so different than himself.

The huge biker laughed. "Jack and I went to college together."

"You went to college?" Emery blurted out before her mouth could stop. "I'm sorry. I didn't mean to insinuate…"

"Ain't the first time that's happened. Can you believe that?" he said laughing. "Follow me and I'll explain what's going on."

"Explain what?" Emery asked.

"Jack told you to meet him here but he's somewhere else. He knew that people would be watching, so he changed his plans. C'mon," he said, taking Emery by the arm and leading her toward a back exit. "By the way, you can call me Tiny."

Emery shook her head not knowing what to think. "That's very appropriate."

"My real name is Frederick. But don't tell anyone that!"

"I don't know if I should leave. I mean, Jack told me to…"

Tiny interrupted and nodded to Emery. "Don't worry. You're in good hands. Jack's waiting on you. But we need to go now."

Unwillingly, Emery followed Tiny through a back door to the outside where a single motorcycle was parked. Tiny picked up a helmet and black leather jacket and told Emery to put them on and to stuff her hair inside the helmet. He also gave her a pair of jeans and boots and told her to slip the pants over the pair she was wearing.

Tiny put his helmet on, stepped over and straddled the bike. With one stroke of his right boot heel, the engine revved up, drowning the wild music blaring from inside. Tiny looked back at Emery and patted the black leather seat of his bike. Emery finished tucking her hair up into the helmet and reluctantly climbed aboard the motorcycle. As Tiny took off, Emery wrapped her arms as far around Tiny's waist as she could but still only made it about halfway. She grabbed hold of his jacket and held on tight.

Fuentes and his partner stared through the binoculars at the front of the bar, waiting for anyone to come out as the Harley-Davidson carrying two passengers passed by directly in front of them. Fuentes looked but paid no attention.

"C'mon. C'mon," Fuentes' partner said, growing impatient for Jack to arrive. "How long are we gonna wait?"

"As long as it takes. All night if we have to," Fuentes said. "All night."

Fully dressed, Jack lay sprawled out on his back, sound asleep across the full size bed at an out of the way hotel somewhere in Dalton, Georgia. The couple in the room next door had to turn on a fan they'd brought along to drown out Jack's intolerable snoring.

Emery twisted the key the clerk had given her into the doorknob. As she pushed the rusted metal door to open it, it creaked slightly. Jack shot straight up and pointed Guido's 9mm pistol at Emery, who took a quick deep breath and clutched her chest. Jack dropped the gun as soon as he realized it was Emery.

Emery stared at Jack who was unkempt. "What in the world happened, Jack?"

Jack hung his head. "I'm sorry. You startled me."

"And how many times will it take before you pull the trigger?" Emery paused. "I don't like guns, Jack. I didn't know you had one. I don't want you to have it."

Jack held the weapon close to his face but pointed away. "It's not mine."

"Then where did you get it?"

"It's Guido's."

"Who?"

"Look. It's a long story. I'm tired and I don't feel like going into it right now."

Emery turned and opened the door.

"Stop!" Jack shouted.

Emery turned and squinted. Jack had never raised his voice to her like that and she wasn't about to let him start. Her look told him so.

"Look. I'm sorry. Alright? Shut the door. It should be closed just in case they're out there."

"In case who's out there?"

"Guido and Sarducci."

"Who?"

"The two Columbians at the house tonight. The ones who tried to kill me tonight. Least that's what I call them."

"That's real cute," she said very facetiously. "But I'm getting my own room."

"Why? What for?"

"Guns. I despise guns and I won't stay in the same room with one."

Jack looked at his gun. "Fine. I'll put it away." Jack searched the room with his eyes until he found a place he could put the weapon. He got off the bed and hid it under several spare blankets supplied by the hotel located on a shelf above the closet. "There. Is that better?"

Emery stared at the blankets. "I guess. But I want you to get rid of it. Okay?"

"I'll get rid of it tomorrow."

Emery half smiled and leaned against the door. "I'm so tired."

"Me too." Jack walked to Emery and held her tight. "You take the bed. I'll sleep on the floor next to the door."

Jack sprawled himself on the floor lengthwise against the door. No more than a few minutes passed when his snoring started. She rolled over on the lumpy mattress and looked down at Jack then at the phone on the night table beside the bed. She slowly reached for the receiver, picked it up and brought it to her ear, but there was no dial tone. She gently pushed the button down several times but could not get a tone. She hung the phone up and reached for the cable running from the back of the phone to the wall jack. She slowly pulled it toward her until she held the cut end in her hand. She looked at Jack who was sleeping soundly with a soiled pillow and thin blanket. Emery rolled over on her stomach and pulled the pillow on top of her head in a futile attempt to drown out Jack's snoring.

It was the first meaningful sleep in days. At least for Jack.

"Whattaya' mean you lost them?" the big, burly SAC shouted at Fuentes, pounding his desk at the same time.

Fuentes sat in the chair directly across from the solid cherry executive desk of the top FBI official in the state of Georgia. He fidgeted a little and ground his jaw back and forth as he and his Squad Supervisor, Richard Meyers, unwillingly accepted the verbal barrage from their superior.

At fifty and eligible for retirement, Frank McMann had twenty-five years in the Bureau. Nineteen of them were spent on the street before he opted for more money, less danger, more prestige, and a desk job. As Special Agent in Charge, he was the top dog. Being placed in Atlanta, a top fifteen office, made his job that much more renowned. As SACs go, McMann was liked by some and hated by more. Unlike many, he was respected in the law enforcement community throughout Georgia. Although many Agents were intimidated by his gruff appearance, he did not micromanage and would not allow himself to become personally involved with any of their cases unless there were nationwide implications. Then it was more for control, publicity and exposure. The Agents appreciated that, but nonetheless were thankful when they were not assigned the Hector Raes case several years back when it was determined that Raes' mode of operation was using plumbing warehouses as points of distribution. McMann had taken a personal interest and demanded weekly briefings from Fuentes. A lot of Agents thought McMann was too involved, and questioned his motives and level of interest. Fuentes didn't seem to mind and didn't say much when asked his opinion, other than it was the SAC's prerogative.

McMann sat back down in his leather, high-back chair and leaned back. "How in the hell could you lose them, Eric?" McMann's voice calmed somewhat but still emphasized each word. "My God! They were right there under your nose. Hell! You knew where they were going to meet. What in the hell happened?"

Fuentes remained silent, not sure if McMann expected an answer or if he was just offering a rhetorical question.

McMann stared back. "Well?"

Fuentes glanced at his supervisor, hoping he would speak up for him, but he just stared back at Fuentes. "I don't know what happened. I can't explain." Fuentes struggled for the right words. "It was dark. It was late. He somehow tripped us up. We lost them. I have no excuse."

McMann turned to Fuentes supervisor. "Richard. Would you mind? I want to talk to Eric alone."

"Sure." Meyers said, actually quite relieved. He had figured he was about to get his weekly butt chewing since the screw up was by one of his squad members. He guessed he either escaped the SAC's wrath or it would come later in the day after Fuentes was severely chastised. Meyers backed his way to the door, opened it, backed out and closed it behind him.

McMann rested his elbows on his desk and nestled his folded fingers on his chin. "Do you realize what you've done?"

"I've got it under control."

"The hell you do!" McMann's nostrils flared as he leaned forward in his chair. "Damn, I hate that cliché. I've always said you know something's out of control when whoever's in charge says it's under control. God! I can't believe I trusted you with this."

Fuentes fidgeted in his seat and tightened his jaw.

"From now on you don't make a move without me. I'm working the case with you. Understand?"

Fuentes rose quickly from his chair. "That's gonna' look funny, Frank. People are going to start asking questions. I don't think that's such a good idea."

McMann looked up at Fuentes who was standing just in front of his desk. McMann motioned with two fingers for Fuentes to sit back down.

Fuentes nodded his head in disapproval but followed the order.

"First of all. Don't call me Frank. It shows no respect. Second. I call the shots. Just in case you forgot, I am the boss. Thirdly. I don't give a shit what anybody says. If any of these agents have the balls to confront me with it, I'll tell them the same thing I'm telling you. Then I'll have their sorry asses transferred to an applicant squad in Minot, North Dakota. You ever been to Minot?"

Fuentes shook his head. "Look, boss. No disrespect meant. I'm not trying to tell you what you can or can't do. I'm just saying SACs don't work cases. It'll look funny and people will ask questions."

"SACs do get involved in big cases, Eric."

"But not on the street level. I'm telling you Fra...boss. It may not look like it, but everything is under con....I've got the matter stabilized. I've got my sources checking around and by this time tomorrow I'll at least have a general idea of where they are."

"Lemme' tell you something, Eric. This isn't your first screw up on this case. You've made some pretty lame blunders. The biggest of which was getting this moron Armstrong involved. I cannot afford any more mistakes. There is a lot riding on this. Not the least of which is yours and my future."

"And if you involving yourself backfires?"

"It won't."

Rising from his chair Fuentes threw his hands into the air. "Fine." He turned and started to leave the office.

"I'm not through yet."

Fuentes turned to face McMann.

"She doing okay?"

Fuentes smiled "She can take care of herself."

"Good." McMann rose from his chair and stuck his hands inside his trouser pockets. "Has Meyers got you working any other case besides Raes?"

"I've got several more, but they're manageable."

"No." McMann shook his head. "I can't afford any more glitches. I'll have Richard reassign everything else."

"That'll make the guys real happy," Fuentes said, tongue planted firmly in cheek. "Look. I can handle my case load. They're my responsibility."

McMann sat back down and pulled out a pocket digital tape recorder. "Sorry, Eric. This is my call. I want your attention focused solely on this one matter. Maybe when the publicity dies down things can get back to normal. But for now, for you and me, this is too important. I'm gonna do a memo to Richard to have all your other cases reassigned."

Fuentes sighed and shrugged his shoulders. "Fine. But I think it's just going to raise more questions we don't need right now."

"I'll handle the questions. You just worry about the players."

Fuentes pressed his lips together and nodded at McMann in submissive approval. Opening the door to leave, he glanced back at McMann, who was starting to record his memorandum to Fuentes' supervisor. Fuentes shook his head slightly from side to side and halfway snickered to himself. He wondered to himself if McMann was right in his first assessment…that things really were out of control and there was nothing he could do about the wall slowly beginning to crumble around him.

The pickup truck sailed along at a comfortable sixty miles per hour as it crossed the Tennessee state line. Jack chose route 411 because he figured the authorities would be watching the interstate like hawks. Even though he wasn't officially a fugitive and wouldn't be one until he failed to show for his trial, he knew the Feds and the Columbians would be constantly searching for him.

Jack glanced down at his fuel gauge and watched the needle bob back and forth between the red danger mark and below empty. "We're gonna have to get gas pretty soon."

"I saw a sign for a Pilot station about a half mile back," Emery said, resting her head against the window. Her eyes were half closed from a sleepless night. "It said it was two miles up on the right."

"Good." Jack looked at Emery who closed her eyes again. The hum of the tires seemed to lull her into a semi-conscious sort of slumber. He saw the next sign and read it to himself. It advertised Fat Eddie's, home of Fat Burgers, cold beer, gas, and the largest fireworks selection this side of the Mississippi River. It was just ahead.

Jack thought he shouldn't take a chance on driving further and decided Fat Eddie's would have to do. Emery stirred and half opened her eyes when the truck dipped as it turned onto the rough parking lot in front of Fat Eddie's.

"Where are we?" Emery asked, rubbing her eyes.

"A place I've dreamed of going for years. I finally made it to Fat Eddies. I can now die a happy man."

Emery didn't laugh. She wasn't amused. She sat straight up in her seat and reached for her sunglasses on the dashboard. Jack did the same. The sun had peaked over the East Tennessee hills and cast a blinding glare on the windshield. But Jack wore the glasses for more than UV protection. Even in the security of the mountain laced countryside, he was afraid of being recognized by the local authorities or by some local yokel that happened to be educated enough to look at another newspaper other than the weekly rag in whatever quiet hamlet he was now in.

Jack pulled his truck up to the gas pump and threw it quickly into park. "Why don't you stay in here and rest while I fill up."

"I need to freshen up. I feel so greasy. There were roaches in the room last night. Roaches for crying out loud! And the sheets were damp. Have you ever slept on damp sheets? I went to sleep for maybe ten minutes and woke up to a roach the size of my foot crawling across my arm. I don't know how much I can take of this."

"I told you not to come. You were the one who insisted on coming. So don't blame me," Jack said in a volatile tone. "What'd you think? That I was gonna reserve us an executive suite in the Ritz-Carlton in downtown Atlanta? Is that what you thought? Well excuse the hell outta me. I've only got the FBI and the Columbian mob after me. Excuse me for trying to save our asses."

Emery glared at Jack. "I'm going to the bathroom. I'll give the clerk my credit card and don't ever talk to me in that tone again." Emery opened her door, grabbed her purse and stepped out of the truck.

"No!" Jack shouted.

Emery turned, and leveled an evil eye at him.

"No credit cards. It'll just create a paper trail. That's all Fuentes needs. He's gonna have to work to find us. I'm not gonna give him any help."   Jack pulled a twenty dollar bill from his pocket and stretched out his hand over the hood to hand it to Emery. "Tell the clerk I'm putting in twenty dollars worth. That'll be enough to get us to Knoxville where we'll switch cars."

Emery cocked her head and her eyes. "You didn't say anything about Knoxville or switching cars there."

Jack paused and looked deeply into her eyes. "Plans change. I had to make some last minute alterations. We're stopping in Knoxville to see an old friend who said he'd help us out. I think we might be able to get the FBI and the Columbians off our trail."

Emery sighed and blew out a long slow breath and smiled. "Fine. But what about our money? We don't have that much. You can't be spending cash every time you need something."

Jack smiled. "That'll be taken care of soon enough."

"Your friend?"

Jack nodded his head.

Emery turned, shook her head and started walking toward the entrance to Fat Eddies.

"Emery!" Jack shouted, as he pulled the gasoline nozzle from the pump. Emery turned back as she put her hand on the metal handle of Fat Eddie's entrance.

"Sorry about....well, you know. We're both tired and all," Jack tried to offer an apology as best he could.

Emery nodded, but refused to smile. She was not a happy person right now. Her hair was beginning to form a slight film. Her makeup had long since faded. Her clothes were wrinkled. And she had forgotten her tooth brush. The only bright side, if there was a bright side, was that she would have no problem mixing in with some of the females at the numerous counters inside shopping for cherry bombs and M-80s and two or three others playing the video poker machines. Emery handed a female clerk, with magenta-red shoulder length hair, the twenty dollar bill and pointed to Jack pumping gas. "Have you got a pay phone?" Emery's cell phone had died the previous day and in all the excitement she had forgotten to charge it back up.

The clerk pointed toward the back corner. "Bock-ar. Taint warkin tho'."

Emery cocked her head and squinted. She had no idea what the clerk just said. "Excuse me?"

"Phone's bock-ar. But taint warkin."

Emery got the gist of where the phone was, but had no idea what 'taint warkin' meant. She then winced slightly at the three or four teeth the clerk still had intact inside her mouth before moving in the direction the clerk had motioned toward. Finally seeing a sign for the pay phone, Emery reached into her purse, desperately digging for a quarter. Ten or so feet from the phone, her fingers finally emerged with one. She was glad that no one was using the phone and upped her stride so no one could beat her to it. Reaching for the receiver, her hand stopped short of lifting it off the hook when she read the faded black words written across the tape. 'OUT OF ODOR'. Appropriate she thought. She also now knew what 'taint warkin' meant. She leaned her forehead against the phone and blew out a long breath.

The gasoline pump registered $15.57 when, from the corner of his eye, Jack saw the police cruiser pull into Fat Eddie's parking lot and park in a space about fifty feet from where he was pumping gas. Jack tried to be nonchalant, but couldn't help glance back and forth at the cop sitting inside the cruiser. The police officer seemed to be watching Jack and talking on his radio. The pump automatically cut off when it reached twenty dollars. With one eye on the cop and the other on the pump, Jack pulled the nozzle out slightly from his tank and shook the last few drops back into it. He replaced the nozzle back into its holder on the pump and silently summoned Emery to hurry up and finish whatever it was she was doing.

The cop looked straight toward Jack's truck, pulled out a piece of paper and pen and wrote something down. Jack's stomach turned. He could feel his heart beating rapidly. He was only ninety miles away from a different license plate number. If the cop was running his tags, it would come back registered to him.

As Emery emerged from Fat Eddie's, three more police cruisers and three or four more unmarked cars with blue magnetic police lights affixed on top, came screeching into Fat Eddie's lot. Jack leaned across the bed wall of his truck and buried his head into his arms. He figured he'd been followed the whole way and was fine until he crossed state lines. His bond stipulated he could not leave the state of Georgia without permission. Now that he'd crossed state lines, he was in violation and a wanted man. They were just waiting for him to make a mistake and now he'd made it.

Six or seven plainclothes cops, with three huge gold letters spelling TBI on the back of dark blue windbreakers, emerged quickly from their unmarked cars. The police officers, just arriving on the scene, quickly exited their cruisers and seemed to be securing the area. Jack watched the activity and waited. He decided he would be a fool to resist. The first cop on the scene, who had watched Jack, got out of his cruiser and attempted to pull his pants up over his belly that hung quite conspicuously over his belt. He placed his western cowboy hat on top of his head and started walking toward Jack. By now Emery saw what was happening. Jack stood up straight and put his hands behind his back to be handcuffed as the fat officer, who was obviously the High Sheriff, approached at the same moment Emery did.

"Scuse me, suh…ma'am. Ah' couldn't help but notice yo' outta state tags." The Sheriff stood straight legged, his toes pointed at ninety degree angles. His thumbs were tucked neatly into his pants underneath his gold star belt buckle. He chewed incessantly at a toothpick hanging from the side of his mouth.

To Jack's surprise, Emery piped in quickly and authoritatively. "Is there a problem with our tags, Sheriff?"

"Well that depends, ma'am."

Jack was about ready to just admit he was the man they were looking for, but the Sheriff kept talking.

"Ya' see. Lots a' you folks from Jawja' likes to cross over the state line bock-ar."

There it was again. That phrase 'bock-ar'. Emery snickered to herself.

The Sheriff glared at Emery. "You may think it's funny Miss, but gamblin' taint' legal in Tennessee. And them video pokah' machines inside Fat Eddie's theyah' is gamblin' devices. And as you can see, these State fellas is conductin' a raid. Now I don't wanna detain you folks none, but if you was a playin' them machines inside theyah'. Well, I'm afraid you may have problems."

Jack lifted his head and smiled. "Oh. No, sir. No, sir. We just stopped for gas. You can go ask the clerk. My girlfriend gave her twenty dollars to pay for it. We've been here all of five minutes."

The Sheriff smiled like he didn't believe Jack. "Okay." He looked around and saw a comrade guarding the door. "Bubba!" he shouted. "Go inside and ask Gladys if'n these two folks was playin' the machines." He turned back to Jack and flashed a toothy grin that was stained yellow by years of tobacco chewing. "I'm sure you folks don't mind waitin'. We gotta be sure bout these things. Understand?"

"Absolutely," Jack said, thrilled he hadn't been nabbed. "Wouldn't wanna violate procedures or anything like that."

The Sheriff nodded and smiled. "Glad you see it that way."

Bubba emerged from the door, his hand never leaving the butt of his pistol. "She says they was just a' gettin' some gas and needin' ta' use the phone. They wasn't playin' no pokah."

The smile faded from the Sheriff's pudgy face. He had hoped to catch someone in a lie.

"Can we go now?" Emery asked politely.

"I reckon so, ma'm. I got nuthin' to hold ya' fur."

Emery opened the passenger door and climbed in, shutting the door behind her. The Sheriff tried to pull his pants up again over his belly as he continued to watch Jack.

Jack turned to the Sheriff as he opened his door to climb into the truck cab. "Sheriff. Can I ask you a question?"

"Go 'head."

"Were you writing down my tag number earlier? Before you came over?"

Emery glared at Jack, not believing he would even bring it up.

The Sheriff nodded. "Reckon I was. Why?"

"Well. Since we were just getting gas and obviously in the wrong place at the wrong time, is there any reason you need to keep it?"

"Why? You gotta reason why I shouldn't?"

"No, sir. It's just we didn't do anything wrong and it's kind of an uneasy feeling you'd have my tag number when I haven't done anything wrong."

"Well, son. If you ain't done nothin' wrong you got nothin' to worry 'bout. You got some reason you don't want me to keep it?"

Emery looked away and rolled her eyes. She couldn't believe Jack had even broached the subject.

Jack cocked his head and squinted his eyes as he jumped quickly into his truck. "Forget it. No big deal. Was just wondering." He cranked his engine and drove away.

"That was pretty stupid," Emery said.

Jack looked at her. "What?"

"Are you serious? You just gave him every reason to run the tag. He probably would have tossed it in the trash. You've only managed to peak his curiosity. I cannot believe you did that."

"Naaaahhhh. He's just a country bumpkin. A large Barney Fife."

"You better hope so."

The Sheriff watched as the truck disappeared from sight. In his palm he straightened the piece of paper with the tag number written on it. He folded it neatly, unbuttoned his shirt pocket and neatly tucked it inside. He refastened the button and patted it twice and grinned before he went inside to join his deputies and the state police.

Sarducci winced with every venomous word Hector Raes could spout over the phone. Guido watched and listened, aware that Raes was just as pissed at him as he was at Sarducci, but thankfully Sarducci was the buffer, which meant he never had to deal with Raes one on one.   Sarducci couldn't get in a word, not that he wanted to. It was just that Raes was doing all the talking, or shouting.

Guido sat on the pink chair in their hotel room halfway listening to Sarducci attempt to explain how they lost Armstrong and halfway listening to Joy Behar and Elisabeth Hasselbeck agree to disagree on *The View*. They hadn't yet checked out of the Atlanta Marriot. It seemed they could do nothing without direct orders from Raes. But Sarducci made a critical error in telling Raes they were still in Atlanta. Guido could hear Raes yelling obscenities violently at Sarducci, who held the receiver an inch or two away from his ear. Raes could not believe they had actually gone back to the hotel and slept when they knew Armstrong was on the move.

"He's a salesman. He sells toilets. You're a hit man. You track people down and kill them. You let a toilet salesman give you the slip," Raes chastised Sarducci in Spanish.

"The man is very clever," Sarducci shot back in Spanish.

"Shut up!" Raes shouted.

Sarducci looked at Guido and rolled his eyes. Sarducci smiled back sympathetically at Sarducci.

"I want you two geniuses to get your lazy asses out of that posh hotel you're staying in and find him. I don't care what it takes or what you have to do. Find him. And when you find him, kill him. No more opportunities for Mr. Armstrong. Is that clear?"

"After he takes us to the cocaine?" Sarducci asked.

"No!" Raes screamed. "Now! Whenever you find him, kill him. And I want him to suffer. Do you understand? He must understand who he is dealing with."

Sarducci silently questioned his boss. Guido flipped *The View* off as Whoopi Goldberg played peacemaker between Behar and Hasselbeck. Guido stood over Sarducci not quite sure what Raes was ordering.

"What about the merchandise?" Sarducci asked.

"To hell with the drugs!" Raes roared. "There's plenty more where that came from. What Armstrong has done is the cost of doing business. But I cannot allow him to win." Raes paused. "You find him and kill him." He paused again. "And I want his head as a trophy. Bring me his head."

Sarducci had probably killed ten or fifteen men in the five years he had worked for Raes. But he had never heard Raes make such as monstrous request. Sarducci had no conscience. He couldn't. Not working in this line of business. But even the mention of doing something as grotesque as severing someone's head made even his stomach turn.

"Did you hear me?" Raes asked.

Sarducci paused. "Yes. Yes. I heard you." He paused again. "Mr. Raes?" Once again he paused, not sure if he should say what he wanted to.

"What is it?"

"I don't know. It's just that I'm not so sure we're after the right man anymore. I don't want to kill an innocent man."

Raes laughed loudly. "That's never bothered you before."

Sarducci did not smile.

Raes' laughter ceased. "Look. Armstrong is guilty. There couldn't be anyone else. No one else had the opportunity. The motive. Isn't that what our sources told us?"

"Yes. But..."

"But what? What else is there? Armstrong did it. Now's not the time to go soft. Don't let his lies get to you."

"He's just so adamant. I mean, like you said, he's a toilet salesman. He seems so honest." Sarducci was almost pleading.

"You have got to be kidding me. What? Are you a psychologist now?" Raes laughed, not quite as hard this time. "Look. There is no one else that could have done it. The U.S. Government has already indicted him. We'll just save them the cost of a trial. I want him dead. If you don't kill him, I will." Raes paused. "Then I will kill the two of you. You don't want that do you?"

"No, sir."

"Now, listen. Don't you get soft on me. You've got a job to do. And I pay you handsomely. I want Armstrong's head. Do I need to come up there and do it myself?"

Sarducci wanted to say yes, because for some crazy reason he believed Jack didn't take the cocaine. But he also valued his own life. He knew Raes would make good on his promise. Raes would kill them both. "No, sir. We'll find him."

"Good." Raes paused. "Have you talked to her?"

Sarducci looked at Guido and thought for a moment. "Yes. But not for long."

"Is she okay?"

Sarducci paused and looked at Guido for help. Guido shrugged his shoulders. "Like I said. We didn't see her for very long but she was fine."

"You will watch her for me. No?"

"Yes. Yes. We will watch her."

Sarducci hung up the phone and made a few more phone calls to well placed sources, while Guido turned the TV back on and caught up on the latest Hollywood buzz on *Entertainment Tonight*. After checking out and grabbing sandwiches at one of the fast food places close to the hotel, Guido and Sarducci were off in their newly rented

Lincoln, racing north up Interstate 75. They made no turns until they were just north of Dalton and saw the signs leading to U.S. Route 411. Their sources were very well placed.

Jack kept one eye on the road and one eye in the rearview mirror. He didn't dare go over the speed limit. Emery slept soundly on a wadded up jacket she had neatly placed between her head and the window.

The large green sign hanging on the interstate overpass told Jack the I-75 and I-40 split was two miles away. He had gotten back on the interstate after passing through Loudon, Tennessee because he wasn't sure if he could remember which route would take him to his friend's. He knew he would recall if he saw the exit signs. It had been several years since he'd been in Knoxville. He looked forward to being there again. He just wished it were under different circumstances. He glanced at Emery sleeping soundly. Jack smiled at her and patted her knee which was tucked neatly into her chest. "Almost there," he whispered.

The left lane forked off to I-40 west to Nashville. The right would lead directly to Knoxville. Jack merged into what was now I-75 and I-40 combined and was surprised at how much more traffic there was, especially tractor trailers. He rested his arms on top of the steering wheel and leaned forward as he read the sign exiting to Watt Road. The name of the road was familiar, but it wasn't the right one. In his excitement the night before, he forgot to ask his friend which exit he was supposed to take. He knew it was in West Knoxville and that he would remember it when he saw it.

"West Hills! That's it!" Jack shrieked, seeing the sign for the next exit.

Emery about jumped out of her skin.

"I'm sorry," Jack apologized. "This is our exit. I didn't mean to wake you, but I guess you'd have to wake up in a few minutes anyway."

"Where are we?" Emery asked, rubbing her eyes and then reaching for her sunglasses.

"Knoxville. And safety. We're just a few minutes away from Doug and Cissy's now."

"Doug? Is that your friend you were talking about?"

"Yeah." Jack turned off the exit and turned right at the traffic light and then another right at the next light. A few turns later and three or four miles further Jack pulled into the high end, tree lined neighborhood.

"Wow," Emery exclaimed, viewing some of the oversized brick homes. "You didn't tell me your friends were rich."

"They're not really rich. They've just made some good investments."

Emery smiled as she looked right and left and absorbed the magnificence of some of the houses in the neighborhood. She wondered silently what some of the people did. There couldn't be that many doctors living in one neighborhood, she thought to herself. There were homes with majestic white columns that seemed to cascade down from the sky. Others which sat on huge lots seemed to stretch for a mile. "What does your friend do?"

"Medical sales. Pharmaceuticals. Things like that." Jack drove slowly, picking his way through the neighborhood, not quite sure the name of the street he was supposed to turn down. He'd been there before, so he looked for the tall Oak tree he'd always used as a landmark when visiting.

"Does his wife work anywhere? Are we gonna have anything in common?"

"Oh! Cissy's great. Real easy to get along with. You're gonna love her. Her only fault is leaving extremely long messages on your answering machine." Jack snickered at himself. "But look. I don't know how long we're gonna be there. So don't worry if for some reason you don't hit it off with her. Doug's getting us another ride and then he's gonna dump the truck so they can't track us. I just need enough time to do some work to prove my innocence."

"And how are you gonna do that up here, Jack?"

Jack paused and shook his head. "I haven't figured that out yet. But I will. For right now I just want to relax a little. Maybe have a beer or two and forget about everything that's happened."

Emery stared at Jack as he searched for the oak tree. He could sense her watching him and glanced at her. "What?"

"Nothing. I just wish this would all be over. That's all."

Jack stretched out his hand and patted hers. "It will. Soon. I promise. Somehow I'm gonna prove I'm innocent, and then it'll be over. I promise."

Emery smiled.

"There it is!" Jack yelped. "The Oak tree. That thing is even bigger than I remember." Jack turned left onto the street and recalled right away where Doug and Cissy's house sat. "There's their house," Jack said, pointing over the steering wheel toward a majestic home. It was immaculate. A red bricked beauty with seven white wide columns running the entire length of the house. The front yard, which covered at least one acre, was akin to a putting green on the finest golf course in America. Four large Weeping Willows drenched the front yard in cool shade.

Jack pulled into the Oak-lined driveway, which from the street to the house seemed like a mile, but was probably closer to a quarter of a mile long. Doug and Cissy stepped out of the front door and onto the front porch. Their two kids, a boy ten years old and a girl, seven years old, dashed from the house and darted quickly toward Jack's truck, racing along beside it. Jack slowed a bit and rolled down his window to hear their squealing voices calling out "Uncle Jack, Uncle Jack!" Jack playfully yelped to the kids how much they had grown since he'd last seen them. He pulled the truck to a halt just behind a shiny silver BMW and white Volvo station wagon, hopped quickly out of the truck and dropped to one knee. There was nothing that could compare to being the recipient of miniature bear hugs around the neck. Jack kissed his quasi-niece and nephew on their smooth as silk cheeks. He stood up and received a firm handshake from his old college buddy. They hugged lightly and patted each other on the back the way guys do when guys hug. It made the hug not quite so feminine.

Emery emerged from the passenger's side and was immediately approached by Cissy, who was labeled by anyone who'd ever met her as the friendliest person on the face of the earth. "You must be Cissy," Emery said, extending her right hand.

Ignoring her friendly gesture, Cissy barged directly into Emery's personal space and gave her a larger than life hug around her shoulders. Emery looked at Jack, not sure how to react. Not sure if she should reciprocate or not, Emery hung in a kind of suspense, her hands slightly raised above her head.

"And you must be Emery. Jack's told us so much about you!" Cissy released her grip and took two steps back, never letting go of Emery's arms. Cissy slid her hands down Emery's limbs until she reached her hands. Like a tail hook on an aircraft carrier latches onto a fighter jet, Cissy's hands clamped onto Emery's hands as she ran out of arms to slide down. "Oh my," Cissy exclaimed, "You're even prettier than Jack said you were."

Uncomfortable, Emery smiled at Cissy and then at Jack. Jack and Doug smiled back.

The children jumped up and down and wanted Uncle Jack to play. Doug told the kids that Uncle Jack was tired and that he would play with them later. He wrapped his arm around Jack's shoulders and started walking toward the oversized front door. "Ya'll take a load off and come on in. You gotta be worn out."

Doug was a month or two older than Jack, but a good six inches taller. A stellar basketball star in high school, Doug's athletic scholarship to LSU had been retracted when traces of marijuana showed up in a mandatory drug screening. Doug had sworn that he was only at a party where it was being smoked, but the powers that be inside the LSU athletic department did not see it that way. Under extreme pressure he finally admitted he had smoked on four or five occasions and that he was only experimenting. That didn't matter. He was kicked out of school before his freshman term began and was put on the next bus back to Knoxville. He tried to talk to the Tennessee coaches, but he was damaged goods. He entered UT as a regular student. He joined a fraternity and helped it win its first intramural basketball championship. Other frats would cry foul because of his talent level. But the rules allowed him to play. The fraternity was where Jack and Doug became best friends. The twenty years that had passed had thinned Doug's dark hair and a noticeable bare round splotch about two inches in diameter was prominent on the top of his head. He was also turning gray around the ears. But he maintained himself in perfect physical condition. Running five miles a day, combined with five hundred sit-ups, kept him looking like a twenty-five year old. His tortoise shell horn rimmed glasses gave him a college professor-like appearance.

Doug dwarfed Cissy. She was small to begin with, but marrying a basketball jock surely did not do anything to enhance her height in the eyes of others. She had gained weight after the birth of their children, but that didn't last long. Within a month after the birth of each child, Cissy was running five miles a day and doing almost as many sit-ups as Doug. Her hair, which had an intriguingly gold tint in the sunlight, was stylishly short. Her green eyes were the deepest green Emery had ever seen. And although Cissy rubbed Emery somewhat the wrong way with her warmer than necessary friendliness, Emery couldn't help but envy the homespun lifestyle Cissy apparently lived.

"The first thing I've got to do is borrow your phone, Doug. With everything that's happened and all, I haven't even called my secretary to tell her I am taking an extended leave of absence. That's of course if I'm still employed."

"Sure. Come on in. I'll get you a phone," Doug said, his arm still draped across Jack's shoulders.

"That's alright, Jack," Emery said, whose left arm was now somehow intertwined with Cissy's as they walked almost ceremoniously behind Jack and Doug. "I already called them for you."

Jack stopped dead in his tracks and turned quickly to Emery. "You did what?"

Emery shrugged her shoulders. "I called them for you."

Jack's expression was not a pleasant one. "Doug. Would you and Cissy mind excusing us for a second?"

Doug looked at Cissy. Cissy looked at Doug and released her grip on Emery's arm. "We'll be inside. Ya'll come on in whenever," Doug said.

Jack and Emery watched as Doug and Cissy disappeared inside the mammoth house. Jack turned and glared at Emery. He was very angry. "Where in the hell do you come off calling my work?"

Emery clenched her jaw. "I've told you before not to use that tone with me. I don't like it."

"I don't care what you like or don't like right now," Jack said staunchly. "You had no business calling Marlowe. None!"

Emery's eyes teared up slightly, but none fell. "I was just trying to help. I figured you had forgotten and they needed to know."

Jack narrowed his eyes. "You figured I'd forgotten? Then why didn't you say something to me about it? Huh? If you thought I had forgotten why didn't you say something? That makes no sense, Emery. None. None at all," he said, shaking his head and looking skyward.

"Look. I'm sorry. Maybe I should have said something. I didn't. I'm sorry. What else do you want me to say?"

"Who did you talk to? What'd you tell them?"

"I guess it was Marlowe or maybe his secretary. I don't know."

Jack turned and looked her squarely in her eyes. "What do you mean Marlowe or his secretary. One's a man. One's a woman. Which was it? Or have you forgotten already?"

Emery clenched her jaw again. "What's that supposed to mean?"

Jack refused to give in. "Who did you talk to, Emery, and what did you say?"

Emery paused and looked up to avoid eye contact. "I guess it was Marlowe."

Jack stepped back and put his interlaced fingers on top of his head. "Oh, geez. I cannot believe this." Jack moved his hands from the top of his head and placed them on his hips, his elbows pointed behind him. "And I suppose you told him I was on the run."

"I told him what happened. That's it."

Jack looked at the sky. "My God!"

"He seemed to understand your predicament, Jack."

"Marlowe doesn't understand anything. When did you talk to him?"

"This morning while you were checking out of the five star hotel we stayed in."

Jack glared, and replied dryly, "Hilarious. Wait a second. How did you call? I cut the..." Jack stopped.

"Phone cord," she finished his sentence. "You cut the cord. Is that what you were about to say?"

"No. I mean it was cut already. When I got to the room I tried to make a call but the cord was cut."

"Uh-huh," Emery said sarcastically. "I wasn't born yesterday. Why didn't you use your cell?"

"Alright look. Fine. I cut the cord. I just didn't want to take any chances."

"I just want you to be truthful, Jack. For this relationship to have any chance you've got to be truthful with me."

"That cuts both ways. Why didn't you tell me you called Marlowe?"

"I forgot. Plain and simple. I slept most of the way up here and didn't even think about it until you just said something to Doug. Is that a crime?"

Jack paused and placed his hands on Emery's shoulders. "Look. It has been a long couple of days. We're both tired. I'm sorry. Okay. But please tell me what you told Marlowe."

"I told him what happened. Everything. About your brother. I told him everything and he seemed to understand. He told me to tell you to take whatever time you needed and that you still had a job when this was over unless..."

Jack furled his brow. "Unless what?"

Emery paused. "Unless you go to jail, Jack. Unless you go to jail."

Jacked loosened his grip from her shoulders. "Yeah." He paused a few seconds. "Does he know where we are? Did you tell him where we were going?"

"I didn't even know where we were going. How could I tell him?"

"Did you tell him what my original plan was?"

"I don't think so. Why?"

Jack thought. "I don't know. Just don't have a good feeling. That's all."

From the corner of his eye, Jack saw Doug inside the house pulling the curtain away from the window. He held up a familiar green bottled Dos Equis beer for Jack to see. Jack smiled at Doug, nodded his head and held up one finger telling Doug he'd be there in a minute. Emery never took her eye from Jack.

"Can we go in now or do you want to keep chastising me out here?" Emery said, with a slight slur in her voice.

Doug had moved away from the window so Jack's eyes skimmed back to Emery. "I'm not going to apologize, Emery. My life. Hell! Our lives are in danger. We have to be careful who we trust. Just do us both a favor and stay away from the phone. Especially your cell. Alright?"

Emery narrowed her eyes. "I don't like your tone Jack, but I understand." She hesitated. "I'm sorry. I really am. But I only did what I thought was right."

Jack stared at her for a moment then smiled. "We're being rude. Let's go inside."

Halfway there the front door opened. Doug paraded out with a Dos Equis beer, steam escaping from the freshly opened top and ice crystals on its side. Doug handed it to Jack. Cissy followed carrying a wicker tray with lemonade, tea and some finger sandwiches perched on top. Neither Jack nor Emery had much to eat in the last twenty-four hours. They both silently hoped this was not dinner.

The muffled voices drifting from down the hallway awoke Emery from a sound sleep. She rubbed her eyes and glanced at the red, oversized digits of the alarm clock sitting on the bedside table. She recognized Jack's and Doug's voices but she couldn't believe Jack would still be up at three in the morning after the grueling pace he had been through the last couple of days. She sat up on the side of the bed and rubbed her eyes again. She stood and reached for her borrowed bathrobe lying neatly across the foot of her bed. Emery tiptoed to her bedroom door that was cracked ever so slightly. She pulled the door six inches or so toward her and poked her ear through the opening to see if she could make out what Jack and Doug were talking about. All she could hear was the same muffled voices that had awakened her.

Emery looked out into the darkened hallway that was lit somewhat by the light oozing from underneath a door on the other side of the square shaped living quarters. She felt like she was staying at a luxurious hotel. When she stepped from her room out into the hallway, a banister formed a perfect square around the entire second floor living area. Down below was the foyer, with its expensive marble floor and priceless antiques adorning it. Across the way was the room with the light on and the mumbling voices wafting out like a distant sputtering motor.

Emery pulled her door but did not shut it completely. She shivered and folded her arms, as a chill ran up her spine for no apparent reason. As she rounded the corner of the banister and started to walk down the oak stairs that formed the center of the house, Emery froze in her tracks when Cissy appeared from nowhere. Cissy carried a pot of coffee and three cups. She lightly rapped on the door of the room where Jack and Doug conferred. Emery stepped back from view and watched as the door was opened. Cissy looked up toward Emery's bedroom before going in and closing the door with the back of her left foot.

Emery slowly peeked over the oak railing to make sure she hadn't been seen. She began making her way down the stairs, stepping as lightly as she could. Although the voices were still muffled, she was able to make out Jack thanking Cissy for the coffee.

Emery reached the bottom of the stairway and grasped the hand carved, mythical oaken figure at the base of the railing and quietly spun herself toward the room. The voices grew slightly stronger with each cautious step she took toward the closed door. But Emery still could not make out the conversation going on from within the room.

She slid her back down the wall as if it were somehow hiding her. She was only a few feet away from the door when she was forced to stop dead in her tracks by the sight of a shadow moving across the light under the door. Her heart raced. She closed her eyes tightly and dug her fingernails as hard as she could into the wall she had now become part of. The doorknob turned a half rotation then snapped back quickly the other way. Emery breathed a quick sigh of relief, realizing whoever was coming out was asked another unintelligible question and would be delayed a few more seconds. Delayed a few more seconds of precious time. Emery extracted her nails from the wall and quietly pulled away. As she reached the bottom stair of the hardwood stairway, the door to the room flung open wide. Holding onto their coffee cups, Jack and Doug stepped outside into the dimly lit foyer. Emery sprung up two steps as quickly as she could, but not before Jack's and Doug's attention was drawn by the movement of her legs catapulting up the stairway.

"Emery!" Jack shouted, as he moved quickly toward the bottom of the stairway. On the fifth step, Emery stopped, shut her eyes and sighed. Busted, she thought to herself. Looking up at her backside, Jack glanced at his watch. "What're you doing up? It's three in the morning."

Emery narrowed her eyes and turned to face Jack. Doug watched and sipped his coffee. "I was about to ask you the same question."

Jack nodded toward Doug. "Doug and I were just talking over old times. That's all."

Emery peered at Doug who smiled, nodded and winked at her. She rolled her eyes. "Why wasn't I invited?"

Jack snickered and took a sip of his coffee. "For one thing it's late, and you need your sleep."

Emery felt patronized. "And you don't?"

"And for another, it's just two old farts telling war stories. No girls allowed." Jack glanced at Doug and smiled.

Emery's ears perked. She jolted her head upright. "So I guess Cissy's just one of the boys?"

Jack shook his head. "What are you talking about?"

"You know exactly what I'm talking about. I saw Cissy go in there with three cups of coffee less than two minutes ago."

"Cissy went to bed three and a half hours ago," Doug said, without looking up from his cup of coffee. "She's like clockwork. As soon as the eleven o'clock news is over, it's lights out for her."

Emery didn't take her eyes off Jack. "I know what I saw and I saw her."

"No you didn't, Emery. You saw Doug bring us two, that's two cups of coffee," Jack said with a little note of sarcasm.

The vein in her neck bulged and her face grew hot. "I know what I saw. Don't tell me what you want me to think."

"What's all the ruckus out here?" Cissy's voice cascaded from somewhere above. "Ya'll are gonna wake the kids," she said, while rubbing her eyes. She emerged from a darkened hallway on the second level and perched herself at the top of the stairway.

Emery watched Cissy as she tied the sash on her robe. She looked back at Jack who gave her one of those I told you so looks.

"It's late. Maybe you were walking in your sleep. Maybe you thought you saw something," Jack said.

"I guess," Emery said, wondering why she was being lied to.

"Go on back to bed. I'll see you in the morning and let you know what our plans are."

Emery stared at Jack for a few seconds then turned and trotted up the stairs. "Night," she said to Cissy as she reached two steps below where Cissy stood.

"Sleep tight," Cissy said as Emery bounded the last two steps and crossed close by her.

"Sorry if we woke you," she said, hoping Cissy would respond.

"Awwwww, that's alright sweetheart. Don't you worry about it. I'll be back to sleep before my head hits the pillow." Cissy glanced quickly at Doug then disappeared back into her bedroom.

Emery smiled. Definitely coffee breath, she thought. "Night," she said as she walked toward her room.

"Night," Cissy said.

"Night, Emery," Doug called out from below.

"Night," she said as she reached her room and closed the door behind her.

Jack looked at Doug who sipped his coffee. Doug and Jack peered up at Cissy who returned their stare, but said nothing. Doug lifted his cup toward Cissy. He and Jack disappeared back into the room and closed the door.

~ 10 ~

"Where are we?" Sarducci asked Guido in Spanish. The rising sun's rays glinted off the windshield and threw several hues of color onto the map of the southeastern United States Guido had spread out on his lap.

Guido moved his finger up and down the several red and blue lined roads on the map, then threw up his arms in frustration. "I don't know. I can't follow these numbers."

Sarducci shook his head, then slowed the car and pulled over onto the shoulder. "Let me see the map."

Guido handed it to Sarducci, then stretched.

Straining his eyes, Sarducci studied the map. He looked closely, but could not seem to find any of the landmarks he was searching for. He looked closely at the top of the map, then frowned at Guido.

"What?" Guido asked.

Sarducci turned the map right side up. "It might help if you didn't have it upside down. We're probably somewhere in Texas by now." Sarducci looked at the road sign perched some fifty feet from where he pulled over. It read Route 411 North. "We're on the right road. But I'm not sure exactly where on 411 we are." Sarducci pushed the crumpled map back into Guido's lap and pulled back onto the road. Several miles down the highway a sign said it was five miles to Loudon. Sarducci smiled at Guido. "We're closer than I thought."

"Cissy, this has got to be the best omelet I've ever tasted," Jack said between bites. "You eat like this every day, Doug?"

Doug peered over the top of the sports section at Jack, who barely looked up. "'Fraid not, Jack. I couldn't keep this girlish figure if I ate like this every day. Only company gets this treatment."

"There's plenty more where that came from Jack. You eat up, ya' hear?" Cissy said, smiling as she fried bacon on one burner and French toast on the other.

"Says here they're looking into more recruiting violations at USC. You'd think they would've learned their lesson the last time."

"Uh-huh," Jack responded, chomping on a piece of bacon.

"Well, she lives!" Cissy made a stab at sarcasm as Emery entered the breakfast room and sat down at the table where a place had been set for her.

Emery piddled with her hair and attempted to comb the snarls out with her finger with little success. "That bed was sooooo comfortable. I could've slept three more hours, but the smell of that bacon was too inviting."

"Well you just dig right on in," Cissy said in her polite southern accent.

"Good morning to you too, Jack," Emery said, with a tone of contempt.

Jack looked up. "Sorry. My mouth was full."

"Morning, Emery," Doug said, still reading his sports page.

"Morning, Doug."

"Sleep well?" Doug asked.

"Like a baby."

"You a football fan, Emery?" Doug inquired.

Emery swallowed a gulp of freshly squeezed orange juice. "Not really."

"Looks like USC screwed up again. Could get the death penalty this time," Doug said, not even paying attention to Emery's answer.

"Didn't you hear her, sweetie? Emery said she wasn't a football fan," Cissy said, popping him on the side of his neck with her dish towel.

Emery watched Cissy playfully flirt with her husband. "Oh, I don't mind. What's the death penalty?" Emery asked, then helped herself to some bacon and French toast on the silver platter in front of her.

"It's when your team basically gets abolished," Cissy answered. "You can't play. You don't have a team. In other words, in the football world you are dead."

"Sounds kind of harsh," Emery responded.

Doug looked over his paper at Emery. "And ninety-nine times out of a hundred the team that gets punished is innocent. They did nothing wrong. It's always some other past player or coach that broke the rules. But the new guys get screwed every time. It'd be like me stealing someone's billion dollar shipment of cocaine, but Jack getting blamed for it. I know that's a stretch, but you get the picture."

"It's just football," Emery said.

Doug stared at her over the top of his paper as Cissy plopped three more pieces of bacon on his plate. "It's just football? Just football?" Football was a religion to Doug.

"Doug," Cissy said firmly. "Don't get started. I'm warning you. Don't get started."

Emery looked at Cissy then at Doug. She quickly realized he wasn't joking. She gulped down two bites of French toast, then wiped the powdered sugar from her lips with the embroidered cloth napkin that had been rolled up neatly in front of her plate. She changed the subject quickly. "Jack. I need to talk to you."

"What is it?"

"I mean in private."

Cissy looked at Emery. Emery looked back, afraid she might have offended her.

Cissy walked over to Doug, whose head was still buried deep into the fourth page of the sports section. "Doug. The kids need some privacy."

"Huh?" Doug said half listening and half reading another article. "Oh, yeah. No problem. Lemme' just finish this one column."

"That's alright. We'll go outside. It's nice out," Jack said, picking up his orange juice and the two pieces of French toast still left on his plate.

Emery stood and followed, but took nothing from the table.

Jack opened the door leading from the kitchen into the backyard which was exquisitely manicured. The grass looked like a putting green. The yard was adorned with Weeping Willows and several islands of colorful flowers and tropical plants. There was even a large man-made orange and white waterfall that cascaded gracefully over smooth mountain rocks into a clear pond filled with koi.

"OK, what?" Jack asked while stuffing an oversized bite of toast covered with grape jelly into his mouth.

Emery grabbed his wrist and pulled him further into the immense backyard. "Let's walk." Emery didn't want Doug or Cissy to hear what she had to say. She led Jack closer to the pond so anything she might say would be drowned out by the sound of the waterfall.

"What is it?" Jack asked, as they reached the waterfall. "What's so important you couldn't say it in front of my friends?"

"I don't like it here, Jack. I want to leave."

Jack stared at Emery in disbelief. He finished chewing his last piece of toast and swallowed it. "Whattaya' mean you don't like it? We've only been here one night. Besides. We're not gonna' be here much longer anyway." Jack paused and wiped the crumbs from his mouth with the back of his hand. "Did Doug or Cissy say something that bothered you?"

"No."

"Then what's wrong?"

"I think we should go back to Atlanta. I think you should go back. You...we can't run forever. If you're innocent you've got nothing to fear. It'll all work out."

Jack glared at Emery. "If.....I'm innocent. If? What's that supposed to mean? I thought you believed me. I thought you stood behind me. I thought that's why you came with me."

"I do," Emery said, making a half-hearted attempt at reconciliation.

"Doesn't sound like it. And as far as nothing to fear, it's not the justice system I fear. Did you forget about Guido and Sarducci? If I go back to Atlanta, I might as well check back into the Fulton County Jail, because I'm dead otherwise. You should know that."

Emery noticed Jack glance away for a second toward the house. She looked back over her shoulder and saw Doug standing in the window watching them. She turned back to Jack. "That's another thing. I don't like him. He gives me the creeps. I don't trust him."

"You haven't given them a chance."

"Why should I trust anybody after last night?"

Jack looked toward the sky and pressed his intertwined fingers on top of his head. "Here we go. So that's it. You're mad about last night. Look, I'm sorry if you were offended, but it was only a couple of old farts talking over old times. That's all."

"That's not all, Jack. You lied to me last night. Cissy was in that room."

Jack smiled. "You're jealous."

"Don't be ridiculous." Emery did not appreciate his attempt to minimize her concern. "I just don't like being lied to."

"Emery. Cissy was not in there. It was just Doug and me. That's it."

"I saw her, Jack. I saw her take three cups of coffee into that room and close the door. And then I heard you or Doug thank her for the coffee."

Jack snickered. "Emery. You saw her yourself on the second floor a couple minutes later. If she was in that room with us, how did she get to the second floor without being seen? I'm telling you it was three o'clock in the morning and you were tired. You were half asleep and were seeing things. She wasn't there, Emery. I'm telling you, it was me and Doug."

Emery glared at him. "I know what I saw, Jack. You're lying and I don't know why. If you think I'm jealous, you're wrong. I really don't care who was in that room. It's just the fact that you're all trying to make me believe something wasn't there when I know it was, and I don't know why you're doing it. That's why I don't trust either one of them. I really think we should go. If not back to Atlanta, at least somewhere else."

Jack sighed. "If you want to go back I'll put you on the next greyhound out of here. But I'm not going back. As long as I'm out I can find a way to prove my innocence and stay alive. If I go back, I'm dead. Then I guess it won't matter if I'm innocent or not, will it?"

Emery stared at him and searched for the right words to say. She looked back over her shoulder. Doug was no longer staring out the window. She peered back at Jack. "I can't go back without you."

Jack smiled and they embraced. Jack's face grimaced slightly. "There's something else I need to tell you."

"What is it?" she said, without releasing her grip around his waist.

"I don't think you're gonna like this."

Emery loosened her arms from Jack's waist, took two steps back and folded her arms across her chest. "What?"

Jack gripped her shoulders with his hands. "Uhhhh. Doug's going with us."

Emery glared at Jack, narrowed her eyes and pursed her lips. Like in a cartoon, he could almost envision the steam about to be released from her ears.

"Just listen, Emery. Just for a minute."

She pulled away from his death grip. "No! That's it. I can't take it. It's bad enough we're still gonna be on the run, but I can't take someone," she motioned with her head toward the house. "Him. I can't take him going with us."

"It won't be for long. I promise. But Doug knows a lot of important people. He can help me."

"Why does he have to go with us? Why can't he just help you from here?"

"In case you haven't noticed, our money is gonna run out soon. Doug has money and resources. He also has the pull to contact influential people that could get me out of this jam." Jack paused and stepped closer to Emery and grasped her shoulders again. "I know how you feel. But I swear it won't be for long. As soon as Doug does what he can, we can go back to Atlanta and back to a normal life. You gotta believe me, Emery."

She stared into his eyes and sighed. Jack knew something else bothered her. She said nothing, but her eyes said differently.

"You know we're gonna get out of this. We are. I know you may not believe me, but I believe the truth always prevails." Jack paused. "What is it? What else is wrong?"

Emery looked at him without blinking. "I don't know. It's just that not one time since we left Atlanta have you mentioned your brother. Are you not gonna go to Seattle?"

Jack loosened his grip from her shoulders and dropped his head. "I can't believe you'd say that to me. I can't believe you would even insinuate I don't care." Jack paused and peered into her eyes. "I love my brother. We were very close and I would've done anything for him. I can't believe you would think any different."

Emery was a little embarrassed, but still confused. "I'm sorry. I didn't mean to insinuate you didn't care. It's just that you haven't said anything about it. It's almost like it didn't happen."

"Did you stop and think that maybe I don't want to talk about it?"

Emery was silent.

"Look. I'm sorry if you think I don't care, but I do. There's nothing more I'd rather do than hop a jet and head to Seattle. But you know as well as I do that they'll be there just waiting on me. As soon as I step off that jet, I'm a dead man. You know they gotta figure I'll show up there. Hell! He's my brother. I should be there. I feel like a turd for not going, but I got no choice. Don't you understand that?"

"Are you gonna at least call your folks? Your sister? Matt's family?"

Jack looked at Emery and shook his head. "I called them last night. Every one of them. I spoke to everyone. I told them everything that had happened and how I wanted to be there. My father told me to stay away. He said he didn't want two dead sons."

Emery sighed and shrugged her shoulders. "I'm sorry. I didn't know. I wasn't thinking."

Jack wrapped his palm around the back of Emery's neck and pulled her slowly to his chest. They embraced for a long time, but said nothing more.

Emery packed the last of her belongings into her small suitcase. Jack and Doug did the same in their respective rooms. Cissy stirred in the kitchen packing some food for the road. The kids played outside on the numerous pieces of playground equipment in the backyard.

Emery zipped up her bag and checked the dresser and floors for the third time, just in case she forgot or dropped something. She swung the bag's strap across her shoulder and walked out into the hallway. She could hear Cissy in the kitchen talking on the phone. Jack and Doug were both behind closed doors. Only this time they were alone. Emery walked slowly down the same stairway where she so angrily stood the night before. She reached the bottom and, like the previous night, pivoted herself around by grabbing onto the wooden sculpture at the bottom of the stairway. As she passed the room where the previous night's incident occurred, she couldn't help but notice the door was slightly cracked. She approached it and thought about going in. She looked upstairs where Jack and Doug were still unseen. Cissy yapped on the phone while bagging up sandwiches. Emery pushed the door lightly and it creaked. She stopped and looked around, but no one was there to notice. She grabbed onto the doorknob and pushed hard. This time there was no audible creak. She stepped inside the room quickly and shut the door. She dropped her bag on the floor and looked around at the wood paneled room.

It was a lovely room, but nothing seemed out of the ordinary. Obviously belonging to Doug, the room was filled with photos of him with various people. There were pictures of Doug standing next to a big swordfish from a deep sea fishing trip he took off the coast of Florida in 1999. There were trophies on a mantle from his high school glory days when he was an all-state basketball star. His most prized possession was a giant picture of him and Bruce Pearl, Tennessee's flamboyant basketball coach who was fired for NCAA rules violations. Nonetheless, Coach Pearl was still probably the most popular man in Tennessee for the leaps and bounds he'd taken the basketball program. Emery looked for anything that might peek her interest about why the three were in this room at three in the morning. But there was nothing that seemed odd or out of place.

She moved toward another vanity picture of Doug toward the end of the wall. It looked like an old college picture. Emery nudged up against the wall and looked closely at the picture. She wondered if Jack was in the picture. She ran her fingers across the numerous faces and, finally coming across Jack's, she touched it with her fingertip. When she did, she noticed the wall seemed to give slightly. She looked closer at the wall and noticed what seemed to be grooves running down to the floor. She pressed a little harder and it gave a little more. She pushed harder and the false door opened. Emery stepped back and gazed into the darkness of whatever was inside. She took a deep breath and pulled some bravery from deep within. She took one step into the darkness and stayed until her eyes could focus a little better. She opened the door a bit wider to let some sunshine into the darkened room. With the light, her suspicions were confirmed. A stairway led to the second floor and another doorway. Emery followed it. She felt like a rat in a maze. The doorway led to a path built inside the walls which seemed to wrap around the shape of the squared hallway. Light came from somewhere and illuminated the secret hidden hallway. As she came to another door, she opened it softly but shut it quickly when she saw Doug in the mirror packing his suitcase. She turned and pressed her back against the door. She breathed deeply as her heart pounded rapidly and loudly inside her chest. She could feel its rhythm pulsating in her throat.

Emery placed her palm on her forehead and then covered her mouth so no sounds would spew forth from it should a sudden noise erupt and frighten her. She could hear Doug inside the room opening and closing drawers. Much like an inquisitive feline, Emery's curiosity got the best of her. She turned slowly back toward the door and moved the hand covering her forehead toward the doorknob. She twisted it slowly and cracked the door open slightly. It creaked. But not before she saw Doug tossing two pistols inside his suitcase.

Doug turned quickly toward the door and stared it down. He bolted as fast as he could toward the door, grabbed it and pushed it open. It banged hard against the wall inside. He peered down the long, dark, hidden hallway and caught a flash of someone dashing around the first corner. He broke away and darted down the shadowy hallway in pursuit of the intruder. As Doug rounded the first corner, he could only make out one leg galloping around the second turn of the hidden passageway. He stepped up his chase one or two notches.

Emery's heart beat so hard her temples ached. She was sick to her stomach and wanted to stop and wretch on the spot. She could hear the heavy footsteps of the big man behind slowly gaining on her. She knew it was inevitable she would be caught. She didn't know what Doug would do. She thought about just stopping and admitting she was curious. But she knew he would know she had discovered that they had lied the night before, and she could now explain how Cissy got from the room downstairs to their bedroom without being seen.

Doug turned the final corner and could hear the sound of footsteps banging quickly down each step of the bare wooden stairway leading to the room downstairs. He turned his pursuit up a final notch and lunged for the door at the top of the stairway. He broke it open with one powerful surge from his oversized shoulder. His breathing was rapid and sweat broke out on his forehead, but he had not been fast enough to catch a glimpse of the spy scrambling through the doorway and into the room at the bottom of the stairway. Doug bounded down the steps three at a time and heard the door to the room slam as he leapt over the last five steps in one thrust and landed at the foot of the staircase. He popped the door open with the butt of his hand, but he knew it was for naught. He wiped the sweat from his brow with his sleeve and blew out a long breath. He rested for less than a minute, his back resting against the frame of the door. His outstretched fingertips clutched the top of the doorframe. He wiped the sweat one more time from his head and disappeared back into the dusky, secret hallway.

Cissy finished bagging up some fried chicken as Emery, breathing hard and sweating, rushed into the kitchen. Cissy still yapped on the phone, but looked at Emery and produced a wiggly, three fingered wave. Cissy did a double take when she saw Emery's demeanor. Emery sat down and placed her small suitcase by the chair.

"Darlin', I've got to go," Cissy told the person on the line. "We have company. One of Doug's college buddies and his girlfriend dropped in." Cissy looked at Emery and grinned. Emery forced a grin in return.

"Okay. Bye-bye now," Cissy said and hung up the phone. She placed her hands on her hips and bent down like a mother lecturing her toddler. "Honey, what on earth happened to you?"

Emery looked down and shook her head. "Whattaya' mean?" Emery knew exactly what Cissy meant.

Cissy stood up straight. "Look at you sweetie. You're all sweaty. You're out of breath. Where in the world have you been, missy?"

Emery despised Cissy's tone as much as her dripping with honey southern drawl. She looked up and stared Cissy square in the eye. "It's a medical condition, Cissy. A hereditary thing. It usually happens in the morning. I sweat uncontrollably. I can't catch my breath. My heart beats twice as fast as it should. If I don't sit down and rest immediately the doctors say it could be fatal." Emery paused to enjoy Cissy's expression of concern and obvious embarrassment for asking the question in the first place. "I'm really sorry. It's very embarrassing for me. I'm sorry you had to see it."

"Oh no, honey!" Cissy exclaimed with one hand on her hip and the other waving in a downward motion toward Emery. "Don't you feel bad. My goodness. I'm the twit that should be embarrassed. I was insensitive for even asking. I am so sorry."

"Nonsense," Emery said, smiling more on the inside than out. "You didn't know."

The saloon styled double doors to the kitchen swung open. Jack and Doug strolled into the kitchen carrying their bags.

"Hey, Emery," Doug said, glaring at her. "Little exhausted are we?"

"Shhhhhh!" Cissy shushed Doug with a deadpanned expression.

"Everything about ready?" Doug asked Cissy, but still staring at Emery.

"Uh-huh. Just a few more minutes," Cissy said, stepping over to where Jack stood still holding his suitcase. "Why didn't you tell us she had a disease?" Cissy whispered in Jack's ear as she breezed by him without slowing down. Cissy ambled on to the pantry and pulled out a few snacks.

Jack said nothing, but his eyes followed Cissy. He had no idea what she was talking about.

"Hope you don't mind the change of plans," Doug said, never taking his eyes from Emery.

"Whatever Jack says," Emery said, wiping the sweat from her forehead and glaring back at Doug.

"We've talked about it already," Doug replied, taking the seat next to Emery. He looked at the beads of sweat on her forehead and cocked his head just slightly. "Is everything okay?" he whispered to her.

"I'm fine," she said, smiling nervously.

"You don't look so good," Jack said a bit louder.

Cissy placed a few more items on the cabinet and kept a concerned eye on Emery.

Doug smiled slightly. "Yeah. She's got kind of a....run down...look." He grinned at his obvious pun.

Cissy spun around quickly with her hands on her hips. "That's enough, Doug! That's enough! She can't help it. Alright?"

Jack turned and looked at Cissy, who by now was standing behind Emery and grasping her shoulders. "Can't help what?"

"Her condition," Cissy said, matter of factly.

Jack's expression was blank. "Condition. What condition?"

"Maybe she's pregnant," Doug said, with all the sympathy of a rock.

Jack swerved quickly and eyed Emery.

"I'm not pregnant and I resent the tone," she growled, leering at Doug.

"She's not pregnant, Doug. You have absolutely no tact," Cissy said. "It's a morning sickness."

"So she is pregnant," Doug said snickering.

Jack's head bobbed back and forth between the conversation like he was at a tennis match. "How could you be pregnant?"

"I'm not pregnant."

"Why don't you tell us what's really wrong, Emery. Tell everybody why you're so tired," Doug said.

Cissy frowned at Doug. "Doug! What is wrong with you? Can't you see she's embarrassed? Now drop it! I mean it!"

"Look everybody," Emery said, standing up. "I'm fine. I'm just a little hot and tired. That's all. Can we just go?"

Cissy nodded and batted her eyes at Doug.

"I'm ready. You ready, Jack?" Doug stood up.

Confused, Jack looked at everybody towering above him. "I reckon."

Cissy handed Jack and Doug two medium sized brown grocery bags with sandwiches, chips and cookies. "There's more in the back of Doug's SUV. This should last ya'll a couple of days. After it runs out, Doug should have plenty of cash to keep you going."

Jack stood and smiled at Cissy. "Cissy. I don't know how to thank you for everything you've done."

"You're like a brother to Doug. You'd have done the same thing for him if he was in trouble. Now ya'll need to go on and get out of here. I'll handle everything on this end."

Jack smiled and hugged her. "Thanks Cissy."

Jack and Emery walked out the door, stopped and looked back at Doug.

"You guys go on," Doug said. "I'll be there in a minute or so."

Jack and Emery headed for the SUV. "You sure you're up to going?"

"I'm fine, Jack. Trust me. I'm fine," Emery declared.

"I shouldn't be gone for more than a week or so," Doug said, as he and Cissy hugged each other.

"Call me."

"I will if I can."

Cheeks touching, Doug and Cissy squeezed each other one last time. Cissy turned and planted a light kiss on his temple. "Be careful," she whispered in his ear.

Doug leaned back slightly to where he could see Cissy's face and smiled. "Careful's not in my vocabulary, sweetheart. You know that."

Cissy smiled back and held his face with her palms. "That's what scares me."

Cissy's arm rocked back and forth like a homecoming queen in a parade as she and the kids waved to the departing trio. As the SUV, whose tags had been changed out by Doug, approached the end of the lengthy driveway, Doug rolled down the window, poked his head out the window and smiled at the sight of his family still waving goodbye. It had always been a tradition in Cissy's family to wave to departing guests or family until they were totally out of sight.

Doug pulled himself halfway through the door and sat in the open window. He held on tightly to the inside and waved to his family he could barely see through the trees. Cissy waved as the kids ran toward the road waving and yelling goodbye.

Emery sighed and smiled at the sight of the two children so far away, chasing after the truck and their father who they loved so dearly. "How can you bear to leave them?" she asked Doug, who climbed back inside the cab and buckled his seat belt.

Doug glanced at Cissy and frowned before snickering. "You've never had kids have you?"

"No."

"Trust me. I need the peace and quiet for a change."

Emery frowned and shook her head in disbelief. She wasn't especially fond of Doug by any stretch of the imagination, but she at least thought he would have a sensitive side when it came to his kids. Emery looked at Jack for his response, but he had none. He had turned on the radio and was trying to find a news station. Jack was obviously paying no attention to Doug, Emery, the kids or anyone else.

The house was a mere dot on the landscape now as Jack turned off the main road and headed toward I-40 West.

Agent Fuentes stood behind the lectern pleading his case to the Judge as SAC McMann sat close by, arms folded, and hanging on every word.

"Your honor," Fuentes begged. "This source has provided us with vast amounts of reliable information in the past. I have no reason to doubt the validity of the information provided now."

"I see," the Judge said, peering at Fuentes over the top of his wire framed glasses that slipped halfway down his nose. "When was the last time this source of yours saw Mr. Armstrong?"

"This morning, your honor. I received a telephone call this morning. The information we received was that not only had Mr. Armstrong crossed over state lines in violation of his bond and a court order, but he was in Tennessee and planning on leaving sometime today."

The Judge tilted his head. "Leaving? Well, is he coming back to Atlanta? I mean technically Mr. Armstrong may be in violation of his bond since he did not inform the court of his intention to leave Georgia. However, I am not inclined to issue a bench warrant for Mr. Armstrong's arrest if his immediate plans are to return to Atlanta."

Fuentes grabbed both sides of the lectern with his hands and turned to look at McMann.

"Throw me a bone, Agent Fuentes. Do you have any information that Armstrong does not intend to return to Atlanta in the immediate future?"

Fuentes' source did not know what Jack's plans were, but McMann wanted Jack back and soon. Other interests were key. "Your honor. Our information is that Mr. Armstrong has no intention of returning here. At least not in the immediate future. It appears his plans are to evade prosecution. He's proven that by fleeing the state in violation of his bond not more than a day after he was ordered to stay in Georgia."

The Judge propped his elbows on the bench, entwining all ten fingers together and resting them underneath his chin. One ink pen protruded from the middle of his fingers. "Very well, Agent Fuentes. I'm going to issue a bench warrant for Mr. Armstrong. I'm also going to issue an Unlawful Flight to Avoid Prosecution charge." He paused. "I've always considered myself a fair judge. But I will not allow a person to flee from his responsibility. I trust the FBI will issue an alert to its field offices regarding the UFAP."

"Yes, sir."

"Good. In addition, any accomplices should likewise be considered for aiding and abetting." The Judge rose and walked down from his lofty perch and into his chambers. The door banged hard behind him.

McMann stood and approached Fuentes, who was turning away from the lectern. "What's wrong, Eric? If I didn't know any better I'd swear you thought you did the wrong thing. Hell! You know he's not coming back here."

Fuentes frowned. "I know that. But we need Armstrong out even if he's not here. The only way we're going to know what's going on is to have Armstrong a free man. If he's caught and put in jail we may lose everything."

"I disagree, Eric. We've had this discussion before. We've gotta have Armstrong under our nose. If we can't track him he does us no good."

"We've got a source doing that already," Fuentes said, with a bit of authority in his voice. "I'm telling you. If Armstrong is in jail he does us absolutely no good. If he's in Atlanta he'll be dead within twenty-four hours. He's better to us if he's out there somewhere on the run."

McMann smiled sarcastically. "That's why I'm the boss, Eric. To make these difficult, executive decisions."

"Yeah? Well, let's hope your executive greed doesn't screw this whole thing up." Fuentes turned and stormed away. He stuck out his arms and plowed his open palms into the large wooden doors at the back of the courtroom.

McMann smiled and shook his head at Fuentes. He believed he was older and wiser and had been around a long time. He was certain what he did was the right move.

Sarducci pounded hard on the door. Guido stood watch a few feet away and down the steps of Doug and Cissy's front porch. Sarducci banged again five times with his fist and pushed the doorbell an equal amount of times. The door jerked open suddenly as he reached for the gold plated doorknob. Cissy peered up at Sarducci who towered high above her. She wanted to tell the dark complected stranger to hold his horses but her throat refused to allow any air to flow.

"Sorry to bother you, ma'am," Sarducci said, with a heavy accent. "But my friend and I are looking for Jack Armstrong." Sarducci motioned toward Guido who nodded at Cissy. "We understand he is here."

Cissy was small but was not intimidated. She crossed her arms across her chest. "And you are?"

Sarducci looked at Guido and back at Cissy. "Friends."

"U-huh. And the Pope's Jewish," Cissy lashed back. "Jack's not here."

"Where is he?"

Cissy laughed out loud. "Do you really think I'd tell you even if I knew?"

Before Sarducci could respond, Cissy's daughter came dashing through the foyer yelling something about her brother picking on her. He couldn't see her, but Sarducci could hear the tender voice. Cissy glanced away, but her eyes shot quickly back to Sarducci's.

Sarducci smiled. "Your daughter is lovely. How old is she?"

Cissy, nervous now, swallowed hard. "She's seven."

"Ahhhhhhh," Sarducci shot back, realizing now he had the upper hand. "Seven is such an impressionable age. Maybe we should talk to your husband."

Cissy's nervousness was apparent now. Beads of sweat formed on her brow. "He's not here just yet."

"Perhaps he is with our friend Mr. Armstrong?"

"No!" Cissy responded sharply.

"So do you know where Mr. Armstrong is?"

Cissy stared at Sarducci. Her heart pounded hard and fast.

"Ma'am. My friend and I mean you nor your family any harm. But we have a job to do and it is essential we find Mr. Armstrong. Now, perhaps you can answer my question. Or perhaps your daughter would like to take a ride with us. It is your choice."

~ 11 ~

Only half of the orange sun was visible on the eastern horizon as Jack pulled into the drive-through of McDonalds to get a cup of coffee. Emery was asleep and leaning on Jack's arm. Doug was slouched against the passenger door surprisingly not waking Emery with his incessant snoring. Three days of non-stop driving on back roads of the Southeastern United States had taken its toll on all three. Jack and Doug's five o'clock shadows had become the unsightly beginnings of beards. Emery's unwashed hair had lost its shimmer.

"That'll be a dollar thirty-nine, sir," the cashier said, while staring more than normal inside the truck's cab.

Jack dug into his pocket and pulled out a dollar. "Hold on a second." He pulled the ash tray open to look for spare change.

The cashier took the money from Jack and handed him his coffee.

Jack took the coffee cup and placed it in the cup holder. "Hey, this may sound like a really stupid question, but where are we?"

"Sir?" The cashier did find it a strange question and the scene inside Jack's cab even stranger.

Jack stared at the cashier, who kept looking back and forth at Jack and his supervisor, who he hoped would eventually look his way. "I asked where we were. Something about that you don't understand?"

"Uhhh. No, sir. Sorry. My mind was somewhere else."

By now Doug and Emery began to stir.

"So where are we?"

"Macon, sir. You're in Macon."

"Macon? Macon, Georgia?" Jack had been driving so long and was so tired he hadn't really paid attention to state lines.

"No, sir. Macon, Mississippi. Actually, you're just outside it."

Doug sat up and rubbed his eyes. He looked out of the front windshield to see where they were. Doug jerked quickly back into his seat. "Jack! What the hell are you doing?"

"Good morning to you, too."

"Get the hell outta here, Jack. Now!"

"What's wrong? I was just getting ready to ask this fella where the nearest motel was. We really need to find a bed to sleep in. We really do, Doug."

Doug tried to talk as calmly and methodically as he could. "Jack. We need to go right now. I'll explain later."

The cashier heard their conversation and any suspicions he had were confirmed. "I'll be right back." He shut his window and darted toward his manager.

"Go, Jack! Get the hell outta here! Now!" Doug shouted.

Emery jerked alert.

Jack floored the accelerator. The tires screeched and sent smoke hurling into the air as he maneuvered the SUV from the parking lot and back on to Highway 14.

"Are you crazy, Jack? Are you friggin' nuts? Have you gone totally whacko?" Doug yelled as they barreled down the two lane highway.

Jack glared at Doug. "What'd I do? All I wanted was a cup of coffee to help me stay awake. Heaven forbid you help out driving a little."

Doug stared back at Jack but let the comments pass. "There's a dirt road up here on the right. Turn on it."

Jack saw the road Doug was referring to and followed his direction.

"Drive as far back as you can. We're surrounded by trees so it should be safe. At least for a while."

Jack drove about a mile into the thick woods dotted with pine trees. He pulled off into what looked like a makeshift camping site and cut the engine. "Now, do you mind telling me what the hell that was all about?"

Emery rubbed her eyes and scratched her head which was beginning to itch from days without washing.

"Look, Jack," Doug let go a long breath and explained. "You've been charged in one of the largest drug heists in the history of the United States. This isn't a story of local interest. It has national. Hell, it has international implications. By now your name and mug has been on every news broadcast, newspaper and talk show in America. That kid back there at McDonalds. Unless he's a hermit, he has seen your picture somewhere whether it's TV or newspaper. Right now you are a fugitive and Emery and I are accomplices. There ain't a cop in this country that wouldn't like to take the credit for gettin' the collar on you. You can't be driving into restaurants and such. If we need food or a place to stay, Emery or I will have to arrange it. Hopefully right now, they don't know we're with you."

Jack opened his door and climbed out. He walked back and forth from the front of the SUV to the back, draped his arms across the hood and rested his forehead on it. Emery slid across the driver's seat and stepped outside. She nudged up next to Jack. "You alright?"

"I'm fine," Jack answered, without looking up.

"We should be safe here," said Doug, now out of the SUV and sitting on the hood. "We'll stay here till nightfall then go find us an out of the way motel somewhere down the road."

"I'm tired of running, Doug," Jack said, still looking down at the ground. "I'm thinking of going back. Just turning myself in."

Doug looked back and smiled sarcastically. He jumped down from the hood and walked back and stood next to Jack. Doug leaned his elbows on the side the same way Jack had his. "I thought the whole reason for this entire escapade was to prove your innocence, Jack."

"Maybe I should do it in the courtroom."

"Maybe not. From what I've seen and heard, the evidence is stacked. And not on your side."

Jack lifted his head and turned his back against the SUV. "I've been running for days now. I don't even know how many. I've lost count. I don't like running. You're right. I came out here to prove my innocence. But all I've done is run. Maybe going back to Atlanta is the right thing to do."

"And who do you think's gonna be waiting on you there? You'll be dead before you have a chance to give yourself up to the Feds."

"Why don't you let him make that decision?" Emery said sharply.

Doug looked at Emery and snickered. "You're just like him. You're tired. You wanna go home. You're both a couple of wimps.

You don't think the Columbians are after you too? You're both as good as dead if you go back. But hey! Don't let me stop you. Go on and go back. I just wish you hadn't involved me. I go out on a limb, put my ass out there to help you, and now you talk about giving up and leaving me hanging out here all by myself."

"I'll explain what happened, Doug. I'll tell them what happened."

"Oh, and I'm sure they'll believe every word of it. I'm sure the Feds will forgive and forget that I aided and abetted you. Do those words ring a bell, Jack? Huh? Aid and abet. It's a federal offense and you can bet me and Emery here will have to answer to it if you go back."

Jack looked toward the sky but did not respond.

"On the other hand, if we can prove your innocence by finishing what we started, it's a pretty safe bet that all charges, current and pending, will be dropped."

"Don't listen to him, Jack. You have to do what you think is right."

Doug leaned over and whispered into Jack's ear. "That's right. You do what you think is right. If you think it's right to go back to Atlanta and have the Columbians slice Emery's throat from ear to ear and to cut you into about three hundred pieces dropped into the middle of the Gulf of Mexico, then go ahead. And if you think it's right for me to go to prison for ten years for trying to help a friend, that's just great." Doug pulled away and walked toward the woods.

Emery stared at Jack, who watched Doug lean against a pine tree. They could hear a single siren in the distance as it obviously had long passed the dirt road they had turned on. "Don't listen to him. You gotta do what you think is right."

Jack snapped his head quickly to Emery. His eyes bulged from their sockets. "I'm tired of hearing what's right and what's not. I'm tired of the FBI. I didn't do anything, but here I am out in the middle of nowhere running from both sides of the law. I'm tired and I just want to get it over with."

"Go back. You don't have to prove your innocence. Fuentes and the U.S. Attorney have to prove your guilt."

Jack looked away and stared at Doug who was crouched, picking up and cracking small twigs with his fingers. "He's right, you know."

"About what?"

"My guilt or innocence doesn't matter. If I go back to Atlanta I'm a dead man. You and Doug go to jail. We all lose."

"You can't prove your innocence out here, Jack." Emery folded her arms and looked around at the woods and the tall pine trees that surrounded them. "Look at us. We're out in the middle of nowhere in the middle of a swamp. Looks like you're making tremendous headway on proving your innocence."

"What's that supposed to mean?"

"Just what it sounds like. You want to prove your innocence, so what the heck are we doing out here? Where is your friend leading us?"

Jack looked cross ways at Emery. "There you go again."

"Jack. For God's sake. Look where we are. We've been traveling for days and now we're in the middle of Redneckville, USA. How in the world are you going to prove your innocence out here?" From the corner of her eye she could see Doug walking toward the truck. "I just think going back gives you the best chance."

Doug jumped up and sat down on the hood of the truck. "We've got to make a decision Jack. You gotta decide what you want to do. Are you gonna stick it out or are you gonna whimper on back to Atlanta and cause all three of us problems?"

Jack glared at Doug. "I don't need your sarcasm. I'm sorry I dragged you into this mess."

Doug sighed and shook his head. "Sorry I wasted my time."

Emery smiled. She was relieved. She wanted to go back.

Jack folded his arms across his chest and turned to Emery. "I'm staying, Emery. I've gone this far. I can't turn back now."

Emery narrowed her eyes and glared at Jack. "But you just said..."

"Doug's right," Jack interrupted her. "By running I've made myself look guilty. Even if I go back, Fuentes and the Feds will make it look like I ran because I was guilty. And that's if Guido and Sarducci don't get to me first."

"You're doing the right thing," Doug said. "And we'll do whatever it takes to clear you of this mess."

Jack touched Emery on the back. She jerked away.

"I'm sorry. I just can't go back now. I'll send you back if you want."

"No!" she said quickly and without moving a muscle.

Doug smiled. "Good move, Emery. The Columbians aren't just after Jack, you know. As far as they're concerned, you're just as guilty as he is."

Emery turned and frowned at Doug. "I really don't care to hear anything you have to say."

Doug pulled back and gave a sarcastic smile. "Oooooh. A little sensitive are we?" he said quietly below his breath, but audible to both. "Look, Emery. I got nothing personal against you, but I think you're just a little out of touch with reality. I know you don't like being out here. Hell! Neither do I. But Jack and I have been friends a lot longer than you care to know. If I can help him prove his innocence, then that's what I plan to do. Whatever it takes. You gotta know what would happen if he goes back to Atlanta. If you care about him, you'll let him do it his way."

Emery glared at Doug. "How dare you insinuate I don't care. I do care. More than you obviously, or I wouldn't have him out here in the middle of Podunk, Mississippi, knee deep in copperheads. Furthermore, if your priorities were straight, you'd be at home with those two kids and that syrupy wife with that sappy southern accent and not out here with a fugitive."

Jack looked at Emery and narrowed his eyes. "Is that how you look at me? As a fugitive?"

She calmed somewhat. "No. It just came out. Sorry. It's just that I've got concerns for a man that will leave his family, for God knows how long, and not even call them. We've been out here three days and you've yet to call your family. Something is wrong with that picture."

Jack turned to Doug. "You haven't call Cissy?"

Doug rested his head on the side of the SUV. "It's too risky. You know that as well as I do. The last thing we need to do is make or answer phone calls where the Feds or the Columbians can trace where our cell uses a signal." Doug turned to Emery. "Don't you ever talk about my wife or family again. They're none of your concern. You got it?"

Emery stared at Doug. She refused to be intimidated. She looked away and into the distant woods.

Jack hoped everything was settled. "We're gonna stick it out. I'm gonna do what I have to do to prove they're wrong. No matter how long it takes."

Doug glared at Emery. She glared right back.

"Take your time, Jack," Doug said. "We gotta hide out a while and let things die down. In a couple of hours these small town hick deputies will assume the kid at McDonalds just thought he saw you and pass it off as a prank. When it gets dark we'll go down the road a bit and find a motel and sleep in a real bed."

Jack smiled. "Sounds good." Jack went twenty or thirty feet into the woods, to where he could not be seen, to pee.

Doug stared at Emery and smiled.

Emery refused to smile back. She did not like Doug. She was closer to despising him.

"Who are you?" Doug asked her.

Emery turned and gave her own sly little smile. "Don't you wish you knew?"

Doug snickered and grinned.

"What makes you think I'm anyone but who I am?"

"Cause not everybody would do what you're doing. And not everybody would go snooping around inside someone else's walls."

"Not everybody has secret inside walls, and if you, Cissy and Jack hadn't lied in the first place, I would've had no reason to go snooping."

"Touché," Doug relented.

Emery paused and turned to face Doug squarely. "So why did you lie?"

Doug squared himself to Emery. "You shouldn't ask questions you don't want to know the answers to." Doug looked away then back at Emery. "You'll know soon enough."

The crunching of the leaves signaled Jack's return. "Have you guys kissed and made up yet?"

Emery rolled her eyes and walked away. "Yeah. And penguins fly."

Jack could do nothing but watch her as she prodded her way into the woods. He turned to Doug for an explanation.

"Don't look at me," Doug said shrugging his shoulders. "She's a woman. I can't explain 'em."

Jack turned back and could just barely see Emery's face through the pine trees. He thought about following her. Then he thought better of the idea. He heard thunder in the distance and looked above at the dark clouds beginning to accumulate. He couldn't help but wonder if this was a premonition.

Guido's head hung back precariously across the top of the front seat. His mouth gaped widely open. Snorting sounds echoed from deep within his nasal passages as drops of rain pelted hard against his windshield. With the gray clouds overhead, dusk had settled in earlier than normal.

Sarducci stood underneath a leaky overhang at a convenience store talking on his cell phone. It was the only way to get away from Guido's snoring. Droplets of precipitation fell from a crack in the canopy and dripped slowly on Sarducci's shoulders. Talking to someone in Spanish, Sarducci tried to motion to Guido, but the fogged windshield prohibited it. After telling his party to hold, Sarducci walked to the car and opened the passenger door causing Guido to stir just slightly and shift positions. "Don't let me bother you," he told Guido in Spanish. He reached across the slumbering Guido and retrieved the road map that sat in the middle of the seat. He stuck it under his shirt so it wouldn't get wet on the way back to the convenience store canopy. He intentionally slammed the door. Guido stirred, but did not wake up.

Sarducci held his cell phone steady against his ear with his shoulder while he looked at the map. He unfolded it and turned it around a couple of times to make sure he was looking at the right section. When he was sure he had it right, he informed the party on the other end of the phone, who obviously was interested in their exact position. Sarducci looked left and right until he spotted the nearest sign identifying the route they were on. "Highway forty-five," Sarducci said in Spanish. He pulled his head back inside out of the rain and listened, running his finger across the map to pinpoint exactly where they were. His right index finger crept slowly south on the red line until it met the town of Macon. "It looks like we're maybe twenty or thirty miles away according to the map," Sarducci told the other party in Spanish. He nodded his head a couple of times and said they would be there within half an hour.

Sarducci closed his cell phone and put back in his pocket. He folded the map as neatly as he could and crammed it in his back pocket. He looked overhead at the pouring rain, pulled his jacket up firmly around his neck and jogged to the car. He got in as quickly as he could and wiped the rain from his head and face. He popped his arms several times to shake the excess moisture from his jacket. He looked at Guido who still slumbered and snored, his arms neatly folded across his chest. Sarducci popped his right arm toward Guido's face. A few droplets splattered against Guido's nose. Never opening his eyes, Guido lightly brushed the drops away, shifted positions, and continued with his nap. Sarducci shook his head and started the car. He started to leave, but not before he was forced to crank up the defroster to full speed to clear the heavily fogged windshield from Guido's heavy breathing. After a minute or two the glass was clear and Sarducci merged onto Highway 45.

Doug, now driving, flipped his right turn signal and pulled into the gravel lot of a grungy motel. Through the rain, the neon sign flashed a red T, E and L. The M and O had burned out years before, but no one cared enough to fix it. The windshield wipers wiped away more rain as Emery leaned forward and peered through the window, checking out the place where she was about to spend the night.

Emery rolled her eyes and flopped back against the seat. "Nothing but the best. Right, Doug?"

Doug glared at Emery, who he disliked more and more every

minute. "Would you rather we stay at the local Marriot where a couple of off duty cops will be working a second job?"

"Where are we?" Jack asked.

"I don't know. There was a sign back there a couple of miles back, but it was raining too hard to read," Doug answered.

Jack looked around at some of the small quaint homes surrounded by thickets of pines. "Somehow I don't think there's a Marriott or Hyatt nearby. Too small."

Doug smiled. "I was kidding, Jack. It was a joke."

Jack looked at Emery. "I knew that."

Doug cut the engine. "I'll go inside and get us a room."

"Wait a minute," Emery said grabbing Doug's arm. "You're not serious are you? We're not staying here."

"You got any better ideas?" Doug asked sarcastically.

Emery glared at Doug. "I'm not gonna stay here."

Doug opened his door. "Fine. Suit yourself. You can sleep in the car for all I care. Makes no never mind to me." Doug stepped his left foot onto the gravel lot.

"Wait," Jack said. He reached for Doug's arm.

Doug stopped, but refused to look at Jack or Emery. "What?"

Jack shrugged his shoulders. "I don't know. Maybe we can find a better place."

Doug turned and looked at both of them. "Look, Jack. We're in God-Knows-Where, Mississippi. This may be the only motel in town." Doug paused. "Look. All we're gonna do is sleep. What difference does it make where we stay?" Doug looked at his watch. "It's almost eleven. I'm tired. All I want to do is climb in a bed and sleep. I don't care whether that bed is at the Hyatt or here or at the...," Doug looked up at the flashing sign. "The TEL. I just want to sleep. If you guys want to sleep out here or drive on down the road, then you go ahead and do it. But I'm gonna stay here."

Jack placed his hand on Emery's thigh and pleaded. "It's just for one night, Emery. Maybe it's cleaner on the inside than it looks on the out."

Emery gave Jack a smug look. "I bet the sheets are clammy and there are roaches running around on the ceiling."

"Just one night. I promise. Tomorrow we'll stay in a nicer place.

And I swear I won't keep you out here long. As soon as I prove my innocence we'll go home." Jack peered into her eyes. "Alright?"

Emery shook her head in disbelief that she was giving in. "Fine. But I want my own room."

Jack shrugged his shoulders. "I don't know if we can do that. You know, the money and all."

"We can do it! No problem!" Doug interjected. "Emery should have her own room." Doug was relieved. He was tired of her whining and really didn't care for spending any more time with her in close proximity. "Money's not a problem here. I'll get the rooms."

Doug climbed the rest of the way out of his SUV and shut the door behind him. He put his arm above his forehead to shield the raindrops from his eyes. He raced toward the glass front door that had a long crack running from top to bottom and stepped into the hotel lobby. An old, wooden desk, probably picked up from some garage sale eons ago, was the sales counter. The floor was yellow vinyl that had never been replaced. It wasn't actually yellow, but years of no waxing or mopping had turned it a permanent yellow. The flooring had cracks and in some places the vinyl had come unglued from the floor and now curled upward. The fluorescent lights, which hung precariously from the tiled ceiling, flickered and hummed, begging to be replaced with new ones.

The lone clerk sat behind the desk in a brown metal folding chair. His crossed feet were propped up on the desk. He hadn't shaved in three or four days and he wore an unbuttoned, flowered, multi-colored Hawaiian shirt on top of a white, round necked wife-beater tee-shirt. "What can I do ya' for?" the clerk said, never taking his eyes off the photograph he was leering at in his *Penthouse* magazine.

"I need a couple of rooms," Doug said.

"How many?"

"A couple."

"That would be two?" the clerk said as he shifted his magazine in different positions to get the best possible view.

Doug stared at the clerk. "Yeah. That'd be two."

"Twenty-nine ninety-nine plus tax for each room, payable in advance."

Doug retrieved his wallet from his back pocket and pulled a

hundred dollar bill from inside and flipped it toward the clerk.

The clerk removed his feet from the desk and flipped his magazine on top of it. "There's an eleven percent tourist tax we have to add on."

Doug furled his brow and smiled. "Tourist tax? You're kidding right?"

"That's what they call it."

"That's fine. I guess we're tourists."

"That'll be thirty-three dollars and twenty eight cents for each room for a total of sixty six dollars and fifty six cents." He slid the hundred dollar bill along the desk and into the top right drawer. He pulled some bills and change out of a metal box and put it on top of the desk.

Doug watched closely. "Out of curiosity, what's the tourist tax for?"

"May seem like a Podunk town to you, but back in 1863 there was a pretty big Civil War battle here. Lots of Civil War buffs from all over the country come here every year for the re-enactment." He slid the change along the top of the desk toward Doug. "Here's your change, mister. Your rooms are fifteen and sixteen. The keys are hangin' over there on the wall." The clerk pointed at a row of nails crudely hammered into the wall. The numbers were written above them in black ink and two sets of keys hung on each nail for the rooms that had not been taken for the night. Most of the keys still clung to their respective nails.

"Alright," Doug acknowledged by turning around and spying the keys. Doug picked up his change and stuffed it in his pocket.

"And you might wanna' grab ya' some towels on the way out."

Doug looked below the hanging keys to a table stacked with unfolded yellowish-white towels simply clumped together. He turned back to the clerk. "Are they clean?"

The clerk peered up at Doug. "Of course they're clean. What kind of place ya' think I run here?"

Doug smiled. "Right."

The clerk propped his feet back on the desk and crossed one on top of the other. He picked up his magazine from the desk and began shifting it in different positions. He smiled.

Giving a look of disgust to the clerk, Doug took the keys from the nails. He grabbed five or six towels from the table, sniffing them to assure they were indeed clean. He stepped back outside into the rain and dashed towards the car.

"What took you so long?" Emery asked Doug, as he climbed back into the SUV and shut the door.

"Why? You anxious to get into your deluxe suite?"

Emery rolled her eyes. "You have a smart ass comment for everything, don't you?"

Doug cupped his ears. "Ooooh, Emery. Please. Your language. Please watch it."

Emery folded her arms and threw herself back against her seat.

Jack shook his head. "What was that phrase Rodney King made famous? Can't we just get along? Yeah. That was it." Jack paused and looked at both of them. "Can't you two just get along for just a little while? Geez!" he said, shaking his head.

Emery reached out her outstretched palm toward Doug. "Just give me my key."

Doug held up both keys. "Which one do you want? Fifteen or sixteen? Sixteen has less cockroaches but fifteen has sheets that have only been slept on three times since they were last cleaned."

"Just give me one," Emery said, certainly in no mood to play games.

"Here," Doug said. He tossed the key with the number fifteen written with black felt tip pen on the oval shaped piece of plastic connected to the key. It landed on her right thigh but scooted off and fell between her and Jack's leg. They both reached for it at the same time which caused their fingers to collide and slightly entwine. They looked up and for a moment their eyes locked. Neither one knew what to say. The stress and strain of the past few days had put everyone on edge. Emery pulled her hand back.

Jack looked down at the seat, picked up the key and handed it to Emery. "Here."

Emery smiled. "Thanks."

"Can we go now?" Doug said sarcastically.

Jack's and Emery's heads turned to Doug. "Yeah. Fine. I'm really tired," Jack said.

Doug looked behind him to make sure it was clear. He backed up slowly because the driving rain made it difficult to see too far in front or in back. Jack softly patted Emery's hand that clutched her key and swore to her it wouldn't be much longer.

Doug eased into the parking space directly in front of room number fifteen and cut his engine. "Here we are."

"Let me get you something to cover your head," Jack said, motioning to Emery.

"No. I'm fine. A little rain's not gonna hurt me."

Doug opened his door, got out and closed the door. Jack did the same, but helped Emery out of his side first. They both then ran the few steps to the door's entrance where Doug was unlocking room sixteen. All three stepped inside and were met with a musty smell that caused all three of their faces to shrivel like a prune. "Geez! What's that smell?" Doug said, covering his nose with his hand.

"Probably the expensive Swedish air freshener they import weekly to keep everything well preserved," Emery said, with a straight face.

Doug and Jack looked at Emery. For the first time in days all three shared a laugh in spite of the putrid lime green walls, stained brown carpet as old as the motel itself, and an air conditioner unit that dinged and pinged like a car engine begging for a higher grade of gasoline.

Emery covered her mouth and let out a lengthy yawn. "I'm really tired. I'd really like to stay up and talk, but I believe if I don't lie down soon I'll collapse."

"I'll walk you to your room," Jack said, reaching for the rusty doorknob.

"Don't forget your towels." Doug pulled two towels from underneath his arm where he had been holding them. "Here. I'm sure they are Downy fresh."

"Thanks," she said, taking the towels. She turned, opened the door and covered her head with the towel to protect herself from the rain. "See you in the morning."

"Right," Doug said, as he sat down on the bed with a dingy, white bedspread. His butt sank deep into the mattress. He pushed down on it with his hands which also sank far below the mattress surface.

"Firm." He fell backwards and let out a lengthy sigh.

"You sure you're gonna be okay?"

"I'll be fine, Jack. All I wanna do is have about eight hours of uninterrupted sleep."

Jack smiled. "I'm sorry it's not what you're used to."

Emery smiled back. "Once I get to sleep I won't know the difference."

"You know where I am if you need me."

"Yeah."

Jack stood silent for several seconds staring at Emery. Emery stared back. Something was on his mind but he didn't know what to say.

"What is it?"

Jack looked down at her face that had several droplets of rain slowly rolling down it. "Nothing. It's nothing."

"You sure?" Emery smiled slightly.

"Yeah." Jack turned, twisted the doorknob and pulled the door to where it was barely open. A few droplets of rain splattered inside.

"Do you wanna talk?" she asked Jack, who stared at the ground and was unconsciously drawing circles on the door with his finger.

Jack looked outside at the pouring rain. "I'm really sorry for dragging you into this."

"Jack," Emery started.

"No," Jack interrupted. "Let me finish." He took a deep breath and continued. "I had no right to make you come."

"You didn't make me come. I made that decision on my own."

"No. I may not have twisted your arm, but I made you feel the pressure." Jack paused. "You shouldn't be out here. By running, I've made myself look guilty. I should've done like you said. I should've stayed in Atlanta and taken my chances that the justice system would work. But like a fool I ran, thinking I could find the proof that Fuentes did it. I didn't realize it was going to be like this. I would've never come, and sure as hell wouldn't have drug you along, had I known all this was gonna' happen."

Emery smiled. "You can't beat yourself up over a mistake, Jack. It's water under the bridge. But you can make it right."

Jack lifted his head. "Make it right? Whattaya' mean?"

"Go back to Atlanta. Turn yourself in."

Jack sat down on the wooden chair with a soiled and ripped plastic orange seat cushion beside the bed. "I don't know."

"If you do it and explain why you ran, I think they'll understand. I mean you were running for your life, for crying out loud. You don't know how many people are trying to kill you. If you tell Fuentes, or anyone, they will have to understand why you ran."

"Maybe they will and maybe they won't. You know, if I do turn myself in this time, I can forget bail. No way they'll give me bail because I would be considered a flight risk."

Emery sat down on the side of the bed directly across from Jack. "You're turning yourself in. Why would you be considered a flight risk? And besides, would it be so awful if you had to stay? At least you'd be alive and all these hit men, or whoever they are trying to get you, couldn't get close to you. Then when a jury finds you innocent, everyone will back off and leave you alone."

Jack laughed. "You really think Guido and Sarducci and whoever their boss is will forget all about me when a jury acquits me? I don't think so. In their minds I'm guilty, and until they kill me they won't give up."

"So what are you going to do? Run the rest of your life? Keep running from town to town until you find someone that can prove your innocence? Is that it? You think that's your best chance? Now that's real quality of life."

Jack buried his forehead into his palms. "I don't know. I don't know anything right now."

"You know what I think? I think if you keep running they're gonna' eventually find you. And I'd rather face a jury than those two baboons. I think out here you have no chance. If you go back, you've at least got a shot. And I think you can do it."

Jack looked up at Emery. He stood and folded his arms. "You're right. I'll go back."

Emery stood up and embraced Jack. "You're doing the right thing, ya' know."

Jack shook his head. "We'll see." Jack walked toward the door. "We'll head back first thing in the morning. We'll have to drop Doug off first."

"Okay."

Jack took a deep breath and let it out slowly. "I'll call Fuentes in the morning and tell him I'll be there day after tomorrow."

Emery loosened her grip from Jack's shoulders and leaned back. "You're doing the right thing."

"I know. It's just that it doesn't seem fair. You know? I mean I didn't do anything. I can't understand why this had to happen to me."

"There's always gonna' be peaks and valleys. You just kind of have to ride along and know right will prevail."

"I guess." Jack turned and took two steps toward the door. "Well. Good night."

Emery reached out and grabbed his sleeve and pulled him back toward her. She planted a soft kiss on his forehead. "Everything's gonna work out. It will."

Jack's lip curled slightly into a semi-smile. "I wish I was as confident as you."

Emery smiled and kissed him on his chin.

Jack reluctantly pulled away. "Lemme' go break the news to Doug."

"You don't want to stay for a little while longer?"

Jack peered into her eyes. "I better not." He gazed a few seconds more. He wanted to stay. "See you in the morning," he said, turning away and leaving the room. He closed the door softly behind him, but not before turning one more time after he was outside. Emery stood watching him from the window, a halo of soft light surrounding her. "Night," he whispered.

Emery waved a three fingered wave. "Night," she whispered back.

~ 12 ~

The rain had eased somewhat, but a steady sprinkle still pelted softly on the hood of the black Lincoln Continental. The blue digits of the analog clock inside silently announced it was 4:12 a.m. Guido's head hung back across the headrest. His mouth hung widely open as snorts and gurgles and other offensive sounds escaped with every breath.

Sarducci sat behind the wheel, and every now and then poked Guido in his ribs to make him shift positions and close his mouth so the annoying sounds might stop for a minute or two. He reached and flipped the switch for the intermittent windshield wipers to brush away the droplets that had accumulated on the windshield. His car sat inconspicuously behind a clump of pine trees about fifty or sixty yards south of the motel. He clutched the steering wheel at the top with both hands, leaned forward and rested his chin on top of his hands. He watched closely as the two figures emerged from their car and walked into the motel office.

The motel clerk slept in much the same fashion as Guido. His legs were propped up and crossed on his desk. His hands were folded neatly across his chest. Strange sounds escaped from within his throat and nasal passages. Like lurching forward when awakening from a nightmare, he was jolted conscious when his feet were so savagely kicked, that it spun him around and almost knocked him out of his chair. He grabbed the corner of the desk to try and stop from tumbling to the floor. Trying to regain his senses, he rubbed his eyes and scratched his head. His eyes squinted as he tried to focus on the two shadowy figures dressed in suits hovering over him.

"Where's Jack Armstrong?" blared a voice with a slight accent.

The clerk rubbed his eyes again and glared up at the two strangers.

"Who?"

"You heard me, you little shit! Where is he?" the voice once again ordered.

"I don't know who you're talking about."

"He checked in here earlier tonight," a different voice said. "Another man and a woman were here with him. They were driving an SUV."

Visions of the SUV sitting outside the office when Doug checked in popped into the clerk's mind. "I can't give out information on guests. It's against policy."

"Oh, yeah. I can tell by the luxurious surroundings here that your establishment here prides itself on the privacy and confidentiality of its guests."

"Yeah. Well." Before he could utter another word, the clerk was pulled up by his ears and had a badge shoved hard into the bridge of his nose. "Hey, hey, hey! Take it easy! Easy!" he shouted, as his back was shoved against the window.

McMann pushed the badge harder into the clerk's face. Fuentes stepped back and watched. "You see this badge asshole, or are you farsighted? Now I'm gonna' ask you one more time where Armstrong is."

"I swear to God I don't know who you're talking about. A guy driving one of them big SUV's checked in late last night and got two rooms but I didn't pay no attention to his name or if anyone was with him."

Fuentes shoved a photograph of Jack several inches from the clerk's face. "Is this the guy who checked in?"

McMann eased his grasp on the clerk and put his credentials back into his pocket.

The clerk looked at the photograph of Jack. "Naah. That's not him. The guy that checked in was tall. Real tall."

"Was this guy in the vehicle with a woman?" Fuentes asked.

"I didn't see. It was raining pretty hard."

"Did the tall guy sign a register? Did he pay with a credit card?" McMann quizzed the clerk.

The clerk straightened his Hawaiian shirt and sat back down at his desk. "He paid cash. And he had a big wad of it, too." He shuffled through a drawer and produced several spiral notebooks. He put them on his desk and fingered through them. "Here," he said pointing to one. "This is the guy, right here."

"Lemme' see it," McMann ordered.

The clerk picked up the spiral notebook and handed it to McMann. McMann read it and smiled. "This guy's dumber than I thought. He signed his real name." McMann handed the spiral notebook to Fuentes.

Fuentes read the name out loud. "Doug Spacey. That's him."

"Name fits him well, doesn't it?" McMann chuckled to himself.

"What room is he in?" Fuentes asked.

"I don't know. Either fifteen or sixteen. Like I said, he got two rooms. I didn't watch to see which one he went into. Ya' know all the kinky stuff that goes on and everything. I just figured it was none a' my business."

McMann pulled a twenty dollar bill from his trouser pocket and stuffed into the clerk's shirt pocket. He patted it three times. "Thanks."

The clerk pulled the twenty from his pocket and looked at it. "Don't mention it."

Fuentes and McMann jumped quickly back into their car and drove slowly, without their headlights, toward room sixteen.

"I don't see the SUV," Fuentes said, doing a visual sweep of all the vehicles parked in the area.

"Maybe he parked in the back," McMann said.

"I don't think there is a back lot. Just looks like woods back there to me," Fuentes said.

"There's room sixteen," McMann pointed to the room, but drove past it. "I'm gonna' drive around the lot again. Maybe we missed it."

"It's possible they dumped it after they were spotted," Fuentes said, offering a possible explanation.

"You sure he's in sixteen?" McMann asked as he drove the loop around the parking lot of the L shaped motel.

"That's what the source said. I'm sure Armstrong's hinky though. He could've changed rooms or maybe they left."

McMann finished checking the handful of cars parked in front of each room. He pulled to the end of the motel next to where the woods began, but to where he could still see room sixteen. "If he changed rooms, Gomer Pyle back there would've had to change it for him. He'd a told us. I think they ditched the SUV just like they ditched the truck back in Tennessee. They'd be stupid if they didn't."

"You want to sit on it awhile? See if a light comes on? Maybe they'll come out."

McMann looked at Fuentes and grinned sarcastically. "What'd they teach you at the Academy about the element of surprise?"

Fuentes rolled his eyes and sighed. "Hit them when they're sleeping. Catch them off guard. Don't allow them to get the jump on you."

"Very good," McMann said, eyeing room sixteen.

"Who's going in first?" Fuentes asked, already knowing the answer.

McMann smiled. "You're the case agent."

Sarducci watched Fuentes and McMann through night vision binoculars. Guido continued to snore, only now in a different position than he was in five minutes earlier. About once every seven seconds the intermittent wipers swept away the drops from the light sprinkling of rain. Sarducci twisted the dial in the middle of his binoculars to bring Fuentes and McMann into better focus.

Sarducci shifted his line of view back and forth between the FBI Agents and rooms fifteen and sixteen. He poked Guido in his side when Fuentes and McMann exited their car and began inching their way toward room sixteen. Guido stirred slightly, but woke up after the third or fourth poke from Sarducci. Guido rubbed his eyes, yawned and turned his head in the direction that Sarducci was pointing.

Their 9mm weapons pulled and pointed upward, Fuentes and

McMann stood on opposite sides of the door with the number sixteen sloppily painted in black paint. Fuentes looked at McMann and nodded his head. McMann reciprocated. Fuentes balled up his free hand into a fist and banged three times on the door with the butt of his hand. "FBI, Armstrong! Open the door!" Fuentes placed his free hand back on the butt of his weapon and waited but, there was no response.

McMann banged a little harder and shouted slightly louder, but other than a few curtains being pulled back from the inside of other rooms close by to see what the commotion was, there was no response from room sixteen.

"Go get the key from Gomer," McMann ordered Fuentes.

Fuentes looked at McMann. Even though McMann was the SAC, Fuentes was getting tired of taking orders. He didn't think McMann should be here in the first place. It didn't look right to the other agents. They were intruding into another field office's territory without notifying it and that was forbidden. And SACs were more public relations men than they were agents. He could see suspension, if not termination, written all over the wall.

"Well?" McMann said, when Fuentes did not jump at his command.

Fuentes blew out a breath through his nose while glaring at McMann. He holstered his weapon and jogged toward the motel office where the clerk watched from the window.

"I need a key to room sixteen," Fuentes calmly told the clerk.

"Ain't got another one. He took 'em both," the clerk said, pointing to the nails in the wall where the keys hung.

"What about your pass key? Give me your pass key."

"Ain't got one."

"You don't have a pass key?" Fuentes said, surprised.

"Lost it a few years ago."

"You didn't have another one made. No spare?"

"Just kept putting it off."

"What do you do if there's an emergency? Never mind. Don't answer that," Fuentes said, before the clerk could respond.

Fuentes trotted back to room sixteen. "Spacey took both keys and Gomer lost the pass key several years ago."

"You gotta be kidding me," an exasperated McMann said.

Fuentes smiled and shook his head.

McMann paused and smiled back. "Like I said. You're the case agent."

Fuentes pounded on the door three more times and announced that the FBI demanded he come out. But there was no response from inside.

"Break the door down," McMann ordered.

Fuentes didn't want to break it down. He didn't really see a need. He had already checked the back of the room and there was no exit point. There were no windows in the back of the room. From the information he had gathered, the trio had slept very little in three or four days and it was likely they were in such a deep sleep that the banging on the door would not stir them. "They're not going anywhere. Let's wait until light and grab them when they come out."

"When it's light other people will be up and about. If you wait, you take the chance of somebody getting hurt, Eric." McMann stared at Fuentes. "Knock it down, now!"

Fuentes looked at McMann a few seconds then shook his head. He backed away from the door to give himself the amount of room he would need to kick the door loose from its jamb. He took a few seconds to prepare himself mentally and to pinpoint the weakest part of the door. Little did Fuentes or McMann know, that if only they had checked they would have discovered an unlocked door.

The bottom of Fuentes' foot met the door at the lock. It flew open and careened into the wall adjacent to it, causing the door knob to jab a gaping hole in it. Termites scurried through the hole and down the wall. McMann quickly flipped on the light.

With weapons pulled, Fuentes and McMann aimed at an empty bed. The covers had not even been pulled down. The beds had not been slept in. There were no clothes, no bags, or articles on the dresser which indicated any sign of life inside the room.

Frustrated, McMann barked his order. "Check under the bed. I'll check the bathroom."

Fuentes lifted the hanging bedspread slowly, got down on his knees and bobbed his head two or three times up and down, just in case there was someone hiding with a clear head shot at him. To his relief, there was nothing under the bed except some crusty, moldy socks left behind years ago.

"Bathroom's clear," McMann announced, still pointing his weapon into the air.

"Same here," Fuentes said pulling himself from the floor. He holstered his weapon.

"Where is he?" McMann queried Fuentes.

"Hell if I know," Fuentes shot back, obviously agitated. "I told you we were better off with him free anyway. Maybe this is the best thing that could've happened to us."

"I'm not gonna' argue with you, Eric. I want the son-of-a-bitch in custody and I want him now. He's been charged with UFAP. We have the right to pursue him and I want his ass back in my custody."

Fuentes glared at McMann. "You know that charge won't stick."

"Judge signed it," McMann grinned.

"Maybe so. But we can't prove UFAP and you know it. Armstrong posted bail. He doesn't have to show until his trial."

"You're right. But as soon as that pissant crossed state lines he basically told the Judge to screw off. He wasn't supposed to leave the state without permission. Besides. Do you really believe Armstrong really has any intention of returning to Atlanta?"

Fuentes narrowed his eyes and glared at McMann. "Yeah. I believe he does. I know he does."

McMann glared back. "And I don't. And I want him in our custody." McMann paused. "Do you realize what's at stake here?"

Fuentes did not take his eyes from McMann. "Yes."

"Then you know why we've got to find him."

Fuentes nodded his head affirmatively.

"He's out there somewhere," McMann said stoically. "We've gotta find him."

They emerged from the room. The rain had stopped. The red moon peeked from behind a cloud. Sarducci watched through his binoculars. Fuentes stopped and gazed at room fifteen where Emery enjoyed a rare slumber.

"Can't do it, Eric," McMann said. "Someone could be watching."

Fuentes caught himself and quickly walked away. He climbed back into the driver's seat of the rental car.

The first rays of morning burst through the long ago worn holes in the faded white curtains hanging in Emery's room. The room smelled musty, the sheets were clammy, and rust colored water dripped from the faucet. But none of that mattered. All she needed was a place to lay her head for six or seven hours. She just needed a little rejuvenation. And despite the conditions, she slept like a baby.

Emery lay flat on her back. She smiled and stretched her arms upward, feeling so much better than just eight hours earlier. She was well rested and was going home. Emery sat up and threw the damp sheets off her body. She frowned for a second, then smiled again, knowing this was about to end. Her body jerked when the phone rang. Cautiously picking up the receiver, she answered. "Hello?"

"Emery. It's me."

"Oh, Jack! I feel so much better," she said, stretching her arms behind her head while holding the phone between her shoulder and neck.

"Listen. There's been a change of plans."

Emery stopped stretching and grabbed the receiver with her hand. "What do you mean change of plans?"

"I can't talk over the phone. You have to trust me."

"What's going on, Jack? I thought we were going back to Atlanta."

"Not now. Not yet, anyway. There's been a change. We can't go back today."

"It's Doug isn't it? He talked you out of it, didn't he?"

"I can't talk about it over the phone. Okay? Now I want you to listen. I want you to get dressed. Get your stuff together and walk about a half mile north on the highway till you see the Piggly Wiggly grocery store. It'll be on the left hand side of the road."

"What's going on, Jack? I don't like this."

"I'll explain later." Jack paused. "I want you to go inside the store and go to the back. You'll see a double set of doors that says *Employees Only*. Go through those doors. You'll walk through a supply area. There will be a lot of boxes. Just come straight back until you see the sign that says loading dock. There's a door right by the dock. Be outside that door in one hour. Alright?"

"Ok, I guess. What's happened?"

"One hour, Emery. We don't have time."

Emery hung up the phone, sat on the edge of the bed and buried her head into her hands. She wanted to scream but didn't have the energy.

After taking a lukewarm, rust colored shower with very little water pressure, Emery jumped out quickly. The stains she could handle. She could stand the cool water temperature. She couldn't stomach the roaches and centipedes crawling along the bathroom floor. In less than twenty minutes she was ready to leave and follow Jack's orders.

Emery closed the door behind her. She placed the strap of the small suitcase she'd brought with her over her shoulder and walked through the puddle filled gravel lot to the highway. She stood still for a few seconds, trying to decide which way was north. She looked to her right and ahead about fifty feet she saw the sign with the highway number and the word NORTH written on top of it. She began walking in that direction and trudged forward until she spied the Piggly Wiggly on the left, across the street. She did not notice the two cars whose passengers watched her from a distance. She let traffic clear and then scooted across the street. She walked through the parked cars of the Piggly Wiggly patrons. Inside the store, only a fraction the size as some of the fancier grocery stores in Atlanta, she walked through the cereal aisle and to the back of the store.

Fuentes and McMann parked across the street from the grocery store and waited. Guido and Sarducci boldly parked in the middle of the Piggly Wiggly parking lot. Neither occupants of either car saw the other. They were very tired and not too alert.

Emery looked at her watch. Fifty-five minutes had passed since she had talked to Jack. She had followed his orders. Other than a young male employee telling her she wasn't allowed in the storage area, she had no problems. She simply smiled and batted her eyes at the pimply- faced sixteen year old, who blushed and walked away.

Sixty minutes passed. Emery paid little attention to the hunter green Ford Focus that pulled up quietly next to the loading dock. She gave little thought to the hand protruding from the driver's window motioning for her to come over. Emery looked behind her, thinking her sixteen-year-old friend might have a visitor, but he wasn't anywhere around. She looked back at the car and saw Jack, who had rolled down the window and was motioning for her to hurry. Emery hurriedly rushed down the steps of the loading dock and jumped into the passenger's seat.

"What the hell is going on, Jack?" she asked authoritatively. "Where did you get this car?"

"I'll explain in a minute. I gotta get outta' here first."

Jack turned the steering wheel hard to the right, looped around, and drove back toward the front of the grocery store. At the same time, Guido and Sarducci approached the front doors of the store, each with one hand inside their jacket. The two Columbian hit men would look extremely out of place inside the rural Mississippi Piggly Wiggly.

Jack waited for traffic to clear and then turned north onto the highway. Just as he did, Fuentes and McMann stepped out onto the road and directly in the path of his car. They froze as Jack slammed hard on his brakes. Jack's heart pumped wildly inside his chest. Emery stared, but said nothing. Jack waited for guns to be drawn, to be jerked from the car, thrown face down on the hard pavement, handcuffed and carted away. Jack's eyes locked with Fuentes' and seemingly Fuentes' with his. But like a fast softball pitcher releases his throw, both Fuentes and McMann swung their arms simultaneously underneath their beltlines telling Jack to hurry it up and go. Not one to argue with authority, Jack followed their instructions.

Fuentes and McMann stepped back and let the car pass by. Not believing he hadn't been seen, Jack turned his face away from them as he passed by. Emery looked at Fuentes squarely. McMann ran across the highway to a grassy area in front of the grocery store. Fuentes froze momentarily, watching as the car drove away.

McMann turned and noticed Fuentes was still standing in the middle of the road. "What are you waiting on? Let's go!"

Fuentes watched the car for a few more seconds. He turned,

unsure of what had just happened, made sure traffic was clear, and caught up with McMann who was entering the Piggly Wiggly.

"What's going on, Jack? Where's Doug?" Emery asked, now several miles down the highway and safely away from the law and the mob.

"I don't know."

"Whattaya' mean you don't know?"

"Last night when I told him we were going back to Atlanta he got all bent outta' shape. He thought we were both crazy. Said we were just giving up."

"Yeah?" Emery asked inquisitively.

"I tried to explain, but he didn't want to hear it."

"Why should he care anyway? It was never his decision to make."

"I know," Jack said, a bit agitated. "I guess he felt I owed him for helping. Anyway, he got ticked off and left. Five minutes later he was back with three thousand dollars cash and gave it to me. I tried to stop him and talk some sense into him, but he said he was going home. Told me to use the money to find transportation."

"Did he go home?"

"I don't know. I told him we'd drive him home, but he just cussed at me and said no. He was pretty pissed off." Jack paused and caught his breath. "Anyway, I went back to bed and crashed. I left the door unlocked in case he changed his mind. I didn't stir til the sun came up. Slept like a baby."

"And?" Emery lifted her arms in the air.

"Like I said. I don't know. He was royally pissed and just stormed away. Anyway, about eight this morning I walked down the road and found a used car lot. This is what I got for the three grand."

Emery narrowed her eyes and threw herself back against her seat. "That's all fine and good, but what I don't understand is why you went to all this trouble if we're going back to Atlanta."

"Cause something's not right."

"What?"

"I don't have a clue, but something just doesn't feel right. You know that gut feeling you have when something's not right?"

"All the more reason to go back to Atlanta."

"Don't be naïve, Emery," Jack said in a patronizing tone. "You saw 'em back there. You saw Fuentes."

"Yeah. So they're following us. They found out where we were. Why not just go ahead and turn yourself in now?"

"You don't get it, do you? You really don't get it."

"Apparently, I don't. Can you fill me in?" she said sarcastically.

Jack narrowed his eyes and glared at Emery. "I think Doug is dead and I think Fuentes and his co-hort back there did it."

Emery belted out a hearty laugh. "Oh come on! Don't be ridiculous. That's the craziest thing I've ever heard. Doug's probably laid up with some floozy somewhere. He'll turn up."

"Don't be so quick to laugh. Let's just say that Fuentes did steal that cocaine. The less people that know about it, the better. I think they found Doug and killed him to shut him up."

"Why would they kill him, Jack? He didn't know any more than whatever you told him."

"Exactly. And I told him about Fuentes. And Doug had the resources to get to the bottom of this debacle. Fuentes knows that."

Emery snickered, but a bit quieter. "I think you're crazy. I think this whole thing has made you so paranoid you can't see straight."

"Maybe so. But I'm not taking any more chances. Somehow I'm gonna' prove I'm innocent. And when I do, I'm gonna' blow the lid off of Fuentes and the FBI and anyone else that might be involved in framing me. If you wanna go back to Atlanta, you can. But I'm sticking it out." Jack paused and looked at Emery. "Should I drive you to the bus station?"

Emery gazed into the thick pine forests on either side of the highway. "No. I'll stay."

Jack was anxious to continue on his mission, but the speedometer never went higher than fifty five. He needed to find some piece of evidence that pointed to his innocence and only he could find it. And he needed his freedom to do it.

~ 13 ~

Quibdo, Columbia

Hector Raes, dressed all in white, spoke in broken English to someone over his white telephone. He sat behind his huge mahogany desk in his pure white surroundings. His servant, dressed in a white paramilitary uniform, brought him a glass of orange juice that he carried on a silver tray draped with a white cloth napkin.

"The situation has gotten out of hand. It must be stopped immediately." There was a lengthy pause. "I must give this Armstrong credit though. He possesses a quarter billion dollars worth of my property and manages to elude my men at every turn." Raes placed his left hand over the telephone mouthpiece and in Spanish ordered his servant to bring some toast. "What we have here is a serious security problem. Not just with my men, but with your outfit. It starts there, my friend. If it is not corrected, it could cause the breakdown of the infrastructure," Raes told the party at the other end of the line. Raes chuckled. "Maybe when this is all over I should hire Mr. Armstrong to manage my security. What do you think? Huh?" Raes chuckled again.

"I don't know, Mr. Raes," the shaky voice on the other end said.

"Well. I don't pay you to make those decisions do I? I pay you, quite handsomely I might add, to act as a distribution point and nothing else. But I expect excellent job performance for the wages you are paid. I do not believe I have received that. What do you think?"

"I do my best. We just let one slip through the cracks. That's all." The voice remained shaky and nervous.

"It takes a pretty large crack for two hundred fifty million dollars to slip through. Don't you think?"

"We think we've corrected the problem."

"That's where you are wrong, my friend. The situation will not be corrected until my quarter billion dollars worth of property is safely back in my possession." Raes' normally calm voice raised just slightly.

"Mr. Raes," the shaky voice continued. "What happened was a fluke."

"Are you telling me that you are responsible for a two-hundred-fifty million dollar fluke?"

"No!" the fearful voice quickly responded.

"Why can't you just admit you made a mistake, Sam? The first step to reconciliation is admitting our errors. Wouldn't you agree?"

"Yes. Of course. Of course. But I can assure you, it was not intentional."

"I don't doubt that, Sam. I would hate to think losing my valuable property was anything but unintentional. But that doesn't change the fact that it is still missing."

"Mr. Raes. Our screening process is designed to eliminate problems. This one just slipped through the cracks."

"Don't use that euphemism again." Raes raised his tone a notch. "It's unbecoming. Besides, two hundred fifty million just does not slip through the cracks." Raes paused. "I'm coming up there. I think we need to speak to one another. Face to face. Mano a' mano."

"I don't think that's necessary, Mr. Raes."

"And tell me why it's not necessary."

A lengthy paused ensued. "It's too dangerous for you. And I believe we have things under control."

"So you've recovered my quarter of a billion dollars?"

"No, sir."

"Then things are not under control. Are they?"

There was no answer.

"Are they?!" Raes shouted.

"No, sir."

Raes' servant re-entered the room and served him two slices of plain toast that rested neatly on top of each other on a silver platter covered with a lily white cloth napkin. He took one bite of the toast and looked at his watch. "It's ten o'clock. I've got business this afternoon I have to attend to. I'll be there tomorrow morning at nine a.m. I'll expect an escort."

"Yes, sir."

Raes hung up his phone and in Spanish ordered his servant to contact his pilot for an immediate trip to Atlanta.

The setting sun rested just above the tree line across Lake Walter F. George in Eufaula, Alabama, as the hunter green Focus turned onto State Highway 431 South. Jack and Emery had not talked much to each other since leaving Mississippi that morning. She was upset and didn't care what Jack's plans were at this particular moment in time.

"I'm really hungry. You think maybe you could stop for five minutes so I could get some crackers or something?" Emery said sarcastically.

Jack looked at his watch. "I guess."

She saw him glance at his watch. "Got somewhere you need to be?"

Jack glimpsed at Emery before looking away. He was tired and did not appreciate her stab at humor.

"Do you plan on stopping for the night, or are you just going to keep driving until you get to wherever it is you're going?"

Jack looked at Emery. "I haven't decided yet. If we stop we take the chance on being seen. If we keep moving we keep ahead of our friends back there at the grocery store."

"I'm sorry, Jack, but I've got to get something to eat."

Jack lifted his chin slightly. "Looks like there's one of those service station restaurant type places up there on the left. That okay?"

"I don't care. I just need something."

Jack flipped on his left turn signal and pulled into the parking lot of the convenience gas store/fast food restaurant. He shifted the transmission into park but left the car running before folding his arms and resting his head back against the seat.

"You not getting anything?"

"I'm not hungry."

"Want me to get you something for later?"

"Thank you, no. I'm not hungry."

Emery rolled her eyes. "Fine." She opened the door, got out and slammed the door extra hard, causing Jack to flinch. She got to the double glass doors of the store before turning around and coming back to the car and opening her door. "I need some money."

Jack dug into his jeans pocket, pulled out twenty dollar bill and handed it to her. "That enough?"

"It's plenty," she said, sharply snatching it from his fingers. She didn't slam the door quite as hard the second time.

Inside the store were several patrons. One was paying for gasoline she had just purchased. Another shopped for candy bars for the three small children she had with her. A young married couple stood in line at the deli watching *Fox News* on the television behind the counter as they waited on their sandwiches to be made by a teenager with greasy blonde hair sticking out of his hairnet. Emery stepped up next to the couple and waited her turn.

"What'll you have ma'am?" the teenage sandwich maker asked Emery.

"Have you got chicken salad?"

"Yes, ma'am. But it's a little old."

"How old?"

"Made it night before last."

Emery sighed. "What do you have that's fresh? As in made today?"

The teenager scanned the trays of meat and sandwich makings spread out across the counter. A fly or two buzzed around the meats. "Uhhhhh. I think the tuna salad was made today."

"You think or you know?"

The teenager let out a goofy laugh. "Yeah. It was made a couple hours ago."

"You sure?"

"Yes, ma'am. I'm sure. Made it myself."

Emery paused and stared at the teenager. He smiled and stared back. "Just give me two hot dogs. Mustard only."

"Coming up!"

Emery shook her head and smiled. Her eyes then shifted to the television as the blonde *Fox News* anchorwoman read the teleprompter. "Remnants of the hurricane were felt as far north as Roanoke, where strong winds caused major damage to residential homes and businesses. A Roanoke man drowned when his car was washed away as he attempted to cross a rain-swollen bridge. His body, still strapped in with his seatbelt fastened, was found along with the car a mile from where it was swept from the road. In the middle box, there are still no new developments into the murder of a prominent Tennessee businessman whose charred remains were found earlier today just outside Louisville, Mississippi. Although the coroner has not made a positive identification, it is believed that the badly burned body is that of Douglas Spacey, President and Chief Executive Officer of Southeast Plumbing and Supply. The body was discovered in the back of his torched sport utility vehicle, found about one mile off the main road in a thicket of woods. It appeared Spacey's throat had been cut and he apparently bled to death before the SUV was set on fire. Authorities arrived on the scene…"

Emery's heart pounded as she stared at Doug's photograph in the top right hand corner of the screen.

"Law enforcement authorities in Mississippi have refused to comment about the murder," the anchorwoman continued. "One official who spoke off the record, said the killing resembled that of a professional hit and that it was possibly drug related. The official said the cutting of one's throat is common in drug circles as a form of revenge or retaliation. We'll have more on the story as it develops. Turning to the third box, the situation in Pakistan has not improved. Talks are underway…"

Emery turned her head slowly and looked out the store's plate glass window to Jack, who looked to be grabbing a few minutes of shut-eye. His head lay across the top of the seat. Emery didn't hear the teenager telling the couple that their sandwiches and her hot dogs were ready.

"Ma'am?"

Emery turned back to the teenager. "What? What is it?"

"Your dogs. Mustard only. They're ready."

Emery paused, then smiled just slightly. "Right. How much do I owe you?"

"Do you want anything else?"

Emery stared at him, not really listening to him. "Uhhhh. Yeah. Yeah. A coke. I'll take a coke." She turned back to look at Jack who had not changed positions.

"Fountain, can or twenty ounce?"

She turned back to the teenager. "I'm sorry. What?"

"Fountain, can or twenty ounce?"

"Can. A can'll be fine."

The teenager reached behind him where a small glass encased refrigerator sat full of soft drinks and beer. He opened the door and pulled the red and white coke can from inside and set it on the counter. He punched a few buttons on the cash register and told her it would be $4.77. Emery handed him the twenty dollar bill she had grasped tightly in her hand. As he was taught by his boss, he laid the bill on the top of the register and counted her change back to her. He then placed the twenty inside its proper slot inside the cash register and closed the drawer.

Emery picked up the white bag containing her hot dogs and her coke from the counter. She smiled and thanked the teenage clerk. He nodded his head back and returned her smile.

Emery pushed the glass door open with her shoulder and stepped outside. She ambled slowly to the car, wondering how she would tell Jack the news...the news that he had already suspected. He looked so comfortable. So peaceful. She laid the bag on top of the car so she could open the door. The sound of the latch release startled Jack. He shot straight up and seemed in a daze.

Emery retrieved her hot dogs from the roof of the car and slid into her seat before shutting the door. She saw the strange look on Jack's face. "You okay?"

Jack rubbed his eyes and stroked his hair back with the palm of his hand. "Yeah. Yeah. Fine. Weird dream I guess."

"What was it?"

Jack shifted the gear into reverse. "I don't know. I dreamed Doug was inside that store. It was real strange."

Pulling her first hot dog from the bag, Emery froze. Jack looked both ways for oncoming traffic and pulled across both lanes when they cleared. He headed south on Highway 431.

"Jack?"

"Yeah?"

Emery stared out the windshield but said nothing.

Jack glanced at her. "What?"

She looked at Jack for several seconds before talking. "You were right."

He trained his eyes back on the highway. "About what?"

Emery stared out the windshield and took a bite from her hot dog. "About Doug."

Jack looked at Emery and narrowed his eyes. "What about him?"

Emery covered her mouth with her hand and once again looked at Jack. "He's dead, Jack. Doug's dead."

Jack slowly rested his head back against the headrest and blew out a long breath. He stared out the windshield and blinked his eyes quickly over and over.

Emery continued. "It was on the news back there. They found his body in the woods. But I think you're wrong about Fuentes. They said it was a hit. Mob style. Drug related."

Jack wiped his mouth with the back of his hand even though there was nothing on it. "Guido and Sarducci. They must've found him. It was the same as my brother. Those guys are crazy. They're friggin' nuts." His voice shook.

"What do you mean the same as your brother?"

"His throat. Just like Matt's. They cut it just like Matt's."

Emery looked at Jack and paused. "How did you know that?"

"Know what?"

"That they cut Doug's throat?"

Jack glanced at Emery. "I didn't."

"But you just said…"

Jack interrupted. "You said it was a hit. Drug related. I just assumed they cut his throat just like they did Matt's."

Emery stared at Jack. He looked out the windshield and continued to drive.

Jack looked back at Emery wondering what was going on inside her head. She took another bite from her hot dog.

Jack shook his head. "How can you eat after what you just heard?"

Emery took another bite of her hot dog. Mustard squirted down the left side of her chin. " I'm starving. Besides. He was your friend, not mine." She reached into the bag and pulled out the second hot dog. "I got an extra in case you change your mind."

Jack shook his head and paused. "No thanks. I'll pass."

Emery wiped the mustard from her chin. "Will the pharmaceutical company Doug worked for take care of Cissy and the kids?"

Jack turned to Emery. "Why this sudden interest in someone you didn't like anyway?" He fixed his eyes back on the road.

"I care about his family."

Jack glanced at Emery then looked back at the road. "Yeah. It's a large company. A good company. I'm sure they'll take care of his family. Doug always talked about what a good company it was to work for."

Emery stared at Jack but had no expression. She wondered why he was lying about Doug working for the pharmaceutical company. Fox had reported he was CEO of a plumbing company. "Good," she said, not ready to confront him on this most recent inconsistency.

Jack drove down the highway glancing every ten seconds or so to observe Emery choking down every last bit of the two hot dogs and chasing it with swigs of coke.

The leer jet was solid white except for the six letters spelling JUAREZ thinly outlined with black paint on the tail. It touched down at Hartsfield International Airport and cautiously approached the white limousine parked adjacent to the runway. Within a minute the latch was loosened and the stairs folded down from the jet by a white clothed employee of the drug dynasty. Hector Raes glanced in all directions before stepping onto the stairs and the cement surface of the tarmac. He shook hands with a man dressed in black and sporting a white pony tail who opened the back door of the limousine and let Raes in. The man with the pony tail and slicked back hair which receded deeply around his temples, closed the door and looked in all directions. He then quickly trotted to the driver's side, hopped in, and drove away. As he drove away, two white Cadillacs flanked the car. There was also one in front and one that trailed.

Through the dark tinted windows Raes peered up at the towering Atlanta skyline from his backseat perch. Sipping a glass of white wine poured from one of the expensive bottles placed conveniently within his reach, Raes watched people on the crowded sidewalks dodging in and around each other. He thought to himself how good he had it. There was also that tinge of jealousy deep inside that he could never be like anyone else.

The lead car stopped in front of the large gray marble building on the right hand side of Peachtree Street. It was followed by the car Raes rode in and the tail car. The two white Cadillacs that flanked Raes' limousine pulled up on the left side of Raes' car and blocked traffic in that lane. Eight men, two from each car, exited their vehicles with ultimate precision. Three guarded the left, or driver's side. Three stood guard on the passenger side. One positioned himself directly in front of the white limousine and the last stood his ground at the rear of it. When all was deemed to be clear, Pony Tail emerged from the limousine and scooted quickly to Raes' door on the back right. Pony Tail rotated his head 180 degrees to the right then to the left to assure one last security check had been performed. He opened the door and assisted Raes from his seat. Like the Secret Service protects the President, the eight men formed a tight square around Raes and led him through the huge electronic door and into the lobby covered with shiny gray marble floors lined with granite busts of influential businessmen of years gone by.

Pony Tail pushed the up button on the elevator. The eight heads bobbed back and forth looking in all directions, anxiously awaiting its arrival. Not one word was spoken. The numbered lights above the elevator's frame indicated it was only a few floors away. When the bell dinged and the doors opened, the eight bodyguards did not want to wait for the three young female occupants to exit. One step inside was as far as Pony Tail could get before Raes asked his sentinels where their manners were. Like a polite motorist gives way to pedestrians, the eight backed up two steps in unison and allowed the three women to exit, pass, and flash toothy grins at Raes.

Inside, all eyes except Raes stared at the flashing numbers above the elevator door. Raes stared straight ahead at the mirrored reflection of his guard force. Twenty six floors later the bell dinged and the doors opened wide into another lobby decorated in pure gray marble. Not as large as the one downstairs, this lobby was equally as impressive with sculptures, original paintings and crystal fixtures adorning the walls. Mahogany furniture graced the large area, which lead into the luxurious offices of the international plumbing company.

"Mr. Raes. I'm so glad you're here. So glad to see you," Samuel P. Marlowe III said, emerging from his two thousand square foot office. He nervously rubbed his hands together and grinned at Raes. Raes did not return the smile. Marlowe motioned to his office. "Would you like to rest a while before we get started? I know it has been a long, tiring trip."

"It took a little over three hours. Hardly tiring, Sam." Raes explained in a deep Spanish accent.

Marlowe's voice was shaky, but not really noticeably so. "Okay. Fine." He rubbed his hands together again. "I guess you gentlemen can go for now," Marlowe said to the eight bodyguards and to Pony Tail.

Even though they worked for Marlowe, all turned to Raes. Raes nodded his head and they disbanded and disappeared in several different directions throughout the lobby.

"Can I get you anything? Coffee? Something to eat maybe?"

Raes glared hard at Marlowe. "I did not come here for tea and cookies. I came to correct your mistake. I came to resolve our problem with your employee. I should not be here. I should not have to be here. Unfortunately, I am."

Marlowe's secretarial staff was located in the lobby. They could hear everything Raes said, but kept their heads down and pretended not to hear.

Marlowe shifted his eyes between the ground and Raes' eyes. He was too intimidated to maintain constant eye contact, a trait Raes despised. A bead of sweat rolled from Marlowe's hairline slowly down his forehead. He wiped it quickly with his coat sleeve. Marlowe motioned to his office. "Shall we go inside and have a little more privacy?"

Raes possessed an evil grin as he passed Marlowe. Second to the money his drug empire had brought him, Raes loved the power of fear he held over every person in his workforce.

Raes made himself comfortable in Marlowe's leather, high-back executive chair. He propped his crossed feet atop Marlowe's oversized cherry desk. Marlowe situated himself in one of the lesser expensive, but still luxurious button studded, leather armless chairs directly across the desk from Raes. He crossed his legs and tried to act calmly, as if Raes was in for a routine annual visit. However, his fidgeting in his seat showed anything but serenity. He dabbed away a few more droplets of perspiration. The wetness from his armpits began to heavily soak his shirt.

"A little nervous are we, Sam?" Raes said, grinning.

Marlowe glanced quickly at Raes then shot his eyes down toward the desk. "No, no. I'm just a little hot. Are you hot? Maybe I should turn the air conditioning up a notch or two." He stood up and reached toward the phone to call someone to adjust the thermostat.

"I'm fine, Sam. Sit down. I'm very comfortable."

Marlowe reluctantly sat back down.

Raes stared at Marlowe, who continued to shift his eyes back and forth from Raes to other objects inside his office. With his fingers, Raes motioned toward his own eyes. "Sam. Look at me."

Marlowe shifted his eyes a few seconds before looking directly at Raes.

"I refuse to talk to a man who refuses to look me in the eye. Not looking at me is not going to make me go away. Do you understand?"

Marlowe froze his gaze on Raes. He shot up straight in his chair. "Yes, sir. I'm sorry."

"I'm not going to hurt you. You haven't done anything to me." Raes paused, entwined his fingers and rolled his thumbs round and round each other. "You are responsible for your employees, but occasionally one comes along that you cannot control. That is not your fault, but you should have been more alert to any signs of trouble."

Marlowe felt a ton of bricks fall from his shoulders. He let out a long, slow breath. He wiped a few more drops of sweat from his brow.

"I trust I have eased your anxiety somewhat."

"Yes." Marlowe's voice shook.

"There is still the question of two hundred fifty million worth of my merchandise still out there somewhere. I won't sleep until I find it, or Jack Armstrong. I don't care which one I find first."

"I've got people searching, but we've had no luck so far."

"I don't want you to worry about Jack Armstrong. We know where he is. We trust that he will eventually lead us to what belongs to us. The only thing I want you to worry about is who you are going to put in Armstrong's place at the warehouse."

"Well. If Jack is found innocent I'm sure he's going to want his job back."

Raes laughed. "Innocent? Armstrong? Are you joking?"

"He may be. I mean, I know all the facts point to him, but there's some other things that happened that may say otherwise."

"Such as?" Raes continued his light laughter.

"Well. The FBI Agent that investigated. Fuentes is his name. It's my understanding that, besides Jack, he knew the combination to the lock."

Raes laughed harder. "Are you out of your mind? An FBI Agent. I hardly think so."

"I know it sounds crazy. And I'm not just taking up for Jack because I know him. It's just that.."

"Just what?"

"Well. I know you're aware of Fuentes' family background."

Raes nodded his head. "I know all about his family. It doesn't mean he's involved."

"Maybe he's in the family business and the FBI is the way he can keep tabs on both sides of the fence."

Raes thought for a few seconds. "Possibly, but the FBI does the most extensive background investigation in the world. He would never make it through the first phase."

"John Walker made it through," Marlowe tried his best to convince Raes. "What about Aldrich Ames?"

Raes smiled. "Sam. I know you want to think Armstrong is innocent. But you are not going to convince me that an FBI Agent...even Fuentes...would do such a thing. It makes no sense. Besides. If Armstrong is so innocent, why is he on the run now?"

Marlowe paused. "Maybe because your people scared him half to death. Did you have to kill his brother?"

Raes stood up and glared hard at Marlowe. "Don't you ever question my motives. Do you understand?"

Marlowe's heart raced. He wondered to himself why he hadn't shut up when he had the chance. He nodded his head affirmatively.

"Good. I will not be questioned by anyone." Raes sat back down. He let himself calm slightly. "Let me ask you a question, Sam. When Armstrong was given that job did you inform him of what we were doing?"

Marlowe shook his head. "No. I didn't."

"And why is that?"

"At the time, I didn't believe there was a need to know."

"At the time? At the time you did not believe there was a need to know. And just when do you think there becomes a time of one's need to know? When would you say that is?"

Marlowe shrugged his shoulders but said nothing.

"Don't you think it's possible that something could go wrong like a toilet breaking and a person like Armstrong who knows nothing about the operation panicking and not knowing what to do? Hell. You didn't even have to tell him the truth. You could have told him things like that had happened at other places by mistake and to call if it did."

"I assumed he would call me if it happened."

"You assumed? You assumed? Well, you assumed wrong didn't you? Instead he called the FBI didn't he?"

Marlowe paused. "That's why I think he's innocent. If he was going to steal that cocaine, why in the world would he call the FBI?"

"You answered your own question. Because it's the perfect cover. If he doesn't call the FBI and the cocaine is stolen, he is the only one who could have done it. By calling the FBI he creates his own alibi."

"True. But that didn't stop him from getting indicted." Marlowe shook his head. "I'm sorry, Mr. Raes. But I just disagree. Jack has worked for this company for over fifteen years. I know him too well. He wouldn't do something like this."

"If you knew him so well, why didn't you tell him about the operation?"

Marlowe thought about it but did not answer.

"Who was the last man you had in that position? Marland? Morrow?"

"Phillip Marcus."

"Yes. Yes. Phillip Marcus. Did he know of the operation?"

Marlowe paused. "Yes," he said reluctantly.

"Oh. So you informed him but neglected to inform Armstrong. Why is that, Sam? Could it be you were unsure if Armstrong would go along with the program?"

"I don't know. I just didn't tell him. No particular reason really."

"Uh-huh. And now you see what situation we are in, don't you?"

Marlowe sighed. "I guess so."

"I'm not going to sit here and argue with you. I didn't come for that. I came to assess the damage and to..." Raes paused. "Relieve you of your position."

Marlowe rose quickly to his feet. "My position?"

"You heard me. I'll be putting my own man in charge beginning tomorrow. Someone I can trust."

"But you can't do that! This is a family business. It's been that way over a hundred years."

"It ceased to be a family business when you asked for my assistance several years ago. If it hadn't been for me your so-called family business would have gone under. Because of me, Marlowe Plumbing is thriving and will continue to do so. But I cannot afford any more multi-million dollar losses. So I am replacing you. But don't worry. I think you will find my buyout will be more than generous and it is doubtful you will ever have to work again, unless you squander away ten million dollars. But I just cannot trust you in this position anymore. I'm sorry, Sam. But it's business. I'm sure you understand. Rest assured that I will maintain every employee and the name of the company will remain intact."

Marlowe was devastated. The company started in the early 1900's by his grandfather was about to slip away.

"Take the rest of the day to clean out your office. My new CEO will move in first thing in the morning. And just so you won't think I'm a cold son of a bitch, you can keep the house we purchased for you when we began this operation."

Marlowe stared at Raes, but could say nothing. He was in shock.

"No need to thank me," Raes said sarcastically. "You have a lot of work to do for now. You can show your appreciation for me at a later time." Raes stood and walked around the desk to Sam and touched him on his shoulder. "You've been a good employee, Sam. But it's time for you to move on. Time to enjoy retirement. Look at it that way, if you must." Raes patted him on the shoulder and walked out of the luxurious office.

Marlowe sat back in his chair and stared out the window at the tops of the skyscrapers dotting the crisp, cloudless blue sky across downtown Atlanta. His stomach hurt as if he'd been hit in the gut by Raes himself.

~ 14 ~

His arms were folded. His head lay precariously back against the top of his seat. The movement of his eyes underneath the eyelids signified a dream of some kind. A five day old beard sprouted from Jack's face as the first rays of the morning sun filtered across the bridge of his nose. Emery lay sleeping in the cramped backseat. Even Jack's snoring didn't bother her anymore. Jack shifted and a wide ban of sunshine glared across his eyes, causing him to stir. After several seconds of trying to get into a more comfortable position, Jack opened his eyes before rubbing them. He looked at his watch then at the backseat where Emery, disheveled and wrinkled, pulled herself into a sitting position.

She rubbed then squinted her eyes at the bright sun glaring off the windshield. She looked around at the palm trees, reeds and moss hanging from a group of old cypress trees. "Where are we?"

"Bout fifty miles north of Miami," Jack answered.

Emery seemed surprised. "Miami? As in Florida?"

"Yep."

"You must have driven all night."

"I drove as far as I could. I couldn't go any further. I pulled off at the first dirt road I saw. Sorry about not getting a motel. But we're running pretty low on cash. I figured we'd better conserve as much as we can."

Emery narrowed her eyes. "Why Miami?"

Jack watched Emery as she climbed from the backseat into the front passenger seat. "Because of something Doug told me."

"What?"

"Fuentes is from Miami."

Emery shook her head. "Jack. When are you going to forget about Fuentes? If you spent half as much time looking at your own men at the warehouse as you have looking at Fuentes, you probably would have solved the case already. Why do you refuse to admit that one of your own employees may have taken it?"

Jack glared at her. "Those men have worked for me for a long time. I know 'em. They wouldn't do it. I trust every one of them with my life. They trust me. Besides, none of them knew the combination to the lock. Only two people in the world knew the combination. Me and Fuentes." Jack paused. "Now, if you'll just hear me out." He paused again. "Fuentes is from Miami."

"I'm listening."

"But not originally. He was born in Columbia. His family left the country when Fuentes was about thirteen or fourteen years old."

Emery leaned back in her seat and rubbed her forehead. "I trust this is leading somewhere."

Jack looked at Emery and sighed. "Fuentes' father was tied up with the drug cartel down there."

Emery looked at Jack, tilted her head and narrowed her eyes.

"Surprise, surprise," Jack said sarcastically.

Emery said nothing but continued to stare at Jack.

Jack smiled slightly. "Cat got your tongue?"

Emery shook her head from side to side but remained silent.

"Fuentes' father was sent to Miami in the early eighties to act as the contact point inside the States for the cartel. Fuentes' father was involved in it up to his eyeballs."

Emery let out a deep breath and shook her head. "That doesn't necessarily mean Fuentes was involved."

"No, it doesn't. But Fuentes' father got caught and thrown in prison in 1990. The same year, incidentally, that Fuentes got into the FBI."

Emery frowned and shook her head. "I don't understand the connection."

"Do I have to draw you a map? It was, and still is the perfect cover for the cartel. Doug said that this Hector Raes fellow is in direct competition with the group that Fuentes' father worked for. What better way to put Raes out business than to disrupt his shipments into the States."

"That's fine. But how would Fuentes know that the cocaine in the warehouse was Raes' cocaine?"

Jack tilted his head and gave her a cocky smile. "He's FBI, Emery. He knows everything."

"It still doesn't make sense to me though," Emery said, scratching her head. "If what you are saying is true, I don't see how he could have ever made it inside the Bureau. I mean their background checks are pretty extensive. They would have known about his family."

"Oh, yeah. About that. I left out the best part."

"What?"

"Eric Fuentes isn't Eric Fuentes. His name is Eric Mendoza."

"He changed his name?"

Jack rubbed his stubbly face and looked in the mirror at it. "Yep."

"So he lied to the FBI?"

"Well. Let's put it this way. He obviously changed his name so they couldn't trace his past. I'd say he had to lie about everything else too, because there's no way they would have let him in if they knew about his family history. With his connections it would have been easy to create a whole other life that would come back crystal clear and clean as a whistle. After his background investigation, I'd say he was as pure as the driven snow."

Emery looked out the windshield at the rising sun. "Do you really believe he's bad?"

Jack let out a deep sigh, grasped the steering wheel and stared straight ahead. "I don't know. I just know that something's not right with him. I know that I didn't do it and somebody's trying to frame me. I know that you know Fuentes and everything, and I know you don't want to think he could do something like that. But I swear I can't think of any other way it could've happened."

Emery gazed at something in the distance and purposefully avoided looking at Jack. "How did Doug know all this?" She thought about the Fox News report she had seen.

Jack looked at Emery, but she maintained her distant stare. "I have no idea. Honest to God, I have no idea. He just knew it."

Emery turned slowly to Jack. "What are you going to do here?"

Jack thought for a moment. "A little research, maybe. If possible, talk to the old man."

"His father?"

"Yeah."

"Why? What for? You really think he'd tell you anything?"

Jack paused. "I don't know. The bind I'm in, it surely can't do any harm to try." Jack reached downward and pulled the key from underneath the floor mat and inserted it into the ignition. "You ready?"

Emery smiled. "Do I have a choice?"

Jack returned her smile. "Reckon not." The engine turned over and Jack cautiously drove the swampy quarter mile dirt road back to the main highway. He turned south on Highway 27 and within an hour was on the outskirts of greater Miami, Florida.

Fuentes sat at his desk in the bullpen style arrangement the Atlanta field office maintained for each squad of agents. There were roughly twenty-five other agents on the narcotics squad, but only three or four besides Fuentes were in the office. They were busily doing paper work or dictation. A look of worry on his face, Fuentes rested the back of his head into his interlaced fingers and stared out the long narrow window overlooking some smaller buildings across the street.

"What's up, Eric?" one of the agents said, noticing his fellow squad member was obviously pre-occupied.

Fuentes heard him but did not immediately respond. "Huh? What?" he said, spinning around in his swivel chair to face his colleague. "Sorry. My mind was somewhere else," he said, his accent very noticeable. He had tried very hard over the years to lose any hint of his Columbian accent but had not been able to shed it completely.

"Something I can help with?"

Fuentes stared at the agent and paused. "No. No thanks. Just some personal problems I'm trying to work out on my own."

The other agent snickered. "What possible problems could you have? You're single, unattached. Not dating anyone. No kids to support or worry about. I'd say the only problem you have is forgetting that you're supposed to fry chicken in oil and not just sprinkle flour on it."

Fuentes looked at him like he was crazy.

"I really had a friend who did that one time. Single guy. Didn't know how to boil water. He actually put the chicken in a pan with no oil. He just sprinkled flour on top of the chicken and waited for the crust to form."

Fuentes smiled. "That's pretty nasty."

"You think that's nasty. Son-of-a-bitch ate it. Can you believe it? He actually ate it!"

"I guess he was hungry."

"I don't know, man. I gotta draw the line somewhere."

"Did he die of food poisoning?" Fuentes asked, not really interested whether the agent's friend did or not.

"Naaah. I think he actually cooked it like that three times before his mother told him what he was doing wrong. Guy was a real idiot. But he ended up marrying a girl that was not only gorgeous, but could cook."

"Good for him," Fuentes answered, his mind a million miles away.

"You sure you're okay, man?" the agent asked.

Fuentes sighed and turned to gaze out the window. "Yeah. I'm fine. Everything's fine. Thanks though."

"Fuentes!" The supervisor's voice boomed from inside his office down the hallway.

Fuentes immediately jolted to his feet and started down the hallway toward Richard Meyer's office. His peers stopped what they were doing long enough to hurl a few good natured verbal touts at him about what to expect when the boss is ticked off. Fuentes smiled and flipped them his middle finger without looking back. They enjoyed a good laugh at his expense.

"Yeah, boss?" Fuentes said, sticking his head just barely inside Meyer's office.

Meyers did not even look up from his desk. "McMann wants to see you."

Fuentes took one step back.

"Wait!" Meyers shouted.

Fuentes stopped and stuck his head around the doorway.

This time Meyers looked up and eyed Fuentes. "Sit down."

Fuentes paused slightly, but then sat down in the uncomfortable wooden chair situated directly in front of Meyer's executive sized desk.

Meyers stared across the desk at Fuentes. "I'm not gonna beat around the bush, Eric. I don't know what's going on and I don't like it. I'm totally out of the loop. Something's not right, and you know it."

Fuentes looked confused. "I'm not sure I know what you mean, boss."

Meyers leaned back in his expensive, brown leather high back button studded chair. "I think you do. McMann is taking a personal interest in this case of yours. I'm ordered to reassign all of your other cases so you can concentrate on this one. McMann goes with you on every lead, every trip. You don't coordinate with other field offices when you go inside their territory. How many offices you been in, Eric?"

"Four."

"How many times did the SAC travel with any other Agent on any lead? Any trip?"

Fuentes paused. "None."

"What is so special about this one? No. Don't tell me. I don't want to know," Meyers said, before Fuentes could even attempt an answer. Meyers leaned forward, put his elbows on his desk and rubbed his hands together. "I knew an agent once that tread where he shouldn't have. Cost him his career. His marriage." Meyers paused. "One piece of advice, Eric. Do your job. Do what you were trained to do. You're a good agent. I'd hate to see anything bad happen."

Fuentes stared directly into Meyer's eyes. "Everything's okay, boss. I assure you everything's fine. You don't have to worry about me."

Meyer's arm motioned upward. "Go on then. McMann's waiting. You know how he is about waiting."

Fuentes rose from his chair and left Meyer's office. Meyers watched and shook his head as Fuentes disappeared down the hallway.

"Get in here!" McMann shouted at Fuentes, who cautiously stepped into the doorway of his office.

Fuentes moved about a quarter of the way inside when McMann rose from his seat and came around the side of his desk. "You gotta' get your ass to Miami!"

"Excuse me?"

"Armstrong's in Miami."

"How do we know?" Fuentes was concerned. "What's he doing there?"

McMann approached Fuentes. They stood face to face. "Don't know. Got a call about ten minutes ago. Didn't Meyers tell you I needed to see you right away?"

Fuentes shook his head. "I got a little sidetracked."

"Yeah. Well. Fine. My secretary's booked you a flight for..." McMann picked up a piece of paper from his desk and read from it. "One thirty-five this afternoon. I can't come. Got a meeting I've got to be at." McMann tossed the piece of paper back on the desk. "Besides. You're right. People are gonna' start talking if I go everywhere with you. You can pick up your ticket at the airport. It's one of those e-tickets or whatever the hell it is they do from the internet. I'll call Miami and let them know you'll be in the area if you need help. You were right about that, too. We need to coordinate from now on if you go into another division's territory."

"No!" Fuentes shouted.

McMann looked stunned.

"I can do it myself. I don't need any help."

McMann stared at Fuentes. He didn't blink. "Fine. Fine. Do it yourself. But I'm still going to let them know you're there."

Fuentes turned to leave.

"Eric?"

Fuentes stopped but did not turn around. "Yeah."

"You alright?"

"Why does everybody keep asking me that? I'm fine," he said curtly, again starting to walk away.

"Eric?"

"Yes," he answered, rolling his eyes, his back still turned to McMann.

"Be careful. Don't try to take Armstrong. Just watch him."

Fuentes turned to McMann. "I thought that was the whole point. I thought you wanted him in your custody."

"I thought about that, too. You were right. We're better off just following him for now."

"No disrespect, sir. But he's gone too far this time. His ass is mine. I'm going to bring him in."

"I don't think that's a good idea."

"You don't know what he knows. What he can find out."

McMann eyed Fuentes and paused. "Maybe I should."

Fuentes paused. "I don't think you want to." He turned and exited McMann's office.

McMann stood frozen in his tracks and watched Fuentes disappear down the hallway.

Jack perched himself in the cushy straight back chair behind the computer at the main branch of the Dade County Library. A clerk at the library showed him how to enter data into the computer to come up with bits of information that could be obtained from the archives. Armed with a pencil and a pad of paper, Jack entered as many facts and figures he had concerning the Mendoza family on the thin computer in front of him. With every bit of information scrolling down the screen, he furiously wrote names, dates and other pertinent data he deemed important. His eyes widened at the voluminous amounts of documents, affidavits, newspaper articles and other public records about the Mendoza family that were readily available through the library and not via Google or other internet search engines.

Carrying two cups of coffee in white styrofoam cups, Emery entered the computer room which was segregated from the main area of the library. She held the door lightly with her foot so it would not make a loud noise when it closed. "I thought you could use this," she said, setting one of the cups of coffee on the table and to the right of the computer keyboard where Jack typed in more data.

Jack peered over his shoulder. "Thanks." He took the plastic lid from the top of the cup and slurped a sip to test its temperature then set it back down. "You're not gonna' believe some of the stuff I'm finding. Tons of news articles, affidavits from the Feds, search warrants, police reports. There's all kinds of stuff here. Doug was right." Jack lifted his pad of paper and flipped through several pages of notes he'd jotted down. "I've got about seventy or eighty pages of documents that are out there and I've barely gotten started."

"Where do we have to go to get all this stuff?"

"Nowhere. It's all right here. All I gotta' do is tag what I want to copy and the library will provide copies for me." Jack turned to the computer screen and smiled. "I'm gonna' nail that bastard for what he's put me through."

Emery was uncertain of Jack's vengeful frame of mind. But she could also understand why. She was concerned that this retaliatory attitude was not in Jack's nature. She was afraid even if he vindicated himself through this new found set of facts, that his innocent but infectious perception of life would radically change him.

Jack hurriedly wrote down a few last tidbits of information spewing from the computer screen. Picking up his pad and pencil, he scooted his chair backwards with his feet, which made a screeching noise across the tiled floor. He stood and looked down at the black streaks he'd just created and then unsuccessfully tried to rub them out with the sole of his shoe. "I guess that's what they pay janitors for," he said looking at Emery.

"I guess so," she said with a straight face.

Jack crossed in front of Emery who still held her cup of coffee. "C'mon. I want to go through some microfiche that's not available on the web based service here."

"Do you want your coffee?" she asked him.

Jack turned and looked at the cup he'd forgotten on the table by the computer he'd also forgotten to turn off. "No, thanks. Cut the computer off for me, will ya'?" He bolted from the door not waiting for Emery to answer.

Emery rolled her eyes and sighed. "Sure." She reached across the table to the back of the computer and flipped the switch to shut it down. Putting the plastic lid back on top of his coffee cup, she picked it up and left the room to follow Jack to his next stop on his trail of revenge. Stepping outside the computer room, she caught a glimpse of Jack as he stepped into a similar looking room across a sea of book racks, card catalogues and study tables dotted mostly with senior citizens reading newspapers.

The air traffic around Miami was heavier than normal. Fuentes sat impatiently in his window seat peering at the stucco houses, swamps, beaches, and miles of highways that looked like black ribbons. The jet circled time and time again until the pilot was finally given the clearance to land by the air traffic controllers below. He rubbed his hands together until they were hot. Then he rubbed his face and massaged his own neck. He could feel a migraine brewing if the plane did not land soon.

As it touched down, Fuentes could hear the screech of the jet's tires and could visualize the smoke billowing from underneath each wheel as it made contact with the surface of the runway. As it taxied toward its assigned gate, Fuentes wasted no time angering the two passengers beside him by forcing himself past their center and aisle seats. He jumped ahead of everyone, opening the overhead compartment to retrieve his small overnight bag. Ignoring their indignant comments, Fuentes grabbed his bag, closed the overhead compartment and made his way toward the front of the jet so he could be the first to deplane. He simply flashed his FBI credentials when confronted by the head flight attendant. As quickly as the passenger loading ramp was positioned and sealed against the jet's exterior and the door unlatched, Fuentes dashed through the tunnel-like hatch and into the concourse. His romp toward the terminal and rental car area while dodging arriving and departing passengers was reminiscent of O.J. Simpson running through the airport in the old Hertz commercials, long before he became notorious and sent to prison.

Slowly twisting the small circular black knob on the bottom of the microfiche monitor, Jack meticulously read every word of every document he pulled up concerning the Mendoza family. To his left rested a pile of documents about an inch thick that he had made copies of from the information on the microfiche. Across the table sat Emery, who dozed off and on while she wasn't making copies of documents for Jack. So far, Jack had read line after line of affidavits and search warrants for the premises of Ricardo Mendoza, Fuentes' father. About the only interesting thing Jack had come across in the affidavits and search warrants was that Ricardo Mendoza was known to keep records and other documents about the cartel he worked for and its associates in his two sons' bedrooms. But the articles did not identify the sons, most likely because they were minors at the time. Jack knew this wasn't enough to incriminate Fuentes. But it was a start.

Jack removed the spool of film from the machine and returned it to its small canister. He pulled another canister from the four or five that rested in front of him. He removed it and carefully threaded it into the machine. As he turned the knob, he realized that this was really what he was most interested in. These were newspaper articles from years ago, not found on the internet. This probably could be the most damaging evidence, if he were patient enough.

Jack checked his notes for the reference numbers on where to find each individual article. The first several were mainly about the investigation, arrest, trial, conviction, post trial motions and appeals regarding the Ricardo Mendoza case. He read each piece in its entirety but found nothing he could use. He perused article after tedious article about Ricardo Mendoza, his associates and the cartel he worked for. There was no mention of Eric Mendoza. Jack sat back in his chair and blew out a long sigh. Rubbing his forehead, he tried to think of other ways to prove his theory. None came to mind. He buried his head into his hands. He was tired and he wondered if it was time to go home. Then he remembered something Doug had told him.

Emery snapped awake and watched in confusion as Jack bolted from his seat, ran out the door, and back to the computer room. She rose and followed him, only she walked. "What are you doing?" she asked, as she opened the door to the computer room.

Jack fired the computer back up and furiously typed something on the keyboard. "Fuentes' father changed his name when he moved the family to Miami." Jack slapped himself on the forehead. "I can't believe I didn't think of this before!"

"What difference does it make?"

Jack continued typing. "I kept looking for something. Anything with Eric Mendoza attached to it. Nothing was there. Then I remembered that before Ricardo Mendoza moved to Miami he was Ricardo Benitez."

"And?" Emery said, totally confused. Her eyebrows arched.

"I assumed Eric Fuentes was Eric Mendoza." Jack slapped himself twice on the forehead. "Stupid. Stupid."

"Eric Benitez?"

"Exactly." Jack typed the last bit of information into the computer. Both he and Emery waited for the computer to spit out any new information it might have concerning the newly entered data. They patiently stared at a blank screen and the bar indicating it was loading information. Suddenly the monitor spilled forth several pages of reference information on the Benitez family, including Eric Benitez. "Bingo!" Jack shouted. He looked around but had forgotten his pad of paper. "Where's my paper?"

Emery looked across the room and spotted some paper in a trash can which she immediately retrieved. She handed it to Jack, who hurriedly wrote down every piece of information listed in front of him on the screen. When he was through, both quickly returned to the microfiche room to pull up the newly found documentation.

Jack removed the film he had been viewing and then threaded the first new spool of film onto the machine. He squinted his eyes and read an investigative reporter's 1988 column about the Benitez family history. Jack learned that Eric Benitez was born in Bogota, Columbia in 1966 and was fourteen when his family moved from Bogota to Miami in 1980. The article chronicled Ricardo Benitez' association with a Columbian based cartel and how he had gradually moved higher and higher in the organization over a period of years. Ricardo Benitez, according to the article, had been detailed to Miami to oversee the Southeastern United States operation. It was a promotion, not only in pay, but in status and rank with the cartel. However, Gloria Benitez, Ricardo's wife, and Eric's mother, remained behind in Columbia. Seems she was an insurance policy of sorts. A guarantee that Ricardo would not get any wise ideas or schemes to break away from the cartel while in the States. Ricardo's two boys, Eric and his younger brother Manny, came to Miami with their father and became U.S. citizens. They both spoke English fluently and Ricardo believed the quality of life would be better for both of them in the United States. It would also be less dangerous.

Ricardo Benitez operated smoothly from 1980 through 1987. The responsibilities he had been given by his superiors in Bogota had been feverishly carried out by him. He followed all orders and requests and was considered one of the best employees within the cartel. He lived a normal middle class lifestyle north of Miami and did not attract any unwanted attention. He was well paid. His style and standard of living were well below his means. Most of the extra money he saved by living moderately went into a savings account for his two sons or to his wife in Bogota, who he saw three or four times a year when he would travel to Columbia for meetings.

Unfortunately for Ricardo Benitez, in 1985 the DEA was lucky enough to infiltrate his end of the operation. Ricardo Benitez unknowingly, and without the knowledge of his superiors, hired an accountant to take over the huge financial dealings that had been one of his sole responsibilities. In the eighteen months prior to his hiring Andrew Fishman, a certified C.P.A., Ricardo's obligations to the cartel had grown larger and larger. He was not offered any help from Columbia to keep up with his duties, so he made an executive decision to hire an accountant to at least take over the books and relieve him of that responsibility. Twenty or so independent accountants were interviewed until he believed he had found the one who could do the work, make a lot of money in the process and keep quiet about the operation. Ricardo never told his superiors in Columbia because he knew they would never approve it. Since his new hire was receiving his paycheck directly from him, he believed it would not be a problem. What Ricardo would eventually discover was that Mr. Fishman really was a C.P.A. He was also an undercover DEA Agent posing as a corrupt accountant whose real name was Special Agent Gordon Fisher. A two year investigation ensued, which shut down the cartel and landed Ricardo a seventy-five year prison term, and that was only because he cooperated with the Government.

The article continued on about the trial and the facts that emerged from it. But there was nothing in the article which implicated Eric Fuentes. However, several paragraphs later on another page, what Jack read sent a cold chill down his spine. After Ricardo had spilled his guts in the courtroom about the cartel, the DEA was able to effectively shut it down, but not without personal affliction for Ricardo and his two sons. During the trial, Gloria Benitez was kidnapped and tortured violently for several days before being murdered. Her frozen head was mailed to DEA Headquarters in Miami. Although he was never arrested for his part in the cartel, Hector Raes was charged by the Columbian authorities with the torture and murder of Fuentes' mother. Raes was one or two notches above Ricardo within the organization and the article surmised that he had fled the country before he could be arrested. An intensive search for Raes was unsuccessful. It was believed that his numerous underground contacts in the country had hidden and protected him from the authorities.

Jack sat back in his chair and took a deep breath. He stared into the screen. Emery read over his shoulder. The theft of the cocaine that had him on the run belonged to Raes, who obviously fled Bogota in 1987 and either started his own cartel or had worked his way to the top of another. Jack locked his entwined fingers on top of his head and tried to sort it all out. For over twenty years, Fuentes had to live with the agony over the murder of his mother by a monster that had escaped justice. "He knew it was Raes' cocaine," Jack said, staring intently into the microfiche screen. "It's all starting to be clear now."

"You think Fuentes stole it to get back at Raes?"

Without taking his eyes from the screen, Jack removed his fingers from the top of his head and scratched his chin. "I think he did it to lure Raes out. He could care less about his cocaine or the money. He knew this would get Raes out of his hole. He has to know Raes will come out eventually. Two hundred fifty million dollars is a lot of money. And it's really more than that. That's just what he stole. The FBI seized the rest. The whole shipment must be worth over four or five billion dollars. Maybe enough to put Raes out of business."

"You think Fuentes wants to kill Raes?"

Jack stared at the screen. "I don't know. Twenty years is a long time. A lot can go through a man's mind in twenty years. I'd like to find this Agent Fisher and talk to him." Jack pushed the print button on the machine and tucked the freshly printed article neatly into his pile. He didn't even check the handful of articles that remained hidden inside miles and miles of microfiche concerning the Benitez family. Gathering up the inch thick stack of documents and stuffing them under his arm, Jack stood and turned the microfiche machine off. "You ready?"

"Yeah," Emery answered.

"We've gotta track down Fisher and talk to him," Jack said, crossing in front of Emery and to the door of the microfiche room.

Emery had never seen Jack so intent. She followed him into the hallway and to the reference section to look for a phonebook. Jack pulled a greater Miami phonebook at least four inches thick and began thumbing through it until he came to the blue section containing the Federal Government telephone numbers. He ran his finger down the page until he found the number for the Miami DEA office. He pulled his cell phone from his pocket and dialed the number.

"DEA," a female voice said, after three or four rings.

"Yes. I need to speak to Agent Gordon Fisher please."

"I'm sorry, but Agent Fisher retired three or four years ago."

"Do you have a phone number or some way to get a hold of him?"

"We can't give out that kind of information."

Jack paused. "What if I give you my number and you call him and you can tell him to call me."

"I can try sir, but I can't guarantee you he will call you back. Can I tell him who is calling or give him a message?"

"Just tell him I have a question about a case he worked over twenty years ago. One of the people involved is trying to kill me."

"I will give him the message. What is your name and number so I can give it to him?"

"Area code 404-555-5498. My name is Jack."

"Thank you. Like I said though, I don't know if he will return your call or not. But I will get him the message."

"I appreciate it. That's all I can ask." Jack pressed the red end button on his phone and put his cell back in his pocket.

"What now?" Emery asked.

"We wait."

Jack sat down in the nearest chair and picked up a newspaper attached to the long wooden sticks used by libraries to hold newspapers. He began reading some articles but paid no attention. Emery sat down beside him and thumbed through a magazine. No more than two minutes passed by when Jack's cell phone began vibrating. He pulled it from his pocket and the number read 'restricted number'. He moved quickly to an area where he wouldn't bother anyone. "Hello."

"Is this Jack?" Fisher asked.

"Yes. Is this Gordon Fisher?"

"It is."

"I really appreciate you calling me back Mr. Fisher. I realize you didn't have to."

"What is it you want? I was told this had something to do with a case I worked twenty years ago. What can I do for you?"

"You don't know me and I don't know you. But I desperately need to talk to you about a matter."

"Well, who are you first? Are you a defendant? A witness? I'm not sure how I can help you."

"No. I just need to talk to you. I need your help."

"Uh-huh." Fisher paused. "Listen, Jack. I'm sorry and I wish I could help, but here's the deal. Considering the work I did for close to thirty years, I don't make a habit of talking to strangers about matters from yesterday, five years ago or twenty years ago. Do you understand? It's just not something that I care to do. If it deals with some case I worked twenty years ago, then you should contact the DEA office and work through them."

"Do the names Hector Raes or Ricardo Benitez mean anything to you?"

Fisher was silent.

"Hello. Mr. Fisher. Are you still there?"

After a few more seconds of silence, Fisher spoke. "I'm here. Alright, Jack. You have my attention. First off. Who are you?"

"I'm a businessman from Atlanta that's been falsely accused of stealing two hundred fifty million dollars worth of cocaine. Cocaine that belonged to Raes."

"And you're still alive?"

"For the time being."

"Look, Jack. That was twenty years ago. We never found Raes and I retired several years ago. I think your best bet is to call the FBI or DEA in Atlanta."

"That's just it. I think the FBI agent I called when all this happened is the one that stole it. That's why I'm calling you."

"Why?"

"Because the agent's name is Eric Fuentes. Otherwise known as Eric Benitez."

Fisher was silent.

"Mr. Fisher?"

"We shouldn't talk over the phone anymore. Where are you now? Are you in Atlanta?"

"I'm in Miami."

"Alright. Listen carefully. Get on I-95 and head north. I'm about seventy miles north of the city in a little town called Jupiter. When you see the Jupiter exit, take it and go east until you come to Highway One. Turn north on one and you'll see a little coffee shop on your left about a quarter mile up the road. It's called Bob's. I'll meet you there in about two hours."

"I'll be there."

"Is anyone with you?"

Jack looked at Emery. "No. I'm alone."

Emery furled her eyebrows.

"Okay. I'll see you in a couple of hours," Fisher said, then hung up the phone.

Jack pushed the red button on his cell phone and turned to Emery.

"Why did you tell him you were alone?" she asked.

Jack frowned slightly, like he wasn't sure he should have jumped so fast into the meeting. "I don't know. Just a precaution I guess."

"Are we going to meet him now?" Emery asked, as they proceeded to walk away from the pay phones and to the exit which led to the covered parking garage.

Jack opened the metal door leading to the garage for Emery. "I'm going to meet with him alone. You're not going."

Emery was upset. "And what am I going to do? Stay here and catch up on my reading? I'm going with you."

Jack drew a long breath and stared at her. He turned his head quickly and looked behind him. "Wait here just a second. I forgot something." He turned and briskly walked toward the interior of the library.

Arms folded, Emery tapped her foot and fumed inside.

Jack returned two or three minutes later with a large brown envelope tucked under his arm.

"Where did you go?"

"I wanted to get something to hold my notes and copies. Don't wanna' lose 'em." Jack pushed the metal door open and they entered the covered parking garage.

"I'm going with you, Jack."

Jack relented quickly. "Fine. You're going with me." Jack looked around at the cars parked in the garage. "Where did we park?"

Emery looked to the left and then to the right. "I think we're down one level."

They found the stairs and made their way to the level below. Arriving at the bottom of the stairs, both looked to the left and right. "There it is," Jack said pointing to the hunter green Focus. He took Emery's hand and lightly tugged her toward the car. Jack unlocked Emery's passenger door and politely opened it for her, helping her inside. He firmly shut the door, walked around to the driver's side, and opened the door that Emery had leaned over to unlock. Climbing inside, Jack shut the door, put the key in the ignition, and started the engine. He leaned back in his seat and started to pull his seatbelt across his chest when he felt the hard steel barrel of a semi-automatic pistol stuffed against the base of his ear. He froze instantly.

"Well, well, well. Look what I found," Fuentes said, grinning broadly as he rose from his hidden position in the back seat of Jack's car. "If it isn't Mr. Jack Armstrong. Otherwise known as my favorite fugitive."

Jack's heart slowed slightly. He closed his eyes and blew out a deep sigh. He looked at Fuentes' reflection in the rearview mirror. Fuentes pressed the gun harder into his ear. "Gee, I wonder how you knew I was here."

Emery shook her head. "I didn't tell him, Jack. I swear I didn't."

"Oh please, Jack. Give me some credit," Fuentes said. "It didn't take a genius to figure out where you'd be once I tracked you here. What other reason would you have to be here except to find all the public records you could about me and my family? Don't blame your woman though. It's your own stupid fault. You'd never make a career criminal, Jack. You don't think like one. Hint of the day. If you're on the run, don't use your cell phone."

Jack rolled his eyes realizing cell phone use could be traced to the nearest tower. "I don't think like a career criminal because I'm not one. Apparently you do."

"I'm an FBI agent. Remember, Jack? I'm paid to think like a criminal." He jabbed the barrel of the pistol harder into Jack's ear.

"What do you want, Fuentes? Or are you going by Mendoza today? Or maybe it's Benitez."

Fuentes laughed. "Cute, Jack. Very cute. But I'm not in the mood for your humor today. I'm here to take you into custody because you're considered a fugitive from justice. And it is my sworn duty to uphold the law, and part of that duty is to apprehend fugitives. And you my friend, are the exact definition of a fugitive."

"I'm no fugitive and you know it."

"According to the federal warrant I have, you are."

"I posted bail."

"Correct," Fuentes shot back rapidly. "But you must not have read the fine print. Your bond strictly stated you were not to leave the state of Georgia without the court's permission. I believe we are in Florida right now." Fuentes looked at Emery. "Tell me, Ms. Carson. We are in Florida. Correct?" He grinned sheepishly.

Emery stared at Fuentes but did not answer.

"Tell me, Jack," Fuentes continued. "Did you receive the court's permission to leave Georgia?"

Jack was silent.

"I'll take that as a no," Fuentes said sarcastically. Suddenly he eyed the brown envelope Jack now had tucked under his right arm. "What's in the envelope?"

Jack looked down at his envelope. He had forgotten he had it. "Nothing you'd be interested in," Jack wisecracked, knowing Fuentes knew what was inside.

Fuentes snatched the envelope from Jack's tight grip. "I'll be the judge of that." Still holding his pistol firmly against Jack's ear, Fuentes tore open the envelope with his free hand and pulled out Jack's notes and the copies he made of the search warrants, affidavits and newspaper articles. He flipped through the various documents Jack possessed. "I'm impressed. You really did your homework didn't you? It's just too bad that I'll have to take possession of all this. Wouldn't want this to get into the wrong hands."

"I'll just get it again. It's public record."

"That's where you're wrong, Jack." Fuentes pulled a document from the inside pocket of his blazer. "This is a Federal Grand Jury subpoena. Perhaps you've seen one before. You know what it's for? I'll tell you. It's for every article or document concerning the Benitez family on file at every library in Miami and Dade County. It also places an order than none of these documents can be released to the public. So you see, Jack. It's going to be quite difficult for you to get what doesn't exist."

Jack stared straight ahead. "I'll inform the authorities. The media. I'll tell them all about your family history."

"Oooooooh, Jack. Stop. You're scaring me." Fuentes laughed hard and poked the barrel even harder into Jack's ear. He stopped laughing. "And who are they going to believe? A fugitive on the run who stole a quarter billion dollars worth of cocaine and wants to claim he was framed by the FBI? Or the FBI agent that tracked his ass down because he was trying to avoid prosecution. Face it. With no documentary evidence, you've got no proof of who I really am. I'm not going to let you ruin my career."

Jack chuckled then broke into laughter. Emery stared at him. "Career? Your career is based on lies. You know who I think is really going to be interested in hearing about your…career?"

"Who would that be, Jack?"

"Gordon Fisher."

Fuentes's smile faded. "Fisher. You've talked to Fisher?"

"Not ten minutes ago."

Fuentes laughed again. "And did former Agent Fisher tell you where he spent two and a half of the past three years?"

Jack didn't answer.

"I didn't think so. Fisher was forced to take a medical retirement three years ago. Up until six months ago, your friend, Agent Fisher, was a patient at Overlook Mental Health Center over in West Palm Beach. He was diagnosed as a manic depressive, I believe it was. His manic episodes included going to his local Wal-Mart, undressing in the produce aisle and singing Michael Jackson tunes while doing the moon walk. Now there's a credible witness." Fuentes chuckled.

Jack shut his eyes tight and squeezed the steering wheel as hard as he could.

"Since you are so into checking records, maybe you could drop in at Overlook on your way to see Fisher and see for yourself what type treatment he's been going through up there." Fuentes laughed. "But then again, that's not public record. Well. Just ask Gordon. I'm sure he'll tell you all about it."

Jack had nothing to say. He felt a pit in his stomach.

"Been a tough day hasn't it, Jack?" Fuentes grinned. "You know what? I almost feel sorry for you. I really do. You know what I'm going to do? I'm not going to arrest you. And I'm not going to arrest your lady friend here for harboring a fugitive. I think you'll do me more good if you're free. For now, anyway. As far as I'm concerned, I didn't even see you today. Let's just say you eluded me. Alright?" Fuentes knew if he arrested him, Jack would squeal like a pig to anyone that would listen. Fuentes needed time to seize every piece of evidence with his name on it. He lowered his pistol and returned it to his holster. He put the documents Jack had copied back into the envelope and held it up so Jack could see it in the rearview mirror. "I'll be holding on to this if you don't mind. You don't mind, do you?"

Jack threw up his hands. "Be my guest."

Fuentes lifted the handle to open his door. He stepped one foot outside. "Oh, Jack. I almost forgot. I thought I'd better ask you again where you hid the cocaine. Per chance you're ready to cooperate."

Jack rolled his eyes. "Excuse me if I don't laugh at your stand-up comedy routine."

"Of course," Fuentes chuckled. "Just thought I would ask. Can't hurt to try." He climbed the rest of the way out of the car. "You folks have a pleasant day. And, Jack. I'm sure we'll see each other again. Soon."

Fuentes stood grinning and watched as Jack backed out of his space and drove out of sight. He chuckled and shook his head. The envelope tucked safely under his arm, he made his way to the metal door twenty feet away at the entrance to the public library.

Subpoena in hand, Fuentes presented his credentials to the Head Supervisor and followed with the subpoena for all documentary evidence and other material relating in whole or in part to the Benitez investigation, family history or any other matter relating in whole or in part to the Benitez name. The subpoena also had an order that the library was barred from releasing any of the same documents to the public and that it should remove any such records from its computer system. The subpoena gave the Miami Public Library one week to comply and it could comply by turning over all said records to Agent Fuentes.

The supervisor advised Fuentes that it would take no more than a day or two to retrieve the requested records. He asked Fuentes to follow him to the computer room where he ran a quick program to pull up all the articles and documents called for in the subpoena. After being certain that he had all the information needed, Fuentes followed the supervisor to the microfiche room. Fuentes watched as the supervisor searched every shelf, drawer, cabinet and desktop in the room. He obviously was concerned. "Is there a problem?"

"I don't understand it. The reference numbers listed on the computer which corresponded to each roll of microfiche you've requested aren't here. They're gone."

Fuentes head jerked upward. "What do you mean they're gone?"

"I don't know. They're gone. They've disappeared. I don't understand where they could be or why anyone would take them."

Fuentes spun toward the door and gritted his teeth. "That son-of-a-bitch!" He flung the door open and bolted out.

"Do you want the records from the other libraries?" the supervisor shouted as he watched Fuentes rush away.

Jack and Emery were twenty miles north of Miami on Interstate 95 by the time Fuentes bolted from the library. Jack held on to the steering wheel with his left hand and reached his right hand down the crotch of his pants.

Emery arched her eyebrows. "Jack. What are you doing?"

Jack pulled a medium size brown envelope from his trousers and flipped it into the backseat. "Always have a backup plan."

Emery looked at the envelope resting on the backseat. "Is that what I think it is?"

Jack smiled. "Uh-huh. Fuentes is probably just now realizing I've got it. I guess he's probably a little pissed off at me right now. Probably changed his mind about not arresting me."

Emery smiled and opened her window to let some fresh air blow in. She reclined her seat and rested her head against the headrest and gradually dozed off.

About two hours later, Jack saw the sign for the Jupiter exit. He turned off and drove the short distance to Highway 1. Turning left onto Highway 1, Jack began looking for Bob's Coffee Shop. Emery remained peacefully asleep, her hair blowing from the open window.

Jack drove slowly looking to his left, but had an uneasy feeling about the whole situation. Between a half and three quarters of a mile up the road on the left sat Bob's Coffee Shop. Jack spied it about a city block before he got there, but decided to drive past it first. He didn't like the feeling in his gut. Parked in the medium sized parking lot, but away from the coffee shop, were three cars with two men in each car drinking coffee. Strange, he thought, that men would be sitting in their cars drinking coffee when they would be much more comfortable inside. The cars they were in also looked official. They were not marked, but obviously were not your normal family sedan. Deciding to drive by the coffee shop, Jack drove about a mile further before turning around and making a second pass. This time he saw another vehicle, a black van with no windows on either side sitting on the opposite side of the road. One female sat in the driver's seat looking directly at the coffee shop. He didn't know what was going on, but he didn't like it. Jack drove two or three miles south on Highway 1 until he found a pay phone on the side of the road next to a rundown service station. He was going to try his best to not use his cell phone unless it was an emergency.

Jack looked for a quarter and found one in the ash tray. He dialed information and got the number for Bob's Coffee Shop and then dialed the number.

"Bob's Coffee Shop," the friendly voice answered. "Bob speaking."

"Hey, Bob," Jack said trying to sound normal. "Is Gordon over there this morning?"

"Fisher? Yeah. Hold on a second."

Jack could hear Bob calling Gordon.

"Yeah," Fisher answered.

"What're you trying to do to me?" Jack asked in a low voice.

"What? Who is this?" Fisher asked.

"You know damn well who it is," Jack shot back.

"Jack? Is that you?"

"What're you trying to do to me?"

Fisher paused. "I have no idea what you're talking about."

"Bullshit!" Jack fired back quickly.

"Hold on, Jack."

"I saw those people out there in their cars. You called 'em, didn't you?"

"Jack, listen. Calm down."

"That's what I thought. Fuentes was right about you. You are crazy. All I wanted to do was talk."

"Who's Fuentes?"

"What?" Jack was very upset. "Fuentes. He's Eric Benitez. The guy I wanted to talk to you about. But I guess that's out of the question now."

"Wait a minute, Jack," Fisher paused. "I know you don't trust me now. But, hell. I don't know you either. How do I know I can trust you? That's why those people are out there. They're not here to arrest you. For all I know, you're part of the Raes organization. Even though it's been twenty years, you still never know who holds a grudge." He paused again. "We can still talk if you want."

"I'll talk over the phone."

"Fine. Whatever makes you comfortable. So you say Benitez is an FBI agent?"

"Yeah."

"They'll take anybody these days." Fisher laughed at his own joke.

Jack wasn't in the mood for humor. "What can you tell me about him?"

"I know that when we busted Ricardo Benitez he was training his two boys to take over his operation one day. They were both twenty, twenty one. Somewhere in there."

"So you're telling me that Eric Fuentes, Eric Benitez, was involved with the drug cartel?"

Fisher snickered. "Up to his eyeballs. At least in my opinion. I just couldn't prove it. There was nothing on paper and no one would testify. I got the old man and that was it. After we convicted Ricardo, Manny, his other boy, went back to Columbia where I guess he still is. Haven't heard much from him. We never knew what happened to Eric until you called this morning. He left Miami and no one ever saw him again." Fisher took a deep breath. "I guess you know about Benitez' mother. What happened to her."

"Yeah. I pulled up some old articles at the library."

"Yeah. It was pretty gruesome. The people Ricardo worked for kept her down there while he was in Miami. They figured he wouldn't do anything stupid while she was still there. Fortunately for the DEA, but not so fortunate for her, Ricardo testified against his boss. They didn't take too kindly to that, and you know the rest of the story."

"Hector Raes killed her?"

"Yeah. He did the dirty work. The guy is cold. I'm telling you, he's got no heart. Benitez has remembered, too. Don't let him fool you. If it takes him a hundred years he'll find Raes. I reckon that may be his plan. Take the coke. Entice Raes up here. That son-of-a-bitch must have really covered up his past really good to get it past the FBI. He must have had some help somewhere."

"I reckon so," Jack said. "But frankly, all I care about now is getting the truth out and vindicating myself."

"How do you propose on doing that?"

"These documents I got. And your story is a start."

"My story? I'm afraid you've got the wrong guy, Jack. I don't mind telling you what I know to help you out, but it shouldn't go any further. I've been living here peaceful now for eight months. I've been out of law enforcement for three years. Nobody's bothered me. I've managed to fit in here. I don't need any trouble. I hate to let you down, but I ain't gonna' be doing any testifying for you or anybody else. I'm through talking. I like living too much."

"So in other words, this conversation we're having is useless."

"I wouldn't put it quite that way. I mean you have the information. You just don't have me saying it. Look. A piece of advice. If you can get them, check his phone records. Wouldn't it be interesting to see who Benitez calls?"

"Yeah. That'd be fine if I had a badge. Somehow I don't think I can get a subpoena."

"You're resourceful, Jack. You'll find a way."

Jack smiled and nodded his head. "Yeah. Thanks for the advice." Jack hung up the phone and got back into his car.

"Who was that?" Emery asked, rubbing her eyes.

"You had a nice nap. You feel better?"

"Much," she said stretching her arms upward and yawning. "Who was that?"

"Gordon Fisher."

"Fisher," Emery said with arched eyebrows. "I thought we were going to meet him at a coffee shop or something."

"Plan got changed while you were sleeping."

"Is he going to be able to help you?"

Jack looked both ways and turned north on Highway 1 when the traffic cleared. "Naah. He doesn't know anything."

Emery looked at Jack with little or no expression. "That's too bad."

"Yeah. A real shame." Jack signaled right, and turned north on Interstate 95.

"Where we going now?"

Jack looked at Emery, but did not smile. "Atlanta."

Emery glanced quickly at Jack and started to smile but did not. "Okay."

~ 15 ~

Atlanta, Georgia

Several weeks had passed since the incident and business at the Marlowe Plumbing Company warehouse had gotten pretty much back to normal. There was still some idle chit chat here and there among the laborers. For the most part, the workers were back into their daily routine.

Jerry, given the amount of years he had worked for the company, was promoted to interim Warehouse Manager until a permanent replacement for Jack could be hired. As Raes had now taken over all decision making functions for the company, he wanted one of his own men in Jack's place. But for the time being, he had no objections to Jerry taking over for a few weeks. Unfortunately, Jerry had the displeasure of a required one on one meeting with Raes where the new, restructured Marlowe Plumbing was described to him. Raes actually just wanted to assure himself that he did not have another Jack Armstrong on his hands. Raes was convinced after the meeting that Jerry was not loyal to Armstrong, but to the company that he had worked for over twenty years. In so many words, Raes described to Jerry how he could pad his retirement should he perform his job just as he was directed. However, should he choose to take the same route as Jack had taken, his twenty plus years would go up in smoke, literally. Raes told him nothing of his operation and its connection with Marlowe Plumbing. He simply told him he was expected to ship and receive all packages in a timely manner and that time was of the essence. He was not to check any packages for quality control. He was simply to send them out to their pre-destined point of delivery.

Jerry smiled and had no problems with his new responsibilities. His paycheck would be fatter and he was promised that it would not decrease when Jack's permanent replacement was hired. The deal was sealed with a firm handshake between Jerry and Raes. When Jerry tried to release the grasp, Raes held on tightly and told an uncertain Jerry how much he was counting on him.

Jerry had worked for Marlowe a very long time and he was very loyal to the company. He would never do anything to jeopardize his livelihood or his looming retirement in about ten years. Jerry was used to working double shifts and he saw no reason to change that now, especially since his income had doubled. He felt he owed it to the company. He also had the strange feeling that something about the company wasn't right. When Raes' associates, now running Marlowe Plumbing, observed the long hours Jerry was putting in, they assumed he was doing it for the company. Those same associates didn't stick around to watch Jerry leave every night.

Every night, very late, when the warehouse was empty, Jerry would check a random sampling of packaged toilets to confirm his suspicions that the warehouse was being used as a distribution point for the storing, shipping and subsequent distribution of billions of dollars worth of cocaine.

Jerry knew that Marlowe Plumbing had been on the verge of bankruptcy when Samuel Marlowe took over the reins. Suddenly, the company seemed to have remarkable financial success, seemingly overnight. What seemed odd to Jerry and other employees was that orders never went up and, in fact, were way down in some quarters. They all wondered how the company had become so successful when there was no evidence to show for it. No one questioned why because they all needed their paychecks. Times were tough and jobs were scarce. Why ask questions? Why upset the apple cart? Why stir up trouble?

Jerry kept his suspicions to himself. He teetered back and forth between telling the FBI or the DEA, or just staying quiet. Every time he thought about telling someone he would remember what happened to Jack and decide to keep his mouth shut. Many times over lunch with his warehouse buddies he wanted to tell them what he believed was going on. But he knew if he did, he could kiss his job goodbye and maybe his life. He liked his pals, but they all had big mouths.

So Jerry maintained his silence and did exactly as Raes directed. He made sure packages destined for certain locations were shipped on time and he confirmed that shipments made it to their destinations with no glitches. He performed his duties admirably and enjoyed the financial rewards that came with it. But somewhere deep within his soul, he knew what he was doing was wrong. Right and wrong played tug of war in his gut. Financial independence on one hand, corruption on the other. Secure jobs and steady paychecks for his friends on one side, deceit and death on the other. He stressed over it with every shipment. He wondered how many lives would be destroyed every time a package was marked cleared for shipping.

Night after night Jerry would leave the warehouse late and drive for an hour or so just thinking about his situation. He put all his friends in his place and tried to play out what they would do but he never came to any logical answer or conclusion. He would lay in bed countless numbers of sleepless nights and pray about what he should do, but no answers came, only feelings of guilt and anguish along with a huge burden to bear.

Like clockwork, Jerry arrived at work every morning earlier than anyone else. Willing, but not eager, he did what was demanded of him. He performed his duties. He executed all tasks without complaint. But his mind and heart were tortured. After days and nights of constant worry, he came to the conclusion that a pulse and a paycheck were better than life on the run and the fear of death that Jack was now experiencing. He figured if he could make it until his retirement eight or ten years down the road everything would be okay. In the meantime, he would have to live with himself. He would have to lay down every night and try to go to sleep. Right now he did not know if he could do either.

~ 16 ~

The old saying goes, red sky at night, sailor's delight. Red sky at morning, sailors take warning. The eastern sky was a dull red just before sunrise. The rays barely cut through the thick clouds that gathered overhead in northern Florida. The rain had not yet begun to fall but was unmistakably imminent.

Emery looked down at the red needle now edging painfully close to the empty line on the gasoline indicator. She was excited to be getting back to Atlanta and Jack was grabbing some well deserved shut-eye for once. They had taken their sweet time getting back to Atlanta, hoping to throw anyone off their tail. She didn't want to stop for anything, but the last thing they needed was to run out of gas. Besides, she was beginning to get hungry and the thought of another Twinkie, which was their regular breakfast of late, made her nauseous. Jack only wanted to stop when it was absolutely necessary. That meant for gas and nature calls. It was expected that emptying of one's bladder would be timed at the same intervals as filling up the gas tank.

Emery was hungry and the car needed gas, so she started looking for signs where the two tasks could be completed in one stop. Driving north on Interstate 75, she was about ten miles south of the Georgia state line. The area she was in now was very rural and she hoped a tall sign of some sort would catch her attention advertising a hot, homemade breakfast and gas to go. She thought about getting off at the next exit she saw to get back on I-75 south and returning the ten or twelve miles to White Springs, where she had seen several fast food places which also sold gasoline. But she figured the interstate always seemed to have at least one or two places at every exit. So she decided to drive on and let Jack catch a few more minutes of sleep. He looked so peaceful, finally. Emery looked at him all reclined in the passenger seat with his arms folded across his chest, his beard almost full now. She smiled, then brushed the hair away from his eyes with her right hand.

The first droplets of rain tapped lightly on the windshield. Not enough to turn the wipers on, but the red glint from the sun through the clouds had all but disappeared and given way to a darker more formidable veil of cover. Emery did not like the feeling she had of driving head on into the thick black cloak of gloomy weather yet to come. Better, she thought, to find a place for gas and food and then let Jack take over the driving. She grasped the wheel tightly with both hands and scooted up in her seat in anticipation of thunder, lightning and heavy rain. She watched as the luminous green signs passed by, informing motorists of what service stations and restaurants lay ahead at the next exit. Something about Big Bubba's Grits and Stuff just did not appeal to her. She would rather navigate in a driving rain than sample the cuisine at a place called Big Bubba's Grits and Stuff.

She watched as the needle got dangerously closer and closer to the red E. The green sign said the next exit was for Jennings, Florida. Emery prayed something would be there because she didn't think the car would make it much further. A half mile before the exit, she smiled when she saw the sign for Cracker Barrel, a warming natural landmark on southern interstates. She knew it would clean, open, and best of all there would most likely be a gas station close by.

The rain pelted down slightly harder as she turned off the exit and onto the two lane highway, driving the half block to the Cracker Barrel entrance. She flicked on the windshield wiper once to wipe away the few droplets that had collected. She turned it off as she pulled into a parking space on the side of the restaurant. It was early morning and not surprisingly there were quite a few cars already parked. Emery turned the key and cut the motor off. With the hum of the engine gone and the car jerking slightly when she parked it, Jack stirred but did not wake.

Emery jostled his shoulder. "Jack. Jack."

He shifted again but refused to wake.

Emery lifted Jack's left eyelid and peered inside. "You in there?" She let it go and it flapped shut.

He moved slightly.

She grabbed his shoulder and shook it back and forth. "Jack," she said louder. "Wake up! It's breakfast time. Time to get up. Rise and shine."

One eye popped open. Jack lifted his head and then the other eye unsealed itself. He rubbed them both. "Where are we? Are we in Atlanta?"

"No. We're still a few hours away. But I was starving and we needed gas. Don't you have to go to the bathroom? It's been at least twelve hours."

"Yeah. I'm starving too." Jack looked around. "Cracker Barrel? Is there anywhere else?"

"You don't like Cracker Barrel? Everybody likes Cracker Barrel. You're un-American if you don't like Cracker Barrel."

Jack rubbed his eyes again and looked around. "I reckon this will do." He got out of the car and tucked his shirt in. Brushing his hair with his hands, he looked up at the dark clouds moving rapidly closer. "Looks like a storm's a' brewing."

Emery closed the driver's side door. "Uh-huh. Let's get inside before it decides to open up on us."

Jack got to the glass door entrance first and opened it for Emery. "Thank you."

"You're welcome," Jack said, stepping inside and past the cash register.

Emery headed for the small hostess' booth to put her name in and was told immediate seating was available. Jack headed for the store section that had all the neat gifts and food items. "Don't you want breakfast?"

Jack turned to Emery. "First things first. Gotta' get some of their taffy. Just order me some eggs, bacon and coffee."

Emery nodded and followed the hostess to their table. She picked up the menu. Jack picked up a box of vanilla taffy and decided he would splurge and buy another box when they left.

Emery ordered breakfast for both of them and waited for Jack. Jack purchased his taffy, then washed his hands before finding Emery and joining her at their table.

"What time is it?" Jack asked.

Emery looked at her watch. "A little before seven."

"What did you order me?"

"Just what you asked for. Eggs, bacon and coffee."

"Do you know how long it's been since I had a good breakfast?" Jack asked.

"How long?"

Jack thought about it and laughed. "I have no idea. I normally don't eat eggs or bacon.   Cholesterol is bad for you, but it just sounded really good."

"You know eggs got a bad rap for nothing. They're actually really good for you. The bacon on the other hand..."

Jack looked at the menu. "Have we got enough money? I know we must be running pretty low by now."

"We've got to eat, Jack. We're fine. Once we get back to Atlanta we'll be fine."

The rain fell harder outside as the dark clouds rolled overhead. A slap of thunder rumbled not too far in the distance.

The very pleasant waitress brought their orders with a smile and hoped they would enjoy their breakfast. Both stared at their meals, not knowing where to start with the plentiful eggs and bacon overflowing on both plates. Emery looked at Jack with a huge grin that quickly faded when she glanced out the picture windows. She put her fork down without taking a bite. She lightly put it on her plate and covered her eyes like she would if the sun were glaring through the window. But the sun was covered by thick gray clouds.

Jack stared at Emery as he took a bite of eggs. "What is it? What's wrong? Is something wrong with your breakfast?"

"It's the police. They just drove up outside," she said quietly, her head still down.

Jack turned quickly to see two burly deputies, with beer guts that hung precariously over their belts, exiting their cruiser. They sat with their guns dangling from their belts, hoping all would see and be impressed. Jack figured they were probably someone's cousins who won the election. Neither looked like rocket scientists, but both were big and sometimes size spoke louder than smart. He turned back quickly and looked at Emery.

"Eat your breakfast. Just act natural. They probably just came in to eat breakfast or get coffee."

The two deputies walked into the entrance. One walked toward the bathroom as the other approached the counter.

"Hey, Bubba!" A slightly overweight waitress at the front of the dining room greeted the deputy.

Jack could hear their conversation and couldn't help but chuckle under his breath at the appropriate name.

"Hey, Charlene," said Bubba.

"What'll it be for you and Junior this mornin'?" Charlene asked.

Emery smiled at Jack. "I wonder if the sheriff's name is Forrest Gump?"

Jack smiled and took bite of bacon.

"Gonna have the special just like always. I reckon Junior'll want the same."

Charlene put the pencil back behind her ear and told Bubba to have a seat and she'd call him when it was ready.

In a few minutes, Junior emerged from the bathroom and joined Bubba, who was standing next to a juke box adjacent to the counter. Bubba searched his pockets for change and borrowed two quarters from Junior. They both agonized over whether to play Brad Paisley or Alan Jackson. Brad Paisley won by a coin toss.

Cracker Barrel was not very crowded on this particular day. Less than half full, Bubba and Junior could have sat anywhere they wanted. They plopped down in a booth right next to Jack and Emery.

Bubba glanced at Emery as he shook his silverware loose from the napkin. "How you folks today?"

Jack nodded his head but didn't look at Bubba or Junior.

Junior glanced and smiled at Jack and Emery who were trying as best they could to act natural. Jack chomped on bacon and Emery sipped some coffee.

"You folks from around here?" Junior asked, trying to friendly.

"No," Jack answered.

"Sort of," Emery said simultaneously with Jack.

"We've been in Florida for a couple days, but it was just business," Jack attempted to explain, without looking at the two deputies.

Bubba looked at Jack hard.

"Uh-huh." Bubba paused but continued to look at Jack. He

rubbed his chin for a moment.

"You look real familiar. Have I seen you somewhere before?"

"I don't think so," Jack said quickly.

"You ain't even looked at him. How would you know if you never seen him before?" Junior badgered Jack.

Jack peered at Bubba very slowly then quickly went back to eating. Bubba and Junior looked at Jack, both their brows furled.

Just as Bubba was about to make another inquiry, their breakfast arrived. Pancakes, bacon, sausage, grits and toast in a bed of grease. Bubba took his fork then cut everything up and mixed it all together.

Junior looked at Bubba's plate and puckered his face like he'd sucked on a lemon. "I swear I don't know how you keep from having a heart attack. Looks more like something my old coon dog coughed up."

Jack and Emery looked at the plate and both agreed with Junior.

"Don't know what you're missing until you try it. All these flavors mixed into one. Ain't nothing like it." Bubba took a huge bite he had scooped up in his spoon. Junior looked away. Jack and Emery just stared at each other.

Bubba kept eating. Yellow streaks from the eggs dripped down the side of his chin. Smacking his food, he glanced again at Jack. "You sure we haven't met somewhere?"

Jack took another bite and shook his head from side to side. "Never been here before in my life."

"What's the name?" Junior asked, eating with much better manners than his partner.

"Jack," he answered without thinking. He and Emery glanced at each other at the same time.

Bubba looked at Junior then at Jack. "Jack who? I know lots of Jacks."

Emery stared at Jack.

"Crockett. Jack Crockett." Jack stared back at Emery, who pretended to enjoy a bite of pancakes. Her heart pounded hard.

Bubba glared at Jack. "Don't know no Crocketts around these parts, but I gotta say you do look awfully familiar. Don't he Junior?"

"What car you drivin' out there, Jack?" Junior asked.

Jack nervously ate another bite and his tension was beginning to show. "The green Ford Focus. Why? You gonna arrest me for not driving a pick-up?" Jack's attempt at a joke fell on unappreciative ears.

"Not gonna arrest you for what you drive. Maybe there's another reason to," Bubba said, staring straight into Jack's eyes. "Do we got another reason to arrest you, Jack?"

"Excuse me?" Jack said, now staring squarely at Bubba.

"Junior," Bubba said. "Run out to the car and get that picture from the dashboard."

Jack's heart sunk.

"Look. I don't know what the problem is, but you boys have got no right to hold us here without probable cause," Emery stated matter of factly, while sliding out of her side of the booth.

"Ain't nobody holdin' you folks ma'am," Junior said, as he passed behind Emery on his way outside.

Bubba looked at Emery. "Ma'am. I know all about probable cause. I don't need you to tell me what it is. I may look big and dumb to you and I may work for a small town Sheriff, but I got reason to believe that Jack Crockett here ain't who he says he is. And although I ain't holdin' you here against your will, I do have a job to do. And Jack here looks an awful lot like a photo I've got in the cruiser. And I don't need probable cause to look at that picture to see if Jack Crockett is really Jack Crockett." Bubba finished the last few bites on his plate and then wiped his mouth with the stack of napkins beside his coffee cup. "Why don't you folks just relax and we'll wait on Junior. Shouldn't take more than a minute or so and hopefully you'll be on your way to wherever it is you're going."

Jack and Emery looked at each other. Both slid back to their seats in the middle of the booth. Bubba leaned back in his booth and picked up his coffee cup, sipping from it slowly.

Jack and Emery watched as Junior crossed in front of the windows eyeing the three by five inch photograph. Junior re-entered Cracker Barrel and made his way toward Bubba. Junior slid into his side of the seat and handed Bubba the photo. "This ain't him, Bubba. This guy in the picture ain't got no beard."

Bubba looked at the photo and looked at Jack. He squinted his eyes. Jack and Emery tried to look at the photo, but could not see it from the angle Bubba held it.

Bubba looked at Junior and smiled. "You're right, Junior. The boy in the picture ain't got no beard."

Jack smiled. A sense of relief flooded over him. He was glad he had not shaved a few days earlier when his new beard started to get itchy.

Bubba turned the photograph toward Junior. "Look at it real close, Junior."

Junior leaned forward and narrowed his eyes to get a better look. He eyed the snapshot for several seconds then leaned back. "Uh-huh. What?"

Bubba covered the face and chin on the photograph and showed it again to Junior. "Look now."

Junior leaned forward and eyed the photograph. His eyes widened when he realized it. "It's him, ain't it?"

Jack's head dipped toward the floor.

Junior pulled his weapon and bolted out of his seat and around to the other side to block Jack from leaving. Bubba remained in his seat cool, calm and collected. He looked again at the photo, and then at Jack.

"I'm afraid I'm gonna have to haul you in, Mr. Jack Armstrong. Seems the Federal boys up in Atlanta are lookin' for you, matter of fact. We just got this photo in this mornin'. Seems you been missin' a while, but for some reason they're just now gettin' around to askin' for help findin' you. Seems our timin' turned out to be pretty good. Least ways for us. Wouldn't you say, Jack?"

Jack took a deep breath. "Look. You fellas got me. But she's got nothing to do with any of this." Jack motioned toward Emery.

"Maybe so." Bubba said. "But we gotta detain her until we can determine that for ourselves. I'm sure you can understand that."

"She's done nothing. Why can't you just let her go?"

"It's okay, Jack. We'll get it all straightened out," Emery said.

"Listen to her, Jack. She seems to have a level head on her shoulders," Bubba said, as he got up from his seat and came around the tables to meet Junior. "You wanna stand up for me Jack, so I can get these cuffs on? You ain't gonna give me no trouble are ya'?"

Jack rose and put his hands behind his back. "I'm not gonna give you any trouble." He looked back as Bubba slapped the handcuffs on his left hand. "Is this really necessary? I'm not gonna try and run."

"'Fraid so," Bubba said. "Department policy. You wouldn't want me to get fired would ya'?"He smiled and finished cuffing Jack.

"I don't think your brother-in-law's daddy's cousin would fire you would he?" Jack joked.

"Huh yuk yuk yuk yuk," Bubba mimicked a redneck laugh. "You're hilarious, Jack. A real card. I may be a southern redneck sheriff's deputy, but I'm gonna be goin' home tonight and sleepin' in my own bed. I reckon you'll be sleepin' in the county jail with an inmate or two who might want you to be their girlfriend."

Jack's slight smile faded. "Touché."

"You want me to cuff the lady?" Junior asked Bubba.

Bubba looked at Emery. "Naw. She's fine. We got no reason to cuff her. She ain't on the list we got." He motioned for Junior to escort Jack and Emery from Cracker Barrel. "Let's get 'em down to the station."

Outside, Bubba turned and walked toward the Ford Focus while Junior began escorting Jack and Emery toward their cruiser. "Where you goin'?" Junior shouted to Bubba.

"The e-mail from the Feds said Armstrong was carrying a brown envelope in his car. We're supposed to seize it and hold it for them FBI boys."

Jack glanced at Emery. He felt his defense slipping slowly through his fingers. His heart pounded hard and his stomach turned sour.

Junior softly pushed Jack and Emery toward the cruiser and then helped them both into the back seat. He left the door ajar and waited for Bubba to return.

Jack and Emery watched as Bubba returned empty handed. Bubba walked to the door that was half opened and squatted down to talk to Jack. "Where's the envelope, Mr. Armstrong?"

Jack looked at Emery, who gave him a quick wink, then back at Bubba. "I'm afraid I don't know what you're talking about."

Bubba smiled. "Look, Jack. I don't particularly care one way or the other. But them FBI boys up in Atlanta sent us an e-mail that said you was carryin' an envelope with some secret shit that I could give a rat's ass about. But I wouldn't be doin' my job proper like if I told them that a search of your car turned up nothin', now would I?"

"You searched my car already. I have no idea what you or the FBI is talking about."

Still squatting, Bubba smiled. He reached in his pocket, retrieved his sunglasses and put them on. "Well, Jack. I reckon you've got a point. I reckon if the FBI wants to come lookin' for themselves, they can do just that." Bubba stood and turned to Junior. "Let's take 'em on in, Junior."

Junior ran to the driver's side of the cruiser and hopped in. Bubba shut the back door and climbed into the passenger side. "If you folks don't mind, we're just gonna keep your car secured here for right now. I locked it up. If everything comes back clear on the lady, Junior will bring her back and she can be on her way. If not, we'll have to impound the vehicle. It'll save you 'bout a hundred and fifty bucks if we can just leave it here. Impound fee and all. You know?"

The county jail was a one room, red brick building with two cells much like the jail made famous in Mayberry, North Carolina. The difference was this building was over a hundred years old and inside it was damp and dingy. The one window air conditioning unit that worked was situated all the way across the room from where the two cells were, causing most of the cool air to be lost somewhere in the middle of the room where the Sheriff's desk sat. There were also a couple of rotary fans whirring from their places on the floor.

Jack and Emery sat on the lumpy cots inside separate but side by side cells. Bubba and Junior sat on opposite sides with their feet propped up on the desk. Bubba had already put in a call to the Florida Department of Law Enforcement to run a criminal history on Emery to determine if they had anything to hold her on. Jack and Emery both wiped drops of sweat from their foreheads. The mildew smell in the building coupled with the stifling heat almost made them nauseous.

Jack stood and walked two steps to the black iron bars. "Bubba!" he called out. "It's been an hour already. Can't you call again and see if they can hurry? They've got no reason for holding her here. She's not done a thing."

Bubba peered over the top of the hunting magazine he was either reading or looking at the pictures in. "I'm sure they'll call when they've checked." Bubba returned to his magazine. "Oh. Them FBI boys should be here anytime now, too. You called them didn't you, Junior?"

Junior woke from his half doze. "Huh? Yeah. Yeah." He rubbed his eyes. "I called them as soon as we got back."

Bubba looked at Jack. "You just take it easy there, Jack. Shouldn't be long now."

Jack sat back down on the cot and buried his head into his hands. Even though he was sitting in a cold, moldy cell, he couldn't help but like Bubba and Junior. If he had to eventually get caught, he was glad it was by two country boys who were as friendly as the day was long. He figured it could have been a lot worse.

Emery sat on her cot which backed up to the bars adjacent to Jack's cell. She leaned back against the bars, her back to Jack. Her eyes shut, sweat building on her face from the stifling heat, she thought about the predicament she was now in. She knew she would be free soon because her name would not show up on any NCIC report or any other network of law enforcement criminal record. But that did not keep her from being miserable in the environment she now found herself in. She opened her eyes and watched as a cockroach made its way underneath the sheet on her cot. She wondered how many other unseen critters currently shared her cell.

Bubba shifted his butt in the hard wooden chair that had a lime green cushion. It had been flattened over the years by other oversized butts so it didn't provide much in the way of cushioning. It just stayed there year after year because nobody ever thought to throw it away. Some joked that the cushion dated back to pre-Civil War days. Bubba, feet still propped on the desk, crossed one leg on top of the other. "You see this Junior?" Bubba flipped back a page or two in his magazine.

"See what?"

"This new contraption they got fer duck huntin'."

Junior, obviously excited about any new duck hunting paraphernalia, pulled his feet from the desk and leaned forward in his chair. He bent his ear toward Bubba. "What is it?"

"Says here they got," Bubba started, just as the phone rang. "Hold on Junior. Lemme' get that."

Junior sat back in his chair. He was truly upset the phone had rung just as he was about to learn new information about duck hunting.

"Sheriff's Office," Bubba announced. "Yeah. Hold on. Lemme' find a pencil and somethin' to write on." Bubba found a pencil lying on the left hand side of the desk. "What's that?" Bubba pitched the pencil back on the desk and flicked some paper out of the way. "Uh-huh. Uh-huh. Yeah. Yep. Uh-huh." Bubba glanced over to Emery and Jack who were both watching him. "Uh-huh. Uh-huh. Yes sir. Yes sir. Will do. Bye now." Bubba hung up the phone. "Well, Jack. I do believe you were right about your female friend here. The state ran all them checks and she's negatory all the way. Looks like she'll be on her way momentarily." Bubba uncrossed his legs and removed his feet from the desk. "Unfortunately for you, Jack, I'm afraid you're gonna have to stay just a little while longer. Least while 'til them FBI boys arrive."

By now, Jack and Emery were both standing at the front of their respective cells, each grasping the cold, vertical bars. "Hey, Bubba," Jack called out.

Bubba was filling out Emery's release form. "Yeah. What is it, Jack?"

"I just wanted to say I appreciate you treating us fairly. Ya' know? Calling about Emery. Getting that taken care of pretty quickly and everything."

Bubba looked up and smiled at Jack. "All in a day's work for us rednecks down here."

Jack couldn't help but smile.

Bubba stood up and got the key to Emery's cell from the middle drawer of the desk. "Junior, I want you to take Miss Carson back to her vehicle. Alright? Drop her off and make sure she gets on her way. Understand?" he said, as he opened her cell door.

"Ten-four." Junior stood and waited for Emery.

"Emery," Jack called to her as Bubba escorted her away from the cell.

Emery turned around as did Bubba.

"Can I talk to her a minute in private?" Jack asked Bubba.

Bubba looked at him and then at Junior. "I reckon. But make it quick."

Emery stepped softly back to Jack's cell and stood facing him on the opposite side of the bars.

Jack stared deep into her eyes and whispered. "The film. Where is it?"

Bubba stood only a couple feet away and tried to eavesdrop. Emery glanced quickly back over her shoulder at him. "Don't worry," she whispered back.

"You ready, Miss Carson?" Bubba asked. He didn't like the whispers.

Emery turned to Bubba. "Yeah. Hold on just a second."

"Hurry it up now," Bubba barked.

Emery turned back to Jack. "What do you want me to do? I don't know what to do."

"I don't know. There's not much you can do. It's over for now. You go on back to Atlanta and stay with a friend. I'm sure Fuentes is on his way. I reckon I'll be there before nightfall. You shouldn't go back to your place until this is all over. Alright?"

"It's time to go, Miss Carson," Junior said, walking up to her. He gently took her elbow, but she jerked it away from him.

"I don't need your help, thank you!" she said, turning from Jack and walking toward the door.

Junior pulled his arm back and looked at Bubba who smiled and shrugged his shoulders. "Yes ma'am. Just tryin' to help."

Emery opened the door, then stopped and looked back at Jack. She ran back and gave him a quick kiss through the cold bars. She smiled, then walked outside into a slight drizzle.

"Would you like an umbrella?" Junior asked, following her outside.

"I don't need an umbrella!" she shot back.

Junior looked back at Bubba, raised up the collar on his green raincoat and shook his head, then closed the door.

Bubba looked at Jack and smiled. "You got a firecracker there, Jack. Is she always that pleasant?"

Jack stared at the door. "She's just tired, Bubba. That's all. Really tired." Jack sat down on his cot and buried his head into his hands.

Hours had passed since Emery had been released. The rain fell harder outside and the gray overcast skies hinted that it was settled in for a while. Jack lay on his back on the lumpy, dusty cot. The back of his right hand covered his eyes. The other hand rested across his belly. He tried as best as he could to doze off, but the surroundings refused to let him. The only sound he heard was the continuous hum and clinking of the air conditioner that might as well have been turned off. Lightning struck somewhere close by and was followed by a deafening clap of thunder. He jumped slightly but maintained his position on his cot. Clearing his mind of all negative thoughts was also not an option. He couldn't help but think if the evidence he had uncovered was gone, he was going to do hard time. There would be nothing to vindicate him. Even though he had fallen in love with Emery, he wasn't sure if he could trust her. He honestly did not know who she really was. She seemed to always know more than she should. Fuentes always seemed to find them. She seemed to have an answer for everything and she kept insisting they go back. It didn't add up, but he wanted to believe that she was on his side.

Outside, another lightning bolt and ensuing drawn out rumble was followed by the shutting sound of two car doors. Jack didn't stir but his heart raced knowing Fuentes had arrived and his time had expired. Bubba, who was catching a couple of winks, put his feet back on the floor and attempted to straighten out his shirt. He looked in Jack's direction.

"That must be Junior and your FBI friends. Took 'em long enough."

Jack twirled his fingers in a circle twice toward Bubba but remained on his back, his face covered by his hand. He heard the front door open and the sound of umbrellas opening and closing several times to shake off the excess precipitation.

"You must be the Sheriff."

Jack narrowed his eyes at the sound of the accent. It didn't sound like Fuentes, he thought to himself.

"No, sir. The Sheriff's outta' pocket for a day or two. I'm acting in his stead until he returns. Name is Bubba Parker. I'm one of his deputies. Pleased to make your acquaintance." Bubba paused and looked across the visitor's shoulder toward the door. "Did my deputy come with you fellas? I thought I heard him outside."

"No. Just us."

Jack listened to the tone of the accent and shot up from his cot. Standing across from Bubba and next to the door was Guido and Sarducci, all decked out in suits, ties, and beige raincoats. They both looked at Jack and smiled when they saw him rise from his cot. Jack backed away from the bars toward his cell wall. Bubba watched, but did not quite understand Jack's reaction.

"I take it you boys are Feds," Bubba said, turning back to Guido and Sarducci.

They both shook their heads affirmatively. "That's right," Sarducci said. He did all of the talking since his mastery of the English language was far superior to Guido's.

"And you boys are here to take custody of Mr. Armstrong over there?" Bubba said, motioning toward the cell.

"That's right," Sarducci answered.

"Have you got the papers?" Bubba asked.

"Papers?" Sarducci looked puzzled.

Jack breathed a sigh of relief.

"Yes, sir. I need some type of release papers or forms from you boys saying you are taking custody of the prisoner."

Jack was beginning to like and appreciate Bubba a lot more than he did at the Cracker Barrel.

"Can't just let him walk out of here with no written notification, boys. Policy and all." Bubba stood firm.

Jack smiled and walked toward the front of the cell. Guido and Sarducci looked back and forth between Bubba and Jack.

Watching Jack the whole time, Sarducci reached inside his raincoat and into the interior of his lapel, pulling out several sheets of paper. "I believe this is what you're looking for, Sheriff." Sarducci stared at Jack, a large grin on his face.

"I'm not the Sheriff, but that's alright." Bubba took the papers and read them over. "Looks official to me." Bubba tossed the papers on the desk, reached inside the drawer, and pulled out the key to Jack's cell.

"Wait a minute, Bubba!" Jack shouted. "I'm not gonna waive extradition."

Guido and Sarducci chuckled.

"You ain't what, Jack?" Bubba asked.

"You heard me. I'm not waiving extradition."

Bubba stood still, key in hand. "Extradition's got nothing to do with this. These boys are the FBI and they got proper papers and all for me to release you into their custody."

Jack's heart raced. He could feel the rhythm of the beats inside his head. "I'm wanted in Georgia. I'm in Florida. I've got a right to not waive my extradition to Georgia."

Bubba stepped a couple of feet toward the cell. "This is a federal case, Jack. It's got nothing to do with Florida. These boys are taking custody of you and your effects. And I ain't got no say so in the matter. Do you understand that?"

"I'm not going. I'm not waiving extradition. I have rights. Check your law book. Call the District Attorney. See if I don't have a right to refuse extradition."

Bubba looked at Guido and Sarducci and then back at Jack.

"Sheriff," Sarducci said. "We are taking custody of Mr. Armstrong. This is a federal matter and Mr. Armstrong has no rights one way or the other concerning extradition. As Federal Agents, we are authorized to cross state lines and take custody of prisoners in federal matters. Now, are you going to release him to us or are we going to have to charge you with obstruction of justice?"

Bubba looked at Jack, not sure of what he could or couldn't do.

"They're not agents, Bubba!" Jack shouted. "They're not FBI Agents. They're two bit thugs from Columbia. Listen to his accent. You ever heard of an FBI Agent with an accent like that?"

Bubba smiled. "In Florida? Actually yeah, I have."

Sarducci smiled. Guido followed suit.

"They're not Agents, Bubba! You gotta believe me!" Jack shouted in desperation as he thought quickly for anything to help himself. "Their credentials! Check their credentials! I'm telling you, they're not Agents!"

The smiles faded from Guido's and Sarducci's face.

Bubba looked at Guido and Sarducci. "You fellas have creds?"

Guido and Sarducci looked at each other, then simultaneously pulled black leather identifications with gold badges on the front from inside their coat pockets. They both flipped them open toward Bubba and revealed the large blue FBI imprinted upon the backing.

Jack grabbed the bars tightly and squeezed his face through the bars. He was stunned. His mind raced. "They're lying, Bubba! Ask 'em! Ask 'em!"

Bubba interrupted. "I'm not gonna ask 'em anything. I think you're just stalling for more time. They showed me papers. They showed me their creds like you wanted. I think that's enough. Don't you?"

Jack backed away from the bars. "They're not who they say they are. You gotta believe me. They're gonna kill me as soon as you let me out of here."

Sarducci laughed. "You see what we've had to put up with, Sheriff? The man is crazy. He's a lunatic that will do anything to keep from being properly tried in a court of law."

Bubba looked back and forth between Jack and the Columbians.

"They'll kill me, Bubba! Just as sure as you're standing there, they are going to kill me. They killed my brother. Ask 'em."

Bubba turned to Guido and Sarducci.

Sarducci smiled. "We didn't kill his brother. The mob killed his brother in retaliation for what this man did to the mob," Sarducci said, motioning toward Jack.

Jack sat down on his cot. "You want my blood on your hands, Bubba? If you let me go, that's what's gonna happen. These men are hired killers. You're gonna have to answer to the FBI when I turn up dead. Think about it, Bubba. The newspapers. The real FBI. Your boss. You want to have to deal with all that?"

Bubba was thoroughly confused. In his eight or ten years of law enforcement, he had never dealt with something like this. Nine out of ten calls were traffic related. "I don't know. I'm not sure what I can or can't do."

"Sheriff," Sarducci said. "If you refuse to release Mr. Armstrong, I'll have no choice but to charge you with obstruction of justice."

Bubba looked at Sarducci then at Jack. "What was it you were saying about extradition, Jack?"

Jack smiled. "That I refuse to waive it."

Bubba put the key to Jack's cell back into his pocket, then turned to Guido and Sarducci. "I'm afraid I got no choice but to keep Mr. Armstrong here until the district judge is in town and can make the proper call. I wouldn't want to break the law or anything."

Sarducci was livid. "I am putting you on notice right now that you will be charged with obstruction of justice for defying a court order for Mr. Armstrong's release to us!" A vein bulged from his neck as he shouted at Bubba.

Bubba shrugged his shoulders. "I'm sorry, gentlemen. If you truly are FBI Agents, you have my sincerest apologies. But if I'm gonna make a mistake I'd rather it be one where nobody gets hurt. And by waiting a couple of days until the judge is in town will assure that."

Sarducci frowned. "And when will this district judge be in town?"

"Day after tomorrow," Bubba answered.

Sarducci frowned at Bubba, then walked over to Jack's cell and peered inside. "You may have won the battle my friend, but the war rages on."

Jack stared up into Sarducci's eyes but said nothing.

"We shall meet again on another day." Sarducci winked at Jack, turned and walked back toward the door. He picked up both umbrellas and handed Guido one. "Thank you, Sheriff," Sarducci said to Bubba, as they walked out into the rain. They knew Raes would be upset that they didn't kill Bubba, but killing cops was not part of the plan. They had waited this long. They were sure they would get Jack in just a matter of time.

"Thanks, Bubba," Jack said.

Bubba walked over to the cell. "You better hope to hell you're telling me the truth. If I find out you're lying about all this, you'll wish you went with those boys."

"I have no reason to lie, Bubba. It doesn't matter how much stalling I do or don't do. I'm gonna have to face a judge and jury. But if I go with those boys there, I'll never see a courtroom."

Bubba stared at Jack. He had no expression. "I hope, for your sake, what you're saying is true. The district judge, he don't take kindly to liars."

Jack peered up at Bubba. They stared at each other for several seconds with straight faces. Bubba turned and walked back to his desk and propped his feet back on top of it. He retrieved his hunting magazine and took up where he left off.

Jack laid back down on the bunk, thankful he had made it one more night.

Fuentes rested his chin upon his folded arms that were laid on top of his white rental car. He stared out at the aqua colored Atlantic Ocean and watched as children frolicked in the warm rays of the South Florida sunshine. His worried expression was as evident as the bright colored sails on the catamarans that drifted by in the medium-sized waves. Pondering what he would tell SAC McMann, his thoughts were shattered by the ringing of his cell phone.

"Yeah. Yeah. It's me. Where are you?" Fuentes waited for an answer. "I don't have time to talk right now. It's all lies anyway." He peered out at the ocean. "Yeah. Well. Who are you going to believe? I'm telling you it's all a front. The man is smart. I'll give him that. But in the long run it makes no difference. I don't care what he found out about my past, I'm going to get him. If he gets silenced or destroyed in the process, then so be it. It's all on him." Fuentes watched and snickered as two teenagers attempted to surf in the small waves. "I guess I'll be heading north then. Don't wait up for me."

Thunderstorms had given way to a moonlit and starry night in Jennings where the county jail was located. There was even a slight chill in the air with the clearing skies. Jack had just finished a plateful of fried chicken, green beans, mashed potatoes, and cornbread, just like Aunt Bea would have made. Not your usual jailhouse meal. But this was a small town with one Sheriff and two deputies. If nothing else, they treated their occasional inmates like humans. That meant a nice warm meal from Aunt Billie's Diner across the street from the jail.

It wasn't often that they had prisoners stay overnight. Usually, if that was called for, prisoners were transported down to Lake City. But Lake City's jail was full and couldn't hold any more that night. Bubba made an executive decision and determined, since it would be no more than a day or two, they were capable of watching after and taking care of one prisoner for as long, or short, as was needed. He thought about calling Tallahassee to see if they could accommodate one more but he'd kind of gotten used to the excitement of boarding a federal prisoner. So he decided against it and settled in for the long night ahead. He sent Junior home to get some sleep because he would be relieving Bubba at six the next morning. And they would be working twelve hour shifts until the judge made a decision on Jack's immediate future.

Jack lay on his cot and looked at the stars through the small barred window in the back of his cell. He could hear the sound of cars passing by on the two lane highway just north of the town. He listened to the faint sound of a train whistle somewhere in the distance. He wished he was on it. He wondered where Emery was right now and what she was doing. He wondered how long it would be before Fuentes got there. He silently laughed to himself that he successfully argued his extradition case to Bubba while knowing nothing about extradition laws. All he knew was he had bought a few extra hours, and maybe even a day or so, to try and figure out how he was going to get out of this mess and prove his case. He knew he couldn't do it from the jail cell.

Bubba took the red checkered cloth napkin from the dish that sat on his desk. He closed his eyes and sniffed the aroma of the freshly baked apple pie his mother had dropped by ten minutes earlier. A small steady stream of steam rose from the still hot apples.

"What's that smell, Bubba?"

Bubba glanced at Jack. "Just what you think it is. I don't reckon you'd want a slice, would ya'?"

Jack sat up and saw the apple pie. "You didn't hear me say this. But I do believe I would plead guilty to whatever they wanted me to for a slice of that pie. I haven't eaten like this in years."

"Sit tight. I'll go see if I can't dig up another plate somewhere."

Jack stood up and approached the bars. He literally had to wipe the corner of his mouth at the thought of what his palate was about to sample. He watched as Bubba disappeared toward the back of the jailhouse. He waited for a minute or two. His eyes danced between the apple pie sitting on Bubba's desk and the dark area Bubba had gone to try and find a plate. "Bubba? You back there?" Jack shouted.

No answer came from the back.

Jack's pulse quickened. "Bubba! Where'd you go? Did you find that plate?" Jack backed away from the bars.

Emerging from the darkly lit back area of the jailhouse was an intruder with a woman's stocking stretched tightly over his head. The intruder held Bubba firmly around the neck with one arm and with the other, shoved a black pistol under his ear. His nose flattened by the hosiery, the intruder forced Bubba toward his desk.

"Where's the key?" the intruder demanded.

Bubba did not answer. The intruder shoved the pistol even harder into the back of Bubba's ear.

"Where is it?"

Jack backed away and buried himself into the back stone wall of his cell. His heart raced uncontrollably. He swallowed hard. He did not want to get hurt nor did he want Bubba to be harmed. He watched as the stranger opened drawers in the desk and finally found the drawer containing the key. When the stranger saw the key, Jack felt his heart leaping from his chest. This is it, he thought. He lived his entire life for it to come down to this.

The stranger handed the key to Bubba. "Open the other cell," he ordered Bubba.

Bubba walked slowly to the second cell and unlocked the door and pulled it open.

"Alright. Give me the keys."

Bubba handed the keys to the intruder.

"Now get in," the stranger motioned for Bubba to get inside the second cell.

Bubba looked at the stranger but couldn't make out a thing because of the way the nylons distorted his face.

The intruder pushed Bubba in the back. "I said get in!"

Bubba was a big boy and the push really did nothing to force him into the cell. He gave the intruder a scowl and then voluntarily stepped inside the cell. The stranger shut the door behind him. He went back to Bubba's desk and searched the drawers for any type of thick tape. In the third drawer on the right he found some white masking tape and a pair of handcuffs. He took them out and approached the cell where he had put Bubba. Jack watched and counted the minutes he had to live.

"Back up to me here," the intruder ordered Bubba. "Now put your hands through the bars."

Bubba backed up and the stranger handcuffed him behind his back. He would be stuck in that position until Junior arrived the next morning to relieve him. The masking tape was applied to Bubba's mouth in multiple layers.

The deputy watched as the stranger fidgeted with the keys and moved awkwardly toward Jack's cell. He could see the fear in Jack's eyes as Jack pushed himself further and further into the stone wall until no space was left between his back and the ancient stones used to build the century old jail

Jack trembled and could do nothing but watch as the intruder inserted the skeleton key into the keyhole of the cell door and turned it. It echoed as it turned the tumblers inside. Opening the creaking door, the stranger slowly raised his gun from his hip and aimed it toward Jack's head. Jack turned his head to the side and squeezed his eyes as tight as he could. He tried to anticipate the exploding round exiting the weapon and then violently ripping through his brain.

"Let's go, Armstrong," the stranger said, motioning with his weapon.

Jack opened his eyes slowly and turned his head toward the stranger. He suddenly felt a surge of courage. "If you're gonna do it, you might as well do it and get it over with."

The stranger took three steps toward Jack. "Do what?"

Jacked arched his eyebrows. "Kill me."

The stranger chuckled. "Why would I want to do that?"

Bubba watched but was confused.

The stranger motioned with his gun again. "Let's go. I ain't got all night."

Jack narrowed his eyes and cautiously pried himself from the stone wall. Moving past the stranger, Jack looked him straight in the eye.

The stranger looked, peered back, but said nothing.

"Where are you taking me?"

"None of your business," the stranger answered. "But I'll be sure and tell Barney Fife over there so he can send out reinforcements like Gomer and Goober." The stranger paused and looked back at Jack. "Whattaya' think, I'm stupid or somethin'? I tell you where I'm takin' you and the entire federal force will be on our asses as soon as Barney over there frees himself."

Jack walked out of the cell and looked back at the stranger who followed closely behind, still aiming the gun at his back. Jack glanced back at Bubba. "Can't ya' give him a chair or something? He's gonna be there all night."

The intruder looked back at Bubba and snickered. He eyed Jack again. "What's this? A soft spot in your heart for the man who put you in here and was about to turn you over to the Feds for something you didn't even do."

Jack turned to the stranger and narrowed his eyes. He tried to look through the nylon to see who this stranger was but couldn't.

The stranger found a stool and unlocked the door to the second cell. He placed the stool underneath where Bubba stood. Bubba nodded his head in appreciation then sat down on the stool.

"Feel better now?" the stranger asked Jack. "Outside, *now!*"

Jack paused for a few seconds then complied with the stranger's request. Stepping outside into the brisk clear night, Jack could see the steam from his breath. Following him outside, the stranger motioned for Jack to follow him around the back and inside an oversized four by four pickup truck with larger than life wheels. The truck looked vaguely familiar, but Jack couldn't quite put his finger on it.

His gun still pointed at Jack, the stranger escorted him to the passenger side and ordered him to get inside. Jack pulled the door open, stepped up and pulled himself into the passenger's seat. The stranger locked the door, slammed it shut, then ran around to the driver's side. He climbed in, looked over to Jack and lowered the gun. He then tossed his weapon underneath his seat.

Jack looked at him, then toward the floorboard, as the stranger quickly started the engine and floored the accelerator, causing the huge tires to scream and smoke. Without looking, the stranger crossed traffic, causing several cars to swerve and barely miss each other. Having a difficult time seeing through the nylon over his head, the stranger drove the truck several blocks away and suddenly pulled it into a darkened alley. Actually feeling somewhat calm several minutes earlier, Jack now began to sweat profusely. His pulse quickened. He froze and waited for the stranger to pull the weapon from underneath his seat, execute him, then dump his body in the green dumpster sitting several feet away.

"Sorry about this, B."

Jack narrowed his eyes and gazed at the stranger.

The stranger took both hands and tucked them firmly under the edge of the nylon circle around his neck. He tugged at it hard and had to stretch and struggle with it to get it over his red goatee.

Jack leaned in toward the stranger. "Jerry?"

He gave the nylon one last swift tug and it came flipping from the top of his head like the snapping of a taut rubber band. Jerry looked at Jack and offered a huge grin. "Hey, Boss."

Jack was in shock. He flung himself back against his seat and quickly placed his open palm firmly against his forehead. "Holy shit! Jerry! Holy shit! Another minute and I would have died of heart failure. Are you kiddin' me? How did you know I was here?"

"Emery called me. She told me what happened. What you'd found out. She said the only way you could prove it was if you were out of there."

Jack shook his head. "Jerry. I love ya' man and I appreciate what you're doing. But you are taking a huge chance. Do you realize what kind of trouble you could be in?"

Jerry smiled. "I'm nothin' more than a good ole Georgia redneck. I've been in trouble too many times to count, Boss. Besides, unless you tell 'em, they won't ever know." Jerry put his truck in reverse and eased back into the road after it was clear. "So whattaya' think, B. Did the FBI guy do it? Is it because of him that you've had to go through all this nonsense?"

Jack laid his head back on the headrest. "I don't think anything,

Jerry. I know it. I know he did it and I have the proof."

"B. Listen. You need to know that this thing has exploded in Atlanta. It's been on the news every night since you were arrested. And man, when you took off, it got even bigger. It's been the top story every night. It's in the paper every day, man. Your mug's in the paper. On the TV. If you go back to Atlanta, you're gonna get spotted. No question about it. Somebody'll see you."

"I've got no choice. I have evidence in Atlanta I need to get."

"Well listen, man. Why don't you stay with me til you done everything you gotta do. I don't think nobody's watchin' me." Jerry saw the sign for Highway 129 North and made his turn. He wanted nothing to do with Interstate 75. He knew if Bubba got loose, the State Troopers would have it covered from the top of Georgia to Miami. He prayed they would have clear sailing and would make it to Atlanta long before Junior relieved Bubba in the morning.

"Jerry. I really appreciate this."

Jerry nodded his head, then looked at Jack. "Listen, B. There's somethin' you need to know."

Eyes closed, Jack was finally able to relax. "What is it?"

"It's about Marlowe."

Jack opened his eyes and glanced at Jerry. "What? They've been wondering where to send my mid-year bonus?" Jack chuckled to himself, closed his eyes and re-rested his head back against the headrest.

"He's in it up to his eyeballs. Has been for years. Didn't know for sure 'til a few weeks ago, but I've always had a gut feelin' he was up to no good."

Jack turned and stared at Jerry. "How do you know?"

Jerry gripped the steering wheel firmly, looked at the floorboard and snickered. "Let's just say I've been doin' some investigatin' on my own recently. We've all know somethin' wasn't right for a long time. We just didn't know what until the day the crapper busted."

"Why didn't you say anything?"

Jerry laughed loud. "Hah! And risk getting fired, or worse?" Jerry paused. "These are the big boys, Boss. It ain't a small operation. We either acted stupid, played along or turned our back. Remember the day the crate busted open and I told you what happened?"

"Unfortunately, it's etched in my mind forever."

"Me and the boys figured what was in there before it even busted open." Jerry chuckled. "Just never said nuthin' cause we didn't know for certain. Guess we liked puttin' food on the table better than we did the thought of unemployment. Then we knew for sure this wasn't a one time deal when our paychecks arrived."

"Whattaya' mean?"

"You wouldn't believe the bonus in our paychecks the next week. It was also accompanied by a visit by some foreigner in a tie that insisted on silence."

Jack pressed himself firmly into the back of his seat and covered his forehead with the palm of his hand. "I can't believe I could have been so freaking blind."

"Didn't you ever wonder how the company could keep operating even though it was losing business year after year?"

"Yeah. But I didn't ask questions. I figured the brass at the top must have been doing something to keep the company afloat."

Jerry laughed and shifted his truck into reverse. "Oh yeah! They were doing something right alright. Marlowe was striking up deals with some drug cartel in South America. He agreed to let some big wig foreign schmo use the warehouse as a distribution point to ship out all his cocaine to parts unknown across the U S of A."

Jack moved his hand from his forehead to his mouth. "And he packaged it inside the toilets."

"Bingo!" Jerry chortled. "And Marlowe made millions. We all stayed employed and lived happily ever after. The end. That is until you brought the FBI in. They've been watching the place like a hawk, Boss. Feds swarm around there every day. They're like buzzards waiting for something to die. They don't even try to hide." Jerry watched for traffic this time and pulled out onto the highway when it was clear. "I reckon the timing wasn't too good for you, though."

"Whattaya' mean?"

"You were sales director, slash warehouse manager, for what? About a year?"

"There abouts. Why?"

"In another year you would have been forced to retire like the rest of 'em."

Jack peered strangely at Jerry as he took one hand from the steering wheel and lit up a cigarette. "My timing? I don't understand what you mean."

Jerry smiled at Jack. "You missed a helluva pension, B."

Jack stared blankly at Jerry and said nothing.

"Remember Phillip Marcus? The guy you replaced?"

Jack looked away from Jerry and out his window. "Yeah?"

"Man retired at forty-four. He drives a Porsche Boxter and has a summer place on the lake. I heard guilt's gettin' to him, though."

Jack looked back at Jerry. A stream of smoked billowed from Jerry's nostrils. "Guilt?"

"Yeah. Marcus was close to Marlowe. I think Marlowe let him in on the company secrets. Marcus was fine with it at first, but then got scared. They retired him early. Gave him a huge pension with endless benefits. All it cost him was his silence. A friend of a friend said he saw Marcus not too awful long ago and that he was all stressed out. Like he was gonna explode if he didn't get it off his chest." Jerry glanced at Jack. "Maybe you should give him a call, B."

Jack stared out at the darkness. "Maybe."

~ 17 ~

Sitting in a worn out twenty-year-old chair covered with a soiled blue bed sheet, Jerry laced up and tied his work boots as Jack slept soundly on the similarly aged couch across the room. Jerry eyed a scrap piece of paper on the floor. Bending over, he finished tying his boots, then snatched the paper between his thumb and finger. With his other hand he went on a search and rescue mission for any pen or pencil hidden deep within the chair cushion. A smile spread across his face when he found what he was looking for. He retrieved it, then scribbled out a quick note telling Jack to make himself at home and to help himself to anything in the fridge. He also wrote down Phillip Marcus' telephone number and then stuck the note on the wall above the toilet. He then leaped over the short metal staircase leading from his trailer to the ground and quickly got into his four wheel drive pickup truck.

Jack twitched slightly, then jerked awake when the mufflers on Jerry's truck revved to a maximum level of decibels, enough to shake the trailer's windows. Sitting up on the side of the couch, Jack simultaneously scratched his head and his stomach. He stood, stretched, scratched his armpit, then walked over to the white vinyl blinds. With one finger he bent one at an angle and peered outside at the sunny, deep blue cloudless sky. The blind snapped back into place and made a popping noise when he removed his finger. He straightened up, stretched again and reached in a contorted way to relieve the itch square in the middle of his back. Jack shuffled over to the small bathroom.

Halfway into his morning ritual, Jack noticed the note over the toilet. He snickered at the thought of Jerry putting the message where he would be sure to find it. After flushing the commode, he tore the note from the wall. Carrying it with him into the tiny kitchen, he opened the refrigerator and knelt down to see what was inside.

Although Jerry had left a pot of coffee on warm, Jack left it. He was more of an orange juice guy.

Moving half empty beer bottles and a soured milk carton out of the way, Jack finally spotted a jar of orange juice that probably had enough left for a small glass or two. He couldn't find any clean glasses in the limited cabinet space. He did see some glasses in the sink, but from the looks of the fuzzy green growth on a few of them, they had probably been there a minimum of three weeks. Jack bristled and took a whiff of the orange juice before deciding it was safe to drink straight from the container. About halfway into his second gulp, he noticed a red hair around the rim of the jar. Making a loud gurgling noise, he jerked it away from his mouth, spit out what liquid was left unswallowed and vigorously wiped his mouth over and over with the sleeve of his tee shirt. He put the twist top back on the jar of orange juice and returned it to its home inside the refrigerator. He kept wiping his mouth again and again until red streaks appeared on both corners. Sitting down on one of the rickety old kitchen chairs, he wiped his mouth several more times.

Jerry's note he'd tossed on the kitchen table caught his eye. He picked it up and read the part about helping himself to anything in the fridge. Jack tore that part of the note away and wadded it up. "I don't think so Jerry, but thanks."

Jack held the note a foot from his face and stared at Phillip Marcus' phone number. "What can you tell me I don't already know?"

"Are you certain he's back in Atlanta?" McMann inquired of Fuentes, inside a closed door briefing.

"That's what she said."

"Do you know where he is?"

"Negative. But I've got a pretty good idea."

McMann smiled. "So the stupid, skinny little redneck did just what we wanted him to."

Fuentes returned the smile. "Just like clockwork."

The TV was turned to *The Jerry Springer Show*, but it was on mute. Springer was talking to obese twins who had been rejected by their mother, who was also having an ongoing affair with the twin's dietician. Jack didn't particularly care for talk shows. He thought they were southern white redneck's only avenue to fifteen minutes of fame. But it was the only station that came in clearly on Jerry's ancient set. So until *The Andy Griffith Show* came on in several hours, it would have to remain on mute. Unless, of course, one of the overweight siblings decided to attack the dietician. That was almost certain. Then Jack might take it off mute.

Jack had tried several times throughout the morning to call Emery. He got no answer at her apartment, which he fully expected. He knew she would be smart enough to stay with a friend. She was not answering her cell phone. The only response he got when he called her work number was to be put on hold and then told she was out. He had picked up the phone several times to call Marcus but always hung up after he dialed the first three or four numbers. He was most fearful of what Marcus would either tell him or not tell him.

Jack jumped when the phone sitting right next to him rang. Jerry had obviously set it on the loudest ring possible. He hesitated before answering, not sure if he should or not since it wasn't his home. He let it ring three or four times before deciding it might be for him. "Hello."

"Jack?"

Jack straightened his back and a broad smile spread across his face. After all they'd been through, his heart always skipped a beat when he heard her voice. "Emery?"

"I see you made it," came the soothing voice on the other end.

"Yeah." He wanted to see her, but knew it probably was best not to be seen together for a while. "Are you okay?"

"Yeah. Maybe just a little tired."

"You sure? You sound a little funny."

"Jerry didn't tell you, did he?"

Jack was confused. "Tell me what?"

Emery sighed. "I didn't think so."

"What? What is it?"

Emery paused slightly. "You were indicted yesterday in Mississippi."

Jack stiffened. He felt his throat shrink to the size of a straw. "What'd they do? Charge me with Doug's murder?"

"Yeah. I just thought you should know."

"I gotta call Cissy."

"I wouldn't, Jack. I'd say the police are monitoring her line."

"But I need her to know I didn't do it."

"I just think that's not a very good idea right now."

Jack sat back on the couch and rubbed his eyes. "What the hell am I supposed to do? I've got the Feds after me. I've got the mob after me. Now I've got the state of Mississippi after me."

"I think you should stay put for now. Let things die down a little."

"Die down? Die down?" Jack laughed. "I'm charged with one of the biggest drug heists of the century and a murder in Mississippi! Writing a bad check dies down. A DUI dies down. Drugs and murder don't." Jack rubbed his forehead feverishly. "I can't stay put. If I stay put I'm as good as dead. I've got to find the evidence that'll clear me. If I get caught while I'm doing it, then so be it. But I can't just sit here and do nothing." He shifted his fingers to his eyelids and rubbed them in a circular motion. "I need the car. What'd you do with it?"

"I parked it in a friend's garage. I figured the FBI is looking for it. So I put it somewhere they won't think of looking."

"Well. Bring it over to Jerry's. I need it."

Emery paused. "I'm sorry, Jack. I'm not gonna do that."

Jack sat up. "Whattaya' mean you're not gonna do it? I need the car, Emery. How the hell am I supposed to gather what I need to show I'm innocent? I can't do it sitting on my ass. Now bring the damn car over, and I mean now!"

Emery paused again and then began very calmly. "I realize

you're under a lot of stress. So I'm going to forgive the little outburst. But believe me, Jack. This is in your best interest. Trust me. Things will die down. Then you can gather your evidence." Emery sighed. "As far as I'm concerned, you got all the evidence you needed in Miami."

"It's not enough. I gotta have more, and now I've got Doug's murder on me."

"Bye, Jack. I'll be in touch."

Jack heard a click. "Emery! Emery! Where are you? How can I get in touch…" Jack listened, but it was too late. There was no response. "Damn it!" he shouted, as he slammed the phone down hard into its cradle.

The crumpled note that bore Phillip Marcus' number sat on the table in front of him. It was wrinkled from the half dozen or so times he had picked it up only to half dial the number. Jack eyed the piece of paper and snatched it with his left hand. He stared at the number for ten or fifteen seconds before picking up the phone and punching out the seven numbers. He listened to it ring eight times and was about to hang up when he heard the answering machine click on.

"You've reached 555-2533," the deep voice bellowed. "I can't come to the phone now, but if you leave a short message at the tone, I will return your call as soon as I can."

Jack waited for the beep, then began. "This is Jack Armstrong. I'm trying to get hold of Phillip Marcus. I hope I've called the right number." A strange click made Jack stop talking.

"Jack?"

Jack sat up straight. "Yes."

"This is Phillip Marcus. I've been expecting your call. Sorry for not answering the phone directly. But I've got to screen all my calls now. I never know who's calling me from one day to the next. I guess you can understand, right?"

"Yeah. I do. I'm glad you picked up."

"I've been keeping up with you through the news. I guess you're sort of a celebrity these days."

"Maybe. But not exactly the kind of celebrity status I dreamed of when I was a kid."

Marcus snickered. "Sorry. Bad choice of words."

"That's alright. At least I'm keeping everybody entertained."

Marcus chuckled and paused before he spoke. "I know you didn't call me to chit chat. I don't know if I can help you or not, Jack. I think you may have gotten yourself in so deep that there may be no way of getting out."

"That's just it. I don't know what I did to get in so deep. I didn't do anything, but yet here I am wondering each day who will catch me first, the FBI or the mob. And what's so crazy, right about now, I really don't care one way or the other. I just wish I knew how this whole crazy thing got started."

"You looked, Jack. You looked."

Jack furled his eyebrows. "I don't know what you mean."

"You broke the rules. You weren't supposed to look."

"Look at what? I don't know what you're saying."

"When you got your promotion to replace me, didn't you find it odd that they put you at the warehouse? I mean, do you really think the National Sales Director of a company with offices all around the nation should be doing grunt work at a warehouse? They did that on purpose. They recruit the people they believe they can trust to do the job they require."

Jack was confused. "I'm not following you."

"This is crazy." Marcus' voice quivered slightly. "If they knew I was talking to you they'd kill me."

"Who is they?"

"You know who."

Jack paused. "Marlowe?"

"Yeah. Until they took him out."

"Until who took him out?" Jack asked.

"Raes took him out after your blunder."

"So it's true?" Jack asked, already knowing the answer. "Marlowe was nothing more than a front for Raes' operation."

"How do you think Marlowe stayed in business? You were there when there weren't enough sales to keep the company afloat. But somehow, Marlowe's profits were higher than most every Fortune 500 company out there."

Jack covered his eyes with the palm of his free hand. "How could I have been so blind? How did I not see it?"

"Because they didn't want you to. They just wanted you to be a good little soldier and mind your own business." Marcus paused. "You remember when you were promoted? You remember being told that the warehouse was just a midpoint and that the crates and packages shouldn't be opened or checked? That they just needed to be inventoried?"

Jack sat back against the soiled couch and thought. He rolled his eyes before he spoke. "Yeah."

"Now you know why. The same thing happened to me that happened to you. The only difference was I called Marlowe and not the FBI. Three million dollars, a full pension, paid benefits, and a day later I became the retired National Sales Director." Marcus paused and blew out a lengthy breath. "It was supposed to make me happy."

"You're not?"

"I've been miserable ever since. I can't sleep. It isn't right what I'm doing. What I know. Always looking over my shoulder. Never answering my phone. Constantly worried they're watching my kids." Marcus paused. "I married my high school sweetheart, Jack. We were married twenty-three years. She walked out on me. Can you imagine that? Three million bucks and she wanted nothing to do with it." He paused again. "Look. I don't feel good talking about this over the phone. You never know who might be listening. There's a lot more I can tell you. Names. Places. I don't know if it'll do you any good, but I guess it can't hurt."

"Can we meet somewhere?"

"Yes. Which direction will you be coming from?"

Jack thought a few seconds. "I'm not really sure. I think from the southeast."

"That's fine. I'm up north of the city."

"I can meet you up there," Jack said. "You just name the place."

"Are you familiar with Buckhead?"

Jack answered quickly. "Yeah. I use to live close by there. Well, I still do. I just can't go there."

"You know where the mall is up there on the corner of Peachtree and Lenox?"

"Yep."

"There's a coffee shop on the upper level."

"The one that has a picture of Juan Valdez on the front?"

Marcus chuckled. "I take it you've been there."

"Been by a hundred times, but never inside."

"Can you be there at nine tomorrow morning?"

Jack knew he'd have to find transportation, but he also knew this could be an invaluable meeting in proving his innocence. "I'll be there."

"Okay," Marcus said. "Guess I'll see you there."

"Wait a minute," Jack jumped in quickly before Marcus could hang up. Jack knew who Marcus was, but had never met him in person. "How will I know you?"

"I just had some eye surgery. I'll have a patch over my left eye."

"Okay. Guess I'll see you in the morning," Jack said with a tinge of nervousness in his voice.

"I guess," Marcus answered.

Neither wanted to be the first to hang up. Only the hum of the phone line could be heard.

"How do I know I can trust you?" Jack asked matter of factly.

Marcus did not answer immediately. "You don't." He paused. "But you're gonna have to."

Jack's lips curled ever so slightly. "I guess you're right."

"See you in the morning then?"

"Yeah," Jack answered. "In the morning." Jack hung up the phone and sat back on the couch. He couldn't help but wonder if he had just made either the biggest mistake or the smartest decision of his life. Whatever the answer was would have to wait until the morning.

Jack lay on the couch pretending to be asleep as Jerry bustled around in the pre-dawn darkness of his trailer trying to find two calf length white socks he could wear with his work boots. Jack didn't tell Jerry about his meeting with Marcus because he thought the less people that knew about it, the better. Of course it also meant he couldn't ask Jerry for a ride. Besides, it would have been way out of Jerry's way.

Jack sat up on the side of the couch and rubbed his forehead and eyes after Jerry hurried out of the door. The red numbered digital clock on the TV stand said it was 4:50 in the morning. Jerry would be the first one at the warehouse.

Without cutting on any lights, Jack walked to the refrigerator and pulled out the jug of orange juice. He brought it to his mouth and suddenly remembered his experience with drink the day before. He shoved the orange juice back into the fridge and slammed it shut.

He laced up his tennis shoes, then stood up and zipped his jeans. Searching through Jerry's closet, he grabbed a windbreaker. Jack looked at his watch as he closed the trailer door. He angled it toward a street light because he couldn't see the hands without some assistance from a light source. It was now 5:05 a.m. Other than a few stray barks from some half-sleeping dogs, everything was quiet as a sliver of orange peeked over the pines.

Jack began his walk down one of the three or four streets that ran through the trailer park. At each car he passed, he glanced quickly through the passenger side to see if some poor fool had forgotten to remove the keys from the ignition. On about the twelfth vehicle he approached, he struck gold. Not exactly what he would have picked had he been shopping, but the thirty-five year old turquoise Gremlin would have to do. He had to make the meeting with Marcus and the chances of finding another car with the keys inside was practically zero. Besides, if he waited much longer, people would be waking up and his chances for 'borrowing' a car for the day would be slim to none. In his mind, Jack was indded borrowing the car. He had full intentions of returning it. Or at least parking it somewhere and calling authorities later to report where they could find it. He even left a note on the trailer door notifying the owner. He just didn't sign his name. Grand Theft Auto never entered his mind. He even planned on leaving a twenty dollar bill on the front seat for gas.

He hopped on I-75 North and drove the twenty or so miles necessary to the Lenox Mall north of Atlanta. Pulling into the huge, empty mall parking lot, Jack was surprised at how smooth the Gremlin drove. He parked in the middle of the lot and looked at his watch. He still had three hours before his meeting with Marcus. The sun was rising above the trees as he yawned and stretched. He folded his arms across his chest and closed his eyes.

The slamming of the car door next to him jarred him awake. Jack jolted upright and saw a sea of cars that hadn't been there before. He looked quickly at his watch. He cursed under his breath when he saw he was already fifteen minutes late to the meeting. Wasting no time, he jumped out of the Gremlin like a fighter pilot ejects from a doomed jet. He ran at full pace toward the closest entrance of the mall he could see. Inside, he looked frantically for the nearest escalator and rushed madly toward it, bounding three steps at a time. He bumped a few stationary passengers enjoying the ride up, which elicited angry scowls. Finally making it to the upper level, he tried to remember which direction the coffee shop was in. He looked both ways and tried to get his bearings straight. He didn't see the coffee shop, but the strong aroma of coffee was there and wafting up his nostrils. It had to be close by. He looked straight ahead. "If it'd been a snake it a bit me," Jack whispered to himself. The coffee shop with picture of Juan Valdez stared him straight in the face about thirty feet away. It was now about 9:25 a.m. Jack prayed that Marcus had not given up and left.

Taking a deep breath, Jack looked around one more time and began walking toward Juan's picture. His heart pounded hard inside his chest. He wiggled his fingers trying to ease the sweating of his palms. Ten feet away from the shop, he peered inside the large plate glass window and to the four booths running alongside the window. He saw customers drinking their morning drug. A few had pastries. Others read their morning newspapers. He pulled the silver handle of the door and cautiously walked inside. He believed he could trust Marcus, but there was something in the back of his mind that begged him not to. He was almost hoping that Marcus had gotten tired of waiting, had given up on him and left. The door swung closed behind him and made a thud. Jack jumped, then scanned the shop for Marcus. At the first booth on his right, Jack established eye contact with a man with an eye patch and wearing a gray beanie. He looked very familiar, but Jack couldn't place him. The man smiled and motioned for him to join him. Jack returned the smile with a slight curl from the corner of his mouth. Still nervous, Jack looked behind him before he ambled over and sat down at the booth across from his nine o'clock appointment.

"Jack Armstrong, I presume?"

Jack reached his arm across the table and shook hands. "Yeah. Sorry I'm late. Traffic was pretty bad."

"That's okay. I assumed that's what happened. What kind of coffee do you want? I'm buying."

Jack shook his head. "No thanks. I'm not really a coffee drinker."

"Sure?"

Jack waved his hand in the air. "No, thanks. I never really developed a taste for it." Jack looked around and then out of the window that ran parallel to the booth.

"Looking for someone?"

Jack turned quickly back. "No. Just a little nervous I guess."

"Me too. I'm not really sure what to expect either."

"You look really familiar," Jack said. "Are you sure we never met?"

"I guess it's possible. Maybe at one of those boring annual sales meetings."

"I guess." Jack looked at the eye patch. "What kind of surgery did you have?"

"Detached retina. Surgery was painful as hell."

Jack nodded his head then noticed something was different. He looked closer at the man across the table. "I thought you said the surgery was on your left eye."

The man touched the patch across his right eye. "Did I say the left? I meant the right. Honest mistake. You sure you don't want something?"

Jack shook his head. "I'm sure." Jack looked hard at the man who said he was Phillip Marcus. "I know I've seen you somewhere."

The man smiled. "Marlowe's a big company. We probably saw each other in the hallway or something somewhere along the way. It's hard to say. But that's not important right now. We need to help you get out of this mess you're in."

Jack continued to stare, but was distracted by the man in the next booth shuffling and crisply snapping his newspaper to a new page.

He looked back at the man across the table from him. Suddenly he did not trust him.

"Before I help you, I've got to know the truth."

The man in the next booth snapped his newspaper hard again.

Jack glanced at the man with the paper, then back at the man across the table. "The truth? Whattaya' mean the truth?"

"I think you know what I mean."

Jack shook his head slightly. "I have no idea what you mean."

The man across the table paused. "The only way I can help you is if you're up front with me, Jack. That means telling me the truth."

Jack shifted in his seat. "What the hell are you talking about? The truth about what?"

"The cocaine, Jack. I have to know if you took it."

Jack slid back in his seat as a frown slowly began to appear on his face. The man in the next booth snapped his paper to a new section. From the corner of his eye, Jack's attention was diverted to a photograph of a man in the newspaper situated just over the shoulder of the man claiming to be Phillip Marcus. His eyes moved slowly to the headline plastered across the top of the paper. His heart pounded unmercifully fast and hard.

BODY OF FORMER MARLOWE PLUMBING SALES DIRECTOR FOUND SLAIN INSIDE HIS HOME.

The name under the photograph read Phillip Marcus. Jack's stomach soured. His palms started to sweat. He slowly shifted his eyes back to the man across the table. His memory seemed to return only in short bits. Jack stared deep into the man's eyes. He remembered the day after the cocaine was stolen when Marlowe came to work and was pissed off because Jack had called the FBI and not him. What Marcus told him on the phone the day before was making more and more sense. Jack tried hard to recall when Marlowe left. The man across the table was there that day. He knew it. "Pony Tail!" Jack blurted out before he could shut himself up.

The man, who pretended to be Marcus, squinted his eye without the patch. "What'd you say?"

Pony Tail twisted around and saw the article. Quickly he jerked back and shed his fake eye patch. His white pony tail fell softly down his back as he flipped off his beanie. His eyes narrowed and an evil grin spread slowly across his face.

Jack flinched. He wanted to run.

Pony Tail grinned and jerked slightly toward the edge of his seat. "Don't even think about it, Jack."

Jack's nerves were shot. He didn't know how much more he could take. He figured he could either run or take his chances with Pony Tail and his band of thugs, whoever and wherever they might be. Jack chose the former. With all the strength he could muster, he placed the butts of both palms underneath the edge of the table in front of him. He counted to three in his head and lifted up and over with as much force as he could muster. In what seemed like slow motion, Pony Tail could only watch as the table was lifted several feet into the air and then came crashing down. Pony Tail lifted his arms in a feeble attempt to protect his head, but it did no good. The edge of the table caught him squarely in the forehead, causing a long thin cut from eyebrow to eyebrow, complete with oozing crimson blood.

Jack came bolting through the coffee shop doors like a horse out of a gate at the Kentucky Derby. He ran ten feet, his eyes frantically searching for a way out. He looked quickly to his right and spotted the escalator. In full stride, Jack sprinted toward the moving stairway but was stopped dead in his tracks by the rabid screams of Pony Tail standing outside the coffee shop, rubbing his bleeding wound and wailing for his thugs to stop him. Jack took three steps toward the escalator and was suddenly eye to eye with Guido and Sarducci. Both grinned, arms folded. Jack turned to his left and sprinted twenty feet before he was met by two men he'd never seen before. Somehow he knew they weren't there to take a friendly mall survey complete with a free prize. One was wearing a black suit with a thin black tie and was completely bald. The other looked more like a biker with a suit. He wore dark sunglasses, looked about seven feet tall and had a beard with ratty spots of gray.

Jack looked behind him. Pony Tail was already half way there. Jack turned 360 degrees, desperately searching for an escape. There was none. He felt trapped. The hoods were closing in on him from all directions. He looked over the banister at the thirty-five foot or so drop down to the first level. That option was out. Trying to run through the thugs was also out. He didn't have that kind of strength. Strike two.

The thugs inched closer. It was still early so the mall was not very crowded. Jack thought about shouting for help, but knew that no one would be willing to help him out, given his predicament. He looked over the banister one more time. The escalator ran parallel to where he stood, but it was still a good fifteen or twenty foot drop. A quick decision was critical and he made it. Just as the gang got within a few feet, Jack sprinted five or six steps toward Guido and Sarducci. He planted his hand firmly on the wooden rail and catapulted himself up and over like a gymnast on a pommel horse. Jack squeezed his eyes as tightly as he could. His toes tingled and his stomach turned as he free fell through the air, hurling toward the downward moving escalator. He tried to anticipate the sudden impact and prayed in midair that no bones would be broken. Guido, Sarducci, Pony Tail and the two newcomers moved quickly to the banister. They all lined up side by side and watched, in what seemed like slow motion, as Jack hurled toward the moving steps. His arms were outstretched like the wings of a soaring eagle. His knees bent slightly awaiting the sudden jolt at the end. They waited for him to die. Or at least break his neck.

The pain shot all the way from his right ankle up through his femur. Jack's butt cracked down hard on one of the steps. He rubbed his thigh and silently thanked God that nothing seemed broken. He looked directly up from where he was and saw the five frowning faces of his adversaries staring down. They looked frozen as if they were waiting to see if he had survived, even though it was clear he had. They even stood there and watched as Jack wasted no time pulling himself up rapidly and bolting as quickly as his trembling legs would allow. The pain was bad, but not enough to stop him.

Pony Tail looked dumbfounded at his subordinates as they watched Jack run away. "What are you waiting on? Get him!" Pony Tail motioned to the thugs Jack had not seen before. "You two! Head him off down that way!" Pony Tail pointed in the direction Jack had run. He then motioned to Guido and Sarducci and ordered them down the same escalator Jack had made his escape from. Drops of blood from his cut drained into his eye and down the bridge of his nose as he shook his head, not believing Jack had escaped again. He pulled a handkerchief from his back pocket and dabbed the blood from his cut. Cussing under his breath, he turned and headed toward the entrance to the mall closest to where Jack's car was parked.

Jack's limp was noticeable as he hobbled down the promenade, constantly looking back over his shoulder about every five seconds. Every store he attempted to duck into had its iron gates down, not yet open for business. It wasn't quite 9:40 a.m., and most of the stores didn't open until ten.

The ankle hurt each time he took a stride, but it was bearable. Jack looked for an alley, an opening, an unlocked door, anywhere to escape. He looked behind and saw Guido and Sarducci about halfway down the escalator running faster than he was able to. Suddenly, somewhere on his right, he heard the clanging of an iron gate. He stopped and spotted a young women's sports clothing store clerk with her key in the gate's locking mechanism. Jack dashed toward the gate and grasped it hard with his ten fingers. The gate clanged loudly which frightened the young clerk. She pulled the key from the lock and stepped back.

"Let me in!" Jack shouted desperately. His voice was high and quivering.

The clerk was terrorized. She stood silently and absolutely still.

Jack looked back at Guido and Sarducci. They were getting too close. Jack turned quickly back to the clerk. "Lemme' in dammit!" Sweat poured from his forehead as his steely eyes burned into the clerk's.

She shook her head. "I can't. I'm not supposed to."

Jack glanced quickly over his shoulder at Guido and Sarducci then on the other side at the two other thugs who he did not know and did not care to meet. His fingers still grasped the gate so hard that it threatened to cut off his circulation. "Those men! They're gonna kill me!" Jack pleaded with desperation in his voice. "You've got to let me in! Please! I'm begging you!"

The clerk looked to the left and right and saw the oncoming hit men but shook her head. "I'm sorry. I can't."

Jack released his death grip, shut his eyes tightly and banged the iron gate with a solid blow from the butts of his palms. His attention was quickly diverted by the sound of another gate behind him. Only this time, the young clerk in a referee shirt was pulling the gate up and had it just above her ankles. Jack looked to the right at Guido and Sarducci about thirty feet away. He looked to his left at the two unknown hoods at about the same distance away. Jack flung himself around and hurled in an all out sprint toward the opening gate. His four pursuers stopped for a second or two, unsure of what Jack was doing. Jack was halfway to his target when the four quickly resumed their pursuit.

The skinny, dark haired adolescent in the referee shirt didn't even see Jack until after he had lunged from ten feet away and slid under the gate that had opened to knee level. Jack reached up and grabbed the bottom of the gate and banged it back to the ground. "Lock it!" he shouted to the clerk.

"What?" the clerk asked, totally confused.

Jack held the gate down as the four killers approached and grabbed it from the outside. They pulled up hard. Jack countered by pulling down. "Lock the gate!" He didn't know how long he could oppose the combined power of the four men. Gritting his teeth and squeezing his eyes, Jack shouted again. "Lock it! Lock the damn gate!"

The clerk pulled the key from her shirt pocket and edged it slowly toward the lock. But the constant motion of the gate moving three inches up and then down again caused his hand to shake.

"Lock it!" Jack shouted. His hands ached and began to cramp.

"I can't!" the clerk shouted back, unable to insert the key into the continuously moving lock.

"Open the gate! FBI!" the bearded hood yelled. "The man is a fugitive. He's wanted by the FBI! Open the gate now and you won't be in any trouble!"

The clerk pulled the key back as Jack maintained his valiant struggle. Jack, lying on his side, looked up at the clerk with pleading eyes. Sweat poured from his brow. Blood began to ooze from his cut fingers. "They're gonna kill me! If you don't lock the gate, they're gonna kill me!"

Jack gritted his teeth as the four forced the door six inches above the ground.

"We're not going to kill him. We just want to talk to him," Sarducci said, in his thick Spanish accent.

Jack's eyes met the young clerk's. The gate rose two more inches. Four more and it would be over. Jack's voice shook. His face was soaked with sweat. "Does that sound like an FBI Agent to you? For the love of God, please lock the gate!"

The clerk stared at Jack. She did not know what to do. The gate rose another inch. With all his might he tried to pull down, but he could he battle no more. His strength was gone.

Jack looked up in desperation. His voice quivered. "You've got to believe me. I'm a dead man. And they'll kill you too!"

The clerk took a deep breath and looked into the eyes of the four men outside the gate.

"We won't hurt ya' kid. Promise," the bald headed thug said, grinning.

The clerk looked back down at Jack. The gate raised another inch. Three of Jack's fingers lost their grip. Jack closed his eyes. "Please help me."

Just at the moment that Jack lost his full grip, the young worker grabbed a metal rod and as hard has she could, whacked the pulley and wheel mechanism designed to roll the gate up and down. The force of the blow bent the structure, causing it to jam in place about four inches above the ground. Outside, the four men struggled to no avail to dislodge the gate. The bald man, the smallest, tried unsuccessfully to fit underneath the gap.

Exhausted, Jack tried hard to come to a sitting position. When the clerk finally helped him sit up, they both were staring into the barrels of two semi-automatic pistols. Jack blinked but barely acknowledged the weapons. The clerk was terrified.

"Open the gate kid, or I'll blow your fuckin' brains all over your sports store," the bearded one ordered.

Jack's eyes were heavy. He blinked slowly and methodically. "He's not gonna hurt you. They don't want you." Jack tried to stand but couldn't. His ankle and thigh were not broken, but the pain was intensifying by the minute. Sensing his need, the clerk helped Jack to his feet.

Guido and Sarducci banged on the gate. "Open the gate kid!

Now!"

The bearded and bald team aimed their guns inside but had no intention of shooting. They'd hoped their scare tactics would intimidate the teenager, but it didn't. They banged on the gate with their guns, watching as the kid helped Jack toward the back of the store.

"Is there a back door?" Jack asked.

"Yeah. There is. But why don't you let me call mall security first to get rid of these guys."

Jack couldn't help but laugh. "Go ahead and call mall security, sweetheart. I'm sure they'll have the matter under control in minutes." Jack paused to catch his breath. "Where's the door?"

The clerk walked to a cloth curtain hanging in a doorless doorway and pulled it back. "Right out here."

Jack stood and looked out the glass door to a half full parking lot. He perused the lot trying to remember where he'd parked his car.

"You sure you don't want me to call you a doctor or something?"

Jack looked at the clerk and smiled. "I'm fine. I just need to leave."

They both looked back at the jammed front gate. The four thugs were gone.

Jack squeezed the clerk's shoulder and smiled. "Thanks. You saved my life."

The young girl smiled. "I don't know about that."

Jack paused and looked both ways before he opened the doorway leading to a back parking lot for store employees that was surrounded by buildings on three sides. Hesitating just slightly, he took off in a half trot, dodging parked cars and looking in every direction with every step he took. Like a ship moving from a harbor into open sea, Jack slowed his pace and cautiously moved into the wide expanse of the customer parking lot. Jack stopped and looked at the mass of vehicles, praying he'd come out on the same side and level where he had parked his pilfered Gremlin. He tried to remember a landmark, but unfortunately had forgotten to complete that task when he arrived earlier. He did remember he parked close to the street closest to Lenox Road and that there was a hotel directly across the street. Slowly scanning his eyes from left to right, he found the hotel. He shaded his eyes from the sun and glared hard in that direction but couldn't find his car. It was too far away. Looking in every direction for any sign of his enemy, Jack began weaving in and out of the conglomeration of multi-hued vehicles until he was about four or five car lengths from the edge of the street. Jack stopped and scanned several rows of cars. He looked into the air and thanked God when he spotted the unsightly auto he had purloined. He looked down and reached into his right pants pocket but came up empty handed. He did the same with his left pocket. He patted his shirt pocket and both pockets on the back of his jeans. Nothing. He thought he had taken his keys but maybe in the rush to make his meeting he had forgotten to remove them from the ignition. He thought hard and tried to retrace his actions. Did he or did he not take the keys? "What difference does it make?" he whispered to himself. "I don't have them."

Jack looked at the Gremlin and began walking toward it, all the way praying he'd left the keys in the car. "Please God. Let 'em be there. Please let 'em be there." He weaved through two cars and was one row away from the automobile, at that moment being reported stolen by its rightful owner. Jack reached the front of the car and edged ever closer to the driver's side window. He was afraid to look. He bent down and peered inside. He blew out a lengthy breath when he saw the keys dangling from the ignition. "Yes! Thank you God!" he said to himself.

Jack looked around him before reaching for the door handle and pulling on it. But nothing happened. Jack stared at the handle, but couldn't believe it. The door was locked. He jerked on it several times with no luck. He shielded his eyes and glared through the driver's side window to the passenger side. It was locked, too. Jack slammed both butts of his hands into the window. He couldn't break the window. That would attract attention and probably get him arrested. He definitely did not have the time to call AAA. Besides, he wondered how he would explain the car which he assumed had been reported stolen already. Jack turned and leaned back against the car door. He looked to the sky and placed his intertwined fingers over his nose and mouth.

"Need a ride?" a voice from behind the car said.

Jack smiled. He knew his trusted friend Jerry was there to save him again. "Why did I know you'd somehow show up?" he said, looking toward the back of the car.

"I have a knack for being at the right place at the right time, Jack," Pony Tail said, as he stepped around the back of the car to face Jack. His steely eyes burned into Jack's.

Jack turned quickly and took one step. Two car lengths in front of him stood Guido and Sarducci. Two car lengths to his right were the new thugs.

"I don't think that's such a good idea, Jack," Pony Tail said, smiling just slightly. He took a handkerchief from his pocket and dabbed at the cut on his head that had almost stopped bleeding.

Jack turned back around to face Pony Tail. "We don't want to hurt you. Never did."

Jack chuckled sarcastically. "Oh yeah." He threw both arms in the air. "And all this time you just wanted to talk. Call me crazy."

"The only thing we ever wanted was what was ours to begin with. We don't want to hurt your girlfriend or anyone else."

Jack's sarcastic smile faded. "Tell that to my brother's kids."

"Your brother was an unfortunate accident."

"Right. I guess his throat just kind of accidentally fell on that knife."

Pony Tail smiled as Guido, Sarducci and the other two thugs watched from their positions. "You only have yourself to blame, Jack. Had you cooperated when you were asked, your brother would still be alive." Pony Tail smiled and took a step toward Jack. Jack backed up one step. "Listen to me, Jack. This can all end today. We can all go home and no one else has to get hurt. But it's your call. It's all up to you. You can't keep running forever. It's got to end sometime. Might as well be today."

Jack stared at Pony Tail and looked around at the others before returning his gaze to Pony Tail. "I can't help you."

Pony Tail took another step toward Jack and Jack reciprocated by taking another step back. "Yes you can, Jack. Think about all that's happened. Think about your brother. His wife. His kids. Think about your girlfriend. Think about all the people's lives you affected because of one stupid decision you made. What about Doug?

Whattaya' think his wife and kids are doing right now because of the decision you made."

Jack stared hard at Pony Tail. "I didn't do anything," he said, shaking his head. "I don't know why you people can't understand that. I never did a damn thing and I don't know why any of you can't get it."

"We can't get it because we know you did it. Do you think we're really that stupid? Do we really look that stupid to you?" Pony Tail took another step closer to Jack just as Jack's eyes shifted to the ground. "Come on, Jack. You can stop running today. This can all be over. Don't you want it to be over? I'm exhausted. I know you have to be."

Jack shifted his eyes quickly back to Pony Tail, who narrowed his eyes. Jack took two steps backwards. "I want it to be over."

Pony Tail reached his hand toward Jack. "All you have to do is take us to where you hid it. Then it'll all be over. You can go home and get on with your life."

Jack paused and stared at Pony Tail. "I can't."

"Yes you can, Jack. You can."

Jack shook his head from side to side. "I can't."

"Why?"

Jack glared hard at Pony Tail without blinking an eye. "Because I'm innocent, you sorry son-of-a-bitch!"

Pony Tail's nostrils flared. His eyes bulged as did the vein in his neck. He reached into his belt and pulled out a black semi-automatic pistol that looked bigger to Jack than it really was. He slowly trained it on Jack's head and closed one eye as he took aim. "Say your prayers, Jack."

Jack's heart pounded but he pretended not to be afraid. "You won't do it."

"Watch me," Pony Tail said.

Guido, Sarducci and the other two thugs watched from a distance, anticipating the bang.

"You need me," Jack said.

Pony Tail steadied his weapon. "You just told me you were innocent. What use are you to me now?"

"I know who took it," Jack said.

Pony Tail lowered his weapon just slightly. "I'm listening."

Jack shook his head. "Not here."

Pony Tail jerked his weapon back up and square on Jack's head. "I'm done with you, Jack. I'll see you in hell."

The next few seconds went in slow motion for Jack. He seemed to focus on Pony Tail's finger pulling the trigger and watching as the bullet exited the barrel rotating cylindrically through the air. In what only took a fraction of a second to occur, seemed to take an hour. And only by the grace of God was Jack able to beat the bullet by diving sideways onto the trunk of the car parked next to the Gremlin. While Guido, Sarducci and the other two thugs ducked for cover and Pony Tail recovered from the recoil, Jack somehow rolled off the trunk and escaped underneath the body of another car.

Pony Tail's arm came down back into position to fire another round, but his target was gone. He panned 180 degrees with his eyes and his weapon. "Damn it! Where is he?" Pony Tail shouted, as patrons of the mall scattered for cover. Some screamed. Others dove behind cars, wondering if it was a gang war or maybe some lunatic was opening fire because he was pissed off at the world.

Their guns drawn, Guido, Sarducci and the two thugs rose slowly from their positions. "Where is he?" one of the thugs yelled at Pony Tail.

Pony Tail went from car to car, bobbing his head and searching underneath each one down the row. His weapon was extended straight in front and held tightly by both hands.

Guido, Sarducci and the other two thugs stood at their positions, pointing their weapons skyward. Pony Tail became irate when he saw them just standing still. "Find him!" he shouted. Veins bulged from his neck as each thug took a row of cars and began searching. Pony Tail leaned back against a car and closed his eyes. He couldn't believe Jack had gotten away. But suddenly and just as quickly as Jack had found cover, Pony Tail saw movement from the corner of his eye. He moved slowly in the direction of the movement, his weapon extended as far out in front of him as it could be. Sirens could be heard in the distance. Fifty feet at ten o'clock, Pony Tail saw a pair of feet slithering from under one car to another. He leveled his weapon, aimed toward the car and fired.

Jack tightened and stiffened every muscle in his body. His eyes shut tightly as he cringed, anticipating the stinging pain as he heard the bullet graze the asphalt and saw the sparks fly two inches from his head. Jack slowly opened his eyes. He felt no pain. No blood was visible. He heard Pony Tail's footsteps echoing like a methodical drum beat as he quickly rolled under the next car, only to army crawl forward to another in front of that one. He could hear Guido and Sarducci yelling to each other in Spanish but he had no idea what they were saying. The intensity of the sirens increased.

He twisted his neck and saw Pony Tail's feet moving closer. He listened and anticipated every move as Pony Tail shouted orders to his underlings. Jack looked in the other direction. Between two cars he could make out a MARTA sign. If he waited for the police, he would be dead. Jack knew his only hope was to somehow make it across the street and onto the train. He looked around and saw Pony Tail moving from car to car. He was three cars away and moving quickly. Jack squeezed his eyes and counted to three before swiftly rolling away from the car and in between two other parked cars. Jack stayed on his hands and knees and four legged it to a retaining wall before standing upright and catapulting himself over the wall and down the sidewalk toward the MARTA station.

"There he is!" Pony Tail screamed. "Get him!"

Jack drove his legs until they burned. Without breaking stride, he looked around and saw Pony Tail and the others in hot pursuit only one hundred feet behind. Thirty feet from the street he would have to cross, Jack weaved in and out of mall, hotel, restaurant and MARTA patrons on the sidewalk.

Pony Tail abruptly stopped his pursuit, leveled his gun, and took careful aim when Jack had to slow down at the intersection because of heavy traffic. The boom of the gun and the resounding echo it caused sent pedestrians running, screaming and flying through the air for cover. Mothers laid on top of their children, protecting them while others dove for the bushes or hid by trees or anything they could find for cover.

Jack never even broke his pace. He weaved in and out of moving vehicles whose occupants slammed on their brakes, honked their horns and cursed madly at the idiot racing across the street. When he reached the other side he stopped and looked back. Pony Tail was twenty-five feet behind the other assassins who had made it to the street and were waiting for any break in traffic. In less than three seconds, Pony Tail caught up with his band of thugs but didn't hesitate a fraction a second before heading into the rapidly flowing mid-morning traffic, again causing brakes to slam, horns to honk and drivers to freeze when they saw the pony-tailed man and the weapon he was carrying.

Jack's eyes widened. He turned and ran down the steps of the MARTA station. He bolted past the manned information booth and the ticket counter and bounded the turnstiles amidst the stares and frowns of several patrons waiting to enter. The lady inside the booth quickly got on the phone to security just as Pony Tail came bounding past her station and likewise high jumped over the turnstile.

An escalator led to a train that was just beginning to pull away. Jack leapt down it five steps at a time. His legs burned and sweat stung his eyes as he tried with every bit of energy left in his body to catch up to the train that was quickly picking up steam. Pony Tail vaulted down the escalator in three strides and slowly gained on Jack. Pony Tail shoved his gun back into his belt when he heard the footsteps of three uniformed MARTA security guards yelling at him and Jack to stop.

Jack did not slow his stride. If anything, he picked up speed as the train seemed to pull further away. Ten feet away from the last car, he pushed his body and his legs to their maximum velocity. Five feet away and pushing even harder, Jack gritted his teeth, pumped his arms and moved to the edge of the barrier separating the train tracks from the staging area. Like an Olympic broad jumper, he pushed off the edge of the cement barrier with his left foot. He spread his arms and legs, shut his eyes and flew spread eagle toward the back of the train. The pain that shot down his legs when his body slammed against the back of the train was nothing compared to the feeling of elation he had when he turned around and saw Pony Tail standing at the edge of the barrier doing nothing but glaring at him.

"That son-of-a-bitch stole my wife's purse," a heavy breathing, perspiring Pony Tail explained to the MARTA security guards.

"We'll need you to fill out a report," one of the guards said.

Pony Tail started walking away.

"Sir!" another guard said. "We're not through. We need you to file a complaint."

Pony Tail refused to turn around. "I've decided not to press charges."

"Sir! Sir!" The security guards tried to summon Pony Tail, who never looked back before bounding up the escalator.

Pony Tail motioned for Guido, Sarducci and the other two thugs to come with him as they disappeared up into the street level area.

Jack held on tightly as the speeding train made its way to its next stop. He turned his head when Pony Tail and the Lenox Station were out of sight. Closing his eyes, he leaned his head against the window of the train and hoped the next station would arrive quickly. Extremely tired, he massaged his cramping hands. Strangely enough, Jack was relaxed but somehow knew it wasn't over. Not by a long stretch. He felt someone's presence. Jack opened his eyes quickly. Standing on the other side of the window, grinning and waving at Jack was Agent Fuentes.

They stared at each other for several seconds. Fuentes peered at Jack with a smart-ass grin. Jack wondered when this would all end. He looked down at the ground moving so swiftly several feet below that it became nothing more than a blur. He looked back up at Fuentes and banged his head against the glass. Fuentes nodded and laughed. Jack looked above him for anything to grab onto. He knew he had to make it to the top of the train or it would all be over, and proving his innocence would no longer matter. The only thing that would be left to ponder would be how Fuentes or the mob would kill him.

Jack searched desperately for anything, any piece of metal to serve as a handle to pull himself up with. The only thing that was a remote possibility was a slight protrusion where a reflector light was positioned. Stretching his right arm as far as was humanly possible, Jack still needed three more inches to even reach it with his fingertips. He looked toward his feet for something to step on to give him the extra inches he needed, but nothing was there. The only thing between the fiberglass bumper on the train, where his feet now rested, and the reflector light ledge was the tiny and narrow ridge of the window he was holding on to. He looked at the speeding ground again, then at the small bulge of the reflector light before turning his attention to a grinning Fuentes.

More than ever, Jack was determined to get away. Fuentes' smile just served to piss him off more than he already was. He looked again at the speeding ground below him. He knew the train would be pulling into the next station within a minute or two. He peered up at the reflector, then inside at Fuentes, who refused to wipe the smile from his face. Bending his knees just slightly, Jack could feel both feet slip closer to the edge of the bumper. He grabbed on tightly to the small window ledge, straightened his legs and carefully regained his balance. By now, Fuentes had broken into hearty laughter.

Jack looked at the ground one more time and shut his eyes tightly. He looked up at the reflector light and at Fuentes shaking his head. Gritting his teeth hard, he slowly bent his knees again and stabilized his feet. With the power of a gazelle, Jack lifted off from the bumper and grabbed solidly onto the small outcropping of the reflector cover with his right hand. Dangling by one hand like a distraught rock climber whose only support is a broken cable, Jack glanced quickly at the speeding ground and down at Fuentes. He kicked frantically at the window, trying desperately to blindly feel for the ledge to get some type of footing, even if only a fraction of an inch. Flailing recklessly from side to side but managing to maintain his grip on the reflector, Jack tried to reach the opposite reflector on the left side of the train. It was too far away. The only thing he could do was to grab onto the reflector with both hands, but there was barely enough room for one. His biceps burned as he held on tightly with both hands. He wondered if throwing himself from the back of the train would be his best alternative. It might kill him, but at least it would be quick and there would be little or no suffering. He'd come too far and gone through too much to give up now.

Jack peered down at Fuentes as sweat dripped down his forehead and stung his eyes. Again, with all the strength he could find, he began to swing himself from side to side until his momentum gradually lifted his exhausted lower body above the curve of the top of the train car. He shut his eyes when his body finally rested comfortably on the edge of the back of the train. His two hands still clung tightly to the reflector. Blood dripped slowly down the window from the webbing between his thumb and index finger.

The grin erased from his face, Fuentes pushed himself hard against the inside window. He banged on it repeatedly and tried in vain to get a glimpse of Jack.

Above, Jack rolled over onto his back and rested. Slinging his forearm across his face, he could feel the fierce wind rushing over the top of his body like wind over the frame of an aerodynamic sports car.

Fuentes pressed his face against the window and looked upward. He could see nothing. Turning quickly, he ran through the car, weaving in and out of passengers while flashing his credentials and screaming for the train to stop. He reached the other end of the car and realized it was as far as he could go. There were no doors on this train which led to the next car. The train's operator was at the other end and there was nothing Fuentes could do about it. Fuentes ran to windows on both sides of the train and smashed his face against them, praying Jack would stay on top of the car he was on.

Rolling quickly from his back to his hands and knees, Jack army crawled his way across the top of the train against the stiff wind created by the speeding train. Watching carefully for obstacles ahead, he made sure his head was always lower than the next tunnel the train traveled through. He wasn't sure exactly what to do but knew he had to get as far up the train as possible and at least have somewhat of a head start away from Fuentes when the train finally stopped. Looking down at the speeding ground and the four foot gap that separated the cars made his stomach turn. On all fours he backed up ten feet and slowly rose to his feet. He looked ahead to make sure no tunnels were in sight which would decapitate him. Four feet didn't seem like great distance, but with a 120 mile per hour wind blowing directly against him he knew he would be lucky to jump a foot. He drew a deep breath and sucked up what little strength remained. Like a horse jumping a fence, Jack leaned forward and ran as hard as he could against the wind, spreading his arms as if in flight and diving headlong toward the next car. His chest thudded hard against the edge of the train and his legs dangled slightly over the back. But he had made it. Slowly he pulled himself up and on all fours until he began the process again.

At the back of the train, his face smashed against a window trying hard to see Jack, Fuentes heard the commotion at the front of the car as passengers pointed and talked about the lunatic on top of the train. Pushing several frightened passengers aside, Fuentes weaved his way back to the front of the train. "Armstrong!" he shouted, his nose smashed against the front window. Fuentes cracked a tiny, barely noticeable smile and shook his head from side to side. "You are one crazy son-of-a-bitch," he whispered below his breath.

Jack struggled hard against the wind. He could barely keep his eyes open against the strong oncoming rush of air as he inched his way toward the front of the car. His stomach soured and his skin crawled when he thought of making another jump from one moving car to the next.

Fuentes watched and wondered why Jack suddenly stopped his snail-like journey toward the front of the next car. He knew what Jack was trying to do. Any head start would help, but Fuentes knew it wouldn't matter. Jack would be dead tired and would not be able to get far once the train stopped at the next station.

The whoosh caused by the northbound train headed in the opposite direction startled Fuentes and made him take his eyes off Jack for an instant. Quickly, he glanced back to the top of the train. Jack was gone. Fuentes put his hands against the glass and jumped onto a seat to get a higher vantage point. But Jack wasn't there. He had simply vanished. Fuentes knew there was no way Jack had time to make it to the front of the next car, much less progress more than a step or two against the furious wind. Fuentes gritted his teeth. Suddenly, he realized what had happened. He turned slowly and gazed upward as the last car of the northbound train sped by. Laying on his belly, spread eagle on the top of the last northbound car, was Jack. Fuentes stared at the train as it grew smaller and smaller and finally faded to a speck in the distance.

"He jumped! The crazy bastard jumped!" Fuentes shook his head, cursed, then pulled his radio from his back pocket. "He's coming back your way."

The train slowed as Jack lay prone, waiting for it to come to a complete stop. He raised his head slightly and looked all around the station for Pony Tail and the other thugs that were after him. He didn't see any of them. The wheels made a grinding, screeching noise as the train finally slowed and came to a halt. Raising himself to a four-legged position, he looked around again before turning and four legging his way toward the back of the train. He firmly gripped the same reflector light overhang he had so tightly grasped only moments earlier on the other train and lowered himself to the bumper. Passengers on the platform waiting to enter the train stared at Jack and wondered what in the world this idiot was up to. Some smiled and thought it must be some publicity stunt or maybe some film company was shooting a Hollywood movie. They looked around for cameras. Jack returned their glances and nodded his head as if nothing was out of the ordinary.

Jumping to the ground below, he was careful not to make contact with the dangerously high voltage electrical tracks. He looked around from his vantage point, which was eye level with the station platform, before boosting himself up and onto it. As passengers on both sides of the station stared at him, Jack brushed himself off and tried unsuccessfully to straighten his hair. He looked around and located the closest escalator leading up to the MARTA entry area and half walked, half trotted towards it. Politely excusing himself to the staring passengers, he quickly bounded the escalator two steps at a time, not meaning to bump anyone. At the top of the escalator, he moved with the crowd into the entry area. He looked all around the area for any sign of Pony Tail. His heart slowed somewhat and his breath was less erratic when he saw no trace of the thug.

On the sidewalk outside the MARTA station, the sun shone brightly as pedestrians made their way up and down the sidewalks. Across the street in the mall parking lot were about ten Atlanta Police Department cruisers with blue lights furiously flashing. Twice as many police officers milled about the area. Some interviewed witnesses. Jack saw one pointing toward the MARTA station. Two police officers were on their knees collecting the expended shells from Pony Tail's weapon. From the corner of his eye, Jack observed three officers heading straight toward him. He lowered his head as they looked squarely at him but passed by and quickly bounded down the escalator steps of the MARTA station.

"Jack!" the voice resounded from somewhere toward the street.

Jack looked at the cars stopped at the traffic light but saw no one calling him. He assumed he was hearing things or maybe it wasn't him that was being summoned. He looked back over his shoulder at the police officers running down the escalator and out of sight.

"Jack!" the voice called louder. "Over here!"

He looked once again at the vehicles, anticipating the light change.

Stepping outside her car in the middle of traffic, waving her arms crossways and above her head, was Emery, trying desperately to motion Jack and get his attention. About the time he saw her, the light turned green. The man in the car behind her laid on his horn and started motioning with his hands for her to move.

Jack dodged the oncoming traffic and approached Emery standing quietly in the middle of the road.

"Need a ride?" she asked.

Jack remained expressionless. "How did you know I was here?"

Emery peered into his eyes.

The man behind her blasted his horn solidly for five seconds. "C'mon! What the hell are you doing? Move the damn car already!"

Emery turned and looked at the angry driver then returned to Jack. "Get in the car."

"I want to know how you knew I was here," Jack barked in a harsh tone, not moving one inch from the space he occupied.

Emery stared at Jack and back at the driver who was gradually losing his patience. "Get in the car, Jack," she said, while turning to get back into her car.

Jack grabbed her shoulder and spun her around to face him. "I'm not going anywhere until you tell me how you knew I was here."

The angry driver twisted his neck to look behind him and waited for any opportunity to present itself for him to change lanes and go around her. As soon as it did, he floored the accelerator, shifted into the other lane, and angrily displayed his third finger to both Jack and Emery. His tires screeched, leaving behind a black streak several feet in length.

"Get in the car, Jack," she said calmly.

Jack stood his ground, his eyes glaring into hers.

Emery pulled away from Jack, who still grasped her shoulder, and climbed back into the car.

Jack watched as she buckled her seatbelt and looked up at him through her open window, silently asking him to please come with her. He stared down at her then looked back over his shoulder, where the police still combed the mall parking lot for any evidence of the reported shooting minutes before.

Emery never removed her eyes from Jack, who was obviously confused. "Jack?"

Jack turned to Emery once more. His eyes silently questioned her.

"You have to trust me on this one. There's not much time."

He stared down at Emery and watched her for at least ten seconds. He ground his teeth which caused his jaw to move back and forth. "Who are you?"

She paused, looked down, then back at Jack. "Get in, Jack. Just get in."

Again, Jack stared at her, not sure of what to do. His head told him to walk away, but his gut instinct was to get into the car.

By now the light had turned red again and cars were beginning to gradually stack up behind Emery's. Emery looked behind her at the nine or ten cars. "In a minute the light's going to turn green and those drivers back there are gonna be pretty ticked off that I'm just sitting here. Now who would you rather confront, the Columbians or a bunch of stressed out, hacked off Atlanta commuters?" She half smiled in her futile attempt to ease the stress written across his face.

Jack returned her half smile and ventured around the front of her car and to the passenger's side. Emery leaned over and unlocked the door. Jack climbed in, closed the door and threw his head against the headrest. He covered his face with his hands and rubbed his eyes, forehead and nose. Emery shifted the transmission into drive and waited five or six seconds for the light to turn green. Passing parallel to the mall parking lot, both watched as the police questioned people and wrote down license tag numbers of every car in the vicinity of the incident.

"You okay?" Emery asked.

Jack looked at Emery, paused then snickered. "What do you think?"

"Sorry. Bad question." She turned left onto Peachtree Street and headed toward downtown Atlanta.

"Where are you going?" Jack asked

"Nowhere really. Just driving."

They drove for what seemed like hours to Jack but in reality had only been several minutes. Emery weaved in and out of traffic and turned down side streets whenever some street seemed to catch her fancy for whatever reason. They both wanted to talk, but neither wanted to be the first.

Jack looked straight ahead, never taking his eyes from the road. "You gonna tell me who you are or are you gonna make me guess?"

Expressionless, Emery looked at Jack. While steering with her left hand and keeping her eyes just over the steering wheel, she traded looks with Jack and the road in front of her. She reached under her seat with her right hand and emerged with a set of black credentials that she pitched on the seat between them. Sunlight beaming through the windshield reflected off the gold badge and in Jack's eyes.

He picked them up and looked at the badge. He snickered to himself before he opened the credentials and studied the large blue FBI letters and emblem with Emery's picture underneath. Shaking his head, he closed the credentials and pitched them back onto the seat next to Emery.

"I can't believe I didn't see it," he said, rubbing the rough growth of beard on his face.

"The phone calls to your work, never catching you in. Whoever answered always stalled me. What an idiot!" Jack glanced at Emery, who kept her eyes on the road as she continued to drive through Atlanta neighborhoods. "Fuentes always showing up at just the right time. How could I have been so stupid?" Jack slapped himself on the forehead. "Hell! You suggested I call him. And I did!" Jack laughed, but it wasn't real. "I should've known no woman in her right mind would go running with me halfway across the South knowing if we got caught she'd be guilty by association." Jack threw his head back against the headrest. "Is it a fair assumption on my part that you're working with my good buddy Fuentes?" He looked at Emery for a response.

Emery glanced at Jack then back at the road. She shook her head yes.

"Oh, God!" he exclaimed, slamming his head back against the headrest.

"For what it's worth, I believe you."

Jack lifted his head from the headrest slowly and stared at Emery. "For what it's worth? For what it's worth? You tell me Emery, or whatever your name really is. You're the FBI Agent. Is your opinion gonna keep me out of jail? I take it that's where we're headed right now."

"No. That's not where we're headed."

"I guess it's also a safe bet we're not dating anymore," Jack said slyly.

"We never were dating."

"What would you call it then? What we were doing, what would you call it?"

Emery looked sympathetically at Jack. "I don't know what you would call it, but for me, it was work."

Jack shook his head. "Oh. Okay. You just happened to pick me out to investigate and fooled me into believing you cared for me in what most people would have considered a relationship."

"I'm sorry if I hurt you, Jack, but it was my job."

"It was your job to hurt me? To fool me? Forgive me if I'm having a hard time understanding how the hell I fit into your plans to stomp the hell out of my heart."

"Look, Jack. Fuentes has been investigating Marlowe for a couple of years. We knew that he'd struck a deal with Hector Raes to be a distribution point for his cocaine operation. Fuentes tried for two years to develop a source inside Marlowe but it was impossible. He knew the only way to even remotely have a chance was to get to the heart of the operation. The warehouse. Eric figured the person that ran the warehouse…"

"That would be me," Jack interrupted.

"That would be you. Eric figured you had to know what was going on and that if he could get to you, you could provide some valuable needed intelligence."

Jack chuckled. "But something strange happened on the way?"

"Whattaya' mean?"

"I didn't know. I didn't know anything about the Marlowe/Raes operation. The first time I knew about any cocaine was when some of my men accidentally busted up a crate one day. And what do I do? I try to be John Q. Responsible and notify the authorities. And instead, I turn out to be a target of your investigation."

"You weren't targeted until after the cocaine was stolen. Eric originally planned on recruiting you as an informant."

Jack laughed. "Oh, that's great! A snitch! You were gonna make me a snitch and I didn't even know anything. What makes you so sure I would've even agreed to be a snitch?"

"We would've paid you."

Jack laughed harder. "I was making six figures. Why would I endanger my life to help you? I didn't need your money."

"Because you could have retired on what we would've paid you."

Jack looked at Emery. His curiosity peeked. "Oh yeah? How much?"

"A million dollars."

Jack snickered. "That's all? Then I would've had to retire and move to Siberia in order to stay alive. There's no amount of money you could have offered me. I didn't know anything."

Emery glared at Jack, not amused at his sarcasm. "I said I believed you."

Jack glared back. "And what good does that do me in the final outcome?"

"It buys you some time."

"So I take it you're not going to arrest me?"

Emery smiled. "Not today."

Jack leaned back against the headrest. "I gotta ask you a question. You don't have to answer it if you don't want to."

Emery looked at Jack, wondering what he wanted to ask her. "Okay."

"You said you believe me."

"Yeah."

"Do you believe that Fuentes did it?"

Just as Jack asked the question, Fuentes tried to raise Emery over the radio. She and Jack looked at each other. Emery leaned over and turned the radio off.

Emery turned to Jack, then back to the road before pausing. "I can't answer that right now."

Jack smiled. "Can't or won't?"

"There is one other thing," Emery said.

"What?"

"Underneath your seat."

"My seat?" Jack asked.

"Yeah. There's a file under there you may need."

Jack leaned over and reached his right hand underneath his seat. He pulled out a manila file folder packed with voluminous documents. Jack stared at the folder, then at Emery.

"It's the stuff you found on Eric down in Miami."

Jack's mouth was agape as he thumbed through the file. "You didn't give it to Fuentes?"

"After you stumbled on all that information, I began to have questions myself. I kept the file hidden. Nobody else knows but you and me."

Jack rested his neck against the seat and closed his eyes. "Oh, man. I would kiss you if weren't FBI. I thought it was gone. My whole case rests on this stuff."

Emery motioned to the file Jack held in his lap. "That information's not gonna exonerate you Jack. I mean it puts Eric's credibility at stake but…"

"At stake!" Jack barked. "At stake! He lied, Emery. He lied about everything. His family. His background. Hell! He lied about his own name, for crying out loud!"

"That doesn't make him guilty of stealing millions or billions of dollars worth of cocaine, Jack."

"But it's a pretty fair indicator, wouldn't ya' say?"

"No comment."

"You saw the connection between Fuentes's family and Raes. You can't sit there and say he didn't have a motive."

"I didn't say he didn't have a motive. I said what you have now is not enough proof to say he did it and not enough proof to say you didn't do it."

Jack stared straight ahead and held on tightly to the file. "You know there's no way I can get the proof either way, don't you?"

Emery paused and made a turn back on to Peachtree Street. "Maybe not the proof. But there may be a way to at least get enough probable cause to start an inquiry and at least take some of the heat off of you."

Emery drove toward downtown. Both remained silent and stared at the road ahead of them. Jack realized that he had not noticed what her real name was on her creds. He wondered what it was, but didn't ask.

~ 18 ~

Assistant United States Attorney Russ Waters flipped through the dense file on top of his desk in front of him. It was surrounded by six or seven other volumes of equal thickness scattered about on his desk concerning the Marlowe/Raes investigation. "I'm sorry I seem so unorganized but I hadn't heard from Eric in a while and got pulled off on some other matters. If you had called before you came I might have had this pulled together and could've gotten the information for you a little quicker."

"I apologize for not calling first. It came up kind of quick," Emery tried half-heartedly to explain.

"Have you discussed this with Eric? Him being the Case Agent and all."

Emery smiled nervously. "Yeah. He was tied up and asked me to come down."

"I thought Eric had already subpoenaed all the numbers he needed. Isn't it kind of late to be subpoenaing more?"

"Like I said. These just came up last minute. We kind of need them in a hurry."

"Whose numbers are they?" Waters asked.

"Don't know. They're numbers Armstrong called."

Waters glanced up quickly from the file. "Armstrong. How do you know what numbers he's calling? I thought no one knew where he was."

Emery fumbled for an answer. Her nervousness was obvious. "They were numbers he called while I was with him in Mississippi and Florida."

Waters stared at Emery. "I thought you said the numbers just popped up. It's been a while since you were down there, hasn't it?"

She could feel the heat throughout her body. The kind of heat when you know you're lying and don't have an answer. A trickle of sweat dripped from her hairline. "Yeah. But things have been kind of hairy, Russ. There's a thousand things to do and only a short window of time to get them done. We're just now getting around to doing this."

Waters paused and stared at Emery. "Do you have any idea why Eric didn't want anyone but himself asking for subpoenas on this case?"

Emery's heart pounded faster. She could feel it beating in her throat. "No. He did what?" She didn't need to hear it again. She just needed more time to think of an out.

"I've never been asked that before. I mean it's kind of a given that the Case Agent leads the investigation and requests whatever sources we can give. But he specifically asked me only to honor his requests." Waters paused. "Any idea what that's about?"

Emery shook her head. "I don't know Russ. I know this case is his baby. He doesn't want to take any chances of screwing it up. All I know is he wanted me to get these numbers subpoenaed." Emery stood up and moved toward the door. "I'll just tell him he's going to have to come down himself."

Russ waved his arm toward Emery. "Sit down. Sit down. That's ridiculous for him to have to come up here when you're already here."

Her breathing eased and her heart slowed to a normal pace again.

"I'll have my assistant draw it up and we'll have it in your hands by tomorrow morning."

"Uhhhh, it's kind of urgent, Russ. If there's any way you could get it for me now. I don't mind waiting."

Russ looked up at Emery and narrowed his eyes. "I guess I can, but I don't understand what's so urgent about phone records. Why can't it wait until tomorrow?"

Emery curled her lip upward and leaned forward. "You know Eric. When he sets his mind to something, he doesn't stop until he gets it. He came across these numbers and decided he wants them yesterday."

"I thought you said you came across the numbers."

"We came across the numbers, Russ. Both of us."

Waters gave what seemed like a false snicker. He stared at Emery but his expression never changed. "I reckon that sounds like Eric. But I still don't understand, because the phone company is gonna take at least a week to get these back to you."

Emery smiled and leaned back in her chair. "Maybe not. I've got a well placed source down there. We'll see."

Half smiling, Waters picked up the phone and punched four numbers, advising his assistant that he was sending down three telephone numbers to be submitted to the phone company via a Grand Jury subpoena. He instructed her to drop whatever she was doing and to draft it up immediately as the FBI, and he, considered the matter urgent.

Emery stood and thanked Waters after he hung up the phone. "I'll see Eric this afternoon and let him know that we got the subpoena."

Waters leaned back in his chair, interlocked his fingers and rested them on top of his head. His expression had changed little if any from the midpoint of their conversation. "Tell Eric to call me if he needs anything else. And keep me posted on what you find out."

"I will." Emery waved and ducked out of his office. She walked across the hallway, where Water's assistant waited for her to bring her the information she needed to draft the subpoena.

"What's so gall-danged important that I had to drop what I was doing?" the assistant asked Emery.

Emery smiled and apologized for the inconvenience. She gushed with kindness and told her how much she appreciated her for getting this done on such short notice.

Thoroughly convinced, the assistant smiled and pulled the papers with the information away from Emery. "Give me that, missy. I'll have it done in a jiffy."

In the covered parking garage below the Federal Building, Jack sat low in his seat but fidgeted, wondering if Emery would make it out before someone in the Federal Law Enforcement community recognized him. Only a few people had passed by but none seemed to pay any attention to him. He figured the last place any FBI Agent would imagine him hiding would be in their own parking garage.

Jack breathed a sigh of relief and sat up in his seat when he saw Emery, carrying a brown manila envelope, walking toward him.

About twenty feet from her car, Emery spotted Jack and smiled as she lifted the envelope high above her head in a show of success and mission accomplished. To her right, she heard a car door bang shut and echo through the cave like surroundings.

"Where the hell did you go? What the hell are you doing!" Fuentes shouted, while rapidly approaching Emery, who stood only ten or twelve feet away from her car.

Jack heard the shouts and saw Fuentes expressing his anger toward Emery. He wanted to get out and pound Fuentes' stubby little nose but instead slumped in his seat, trying his best to get his head below window level.

Fuentes was angry. His face was tight as he got nose to nose with Emery. "What the hell are you doing? I've been trying to raise you over the radio for the last two hours. Why the hell didn't you answer?"

Emery paused as she searched for an answer. "I didn't hear you. It must be on the fritz. I've been having problems with it."

Fuentes refused to back away. "On the fritz, hell! I want to know what's going on. You couldn't have missed him out there. And why the hell didn't you meet us back where we agreed to? You know you didn't follow procedure. For all we knew you were laying out there dead somewhere. Something's going on in that pretty little head of yours and I want to know what it is."

Fuentes was not much taller than Emery, so they stood eye to eye. "If you don't get out of my face right now you'll be looking at one of the biggest sexual harassment cases in the history of the FBI."

Fuentes didn't blink or back away. "You go right ahead and file whatever it is you want to file. But it won't work. You're wrong on this one and you're getting in way over your head."

Nose to nose with Fuentes, Emery refused to back down. "No, Eric. I think you're wrong. And I think you're going down on this one."

Fuentes narrowed his eyes. "What the hell is that supposed to mean?"

Emery took one step backwards. "I was in Miami, Eric. See if you can figure it out."

Fuentes stared back at her as Emery cautiously walked toward her car. He could not see her worried expression, concerned if he got closer, he would see Jack.

"What's in the envelope?" Fuentes shouted at about the same time Emery reached for her door handle.

Emery froze for a second or two. "A subpoena on one of my cases. Any other questions?"

Fuentes took a step toward her car. "Let me see it."

Emery opened her door quickly. "It's my case."

Fuentes took several more steps and was now about five feet away from Emery who had just climbed into the car. "I want to see it, Margaret."

She shut the door hard and locked it with her left elbow. "I said it's my case! It's none of your concern!" she shouted through the half cracked window, as she started the engine and shifted into drive. Jack was tucked about as low in his seat as he could get.

Fuentes chased the car and banged on the trunk as it quickly pulled away. "You're off the Armstrong case! You hear me! You're off the case!" He watched as she made the loop around the garage. The screech of her tires echoed throughout the entire cavernous lot.

"That's what he thinks," Emery said, a slight smile appearing.

"Did he see me?" Jack asked from his crouched position.

"I don't think so. But stay down. He might try and follow us."

"Margaret? So that's your name?"

She glanced at Jack, but said nothing before speeding away.

Standing in the middle of the parking garage, Fuentes was silent but fumed inside. Two cars that were stopped behind him waiting for him to move lightly tapped their horns. He turned and flashed his credentials in their direction. "What!" he shouted in anger. Fuentes stormed over to the first car. "Do you want something? You honked your damn horn! Is there something you need?" Fuentes shouted at the top of his lungs.

The driver moved away from the window and nervously shook his head no.

"Then get the hell out of here!" Fuentes yelled and kicked the back bumper as it quickly pulled away. He kicked at the second car but missed. He walked over to the back of his car and pounded the trunk before lying across it as if admitting defeat.

Comfortable in the fact that Fuentes had not followed them, Jack sat up in the seat and stretched out his arms and legs that were sore from being cramped up from squatting near the floorboard. "So what do we do now?"

"We've got to get these records before Eric figures out what we're up to," Emery explained. "I just hope I can get them today. Normally the phone company has thirty days to respond to a subpoena."

Jack turned sharply to Emery. "Thirty days? I don't have thirty days! I'll be dead, or in jail, in thirty days!"

Emery turned to Jack but said nothing.

Fuentes bolted from the elevator and bounded to the bullet proof partition that separated the United States Attorney's Office reception area from the general public. Banging on the thick glass, Fuentes shouted through the circular piece of metal with holes in it. "I've got to see Russ Waters! I've got to see him now!"

Fuentes looked familiar to the receptionist behind the partition, but his demeanor shocked and scared her at first. She looked around for someone to help but no one was there. She knew she was protected but she still apprehensively reached for the button to speak. "Can I help you?" she asked with a tinge of concern in her voice.

Fuentes breathed hard and sweat streamed into his eyes. "Russ Waters! I've got to see Russ Waters now."

"Do you have an appointment, Sir?"

"No! I don't have an appointment!" Fuentes barked. Fishing for his credentials, he pulled them from his pocket and slammed them against the bullet proof glass. "It's urgent that I see him now." His voice calmed somewhat, but he was still obviously desperate.

Remembering now that Fuentes was indeed an FBI Agent, she reached under her desk and pushed a blue button that released the lock on the security door. A buzzing noise followed by a click indicated it was unlocked. Fuentes quickly pulled the door open, stepped inside and returned his badge to his pocket.

"He's in the middle of a meeting. If you'll just have a seat, he should be out..."

"I don't have time to wait!" Fuentes fired back before she could finish speaking. He walked by her without even glancing her way. He walked through a doorway which led to a hallway and to the large conference room where all meetings were held. Paying no attention to the sign on the door confirming an ongoing meeting, Fuentes boldly barged through amid the stares of the surprised attorneys. Out of breath, and with sweat running down his face, he quickly located Waters and pointed in his direction.

"I need to see you," he said, with desperation in his voice. "I have to talk with you now."

Most of the attorneys present at the meeting knew Fuentes, or at least knew who he was. But they had never before seen him in this frantic condition.

"I'm right in the middle of a meeting, Eric. Can't it wait for an hour or so?"

"No!" Fuentes shouted. "It can not wait. I have to see you now!"

Waters stared at Fuentes for a few seconds and then at his shocked peers sitting around the large rectangular oak conference table.

Sensing the urgency of the matter, the attorney leading the meeting half rose from his chair and glanced at Waters. "Let's take a ten minute break, alright?"

The twenty or so attorneys rose from their cushy seats and filed out one by one past Fuentes. A few acknowledged his presence. Most looked the other way pretending not to notice. Waters stood but remained at the table. When everyone but Waters had cleared the room, Fuentes took a couple steps in his direction.

"What's going on, Eric? Margaret said you were tied up. What's wrong?"

"What did she do?" Fuentes asked, his glance drifting toward the floor.

"What do you mean?"

"Why was she up here?"

"She said you sent her to get a subpoena and that it was urgent."

Fuentes looked at Waters. "I thought we had an understanding. I thought it was understood that I called the shots on this case. That no one got anything without going through me first."

"She said you were busy. She said you were tied up and that you sent her down. I assumed since she was working on the case, it was legitimate."

Fuentes' voice became very calm. "She wasn't. She lied. She's become sympathetic to Armstrong. It's possible she's fallen in love with him and will stop at nothing to vindicate him." Fuentes paused. "What information was on the subpoena?"

Waters scratched his forehead. "Uhhhhh. Three numbers. Three phone numbers. She said they were numbers Armstrong had called."

"Was one 770-555-1482?" Fuentes asked, his eyes drifting back and forth between Waters and the floor.

Waters walked toward Fuentes then out the door. "My assistant has a copy on her desk. Let's go see."

Fuentes turned slowly and followed ten feet behind a rapidly moving Waters.

Waters rounded the corner of the square shaped office layout and entered the second cubicle on the right. "Mona. Where's that subpoena Margaret Lewis picked up just a little bit ago?"

Mona reached toward the left hand corner of her desk and retrieved it right away. "Right here. But it's just a copy," she said, handing it to Waters.

Fuentes watched as Waters browsed the subpoena with his index finger.

"Yep. Here it is. 770-555-1482." Waters looked at an obviously distraught Fuentes. "What's going on, Eric? Tell me what's happening here. I need to know."

Fuentes stared at his privately listed number on the official piece of paper. "Can you cancel the subpoena?"

"Cancel it? Why?" Waters said, with surprise in his voice.

"Because she's trying to implicate me. She's got it in her mind that I'm the real target and that Armstrong is innocent. He has obviously brainwashed her into thinking he is innocent. You have to cancel that subpoena before they get there."

Waters stared hard at Fuentes. He didn't know who to believe or what to do. He'd known and worked with Fuentes for several years and had come to trust him, but there had always been an air about him that Waters did not like. And even though he never questioned him about it, he often wondered why Fuentes had insisted that only he be allowed to make requests for assistance and resources on this particular case. Something was not right, but he had let it go.

"I can get it cancelled, Eric. You're the Case Agent and your name is on all the subpoenas."

"Uhhhhhh. Not this one," Mona interrupted. "Agent Lewis had me put her name on it. She's the requesting Agent and the phone company is required to supply the information directly to her. She did the same for the bank records subpoena."

"The what?" Waters asked.

"Bank records," Mona answered.

"Whose bank records?" Waters inquired.

Mona eyed Fuentes. "His," she said, nodding her head toward Fuentes.

"Why didn't you say something, Mona? For crying out loud."

"She came from your office. She said you okayed it. I don't ask questions."

Fuentes eyed Waters, who shook his head. "I can't cancel them. She's the only one who can."

Fuentes spun quickly, bolted around the corner by the conference room, and out the door. The receptionist was busily telling her co-workers how she had been so rudely treated by the FBI agent. Fuentes pounded on the down elevator button over and over until he lost his patience and disappeared down the stairwell adjacent to the three elevators.

Inside Bellsouth headquarters, Emery leaned across his desk and batted her green eyes at the custodian of records who she'd dealt with on two or three other subpoenas. He spent his time reading the subpoena and glancing up at Emery, who rested her chin in her palm and smiled at him every time he looked up. The custodian, two years out of college and incurably horny, turned red and smiled back. "I can have this for you by the end of the week. I won't need thirty days," he said nervously. He wiped one bead of sweat from the middle of his forehead.

The smile faded from Emery's perfectly formed lips. "This is really important. I really need the information sooner than that," she said in a manufactured, but well performed sexy voice.

The custodian felt the temperature rise about ten degrees inside his office. He dabbed at a few more beads of sweat building up above his eyebrows. "Well. I've got some other requests I'm working on. I guess I could work yours in and get it to you by the end of the day."

Emery stood and moved softly to the custodian's side of his desk. He pretended not to notice. She leaned over and laid her hand on top of his. "Is there any way you could get it to me quicker than that?" she said in a sultry voice.

The custodian stared at his hand, now covered by the soft skin of a woman he thought was way too attractive to be a cop. "I guess if it's that important, maybe I can get it for you now, if you don't mind waiting."

"I don't mind at all. I really appreciate this," Emery said, her hand still resting comfortably on top of the custodian's.

He turned in his swivel chair toward the computer that rested on a table to the right of his desk. However, his left hand remained solidly positioned on the desk with Emery's on top. Sitting in front of the computer, he peered up at Emery. "Uhhhhh..." he muttered, glancing at Emery first and then at their hands pressed together.

Emery acted embarrassed, but it was merely a performance. "Oh," she said, lifting her hand from his. "I'm so sorry."

The custodian turned again to the computer then glanced one more time over his shoulder at Emery, who batted her eyes and smiled. He turned back to his computer and began inputting data. "Whew," he said under his breath. 'Tough job,' he thought to himself.

Fuentes weaved in and out of traffic and dodged pedestrians as he advanced as quickly as was humanly possible through the downtown Atlanta traffic. Only one thing was on his mind and that was to get to Emery before she got the phone records. Fuentes knew what she would find and he knew he couldn't let her complete her mission.

"Headquarters to 509," the radio crackled.

He tried to ignore the call at first, but finally picked up after the third call. "509. Go ahead," Fuentes answered, stopping at a red light.

"509. 102 requests your presence in his office ASAP."

Fuentes did not feel like talking to SAC McMann now or anytime in the near future. "Tell him I can't right now."

"That's a negative 509. 102 advises this is not a request. It's an order."

Fuentes held his radio mouthpiece against his cheek as he waited impatiently for the light to turn green and thought hard for a response. "Advise 102 that I am unavailable at the present time."

"Fuentes! Get your ass in here now! Do you understand me?" McMann's angry voice cracked over the radio.

Fuentes buried his face into the palm of his hand. It was obvious McMann had talked to Waters and had been standing over the radio operator the entire time. Composing himself, Fuentes lifted the mike to his mouth. "102. I can't come right now. I've got business to attend to."

McMann was angry as a raging fire. "The only business you have to attend to is here! Now I'm ordering you back here now! We can handle this matter from inside."

Fuentes gunned the accelerator as soon as the light turned green.

"The only way it can be handled is on my terms."

"Damn it, Eric! You don't know what you're doing!" McMann shouted through the radio. "For the last time I am ordering you…"

Fuentes reached down just under the floorboard and jerked out every wire leading from the radio as McMann's voice trailed away. Fuentes smiled. "I didn't get that last command, boss. Radio went out."

The custodian handed Emery the last of the phone records his printer spit out. "A couple of your boys there tore up the lines to Columbia."

No longer smiling or pretending to be sexy, Emery casually flipped through the pages and pages of phone calls made from the telephones of Fuentes, Doug Spacey and Jack. If there was any good news about the records, at least as far as Emery was concerned, it was that there were no calls to Columbia made from Jack's phone. The hundreds of calls placed to several different numbers in Columbia all originated from either Fuentes' or Doug Spacey's phone numbers. But there was still some unsettling information in Jack's subpoenaed records that Emery wanted answers for. She thanked the custodian for his time and for generating the records she needed so quickly. He turned around with a smile as big as Texas, hoping for more conversation, but Emery was halfway out the door, leaving him with his mouth partially open, fully prepared to deliver a pick-up line.

Outside, parked close by but far enough away not to be noticed, Jack slumped in his usual position. His eyes were high enough above his dashboard to watch Atlantians go about their business, but low enough not to be seen.

Records several inches thick in hand, Emery emerged from the double glass doors in front of the phone company. She looked left, then right, before breaking into a swift trot toward her car. With twenty-five feet to go, she heard the car and its screeching tires zeroing in on her position. She didn't have to look back. She knew it was Fuentes. Her trot turned into a full gallop, but it was too late. Fuentes' car had blocked her path. Fuentes slammed on his brakes and his car came to a screeching halt. He erupted from his car, his 9mm pistol poised on top of his car and aimed directly at Emery. She froze, not daring to look at Jack, who nervously observed from his crouched position. She did not look at Fuentes either. She simply stared at the ground.

"Give me the records, Margaret," Fuentes said calmly, his face soaked with perspiration.

She shook her head no. "No, Eric. Game's over." She took one step toward her car.

"Not by a long shot. You take one more step and I'll blow your head off."

Emery froze, then turned to Fuentes. "You wouldn't do it."

"Don't try me. I *will* do it," he said, his nostrils flaring.

She stared at Fuentes, turned and took one more step toward her car.

Like an explosion, the bullet tore through the left back door of her car. The deafening blast sent a chill through her spine and a ringing in her ears. Inside, Jack cringed, his mind searching for a plan.

"The records. Put them on the ground."

Emery turned back to Fuentes. Again she shook her head no. "Not this time, Eric. You're going to have to kill me." She took one more step, but was stopped by another bullet penetrating the back door just above the entry point of the first round shot.

"I swear to God, Margaret. The next one will be between your eyes. You're not leaving with those records."

Turning to Fuentes, she shook her head again. "Go ahead. Either finish the job you came here to do or let me go and do mine."

Fuming, Fuentes stared at her. He had no intention of shooting her. He only hoped he could intimidate her into giving him the records. "You know you're going to crucify me with those records."

"You crucified yourself. I had nothing to do with it." She turned from Fuentes and walked the last few steps to her car as he watched in silence, his gun still steadily aimed at her. She opened her door just enough to squeeze in. She did not want Fuentes to see Jack. His gun followed her every move.

"I know he's in there. You can stop being so careful," Fuentes said smiling, even before she shut her door. "Just tell him he hasn't won. Not yet." Fuentes removed his weapon from the top of the car and replaced it in his shoulder holster.

Jack sat up in his seat. His eyes met Fuentes' as Emery backed from her parking space, pulled away and drove off into the Atlanta skyline.

"What's your last name? Or is that classified?" Jack stared at the woman he had known for so long as Emery.

"Lewis. Margaret Lewis. And I hope to God you're telling the truth."

~ 19 ~

It didn't matter if Emery was really Special Agent Margaret Lewis. In Jack's mind, she was still Emery Carson. In a cheap hotel room on the south side of Atlanta, Jack and Emery perused over phone and bank records all night and early into the morning. White Styrofoam cups with coffee stains littered the puke-green soiled carpet. Jack stretched out on one of the double beds, staring at the ceiling. His eyes had begun playing tricks on him a half hour earlier, most likely caused by a mixture of tediously reading hundreds of tiny entries and the flashing yellow neon sign outside their window advertising all night entertainment. Emery sat on the floor, records strewn all around her. For about the tenth time she scrutinized each call Fuentes had made, trying to match up telephone numbers that had arisen during the investigation. In the previous year alone, Fuentes had made 429 long distance calls to eight different numbers in Columbia. Emery cringed when she thought of what had been going on practically right in front of her. She hadn't even started going over the bank records they picked up after they left the phone company.

Jack sat up on the side of the bed and rubbed his neck. "Sorry about that. My head's splitting."

"That's alright," Emery said, without looking up from the records she continued to pour over. She shook her head.

"What?" Jack asked.

"I just can't believe what's been going on right under my nose. And I never suspected it. Not for one second."

Jack slid down from the bed and sat beside Emery. "What've you found so far?"

"Over four hundred calls last year to eight different numbers in Columbia. And I haven't even checked the year before that yet."

"Are any to Raes?"

"I don't think so. A couple of the numbers look real familiar, but I can't put my finger on them. I'm gonna have to go to the office and pull up the numbers that came up during the investigation and see if any of them match up. I just can't remember right now." She looked at her watch. "It's not quite three yet. I'd kind of like to go over the bank records first, but I probably should go to the office before anyone gets there."

Jack acted surprised. "You're gonna go now?"

"I have to. I'm sure by now Eric's smoothed things out with the SAC and they're not gonna let me touch that file. I've got to get a hold of it and the only way is to go now before anyone gets there." She looked at her watch again. "I've got about three hours before any agents start filtering in." She pulled her briefcase from the foot of the bed and unlatched it. After writing down the eight numbers on a scratch piece of paper that Fuentes had called in Columbia, she stuffed the note into her pocket. Jack watched as she meticulously straightened all the phone records scattered about and placed them neatly on top of the bank records inside the briefcase. "I'll be back before sunrise. You stay here and get some rest," she said, standing up and attempting to smooth out the wrinkles in her pants.

Jack stood alongside her. "No. I'm going with you."

Emery laughed. "You can't go with me. The subject of the case? The target of a massive manhunt walks right into the middle of the FBI office? I don't think so, Jack."

"I'm not staying here. I'll ride along. I'll stay in the car. But I'm not staying here. I've got a weird uneasy feeling about this place. I just don't like it."

Emery smiled sarcastically. "That's ridiculous. Besides, you've got a headache. You need some rest."

"I'm going, Emery! Margaret. Whatever your name is. I'm not staying here."

Emery shrugged her shoulders. "Fine. Suit yourself. And, it's Margaret," she said, as she set the briefcase on the foot of the bed and snapped the latches closed. "Let's go."

Pitching her briefcase onto the middle of the front seat, Margaret peered at Jack over the top of the car. "You ready?"

"As ever."

Margaret smiled, got in the car and leaned over and unlocked Jack's door.

Neither talked much on the ride up the interstate to downtown Atlanta. For the most part, Jack reclined his seat halfway and dozed off and on for the fifteen minute trip.

The large digital clock on top of one of the downtown banks flashed 3:21 as their car pulled into the darkened parking garage utilized by the FBI and other Federal agencies. Margaret checked her watch to see if her time matched. As if on cue, Jack opened his eyes, then brought his seat back to its normal position. He rubbed his eyes then the back of his neck.

"Is your head better?" she asked, pulling into a parking space in the near empty garage.

"Yeah. A little I guess. What time is it?"

"Almost three-thirty," Margaret answered, as she opened her door and stepped one foot outside onto the cement floor. "This shouldn't take long. No more than thirty minutes."

"Will anyone see you?"

"Naaah. Just the night clerk and they don't ask questions." She stepped all the way out of the car and put her hand on the door to close it.

"Got the numbers?"

Margaret tapped her pocket twice. "Right here." She shut the door quietly, crossed the shadowy confines of the enclosed garage, and disappeared up a stairwell.

Jack watched her all the way until she was swallowed by the darkness. After her barely visible figure rounded a corner and charged up the stairway, he swiveled and slowly panned his eyes to the briefcase sitting beside him in the middle of the front seat. He turned and looked behind him before shifting back and eyeing the briefcase again. Slowly, he moved both hands toward the latches that he gripped with his thumbs. Pressing ever so slightly sideways, the latches released and popped against the hard brown leather top. Jack twisted his neck and looked one more time toward the stairwell. He turned the briefcase and lifted the top of it. With his thumbs, he pushed the inside arms forward to keep the top half locked in place.

Flipping through the phone records toward the bottom of the

stack, Jack pulled out a sampling of Fuentes' bank records. The only light available came from the streetlights outside the garage. But they weren't enough to read the small print. Jack assumed correctly that all good FBI agents carried a flashlight in the glove compartment. He retrieved it and held the records close to the floorboard so he could not be seen by anyone that happened to be up at this hour. The only person Jack could see was a homeless man about a hundred yards away, who was comfortably snoring on top of a grate where a gracious amount of steam poured forth, keeping him warm for the night.

The beam from the flashlight cruised along line after line, entry after entry, of Fuentes' banking practices during the month of July of the previous year. It just happened to be the one Jack had pulled from underneath the stack. He could not believe his eyes. In the month of July alone, Fuentes had six deposits totaling $235,000. And that did not include his savings account or his paychecks that were direct deposited. He edged the flashlight toward the bottom of this particular statement, which indicated Fuentes' ending July balance was $342,867. Jack could not believe that Fuentes hadn't even made an attempt to hide his financial dealings. All six deposits were always way above the $10,000 cap required to be reported to the proper financial authorities. Jack wondered aloud why Fuentes would make deposits above the reportable limit.

Jack took the page he was looking at and put it on the bottom of the stack in his hand. On the next page were the figures of Fuentes' savings accounts. He had three. One was in his name and two were in names of persons Jack had never heard of. He edged his flashlight toward the bottom of the statement where the figure he saw was nothing short of astounding. Fuentes' savings, CD's and other accounts were just under three million dollars. Jack turned off the flashlight and leaned back in his seat to catch his breath. He threw the records he was looking at into the briefcase and pulled another stash of banking records from underneath the phone records. This stack, from the second of four banks where Fuentes had additional accounts, read much the same as the first. He had a $154,427 balance in his checking account, four savings accounts, and several CDs, which totaled close to four million dollars. The October statement had five deposits totaling just under $300,000. Like the first bank, every deposit was above the $10,000 cap. Jack silently wondered how Fuentes explained the large deposits to authorities.

Margaret quietly stepped out of the elevator and into the dimly lit foyer that led to the Atlanta FBI office. She crept silently toward the Agent's entry complete with a number coded keypad and two cameras perched on either side of the foyer, monitored by a night clerk. Margaret knew the night clerk usually stayed busy filing or catching up on his reading, so chances were he would not see her on the monitor. Even if he did, it wouldn't matter. She had every right to be in the office, no matter what time it was. With her index finger, she punched in the five digit code which electronically released the lock. She entered the hallway and heard the latch lock a second or two after the door closed. Margaret was safely inside the corridors of her office. She plodded softly one step at a time, around two corners toward her squad room and the rotor where the files were kept.

"Hey, Agent Lewis!" The voice echoed through a dimly lit hallway around yet another corner from her squad area.

Margaret stood upright. Her heart pounded in her throat. She turned toward the corner and saw a head peeking around the corner. She breathed a sigh of relief when she saw the nineteen-year-old intern, his curly blonde locks pouring down the back side of his neck. "Is that you, Carlton?"

"Yeah. It's me. I thought that was you out there. Just wanted to make sure."

"Yeah. I couldn't sleep. Thought I'd come on in and get an early start."

"Man, you Squad Five guys like burning the midnight oil, don't cha'?"

"Well, you know what they say about the early bird."

"Well, I'm just up here doing some filing," Carlton explained. "If you need me, I'll be in the ASAC's office."

"Thanks," she said, her voice shaky, but not noticeably. "I think I'm okay right now."

"See ya'," Carlton said, as his head disappeared around the corner.

Margaret turned to make sure Carlton had indeed left the area. She moved swiftly to the rotor area behind the Squad Five secretary's desk and switched on the light. With her hand, she rolled the eight volume case file around until it reached the front. Margaret reached in, grabbed four volumes, and carried them to her desk. She sprinted quickly back to the rotor and pulled the other four volumes. Each volume was two inches thick and she had no idea which of the eight files had the numbers she needed to match up. She found volume one and started flipping page by page, looking for a document or report that contained the phone numbers. She knew the pin register that had run for the duration of the investigation had registered numerous numbers in Columbia. Her gut feeling was that one or more of the numbers from Fuentes' phone records would be listed on a document somewhere. The only problem was, each file contained around three hundred pages. She just hoped that the numbers popped up before the last document in volume eight.

Five minutes into it, and halfway through volume one, the numbers still had not appeared. However, the process was going a little quicker than she'd hoped for. All in all it was a fairly simple task just looking for numbers. She knew they were there somewhere. The quiet of the early morning hours made her eyes drowsy.

"Finding what you need?"

Margaret jumped from a half sleep. She felt her heart skip several beats then begin racing. "Carlton! Don't sneak up on me like that," she ordered, turning around to face him. She cocked her head and narrowed her eyes. In the dimly lit squad room she could only see the outline of a human figure. A figure that had no blond, curly locks. A figure that caused her blood to run cold.

Fuentes firmly grabbed and spun her chair around to where her face met his beltline. He was short, but at this moment he seemed to tower high above her. She was powerless to do anything but stare up at him. "Surprise, surprise," he said, grinning down at her. "And what have we got here?" He picked up the file she had been reviewing and looked at it. "Well, damn. If I didn't know better, I'd swear these are the case files from my case." Fuentes threw the file on the center of her desk. The sound of the file smacking against the metal echoed throughout the empty office. "What are you looking for, Margaret? Names? Phone numbers, perhaps? Maybe where Raes keeps his banking records?" Fuentes shook his head. "Armstrong's got you snowed, doesn't he? He has totally brainwashed you and turned you against the truth."

"The evidence speaks for itself, Eric. How do you explain it?"

"I don't have to explain anything!" he barked, leaning close to her face. "I haven't done anything wrong."

Margaret chuckled and shook her head. "I don't get you, Eric. Are you in total denial? I was in Miami. I saw what you did. Who you were. Who you are. Where you came from. I've seen the phone records. I've got your bank records. You can't get away with it."

Fuentes refused to give ground. He hovered over her, invading her personal space. "McMann suspended me indefinitely. At least until it all blows over."

"It's not gonna all just blow over, Eric. And if you're suspended, why are you here?"

"Shut your mouth you stupid little traitor...!" Fuentes shouted as he raised his fist to backhand her across her face. He stopped himself two inches before impact.

Margaret flinched. Her eyes shut tightly waiting for the blow to land.

Fuentes pulled his hand back.

Margaret opened her eyes and peered up at his. Her breaths were like the slow pant of a dog. She was scared. "Go ahead if it makes you feel any better."

Fuentes glared down hard at her. His jaws grounded together. "Why?" he angrily muttered. "Why are you doing this to me?"

She stared up at him. His eyes seemed genuine. "I'm just searching for the truth. That's all. Just the truth."

"That's just it. You won't accept the truth. You think you're going to make a name for yourself but you're wrong." He kept a tight grasp on both arms of the chair she was sitting in, his face still only inches away from hers. "You want the truth? Is that what you want

Margaret....Agent Lewis?"

She paused and gazed upward into his raging brown eyes. "Yeah, Eric. That's what I want. That's exactly what I want."

Fuentes released his grasp on the arms of the chair, grabbed her left arm and with a forceful jerk, pulled her from the chair. "You want the truth? I'll give it to you." Pulling on her arm, he drug her across the squad room and toward a hallway. Fear spread across her face like wildfire across a dry forest. Just as he turned the corner, the phone on his desk rang. Fuentes stopped. Maintaining a tight grasp on her arm, he looked back at the phone, then at Margaret. She never took her eyes from his. The phone rang a second time.

"Aren't you going to answer it, Eric?"

It rang a third time. Fuentes stared at the phone.

"I can't imagine who would be calling you at four in the morning here at work. And you just happen to be here. My God! How lucky you just happened to be here. It couldn't be that maybe you were expecting a call, is it?"

The phone rang for the fourth, fifth and sixth time. Fuentes took turns glancing between the phone and Margaret.

"Better get it, Eric. Never know. Could be the Director wanting a briefing on your case. I heard he likes to call Agents for briefings in the middle of the night."

The phone rang for the eighth time. Fuentes slightly loosened his grip from her arm.

"Go ahead. Don't let me stop you. This could be the call that makes your case or your career."

Fuentes released his grip and walked casually over to the phone ringing on his desk for the ninth and tenth time. He glanced at Margaret, who stood still and watched him before he answered. "Fuentes."

She watched as Fuentes sat down in his chair but was puzzled when he looked back and smiled at her.

"Why, hello Jack," Fuentes answered.

Margaret narrowed her eyes and turned an ear toward Fuentes.

"I take it you're looking for Margaret. Or do you still know her as Emery? I guess it doesn't make any difference now, does it?"

She watched from the corner of the hallway as Fuentes paused and stared at her, grinning.

As quickly as Fuentes' goofy grin appeared it was suddenly gone. "When and where do you propose this…this…this meeting to occur?" Fuentes listened for an answer then glanced at his watch. "I'll be there in twenty minutes."

Margaret patted her pocket for her keys. She'd left them in the car. She had no cell phone. She was clueless about what conversation had just taken place. Nonetheless, she was severely pissed off that Jack would take off in her bureau car without saying anything. This was a fireable offense and now Fuentes would have the goods on her. She could only assume Jack knew Fuentes was there and he was trying to draw him out or divert his attention in some way.

Fuentes hung up the phone and walked toward Margaret. "You still want the truth?"

She nodded yes.

"Let's go then."

Fuentes walked past her and was ten or fifteen feet down the hallway before he looked back and saw that she remained glued to her spot on the corner. In the back of her mind, she wondered if this was a trap. Maybe Fuentes was simply luring her away so he could dispose of her. She figured if he was capable of stealing 250 million of dollars worth of drugs, he could also be capable of murder.

Fuentes froze, stared at her, then paused. "If you want the truth you're going to have to trust me. You have to come with me now. I've got nothing to lose at this point."

"And what about me?"

Fuentes smiled. "I'm not gonna hurt you. I'd have done it already if I was going to."

"How do I know that? How do I know this just isn't a trap?"

"You just have to trust me."

Margaret hesitated. Then against all her instincts, she stepped slowly toward Fuentes. They entered the darkened garage and approached Fuentes' bureau car that he was not supposed to drive now that he was officially suspended. It was parked on the same level but on the other end from where she and Jack had parked. In her haste to get up to and inside the office, she hadn't even noticed it was there. She looked at the empty parking place formally occupied by her bureau car. Fuentes saw her shaking her head.

"I know what you're thinking," Eric said.

Margaret looked at Fuentes who had opened the trunk and was fishing for something inside it.

Fuentes smiled. "You can screw up an investigation. A conviction, maybe. You can just about screw up anything about your job. But don't ever screw with the bureau car."

Margaret didn't remove her eyes from the empty space. "Is it thirty or sixty days on the bricks?"

Fuentes pulled a medium-sized brown briefcase from the trunk and the shut it. The sound echoed throughout the garage. He took the briefcase with his right hand and glanced down at his watch on his left wrist. "In about fifteen minutes it won't matter. You'll be a hero either way this works out."

Margaret turned but refused to smile. Her solid glare did not intimidate Fuentes at all. "What's that supposed to mean?"

Fuentes smiled and moved to the driver's side door, unlocking it. He stared at Margaret, who followed him with her eyes, but whose body was transfixed to one spot. "Are you coming or not?"

She turned, opened the passenger door, and climbed in.

The wailing of the spinning tires bounced off the garage walls. Fuentes' car bolted from the garage onto the empty downtown Atlanta streets. The only light came from the streetlights that lined the vacant sidewalks. Eric quickly turned down a main street and then swiftly accelerated into the north bound ramp of Interstate 75.

"Where are we going?" Margaret asked.

"Your boyfriend wants to meet me at a coffee shop up at the junction of 75 and 285."

Margaret propped her elbow against the window and leaned her temple on two of her fingers. "He's not my boyfriend. And I'm beginning to resent the accusations."

Fuentes looked at her and smiled. "Whatever."

"What did he say when he called?" Margaret refused to make eye contact with Fuentes.

"He said he needed to talk to me and that he didn't want you around to hear whatever it is."

"So why are you taking me?"

"Because I think you need to hear. I think you are entitled to the truth."

"Lucky me," she said sarcastically, peering out her window. She wanted absolutely no eye contact with him.

Fuentes veered his car up the ramp, immediately following the sign indicating the 285 bypass was the next exit. He wound around the cloverleaf and took the first exit. Driving into a convenience store, he pulled into a space in the back and threw the transmission into park. Margaret looked around but did not see her car.

"He's not here, if that's what you're looking for."

"Then what are you doing?"

Fuentes opened the briefcase that sat between him and Margaret. He pulled out a tiny disc about the size of a dime. It was attached to some wires. He laid it on his lap before pulling some white medical adhesive tape from another section of the briefcase.

"A wire?"

"Yep." Fuentes tore a piece of tape from the metal roll and placed the disc and wires across his chest. He taped down the wires and refastened the buttons on his shirt. Pulling the transmitter from the corner where it had slid in the briefcase, Fuentes flipped a tiny switch and placed it on the seat next to Margaret.

She looked at the transmitter like it was a live grenade. She then peered at Fuentes and shook her head. "What do you expect me to do?"

Fuentes jerked the gear shift into reverse, backed up and made sure he was clear of the convenience store gas tanks before he shifted into drive and casually drove toward the street. "Nothing. All you have to do is listen." Fuentes pulled onto the street, crossed the bridge to the other side of I-285, and entered the ramp heading in the opposite direction. Crossing over I-75, both looked down at the few cars below on the road that within two hours would be teaming with bumper to bumper rush hour traffic.

After several minutes, Fuentes reached the fourth exit off I-285. He came to a halt at the red light at the end of the ramp that turned green as soon as he stopped. He turned left and crossed back underneath the I-285 overpass. His eyes danced back and forth from one side of the road to the other in a diligent search for the coffee shop. Finally, ahead on the right about a quarter of a mile, he spotted it. "There it is."

Margaret looked up. "The Waffle House?"

Fuentes smiled. "Yeah. Don't let anybody ever tell you your boy Armstrong doesn't have any class. I bet he'll even spring for the coffee."

Margaret was not humored.

Fuentes quickly pulled his car into another all night convenience store that was situated three buildings down, but on the same side of the road. Pulling in the back where the car would not be visible, he cut the engine but left the keys in the car. Patting his chest to assure himself that the wire was still there, Fuentes opened his door and stepped outside. "I assume you've used one of these things before," he said motioning toward the receiver that still lay beside her.

Margaret scowled at his patronizing tone.

"Then I won't explain. I hope you enjoy what you are about to hear." Fuentes shut his door and disappeared into the shadows of the pre-dawn morning.

Margaret slumped down into the seat and listened to Fuentes' footsteps. She could hear his breathing grow faster and heavier the further he went.

Inside the Waffle House and seated in the booth nearest the back, Jack nervously sipped on a cup of coffee. His head darted back and forth, checking every car that drove past on the street outside. His whole body stiffened when he heard the waitress behind the counter give the customary 'Mornin'! greeting as the door opened.

Fuentes looked left, then right, where he spotted Jack sitting in the back. He looked around, winked at the waitress behind the counter, and slowly began making his way toward the booth. When he finally approached, he stood at first, looking down on his nemesis. A slow grin appeared on his face. "Hello Jack." Fuentes was winded from his walk and his rapid breathing showed it.

Jack looked up. A non-verbal staring contest ensued for several seconds.

"Damn, Jack. You think you could have found a table a little closer to the back? The walk back here about wore me out."

"Yeah. I can tell. Sounds like you're in great shape there, Fuentes.

I thought the FBI had physical standards you Fed boys had to meet. They must have thrown them out when your class went through the Academy."

Fuentes sat down across from Jack. "You're a barrel of laughs, Jack. You ever thought about going into comedy? Maybe do some standup? Then again. I don't guess you'll have to worry about a career when this is all over will you?"

Jack shook his head. "You still refuse to understand anything."

"Understand what? Understand? What's not to understand? You are guilty as hell but aren't man enough to admit it."

Jack glared across the table at Fuentes.

The waitress that Fuentes had winked at approached their table. She removed the pencil from behind her ear and produced a green order pad from her skirt pocket. "Can I get 'cha anything, sugar?"

Fuentes looked up. "Cup of coffee. Black."

The waitress pulled a white saucer with a chip on it and a cup to match from underneath the counter adjacent to where Fuentes and Jack were seated. She placed them in front of Fuentes and pulled a coffee pot from the counter, pouring him a cup. "There ya' go, hun."

Fuentes looked up and smiled at her. "Thanks."

The waitress put the coffee pot down and walked away to check on the six or seven patrons that were all drinking coffee or eating waffles.

Fuentes scooted forward in his seat and leaned slightly across the table. "You really want to know what I understand, Jack? I'll tell you." Fuentes paused and drank a sip of coffee. "Are you old enough to remember George Carlin when he was doing standup comedy? You should. I mean you're such a funny guy."

"What's your point?"

Fuentes took another sip of coffee. "Well. I remember he had this routine. And I remember laughing real hard when Carlin said that if two people are on an elevator and one of them farts, everyone knows who did it. Get it? You get it, right? I mean I don't get on an elevator to this day that I don't think of that line."

"What are you getting at? Is there a point to your drivel?"

Fuentes smiled and shook his head. "Don't you get it, Jack? Do you really not get it at all? Two people. Elevator. One farts." Fuentes paused. "You and I were the only ones that could have stolen that cocaine. And you and I both know it wasn't me. In other words, Jack. You were the one who farted in that elevator. Get it?"

From the car, Margaret listened to every word.

Jack stared across the table at a smiling Fuentes. "I've got enough to bury you."

"With what, Jack? You haven't got shit. Oh, the stuff you found might look funny but it proves absolutely nothing. It might cause people to question my past. I guess it could even cause me to lose my job. But it's all legal and it doesn't mean a damn thing."

"How much is your reputation worth? Huh? Can you put a price on reputation? How are you going to explain all those calls to Columbia? Huh?"

"I guess you were pretty impressed with my bank records, too. Right? But it's all legitimate. You didn't even scratch the surface of my wealth. If you play the market right, buy at the right time, take chances and make the right choices, you'd be amazed at the returns you could see. Too bad you couldn't subpoena my bank records in Switzerland and the Grand Caymans. I'm worth millions. But I did it all legally. Every fucking penny I've made is legit. Every damn one of 'em. Unfortunately, Jack," Fuentes paused. "I can't say the same about you."

Jack leaned across the table. Their faces were separated by six inches. "I don't care if they're legitimate or not. The appearance of it. The phone calls. The bank records. What I've got will bury you alive."

"Dream on, Jack. They're all legit." Fuentes paused. "Sure. The appearance is not so good. I might be suspended while they investigate internally. But in the end, I'll be cleared and you'll still be rotting in a prison in the middle of Kansas."

Jack smiled. "You're forgetting something. Maybe all of it is legit, but your ass still belongs to me."

"How do you figure that?"

"Miami. Quibdo. Columbia. Does the name Enrique Montalvan ring any bells?"

Fuentes stared at Jack but said nothing.

Jack leaned back and folded his arms. "Oooooh. If I didn't know better I'd say I've struck a nerve."

Fuentes frowned. "That was a long time ago."

"You lied to the FBI about everything. You think maybe they'd like to compare your resume' to the information I recovered in Miami? Did you change your name because of the family business or because…"

"That's enough!" Fuentes shouted. Everyone inside the Waffle House looked at him. "I did nothing wrong and you know it!" Fuentes said quietly, but with emphasis.

Jack grinned. "Touchy, touchy."

Fuentes glared across the table. "What is it you want?"

Jack reached in his pocket and pulled out a key with a number on the green plastic key ring. He held it six inches from Fuentes' nose. "This is one of two keys that fits a locker somewhere in the greater Atlanta area. A good friend holds the other one and is waiting to hear from me. In that locker are three folders. Inside those folders are three stamped envelopes with every detailed piece of information I got from Miami about you and your family. One envelope is addressed to your office. One is to FBI Headquarters in Washington and one to the Atlanta Journal Constitution." Jack reached into his shirt pocket and pulled out a small square piece of paper with a seven digit number written on it. He handed it to Fuentes. Jack looked at his watch. "What time do you have?"

Fuentes looked at his watch. "It's almost four-thirty."

"By noon today," Jack began, glancing at his watch, "you're going to wire ten million dollars into this account number at the International Bank of Zurich in Switzerland. From what I've seen, that's a drop in the bucket for you, Fuentes."

Fuentes laughed out loud. "Forget it, Jack. It's not going to work."

"If the money is not in the account by noon, my friend takes the envelopes and drops them in the United States Mail and your career and your….uhhh, good name…is over."

Fuentes laughed hard and then faded into a smile. "You don't understand, Jack. You're right. I love my job and I will be cleared no matter what scam you pull. But I don't need the job. I'm independently wealthy. I won't cave into your threats."

Jack smiled back. "You may not need the job. But what about your reputation? What will all those trusted friends, neighbors and all your FBI comrades say about your tainted past, not to mention the appearance of your present and future?"

Margaret straightened up in her seat and stared out the windshield.

"What's in it for me?" Fuentes asked.

Jack gazed across the table. "As soon as I confirm the money is in that account I'll contact you and let you know where the locker is. If it's not, I contact my other friend. Very simple."

"And what about the cocaine?" Fuentes asked Jack.

"You didn't let me finish. That's the best part. For ten million dollars you're gonna get more than just the Miami files. You're gonna get what might be the largest cocaine bust in United States history, certainly in Atlanta."

Fuentes smiled facetiously. "And just think, I have you to thank for that."

Jack smiled. "You're a smart ass. But I'm not gonna hold that against you." Jack paused. "Let me try to explain this so even you can understand it. Agent Carson, or whatever the hell her name is..."

"Lewis. Special Agent Margaret Lewis," Fuentes interrupted.

"Whatever," Jack waved his hands and nodded his head. "Lewis was very conscientious. She didn't think I knew that she subpoenaed Doug Spacey's phone records, but I did. Anyway, being the astute Agent she is, she subpoenaed Doug's records because she still didn't know whether or not she could trust me or whether or not I was telling the truth. I guess all you Feds are skeptics. I guess something in the back of her mind told her that maybe, just maybe, that I was guilty. But she left all of her information just laying out there for me to see it. If I didn't know better, I'd have sworn she'd done it on purpose."

Margaret stared out the car window. She was motionless.

"Anyway," Jack continued. "Doug was no pharmaceutical rep. Hell. He was doing the same damn thing Marlowe was doing. He was nothing more than another distribution point for Raes."

"You knew it all along?" Fuentes asked.

Jack smiled. "Not until after I was arrested. Oh, I had heard what he was doing but I didn't believe it. When it happened to me, I thought maybe what I had heard was true all along. So, I called him. Then I found out it really is a small world after all." Jack leaned back. "Doug was in on it, but Raes barely paid him after the first year. Doug knew if he called the authorities, he was a dead man. And then Raes dramatically dropped his profit margin. Doug lived fine but he wanted more and he felt Raes had screwed him. Doug had gobs of information about everyone involved and we devised a plan beneficial to all. Well, beneficial to Doug and me, of course." Jack paused. "And you of course. That's where you come in. As we speak, Raes is wiring his half of my inheritance to the same account number that you will too, as soon as your bank opens. For him, it's a small price to pay for two-hundred and fifty million dollars worth of cocaine."

Margaret pulled the wires from her ears. She had heard enough. The SOB had fooled her. He had totally scammed her.

"There is one small glitch that Raes isn't aware of." Jack paused and grinned. "He has no idea I'm talking to you." Fuentes smiled nervously, still unsure of the events unfolding before him.

"As soon as I confirm Raes' deposit, he'll be made aware of where I hid his merchandise. As soon as I confirm your deposit, you'll be made aware of the same location."

Jack smiled and lifted his hands in the air and spread them apart. "Think of the press. I can see the headlines now. Special Agent Eric Fuentes responsible for the largest cocaine seizure in United States history. Agent Fuentes stings the world's largest drug cartel."

Jack paused. "You also bury the man who murdered your mother." Jack paused again and put his hands back on the table. "On the other hand, if the money is not wired by noon today, Raes gets his cocaine back. I'll still be rich, but the headlines will read something a whole lot different. The question is. Are you willing to accept the latter? I guess it's a question of dignity, Eric. Do you keep it, or do you give it up? You have to ask yourself if your dignity is worth my asking price."

Fuentes stared deep into Jack's eyes.

Jack softly reached for and pulled Fuentes' hand toward his, placing the key into his palm. He then balled Fuentes' fingers around the key. "You'll be needing this." Jack slid across his seat and stood up. He pulled five dollars from his pocket and pitched it onto the table. "Coffee's on me."

"You're so generous, Jack."

"Don't mention it," Jack said, as he started to walk away. "It's the least I can do."

Fuentes turned back to face Jack but remained seated in the booth. "Jack?"

Jack stopped and turned to Fuentes.

"I gotta know why. Why did you do it?"

Jack paused and smiled at Fuentes. He shrugged his shoulders. "Why does anyone do anything? Because it was there? Greed, maybe? Impulse, for sure. Tough question." Jack paused. "Bottom line? I never thought you'd count all twelve thousand bricks again. I thought I'd get away clean. Guess I was wrong about that. If you just hadn't counted all those damn bricks again, we wouldn't be sitting here." Jack walked out of the Waffle House.

"It would have caught up to you, Jack. Sooner or later it would have caught up to you." Fuentes watched as Jack pushed open the door and climbed into Margaret's confiscated bureau car. He resented the cocky smile Jack now wore. He patted his chest where the wire was taped. "Do you still believe him?"

Fuentes half walked and half trotted back to the convenience store where he had parked the car. Somehow he wasn't surprised when he arrived that his car and Margaret were missing.

~ 20 ~

The sky was a deep blue over Hartsfield International Airport. Not a cloud in the sky. It was a perfect day for flying. People buzzed about pretending not to notice each other as they passed by in the airport concourse like ships in the night. The temperature was perfect. Seventy-two degrees and a nice little nip in the air. After confirming the first deposit into his account in Zurich, Jack leaned into a booth used for computer users and whispered directions, the number of a storage unit, and the combination of the padlock. Calmly he gave the crucial information to Hector Raes, who promised if Jack tricked him he would track him down and make him regret the day he was born.

A second call to the International Bank of Zurich confirmed the second deposit of ten million. A wide smile and a small shoulder bag were the only possessions Jack would carry on his flight to Switzerland. Placing a call to Fuentes and giving him the location of the locker along with the same information he provided Raes, Jack cockily insisted that Fuentes not thank him for what was about to be the largest drug bust in U.S. history. Fuentes, who had been cleared by the SAC and was off suspension, laughed and told Jack not to be so brazen. He informed him somewhere along the line, what he had done would catch up to him. Jack shrugged off the comment and told Fuentes he had a bonus for him inside the locker that would make him famous. Fuentes would discover later, that inside the Miami files, Jack had placed the names of every plumbing warehouse and executive involved with the Raes organization and all scheduled deliveries.

Jack chuckled. "Hey. I've done the honorable thing. You get your cocaine, make your arrests, and the bad guys go to jail."

"All except for one," Fuentes retorted.

The smile disappeared. "Yeah. All except for one. But can you blame me for cashing in at the expense of a Columbian scuzball billionaire dope dealer? Ten million dollars is nothing to him."

"What difference does that make, Jack? You are still wrong and you know it. You're the one who has to live with yourself."

"You're no angel either. You lied to the FBI about everything. I guess that's the price you pay for dishonesty."

"I gotta go, Jack. Got more important matters to attend to. But listen. Wherever it is you're headed to, have a pleasant trip. I'm sure we'll meet again someday."

Jack pressed the end button on his cell phone and stared straight into the wall for ten or so seconds. He then adjusted the strap on his shoulder and headed toward the gate and jet that would whisk him away to lengthy layovers in New York and London before carrying him on to his final destination to Zurich. The entire trip would take over twenty-four hours, but he had twenty million reasons why not to worry about the long trip ahead. He eyed Gate B-21 in the distance.

He glanced at his watch and saw he had twenty minutes before takeoff. Some reading material would be appropriate for the long flight he was about to embark on. He stopped in the small store fifty or so feet from his gate where he could spy passengers already lining up to board. A copy of USA Today, Time Magazine and the latest Sports Illustrated would keep him occupied for at least part of the trip. He hoped he could also get some well deserved shut eye once the time barrier was passed and darkness enveloped the plane. Third or fourth in line, Jack darted his head back and forth between the store clerk and the line of people for his flight to make sure he wasn't being left behind. Finally, when it was his turn, he quickly dished out a twenty dollar bill and told the clerk to keep the change. Dashing from the store in full stride, his shoulder bag bouncing with every step, Jack approached the entrance to the gate. Somehow he wasn't really surprised at who was standing there blocking his path.

"Nice job, Jack. I gotta admit. You had me snowed big time. Scam of the century," Margaret said, smiling and shaking her head.

Jack nervously looked all around and waited to be pounced on by every FBI agent in Atlanta.

"Don't worry. I'm alone. Nobody else knows. Nobody's gonna touch you. You're gonna hop on that plane as free as a bird. A rich bird. Besides, you'd be in Zurich and gone before I could finish all the international paperwork."

Jack looked serious. "I'm sorry."

"No! Don't even start, Jack." Margaret paused, then laughed. "You won. We know when to admit defeat. I mean what a con job. You pulled it off. I believed you. Especially after Miami. You had me convinced that Fuentes was the one. You saw right through me and played me like a freaking fiddle. Enjoy your victory, for now."

"For now?"

Margaret smiled. "Figure of speech, Jack. Just a figure of speech."

Jack peered across Margaret's shoulder at the moving line.

She looked back and glanced at her watch. "Don't worry. They'll hold it for you. You still have fifteen minutes. Zurich's not going anywhere."

Jack looked at Margaret and narrowed his eyes. "How did you know I was going…"

"I'm FBI, Jack. I get paid to know these things." Margaret paused and looked at the ground, then back at Jack. "There's something I gotta know before you go."

Jack actually felt guilty for how she felt. "Anything."

"Eric's a good agent. What he did. Lying and all was wrong. But he was never on the bad side of his family. He wanted out. He would've never made it if he'd told the truth. He hated Raes for what they did to his mother but he never set out to get Raes out of revenge. He was gonna get him the right way."

"He will get Raes. Eventually."

"He won't get Raes. He's untouchable. He might get some of Raes' men. But Raes is way too big."

"But when it happens it'll be big, Emery. Margaret. Sorry. You'll always be Emery to me."

"What you did to Eric was wrong. Don't you get it? You wanna mess with Raes, that's your business. But Eric's an honest man."

Jack shook his head, looked over Margaret's shoulder at the slowly diminishing line, then back at her. "I'm sorry for what I did but I only did what I had to do."

"What you had to do? Nobody held a gun to your head, Jack. I can't believe I trusted you." She shook her head and narrowed her eyes. "When did you know who I was?"

Jack grinned. "I suspected it sometime after I was released on bail. Didn't take a rocket scientist, ya' know. Some of the stuff you said. Some of the stuff you knew. But I still didn't know for sure until you showed me your credentials. I wanted to believe you were with me because you cared. Guess that was a big joke, huh."

Margaret cocked her head. "Doug. Did he know?"

"He was pretty sure you weren't who you said you were. He thought I was a fool to trust you."

"What about Cissy?"

Jack tilted his head slightly. "Are you gonna arrest her?"

Margaret snickered. "On what grounds? There's no evidence against her."

Jack smiled. "She was in it up to her eyeballs."

"Did you kill Doug?"

Jack's smile faded. He stared at Margaret before answering. "No."

Margaret shook her head and glared at him. "Then who did?"

"I don't know. I honestly don't. Look. I'm not stupid. I know what Doug and I did was wrong in the eyes of the law. But I'm not a killer. I could never do that. Doug followed the plan. His leaving us in Mississippi was planned. Thought it might throw Guido and Sarducci off, but apparently it didn't. I don't know what went wrong. I'm really sorry for Cissy and the kids. But he knew what he was into. He knew the risks. I knew the risks. Cissy knew what could happen."

Jack looked at his watch and at the passenger line that was dwindling down to only a few passengers. The flight attendant picked up the microphone and announced a last call for passengers on the flight. "If you're gonna' arrest me, do it. I can't miss my flight."

"You know I can't arrest you." Margaret paused. "One more question before you leave. "Why didn't you kill me when you had the chance?"

Jack chuckled and took a couple of steps toward the line that only had two or three people left in it. "Kill an FBI Agent? Are you kidding me? That wouldn't have been the right thing to do, now would it? I told you. I don't kill people. Besides. I needed you.

Without you, I never knew where Fuentes was. With you, I was always one step ahead. You were also way too pretty to kill."

Jack paused. "Now let me ask you a question. Did you ever, at any time, feel something for me? Or was it all work to you?" He waited for the answer, but it never came. He wasn't able to read anything in those beautiful eyes of hers.

With two of his fingers pressed against his right eyebrow, Jack saluted her. "Alright, then. Until we meet again." He pulled his boarding pass from his shoulder bag and handed it to the flight attendant. He was the last passenger in line.

Margaret watched as he entered the long white chute leading to the jet. Barely inside the entrance, Jack turned and his eyes locked with hers. He smiled and saluted again before disappearing into the long tunnel.

She ambled slowly over to the large plate glass window and marveled at the huge jumbo jet. Panning every small window on the jetliner, she was unsuccessful in spotting Jack.

From inside the jet Jack could see her. He thought of how beautiful she was. He wondered if in another place, another time, it might have been different. His ultimate goal was to commit the crime of the century and get away with it. But he had found himself during the mission, at least for the moment in time, falling in love with her. Reality would set in. Priorities would be set. And he wouldn't allow love to rear its ugly head. He believed that she had fallen for him, too. Yeah. Sure, she was an FBI agent but she believed him to be innocent. And if he was innocent, why couldn't it have worked? FBI agents fall in love, too. But it was a moot point. Jack snickered to himself. He wasn't innocent. He was guilty as hell. He'd gotten away with it.

Jack looked at his watch and saw the chute being pushed back against the outer walls of the terminal. The tug of the jet as it was pushed backward caused him to look downward. When he returned his glance at the window, she was gone.

The giant jet rumbled down the runway and pulled away from the earth. In all his years of flying, Jack had never understood how a monstrous jetliner could get off the ground or how a ship or aircraft carrier could float. He smiled and thought he'd now have the time to ponder such great questions. Looking out his window, he saw the shadowy Atlanta skyline. He knew he would never see it again and watched until it was out of sight.

Inside the briefing room at the FBI office in Atlanta, Fuentes went over final preparations for the bust that would take place in a few hours. In the back of his mind he couldn't help but feel frustration for what had happened. Not so much for his personal wealth. There was plenty of money left over. He was angry that the system had failed. He was angry with himself for not producing the evidence that would have convicted Jack. He believed he had failed to do what he had trained and worked so hard for. Inside, he beat himself up over what he could have done or what he did not do right. Probably the hardest thing was that he couldn't even tell his fellow agents the truth. Only he and Margaret knew. The other agents would hear at the briefing that the evidence would only show that Raes' own men had stolen the cocaine and that a well placed anonymous informant provided a location.

Fuentes went over the details of how the surveillance and arrests would go down. He gave biographies of those likely to be at the location. Each agent was given specific assignments and placements.

Margaret was absent from the briefing. She had called earlier and left Fuentes a message on his voice mail. She apologized for taking his car and leaving him stranded at Waffle House. She asked his forgiveness for not believing him. She told him that as far as she was concerned, the Miami files never existed. Agent Lewis asked to be excused from the raid, telling him that she was taking some leave and would call him in a week or so. He was sad that she hadn't given him the chance to say that they were okay. He was sad he couldn't tell her that everything was alright.

Fuentes adjourned the briefing and directed everyone to meet back at the office at six o'clock. He had everything timed perfectly for when Raes' men were likely to show up to retrieve their cocaine. For the rest of the afternoon, Fuentes went home and secluded himself from everything. He sat in his favorite chair and stared out the window, pondering what might have been.

The bust went as planned. No screw-ups. No casualties. Not even a single gunshot fired. The Columbians were taken totally by surprise. The best part of the night was the look on Guido and Sarducci's faces when they were surrounded by FBI agents after they broke the lock and jumped in amongst the mounds of bricked white powder.

The headlines the next morning would tell how Special Agent Eric Fuentes single handedly made the largest cocaine bust in Georgia, and possibly U.S. history, when it was combined with the bust weeks earlier. That night, Fuentes would be credited with seven arrests in Atlanta alone and a drug seizure worth over two-hundred and fifty million dollars, not to mention the confiscation of four luxury Lexus vehicles and multiple cases of weapons owned by the most powerful drug cartel in the world. The news the next morning would inform Atlanta and the nation of the huge sting, and how Raes ran his operation using plumbing warehouses throughout the nation. NBC, CBS, ABC, CNN and FOX News dispatched crews from all around the country as the FBI rounded up executives from the companies that were involved in the conspiracy with Raes and seized well into the billions of dollars worth of cocaine that was stored in the respective warehouses.

Fuentes would eventually be summoned to FBI Headquarters to be personally congratulated by the Director. He would also be requested to testify before a Congressional hearing on the devastation caused by drug cartels. His name would be plastered across the headlines of every major newspaper in America and abroad. His face would become well known within the FBI family and within a year it would bring him that cushy job of instructor at the FBI Academy in Quantico, Virginia, that he'd yearned for.

Weeks would pass and he would think of Jack some and wonder where he was. As the months passed, he seldom, if ever, thought of him. After a year, Jack was merely an afterthought. He did talk about him to the new agents' classes he taught. From time to time Jack would show up in a dream and threaten to expose him unless he wired more money. Fuentes would wake in a cold sweat and thank God that Jack was on some South Sea island or at some winter resort in the mountains of Switzerland.

Fuentes despised Jack for what he had done. He didn't know if forgiveness was possible. Probably not. He tried as time passed to not concern himself with the saga of Jack Armstrong. Instead he immersed himself in his work, because that was his life. Jack Armstrong was in the past, and there it would stay. And Fuentes prayed for that every night.

It was 8:10 a.m. in London. Jack, in the middle of a five hour layover, dozed off and on by stretching out the best he could across two plastic seats that were not conducive to sleeping. Jolted awake by the announcement of an arriving flight, he looked at his watch and calculated what time it was in Atlanta. He smiled when he figured that right about now Fuentes was probably making the biggest arrest of his career and he had Jack to thank for it.

Jack sat up and rubbed his eyes. He still had a couple hours before his flight to Zurich boarded. When he had arrived at the gate there were only a handful of people there. More people were starting to file in now. Jack looked at each one, smiled and wondered how many were going to check on bank accounts as large as his. He laid his head back and maneuvered it back and forth several times before he finally got it somewhat comfortable. He would manage to doze a minute or so at a time before the call was made that his flight to Zurich was boarding.

There wasn't a cloud in the sky as Jack gazed at the green earth some 25,000 feet below. He'd always wanted to travel to Europe, but could never seem to find the time much less afford it. Marveling at the lush rolling hills and black highways that looked more like dark narrow ribbons, Jack rested his chin in the palm of his hand and pondered whether he would buy a place in the country or maybe live right in the middle of downtown where all the action was. He snickered to himself. He hadn't even decided where he would live. The only requirement was that it had to be far removed from the life he left behind in Atlanta. Taking one last look at the dense and abundant greenery below, he closed the shade on his window, reclined his seat, laid his head back and slept sounder than he had in weeks.

"Sir," the flight attendant nudged Jack.

Jack woke from his slumber not sure where he was. He gazed up and saw the pretty smile of the flight attendant.

"We are about to land, sir. You'll need to return your seat to its upright position."

Jack rubbed his eyes and followed the flight attendant's directions. Raising the shade on his window, the bright sun shone through, causing him to shield his eyes. He smiled when he could see his future rising slowly to meet him.

The head flight attendant made her announcements about the overhead compartments, connecting flights and keeping seatbelts fastened until the plane came to a complete stop. Of course, no one listened and as usual, as the jet taxied about fifty feet from the gate the majority of the passengers rose and began opening the overhead compartments to retrieve briefcases and other small packages. Jack remained seated. He was in no hurry. His only concern was getting a rental car and finding the International Bank of Zurich.

Standing motionless, passengers clogged the aisleways and waited impatiently for the door to open which would allow them access to whatever business they had in Zurich. Finally, movement began and when the aisle was mostly clear, Jack inched from his window seat and retrieved his shoulder bag from the overhead compartment. He filtered in behind the last few passengers waiting to deplane. Reaching the front of the jet, the pilot nodded his head and thanked Jack and the other passengers for choosing to fly his airline. Jack smiled and nodded back, then began his journey through the chute leading to the gate.

He looked around the terminal as he completed his trip through the maze as he had always referred to it. He had no idea where he needed to go but figured he was in no hurry. He followed a few Americans he had met on the flight and figured they would at least lead him in the right direction.

"Jack!" He heard his name being called in a deep but familiar voice from what seemed like a long distance.

Jack no sooner had gotten to the edge of the gate when he noticed a blonde haired, blue eyed, young and beautiful Swiss woman holding up a poster board that read JACK ARMSTRONG in huge black letters. Standing right beside the blonde was Doug. Jack looked toward the sky and thought of the beer commercial that reminded its viewers that "it doesn't get any better than this." He smiled, approaching the ravishing lady and his good friend.

"I believe this is our ride," Doug laughed.

"Mr. Armstrong," she said in a Swiss accent.

"That's me."

"From Atlanta, Georgia?"

"Yes. Can you give us a second?" he said, a broad smile breaking across his face.

She backed away a few steps.

Jack looked at Doug. The two friends shook hands and then hugged. "Doug, man! We thought you were dead."

"Naaaaah. I'm alive, and assume with you safely here, now rich as hell."

"They found your car, Doug. There was a body inside it."

"Wasn't mine."

Jack shook his head quickly, surprised at his callousness. "Then whose?"

"I don't know. Some poor schmo who had the unfortunate timing of meeting me while I was trying to cover my tracks."

"Why? You didn't have to kill anyone, Doug. That was never in the plan. Why would you do that?"

"Doug Spacey no longer exists, man. I'm rich beyond my wildest dreams and everybody assumes I'm dead. You, my friend, are rich beyond your wildest dreams but you are still very much alive. I only did what I felt I had to do. Pretty simple, really. You should start thinking like I do."

Jack stared at him, not sure of what to say.

Doug put his hands on Jack's shoulders. "Don't be so shocked, Jack. This ain't the florist business we got ourselves into." Doug turned to look at the blonde who was still holding the sign. "C'mon, man. Let's go get our just desserts."

"What about your family, Doug?"

"They'll be here next week. Just letting things die down a bit." Doug looked back at Jack. "You worry too much, man. Chill out. It's time to enjoy life to the fullest!" Doug turned and walked toward the gorgeous blonde Swede.

Jack looked at her and forced a smile. The beautiful woman smiled back. She extended her hand to Jack. Her voice was smooth as silk. "Mr. Armstrong. It is such a pleasure to welcome you to Zurich. My name is Iva and I'm with the International Bank of Zurich. I've been assigned to show you around, bring you to the bank, and escort you to wherever you may have business while in Zurich. I trust you won't mind me escorting you. The bank makes it a policy to entertain all new depositors in yours, and of course, Mr. Spacey's category."

"What was your name again?" Jack asked with no expression, still stunned by Doug's trivial excuse for murdering an innocent person.

"Iva."

Jack extended his palm toward the exit. "Thank you, Iva."

Iva put the poster with Jack's name on it next to a trash can and told Jack and Doug to follow her. Jack told her he had no baggage, just the one on his shoulder. She led them through several concourses and finally out the huge glass doors in the front of the drop off and pick up area. Jack and Doug grinned when they saw the white stretch limousine parked directly in front of them and Iva heading in that direction. Iva opened the back door, gazed up and smiled at them while she extended her arm inviting them into the luxurious vehicle. Jack slid into and across the fine soft white leather seats with interiors to match while Doug followed. Iva shut the door. Doug looked out to wave to her, but she couldn't see him through the tinted windows. Too busy touching the fine leather, neither Jack nor Doug even noticed the person sitting across from them in the other seat that faced them.

"Jack. Mr. Spacey, I presume. I was not expecting both of you. Two for the price of one I guess you could say," the dark- skinned man in the white suit said, while extending his hand toward Jack to shake. "Welcome to Zurich."

Alarmed, both their heads snapped toward the man who wore sparkling white shoes, white socks, white shirt and white tie to match. Jack paused slightly, then extended his own hand.

"Allow me to introduce myself," the man said, while staring at Jack, but no longer smiling. "My name...is Hector Raes."

Jack released his grip. His blood ran cold. His hands became clammy and pale. Staring into the cold black eyes of Raes, Jack became nauseous. Doug said nothing as the hairs on the back of his neck rose.

Never taking his eyes from Jack, Raes smiled and knocked on the glass that separated the driver from the back section of the limousine. The driver pulled away from the curb and drove about forty or so feet further down before stopping. "You don't mind if we pick up another party do you?"

Jack said nothing. His body was numb and his mind was in shock. Doug's heart pounded.

"I didn't think you would."

The door beside Jack opened. The passenger climbed in and sat down next to Jack. "Hello, Jack. Well, Doug. What an unexpected, but lovely surprise. So glad you could make it, too."

They knew the voice immediately. Both looked slowly toward her.

Margaret smiled and patted both their legs. "I see you both met my husband."

As the limousine pulled away and headed into the traffic, business carried on as usual for passengers scurrying from gate to gate, concourse to concourse, hoping to make flights and stick to schedules in their common, ordinary lives.

Terry and Margaret Moran

- Title: *My Enemy's Face*™
- Author: Terry Moran
- Price: $27.95
- Publisher: TotalRecall Publications
- Format: HARDCOVER, 6.14" x 9.21"
- Number of pages: 256
- 13-digit ISBN: 978-1-59095-660-1
- Publication: 2012

Billy Ray Sawyer is the All American kid. The high school football hero from the "right" side of the tracks is son of the powerful and wealthy Mayor who has raised Billy Ray to accept his racist and narrow-minded ways in 1960's Alabama.

Noah Franklin is the polar opposite of Billy Ray. A black son of poor parents, Noah doesn't have racist bone in his body until the Government forces integration. Billy Ray and Noah clash on the first day of school, and through what can only be explained as an Act of God, are forced to live their lives through the other's eyes.

Both their spirits and faith are tested through triumphs and failures in a community not ready for change or unity. Hate turns into friendship, as the two boys try to deal with their new circumstances. In an ultimate act of sacrifice, one will be forced to lay down his life to save the other. In an act of love, the other races against time to save him.

www.ingramcontent.com/pod-product-compliance
Lightning Source LLC
Chambersburg PA
CBHW020300120726
47904CB00001B/277